TRISH TODD
VICE PRESIDENT
EXECUTIVE EDITOR

SIMON & SCHUSTER, INC.
1230 AVENUE OF THE AMERICAS
NEW YORK, NY 10020
VOICE 212 698 4659 FAX 212 698 7066
trish.todd@simonandschuster.com

SIMON & SCHUSTER

August 30, 2012

Dear Reader:

I first began to feel we might have a winner on our hands when the art director called me in the middle of the work day, gasping and sobbing, "I've just . . . read . . . the . . . letters." She was at her desk, glued to the end of this big, sweeping story about a love triangle spanning the first half of the twentieth century. Mind you, our art director has read *a lot* of books, so I was thrilled that *Motherland* reached her on such a personal level. Then others in the company began texting each other during weekends and missing subway stops as they read *Motherland*. The rising tide of in-house enthusiasm elevated *Motherland* to a lead position on our Spring 2013 list.

While it is a love story, *Motherland* also grapples with some of the big issue of life, like faith and duty and honor. There are frightening war scenes, pageantry and politics, questions about art. There are also quiet, intimate moments of passion, doubt, and longing. Somehow, William Nicholson writes women and men with equal understanding and empathy. The plot compels you to turn the pages, but there's a big, profound undercurrent, too—making this the perfect book for readers of Sebastian Faulks or William Boyd.

You may recognize William Nicholson's name because he is a well-known screenwriter. He was nominated for an Academy Award for *Shadowlands* and *Gladiator*, and he has written the scripts for the upcoming *Les Miserables* and *Mandela: Long Walk to Freedom*. He has published YA and fantasy novels and three adult novels that received stellar reviews but have not been widely distributed in the United States. We believe this is his very exciting breakout book.

I hope you can find the time to enjoy *Motherland*. If you'd like to share your thoughts with us, please e-mail jessica.abell@simonandschuster.com.

Best wishes,

Trish Todd

Also by William Nicholson

*The Golden Hour*
*All the Hopeful Lovers*
*Rich and Mad*
*The Secret Intensity of Everyday Life*
*The Trial of True Love*
*The Society of Others*

Wind on Fire trilogy

*The Wind Singer*
*Slaves of the Mastery*
*Firesong*

Noble Warriors trilogy

*Seeker*
*Jango*
*Noman*

# MOTHERLAND

*William Nicholson*

*Simon & Schuster*

New York London Toronto Sydney New Delhi

Simon & Schuster
1230 Avenue of the Americas
New York, NY 10020



First Simon & Schuster hardcover edition April 2013



Manufactured in the United States of America

1 3 5 7 9 10 8 6 4 2

Library of Congress Cataloging-in-Publication Data

ISBN 978-1-4516-8713-2
ISBN 978-1-4516-8714-9 (ebook)

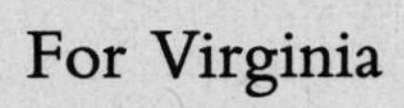

For Virginia

Our parents have loved before us, and their parents before them. For all we know we inherit our ways of loving along with the colour of our eyes. The joys we feel have been felt before; the mistakes we make have been made before. We carry within us the hopes and fears of the generations that have formed us. This is the unknown motherland from which we are always escaping, and to which we will always, helplessly, be true.

# PROLOGUE

## 2012

Alice Dickinson sits in the back of the Peugeot, though she would prefer to sit in the front, watching the orchards of Normandy roll by. The driver, a heavy middle-aged man with sad eyes, was waiting at the ferry port holding a sign displaying her name. Her clumsy prep-school French was met with incomprehension. Now he sits stooped over the wheel, one finger tapping out some inner rhythm, brooding on some secret unhappiness. She has no idea of his role. He could be an employee, he could be a member of the family. He's driving her to the grandmother she has never met, whose name is Pamela Avenell, who didn't know she existed until ten days ago.

The car turns off the main road onto a smaller road that runs along the east bank of the Varenne. Now the streets of steep-roofed houses give way to stands of mature beech trees, their broad leaves dusty in the mid-August sun. The late hot summer disturbs Alice. This is the weather for lying in long grass beside your lover, not the season for ending an affair.

You lead the life you choose to lead. It should be simple but it's not. Her own mother's love life, for example. She was just the age Alice is now, twenty-three, when she had an affair with a man who didn't love her, or not enough to want her baby. 'Get an abortion,' he told her. 'I'll pay.'

My father, Guy Caulder, the bastard. And me, the not-abortion. The genuine bastard, to be precise.

The strange thing is she doesn't hate her father. For some time she thought she despised him, which is different. Guy is handsome, selfish, shameless. He has played no part in her life: not a secret, but not a real person, either. An idea, a few anecdotes, and a genetic legacy.

That's what hooks you in the end. That's what reels you in. One day you wake up thinking: half of me comes from him. What if I take after him after all? That's when you start to want to know more.

'Why are you such a bastard, Guy?'

She asks the question without rancour, and he takes no offence. He's buying her lunch in one of the restaurants in Charlotte Street he favours; this one is called Mennula, smart Sicilian.

'Usual reason,' he says. 'My mother didn't want me.'

Of course. Blame the mother. The father can fuck off and no one blinks, but the all-nurturing mother must never stop giving. Give birth, give suck, give unconditional love.

So back it goes, another generation.

Alice has seen so little of Guy in her life that she knows nothing at all about his family. Now she has started to want to know.

'Why didn't your mother want you?'

'Oh,' says Guy, as if the whole affair lost its interest long ago, 'my mother married the wrong man, the way people do.

Probably because her mother married the wrong man. So you see, you come from a long line of mistakes.'

I come from a long line of mistakes. Thanks for that.

'Is she still alive?'

'God, yes. Very much so. She's only just seventy, not that you'd know it. Still a very good-looking woman. Still getting her own way. Mind you, I haven't actually seen her for years now.'

'Why not?'

'It works out better for both of us that way.'

More than this he will not say.

This story of a chain of unsuccessful marriages haunts Alice. She tells Guy she wants to meet this grandmother she's never known, who *gets her own way*.

Guy says, 'She has no idea you even exist.'

'Would you mind?'

He has to think about that one. But of course he has no real choice.

'All I've got is an address,' he says. 'In Normandy.'

The Peugeot has no air-conditioning, but the sad-eyed driver has his window fully open, and the speed-wind ruffles Alice's hair. She has dressed with care for this trip, wanting to appear smart but not over-eager to impress. She's wearing fashionably tight jeans and an off-white linen jacket. Her modest luggage is a canvas tote bag printed with a Caillebotte painting of Paris on a rainy day. She has a notion that Pamela Avenell is stylish.

The beech trees screen the road on both sides now. They pass a road sign pointing to the right, to St-Hellier and Cressy. The driver half-turns towards her.

'Après Bellencombre nous plongeons dans la forêt.'

We plunge into the forest.

The beech trees are spaced well apart from each other, but they recede as far as the eye can see. The columns of light and shade form shifting avenues that appear and disappear as they pass. Why would anyone choose to live in a forest?

But now the trees are retreating, and the bright afternoon sunlight is flooding a wide roadside meadow. They turn off the road and bump over an unmade track that climbs a gentle rise. And there at the top, commanding an immense view of the forest, stands La Grande Heuze: a steep-roofed many-gabled manor house, with cream-coloured walls striped by close-set vertical beams of grey wood.

The Peugeot rolls to a stop by a front porch that is dense with overhanging clematis. The driver stays in his seat.

'Voilà,' he says. 'Vous trouverez Madame dedans.'

Alice gets out, and the car drives away round the back of the house. A golden retriever appears and gives a token sleepy bark. The door within the porch is open. There is no doorbell.

She knocks, then she calls.

'Hello? Mrs Avenell?'

Ahead she sees down a wide dark hall to a doorway that is bright with daylight. The only sign of life is the dog, which has crossed the hall and disappeared into the room beyond.

'Hello?' Alice calls again. 'Anyone in?'

Still no answer. She follows the path taken by the dog and enters a long room with two sets of French windows that look onto a garden. The windows stand open. The dog lies in the sun on the terrace outside.

Alice goes onto the terrace and sees, across an expanse of lawn, the beech trees of the forest begin again. Where is her grandmother? She has the uncomfortable sensation that she might be watching her, even now. With this comes a new thought: what if her grandmother doesn't like her? This hasn't occurred to Alice before. She realises that unconsciously she has supposed herself to be a surprise gift. *Look! A real live granddaughter!* But just as Guy never wanted a daughter, perhaps this grandmother who gets her own way never wanted a granddaughter.

She is not arriving unannounced. There has been an exchange of letters. But her grandmother's letter of invitation was not effusive. Curious to see her, certainly, but guarded, cool.

She crosses the lawn to look into the trees, as if there might be some secret there: a leftover impulse from childhood fairy tales. There is no wall or fence. The garden is a glade in the forest. A few years' neglect and the tall beeches would advance to the very steps of the old house itself, and press like bars on its windows and doors. And yet it doesn't make her afraid. This is not the tormented forest of nightmares. Beech alleys form spaces that are light-speckled, domesticated, a chain of rooms that go on for ever. You could go wild here, and be safe.

Turning back, she sees a figure standing in the open French windows. She's slim, with short-cropped silver hair and smooth lightly tanned skin. A long white blouse loose over jeans. Her arms raised in a gesture of welcome.

'You've come! How wonderful!'

Wide brown eyes watch Alice cross the grass towards her. Shining eyes that give full attention, that want to know everything. No holding back here.

'Darling one!' she says. 'What took you so long?'

Alice is flooded with an inexplicable wave of happiness. This silver-haired woman, this never-known grandmother, is simply beautiful. Alice, who has never been beautiful, sees in her at once herself as she could have been; herself as maybe one day she could be.

Pamela Avenell takes both Alice's hands in hers and studies her with rapt wondering attention. Alice feels infinitely precious under that gaze.

'You've got my eyes.'

'Have I?' says Alice.

'Of course you have. I saw it at once.'

'I can hardly believe it,' says Alice. 'You're so beautiful. How can you be my grandmother?'

'I'm sixty-nine, darling,' says Pamela. 'But don't tell a soul.'

'I just can't believe it,' says Alice again.

They stand there like fools, holding hands, grinning at each other, looking and looking. Alice doesn't know why this makes her so happy, nor does she ask herself.

'Come into the house,' says Pamela. 'Let's have a drink and tell each other everything. It's far too hot outside.'

In the house she calls out, 'Gustave!' and the driver appears from an inner room. She speaks to him rapidly in excellent French, touching him lightly on one arm before he departs to carry out her orders.

'Gustave is an angel,' she says. 'I simply don't know how I managed before he came.'

They're sitting down and her big brown eyes are fixed on Alice once more.

'So you're my granddaughter,' she says. 'How cruel and wicked of Guy to hide you away from me.'

'He hid me away from himself,' says Alice. 'He never wanted me. I was an accident.'

'He never wanted you.' Her gaze is penetrating ever deeper into Alice, past all her defences. 'Oh, my dear. I know all about that.'

'I'm not blaming him. My mother says it was all her own choice.'

'No, there's nothing to be gained by blaming people. But that doesn't stop us doing it.'

Gustave comes back into the room carrying a tray of drinks. He sets it down on the low table between them. There's a bottle of Noilly Prat, two glasses, a plate of biscuits.

'Chilled vermouth,' says Pamela, pouring golden liquid into the glasses. 'Just right for a hot day.'

She thanks Gustave with a quick smile, and he departs again. Alice takes her glass.

'To accidents,' says Pamela.

She's wearing no make-up, Alice thinks. Her hair isn't dyed. How can she be almost seventy, and so beautiful?

'I don't understand why Guy hasn't told me about you before,' Alice says. 'He should be so proud of you.'

'Ah, well. These things go back a long way. But I don't want to talk about me. I want to know all about you.'

Under her grandmother's intoxicating gaze, Alice tells her life so far. How sometimes a love affair ends for no reason except it's your first and you're too young and there's so much more you need to find out about yourself. How you drift apart and only know it's happened when the space between you has grown too wide, and you reach across and find you're no longer touching. How the old questions which you thought had gone away turn out to have been waiting all along, as unanswerable as ever. What do I really want? Who am I when it's just me? When I love again, will I love with all my heart?

She hears herself say, 'If I love only him, I'll be a smaller person than I know I can be.'

'How wise you are, my darling,' says Pamela. 'I wish I'd known that when I was your age. How old are you? Twenty-one?'

'Twenty-three.'

'When I was twenty-three I had a husband and a baby.'

The husband was Alice's grandfather. His name was Hugo Caulder. This much Alice knows. The baby was Guy. The baby is Guy.

'Guy said something about you marrying the wrong man.'

'Yes, I did. As a matter of fact, I've done it three times. You'd think I'd learn.'

'I want to learn,' says Alice.

'Not from me.' Pamela laughs. 'Unless you study everything I've ever done and do the opposite.'

'I want to learn about who I am. Some of me comes from Guy. And some of him comes from you.'

'Well, yes,' says Pamela. 'It's all rather devastating, isn't it? You see the patterns more clearly as you grow older.'

'Guy says I come from a long line of mistakes.'

'Does he, now? What a little beast he is. I bet he didn't tell you our one true love story.'

Our one true love story. Like the unicorn: beautiful, impossible, long sought but never found.

'Is it yours?'

'Mine? No, it's certainly not mine.' She refills their glasses with vermouth. 'It's my mother's story. Your great-grandmother's.'

She raises her glass, as she did before.

'To mothers,' she says.

'And grandmothers,' says Alice.

They both drink. Alice feels the vermouth warming her inside.

'I adored my mother,' says Pamela. 'You can't imagine how much I adored her. Then later, I envied her. I wanted to be loved as she was loved. Don't you find the trouble with love stories is that they make you sad? You want to have a love story like it for your very own. You go on looking for it and looking for it. And you don't find it.'

'But your mother did.'

'Yes, she did.'

She gets up and takes a framed photograph off the wall. The frame is far too grand for the photograph, which is an old snapshot of three young people: a woman between two men. The woman is young and pretty, in the slightly artificial manner of the 1940s. The men gaze at the camera with that bold self-confidence that is somehow so heartbreaking to see today: boys who believe themselves to be men. One of them, the good-looking one, doesn't smile. The other smiles.

'That's my mother,' says Pamela. 'She was called Kitty. That's my father, Ed Avenell. And that's my father's best friend, Larry Cornford.'

'Your mother was very pretty,' says Alice.

'Your great-grandmother. And wasn't my father handsome?'

'Very.'

'He won the Victoria Cross.'

'How?'

'I'll tell you. And what do you think of Larry?'

Alice studies the friendly smiling face in the photograph.

'He looks nice,' she says.

'Nice. Poor dear Larry. How he'd hate that.'

# PART ONE
# WAR

1942–45

# I

The staff cars are pulled up by the coastguard cottages, close to the cliff edge. A steady drizzle is falling and visibility is poor. A cluster of officers stand in glistening greatcoats, binoculars raised, tracking the movements on the beach below.

'Bloody mess as usual,' says the brigadier.

'Better than last time,' says Parrish. 'At least they found the beach.'

Seven assault landing craft are rolling in the grey water of the bay, as men of the Canadian Eighth Infantry Brigade flounder ashore. Each man wears an inflated Mae West and carries a rifle and a full battle pack. They move slowly through the water, blurred by rain, like dreamers who stride ever onward but never advance.

The watchers on the clifftop command a view that is almost parodic in its Englishness: a river winds through green meadows to a shingle beach, framed by a line of receding hump-backed white cliffs. They are known as the Seven Sisters. Today barely two of the Seven Sisters are visible. The beach is defended by concrete anti-tank blocks, scaffolding tubes and long rolls of barbed wire. Small thunderflashes explode among the pebbles at random, and to no obvious purpose. The popping sounds rise up to the officers with the binoculars.

One of the landing craft has cut its engine out in deep water. The tiny figures of the men on board can be seen jumping one by one from the ramp. Parrish reads the craft's identifying number through his binoculars.

'ALC85. Why's it stopped?'

'It's sunk,' says Colonel Jevons, who devised the exercise. 'Further out than I intended. Still, they should all float.'

'A couple of six-inch howitzers up here,' says the brigadier, 'and not a man would make it ashore alive.'

'Ah, but the advance raiding party has cut your throats,' says Jevons.

'Let's hope,' says the brigadier.

Behind the staff officers the two ATS drivers are seeking shelter at the back of the Signals truck. The Signals sergeant, Bill Carrier, finds himself in the unfamiliar situation of being outnumbered by women. If a few other lads from his unit were with him he'd know how to banter with these English girls, but on his own like this, unsure of his ground, he's feeling shy.

'Look at it,' says the pretty one. 'June! You've got to admit it's a joke.'

She laughs and wriggles her whole body, as if the absurdity of the world has taken possession of her. She has curly brown hair, almost touching her collar, and brown eyes with strong eyebrows, and a wide smiling mouth.

'Don't mind Kitty,' says the other one, who is blonde and what is called handsome, meaning her features are a little too prominent, her frame a little too large. She speaks through barely parted lips, in the amused tones of the upper classes. 'Kitty's perfectly mad.'

'Mad as a currant bun,' says Kitty.

The rain intensifies. The two drivers in their brown uniforms huddle under the shelter of the truck's raised back.

'Christ, I could murder a cup of tea,' says the blonde one. 'How much longer, O Lord?'

'Louisa was going to be a nun,' says Kitty. 'She's tremendously holy.'

'Like hell,' says Louisa.

'Sorry,' says the sergeant. 'We're still on action stations.'

'Only an exercise,' says Kitty.

'My whole life is only an exercise,' says Louisa. 'When do we get to the real thing?'

'I'm with you there,' says the sergeant. 'Me and the lads are going nuts.'

He answers Louisa but his eyes are on Kitty.

'All you Canucks want to do is fight,' says Kitty, smiling for him.

'That's what we come over for,' says the sergeant. 'Two bloody years ago now.'

'Ah, but you see,' says Kitty, pretending seriousness, trying not to laugh, 'that's not what Louisa's talking about at all. She's talking about getting married.'

'Kitty!' Louisa pummels her friend, making her crouch over, laughing. 'You are such a tell-tale.'

'Nothing wrong with wanting to get married,' says the sergeant. 'I want to get married myself.'

'There!' says Kitty to Louisa. 'You can marry the sergeant and go and live in Canada and have strings of healthy bouncing Canadian babies.'

'I've got a girl in Winnipeg,' says the sergeant. He thinks how he'd ditch her in a flash for Kitty, but not for Louisa.

'Anyway,' says Kitty, 'Louisa's tremendously posh and only allowed to marry people who went to Eton and have grouse moors. Did you go to Eton, Sergeant?'

'No,' says the sergeant.

'Do you have a grouse moor?'

'No.'

'Then your girl in Winnipeg is safe.'

'You really are quite mad,' says Louisa. 'Don't believe a single word she says, Sergeant. I'd be proud and honoured to marry a Canadian. I expect you have moose moors.'

'Sure,' says Bill Carrier, tolerantly playing along. 'We hunt moose all the time.'

'Isn't it meese?' says Kitty.

'They're not fussy what you call them,' says the sergeant.

'How sweet of them,' says Kitty. 'Dear meese.'

She gives the sergeant such an adorable smile, her eyes crinkling at the corners, that he wants to take her in his arms there and then.

'Stop it,' says Louisa, smacking Kitty on the arm. 'Put him down.'

A ship's horn sounds from the bay, a long mournful blare. This is the signal to the men on the beach to re-embark.

'There she blows,' says the sergeant.

The two ATS girls get up. The officers on the clifftop are on the move, talking as they go, huddled together in the rain.

'So what's your names anyway?' the sergeant says.

'I'm Lance-Corporal Teale,' says Kitty. 'And she's Lance-Corporal Cavendish.'

'I'm Bill,' says the sergeant. 'See you again, maybe.'

They part to their various vehicles. Kitty stands to attention by the passenger door of the brigadier's staff car.

'Ride with me, Johnny,' the brigadier says to Captain Parrish.

The officers get in. Kitty takes her place behind the wheel.

'Back to HQ,' says the brigadier.

Kitty Teale loves driving. Secretly she regards the big khaki Humber Super Snipe as her own property. She has learned how to nurse its grumbly engine to a smooth throb on cold early mornings, and takes pleasure in slipping into just the right gear for each section of road, so that the vehicle never has to strain. She carries out the simpler operations of car maintenance herself, watching over oil levels and tyre pressures with an almost maternal care. She also cleans the car, in the long hours waiting at HQ for the next duty call.

Today, driving home through the little towns of Seaford and Newhaven, she resents the drizzle because she knows it will leave a film of grime over every surface. At least she's not in convoy behind an army lorry, enduring the spatter of mud from high back wheels. Louisa, who is following behind her in the Ford, will be getting some of the spray from her wheels. But Louisa has no sense of loyalty to the car she drives. 'It's not a pet,' she says to Kitty. 'It's got no feelings.'

To Kitty, everything has feelings. People and animals, of course. But also machines, and even furniture. She's grateful to the chair on which she sits for bearing her weight, and to the knife in her hand for cutting her bread. It seems to her that they've done her a kindness out of a desire to make her happy. Her gratitude is the tribute she pays, as a pretty child grown accustomed to the kindness of strangers, afraid that she does too little to deserve it. She's been brought up to believe it's wrong to think herself attractive, and so is caught in a spiral of charm, in which those who seek to please her must be pleased by her in return. This gives rise to frequent misunderstandings. Unable to offend, she is forever encouraging false hopes. There's a young man in the navy who supposes her to be his girlfriend, after two meetings and a dance. It's true they kissed, but she's kissed other boys. Now he's written her a passionate letter asking her to meet him in London this Friday, when he has twenty-four hours' leave.

The officers in the back are talking about the coming big show.

'All I pray is the flyers do their job,' says the brigadier. 'I want those beaches bombed to buggery.'

'Do we have a forecast?' says Captain Parrish. 'This is no good to anyone.'

He indicates the rain blurring the car windows.

'Supposed to clear by tomorrow,' says the brigadier. 'Then we have to wait for the moon. We've got a few days. Not that anyone ever tells me anything. Bloody liaison officer knows more than I do.'

The Humber turns off the road up the long drive to Edenfield Place, where the battalion is based. The great Victorian Gothic mansion looms out of the drizzle. Kitty pulls the car to a gentle stop before the ornate porch, and the officers clamber out. Behind her, Louisa brings the Ford to a noisier halt on the gravel.

'Thank you, Corporal,' says the brigadier to Kitty. 'That's all for today.'

'Yes, sir. Thank you, sir.'

He signs her work docket.

'If you have a moment, be nice to our friend George. The boys have made a bit of a mess of his wine cellar and he's rather cut up.'

The rightful owner of Edenfield Place, George Holland, second Lord Edenfield, has opted to go on living in the house through this period of wartime requisition. In the sacrificial spirit of the times he has retained for himself a modest suite of three rooms that were formerly occupied by his father's butler. George is barely thirty years old; soft-spoken, shy, in poor health.

'Yes, sir,' says Kitty.

She drives the car round to the garage at the back, followed by Louisa in the Ford. They go together to hand in their work dockets at the Motor Transport Office.

'Fancy a drink at the Lamb?' says Louisa.

'I'll just give the car a wipe-down,' says Kitty. 'Meet you in the hall in half an hour.'

She takes a bucket and cloth and swabs the Humber's flanks, patting the metalwork as she goes. Then she fills the petrol tank back up, and finally immobilises the car by removing its rotor arm, as required by regulations.

Her route through the big house takes her down the cloister, across the galleried hall, past the organ room to the nursery stairs. The room she shares with Louisa is on the second floor, under the eaves, in what was once the night nursery. As she goes she ponders the best strategy to deal with Stephen and Friday. She could say she's run out of travel warrants, which she has, but she's always hitch-hiked before. And anyway, she'd like to see him. They could go to the 400 Club and dance and forget the war for the night. Surely there's no harm in that?

In the attic nursery Kitty sits on her bed and unrolls her regulation lisle stockings. She stretches out her bare legs, wiggling her toes, relishing the sensation of cool freedom. She possesses one pair of rayon stockings, but they won't last for ever, and she has no intention of wasting them on the crowd in the Lamb. Friday, maybe, if she does decide to go up to town.

She sighs as she touches up her lipstick. It's all very well having boys be sweet on you, but why must they all try to own you? Louisa says it's because she smiles too much, but what can she do about that? You're allowed to smile at someone without marrying them, aren't you?

At No.2 Motor Transport Training Centre in North Wales there'd been a girl her age who said she'd done it with four different men. She said it was ten times better than dancing. She said the trick was to pretend to be tipsy, then afterwards you say you don't remember a thing. She said if you were lucky and got a good one it was heaven, but you could never tell from the outside which ones would be good.

On the way back down the narrow carpetless stairs Kitty meets George himself, loitering on the first floor. Somehow since being billeted in Edenfield Place she has befriended its owner, rather in the way you take in a stray dog.

'Oh, hullo,' he says, blinking at her. He has poor eyesight, apparently. 'Are they still keeping you hard at work?'

'No, I'm off now,' says Kitty. Then remembering the brigadier's request, 'I'm really sorry about the wine.'

'Oh, the wine,' he says. 'All the '38 Meursault is gone. I'm told they drank it laced with gin.'

'That's terrible!' Kitty is more shocked by the gin than by the theft. 'They should be shot.'

'Well, not shot, perhaps. You know the Canadians are all volunteers? We should be grateful to them. And I am grateful.'

'Oh, George. You're allowed to be angry.'

'Am I?'

His unfocused eyes gaze at her with silent longing.

'I suppose they meant no real harm,' says Kitty. 'They're like children who don't know what damage they're doing. But even so. You'll get compensation, won't you?'

'I expect I'll be paid something.' Then with a sudden rush, 'The thing is, Kitty, I was hoping we could find a moment to talk.'

'Later, George,' she says. 'I'm late already.'

She touches his arm and gives him a smile to soften the implied rejection, and runs on down the main stairs. Louisa is waiting by the ornate fireplace in the great hall. She's wearing her now-obsolete FANY uniform, made for her by her father's tailor, with the lanyard on the left, yeomanry-style, in the FANY colours of pink and blue. Kitty raises her eyebrows.

'To hell with them all,' says Louisa cheerfully. 'If I have to wear uniform when I'm out in the evenings, I'll bloody well wear one that fits me.'

Kitty and Louisa both volunteered for the FANYs, so much more socially acceptable than the ATS, and met at the training camp in Strensall.

'I don't mind being bossed about by lesbians in trilbies,' says Louisa, 'so long as they're my own class.'

Two years ago the proud FANYs were merged with the ATS, which is not at all Louisa's class, and has the least fetching uniform of all the services.

Outside the rain has stopped at last. There's a crowd of

Camerons by the pub, sprawled on the damp grass strip between the door and the road. From inside come cheers and waves of laughter.

'You don't want to go in there, darling,' one soldier calls out to them.

'I don't see any drinks out here,' responds Louisa.

They go into the saloon bar and find a mixed bunch of Camerons and Royals banging on the tables, roaring out encouragement. A trooper from the Fusiliers Mont-Royal is dancing on a table.

'Frenchie! Frenchie! Frenchie!' they chant. 'Off! Off! Off!'

The trooper, a gangling French-Canadian with a craggy stubble-dark face, is performing a mime striptease. Without removing a single actual garment he is managing to create the illusion that he's a sexy young woman peeling off layer after layer.

Kitty and Louisa watch, mesmerised.

'Bravo, Marco!' shout his comrades. '*Baisez-moi*, Marco! Allez Van Doo!'

The trooper writhes with seductive sinuousness, as little by little, with careful tugs, he eases invisible stockings down his legs. Now mock-naked but for brassiere and panties he plays at coyly covering his crotch with his hands, opening and closing his legs. Looking round the faces of the watching men, Kitty realises they're genuinely aroused.

'Show us what you've got, Frenchie!' they call out. 'Knickers down! Off, off, off!'

Teasing inch by teasing inch, down come the imaginary knickers, while the performer remains in full khaki battledress. Kitty catches Louisa's eye and sees there the same surprise. It's only a joke; but the male sexual hunger on display is all too real.

Now the knickers are off. The legs are tightly crossed. The ugly soldier who is also a gorgeous naked woman holds his audience spellbound with anticipation. Now at last he throws up his hands, parts his legs, thrusts out his crotch, and a great sigh of satisfaction fills the smoky air.

The show over, the young men packing the bar become suddenly aware that there are two actual females in their midst. Laughing, jostling, they compete to get close.

'Look who's here! Let me buy you a drink, gorgeous! This one's on me. Budge up, pal! Give a guy a chance.'

Kitty and Louisa find themselves pushed back and back until they're pressed to the wall. The friendly attentions of the excited soldiers become uncomfortable.

'Take it easy, boys,' says Kitty, smiling even as she tries to fend off reaching hands.

'Hey!' cries Louisa. 'Get off me! You're squashing me!'

None of the soldiers means to push, but the ones behind are surging forward, and the ones in front find themselves thrust against the girls. Kitty starts to feel frightened.

'Please,' she says. 'Please.'

A commanding voice rings out.

'Move! Get back! Out of my way!'

A tall soldier is forcing himself through the crush, taking men by the arm, pulling them aside.

'Idiots! Baboons! Get back!'

The crowding soldiers part before him, all at once sheepishly aware that things have got out of control. He reaches Kitty and Louisa and spreads his arms to create a clear space before them.

'Sorry about that. No harm done, I hope?'

'No,' says Kitty.

The man before her wears battledress with no insignia of any kind. He's young, not much older than Kitty herself, and strikingly handsome. His face is narrow, with a strong nose over a full sensitive mouth. His blue eyes, beneath arching brows, are fixed on her with a look she's never encountered before. His look says, Yes, I can see you, but I have other more important concerns than you.

The soldiers he has displaced are now recovering their poise.

'Who do you think you are, buddy?'

The young man turns his faraway gaze on his accuser, and sees him raise a threatening hand.

'Touch me,' he says, 'and I'll break your neck.'

There's something about the way he says it that makes the soldier lower his hand. One of the others mutters, 'Leave him alone, mate. He's a fucking commando.'

After that the crowd disperses, leaving Kitty and Louisa with their rescuer.

'Thanks,' says Kitty. 'I don't think they meant any harm.'

'No, of course not. Just horsing around.'

He guides them to the bar.

'Got any brandy?' he says to the barman. 'These young ladies are suffering from shock.'

'Oh, no, I'm fine,' says Kitty.

'Yes, please,' says Louisa, treading on her foot.

The barman produces a bottle of cooking brandy from under the counter and furtively pours two small shots. The soldier hands them to Kitty and Louisa.

'For medicinal purposes,' he says.

Kitty takes her glass and sips at it. Louisa drinks more briskly.

'Cheers,' she says. 'I'm Louisa, and this is Kitty.'

'Where are you based?'

'The big house.' Louisa nods up the road.

'Secretaries?'

'Drivers.'

'Take care at night,' he says. 'More killed on the roads in the blackout than by enemy action.'

Kitty drinks her brandy without being aware she's doing so. She begins to feel swimmy.

'So who are you?' she says. 'I mean, what are you?'

'Special services,' he says.

'Oh.'

'Sorry. I don't mean to sound mysterious. But that really is all I can say.'

'Are you allowed to tell us your name?'

'Avenell,' he says, pushing back the sweep of dark hair that keeps falling into his eyes. 'Ed Avenell.'

'You're a knight in shining armour,' says Louisa. 'You came to the rescue of damsels in distress.'

'Damsels, are you?' Not a flicker on his pale face. 'If I'd known, I'm not sure I'd have bothered.'

'Don't you like damsels?' says Kitty.

'To tell you the truth,' he says, 'I'm not entirely clear what a damsel is. I think it may be a kind of fruit that bruises easily.'

'That's a damson,' says Kitty. 'Perhaps we're damsons in distress.'

'You can't distress a damson,' says Louisa.

'I don't know about that,' says Ed. 'It can't be much fun being made into jam.'

'I wouldn't mind,' says Louisa. 'You get squeezed until you're juicy, and then you get all licked up.'

'Louisa!' says Kitty.

'Sorry,' says Louisa. 'It's the brandy.'

'She's really very well brought up,' Kitty says to Ed. 'Her cousin is a duke.'

'My second cousin is a tenth duke,' says Louisa.

'And you still a mere corporal,' he says. 'It just isn't right.'

'Lance-corporal,' says Louisa, touching her single stripe.

The young man turns his steady gaze on Kitty.

'And what about you?'

'Oh, I'm not top-drawer at all,' says Kitty. 'We Teales are very middle-drawer. All vicars and doctors and that sort of thing.'

Suddenly she feels so wobbly she knows she must lie down. The brandy has come at the end of a long day.

'Sorry,' she says. 'We were up at four for the exercise.'

She starts for the door. Apparently she staggers a little, because before she knows it he's taking her arm.

'I'll walk you back,' he says.

'And me,' says Louisa. 'I was up at four too.'

So the gallant commando takes a lady on either arm, and they walk back up the road to the big house. The soldiers they pass on the way grin and say, 'Good work, chum!' and, 'Give a shout if you need help.'

They part by the porch.

'Corporal Kitty,' he says, saluting. 'Corporal Louisa.'

The girls return the salute.

'But we don't know your rank,' says Kitty.

'I think I'm a lieutenant or something,' he says. 'My firm isn't very big on ranks.'

'Can you really break people's necks?' says Louisa.

'Just like that,' he says, snapping his fingers.

Then he goes.

Kitty and Louisa enter the cloister and their eyes meet and they both burst out laughing.

'My God!' exclaims Louisa. 'He's a dream!'

'Squeezed until you're juicy? Honestly, Louisa!'

'Well, why not? There's a war on, isn't there? He's welcome to come round and lick me up any time he wants.'

'Louisa!'

'Don't sound so shocked. I saw you simpering away at him.'

'That's just how I am. I can't help myself.'

'Want to come into the mess?'

'No,' says Kitty. 'I really am bushed. I wasn't making it up.'

Alone in the attic nursery Kitty undresses slowly, thinking about the young commando officer. His grave amused face is printed clearly on her memory. Most of all she recalls the gaze of those wide-set blue eyes, that seemed to see her and not see her at the same time. For all his staring, she never felt he wanted something from her. There was no pleading there. Instead there was something else, something vulnerable but all his own, a kind of sadness. Those eyes say that he doesn't expect happiness to last. It's this, more than his good looks, that causes her to keep him in her thoughts right up to the moment she finally surrenders to sleep.

## 2

The rear wheel of the motorbike slews on the chalk slime of the farm track, making the engine race. Its rider swerves to regain traction and slows and leans in to the turn, swinging round the barn end into the farmyard. Chickens scatter, squawking, only to return as soon as the engine cuts out. This is the time that kitchen scraps are thrown out. There are crows waiting in the birches.

The rider pushes his goggles up and rubs at his eyes. The roads have been slick and dangerous all day, and he's thankful to be off his bike at last. Mary Funnell, the farmer's wife, opens the farmhouse door, one hand holding her apron hem, and calls to him, 'You've got a visitor.'

Larry Cornford pulls off his helmet to reveal a tumble of golden-brown curls. His broad friendly face looks round the yard, his eyes blinking. He sees an unfamiliar jeep.

'Thanks, Mary.'

The farmer's wife shakes out the contents of her apron and the chickens make a rush for the scraps. Larry pulls his satchel out of the motorbike's pannier and strides into the farmhouse kitchen, wondering who his visitor might be.

Rex Dickinson, the medic with whom he shares this billet, is sitting at the kitchen table, smoking his pipe and laughing uneasily. With his owl glasses and his long thin neck and his teetotalism Rex is always the butt of jokes, which he takes with patient good humour. Everyone likes Rex, if only because he wants so little for himself. He's so modest in his needs that he has to be reminded to use his own rations.

Facing Rex, dark against the bright rectangle of the kitchen window, is a lean figure Larry recognises at once.

'Eddy!'

Ed Avenell reaches out one lazy hand for Larry to grasp.

'This housemate of yours, Larry, has been putting me in the picture about divine providence.'

'Where in God's name have you sprung from?'

'Shanklin, Isle of Wight, since you ask.'

'This calls for a celebration! Mary, put out the cider.'

'Cider, eh?' says Ed.

'No, it's good. Home-made, with a kick like a mule.'

Larry stands beaming at his friend.

'This bastard,' he says to Rex, 'ruined the five best years of my life.'

'Oh, he's one of your lot, is he?' says Rex, meaning Catholics. He himself is the son of a Methodist minister. 'I should have guessed.'

'Don't put me in a box with him,' says Ed. 'Just because we went to the same school doesn't mean a thing. The monks never got to me.'

'Still protesting?' says Larry fondly. 'I swear, if Ed had been sent to a Marxist-atheist school, he'd be a monk himself by now.'

'You're the one who wanted to be a monk.'

This is true. Larry laughs to remember it. For a few heady months at the age of fifteen he had considered taking vows.

'Has Mary fed you? I'm starving. What are you doing here? What outfit are you in? What kind of uniform do you call that?'

The questions tumble out as Larry settles down to eat his delayed supper.

'I'm with 40 Royal Marine Commando,' says Ed.

'God, I bet you love that.'

'It gets me out of the army. I think I hate the army even more than I hated school.'

'It's still the army, though.'

'No. We do things our own way.'

'Same old Ed.'

'So how are you winning the war, Larry?'

'I'm liaison officer attached to First Division, Canadian Army, from Combined Operations headquarters.'

'Combined Ops? How did you get in with that mob?'

'My father knows Mountbatten. But I don't do anything interesting. I get a War Office-issue BSA M20 and a War Office-issue briefcase and I ride back and forth with top secret papers telling the Canadians to carry out more exercises because basically there's sod all for them to do.'

'Tough job,' says Ed. 'You get any time to paint?'

'Some,' says Larry.

'First he wants to be a monk,' Ed says to Rex, 'then he wants to be an artist. He's always been a bit touched in the head.'

'No more than you,' protests Larry. 'What's this about joining the commandos? You want to die young?'

'Why not?'

'You're doing it because you want to give your life to the

noblest cause you know.' Larry speaks firmly, pointing his fork at Ed, as if instructing a wayward child. 'And that's what monks do, and that's what artists do.'

'Seriously, Larry,' says Ed. 'You should have stuck with bananas.'

Larry bursts into laughter again; though in fact this is no joke. His father's firm imports bananas, with such success that it has achieved a virtual monopoly.

'So what are you doing here, you bandit?' he says.

'I've come to see you.'

'Is your journey really necessary?'

These days it takes real clout to wangle both a jeep and the petrol to run it.

'I've got an understanding CO,' says Ed.

'Will you bunk here tonight?'

'No, no. I'll be on the road back by ten. But listen here, Larry. I was trying to track you down, so I stopped at the pub in the village. And guess what happened?'

'He's been struck by a thunderbolt,' says Rex. 'Like St Paul on the road to Damascus. He was telling me.'

This is Rex's dry humour.

'I met this girl,' says Ed.

'Oh,' says Larry. 'A girl.'

'I have to see her again. If I don't, I'll die.'

'You want to die anyway.'

'I want to see her again first.'

'So who is she?'

'She says she's an ATS driver from the camp.'

'Those ATS girls get around.'

Arthur Funnell appears in the doorway, his shoulders slumped, his face wearing its habitual expression of doom.

'Any of you gents seen a weather forecast?' he says. 'If it's more rain, I don't want to know, because I've had enough and that's the truth.'

'Sunny tomorrow, Arthur,' says Larry. 'Back into the seventies.'

'For how long?'

'That I can't tell you.'

'I need a week's sunshine, you tell 'em, or the hay'll rot.'

'I'll tell them,' says Larry.

The farmer departs.

'He wants help bringing the hay in,' says Rex. 'He was telling me earlier.'

'He should get himself some Canucks,' says Larry. 'They're all farm boys. They're bored to death in the camp.'

'Who cares about the hay?' says Ed. 'What am I going to do about this girl?'

Larry pulls out a pack of cigarettes and offers one to Ed.

'Here. Canadian, but not bad.'

They're called Sweet Caporal. Rex lights up his pipe as Larry pulls gratefully on his after-dinner cigarette.

'I'm stuck in bloody Shanklin,' says Ed. 'There's no way I can get back over here till the weekend.'

'So see her at the weekend.'

'She could be married by then.'

'Hey!' exclaims Larry. 'She really has got to you, hasn't she?'

'How about you find her for me? Give her a message. You're the liaison officer. Do some bloody liaising.'

'I could try,' says Larry. 'What's her name?'

'Corporal Kitty. She's a staff driver.'

'What's the message?'

'Come to Sunday lunch. Here at your billet. You don't mind, do you? And the other girl can come too. The horsey one.'

'How's she horsey?'

'Looks like a horse.'

He stubs out the last of his cigarette. He's smoked it twice as fast as Larry.

'Quite decent,' he says.

'So who's laying on the lunch?' says Larry.

'You are,' says Ed. 'You're the one billeted on a farm. And Rex too. I'm issuing a general invitation.'

'Very big of you,' says Larry.

'I'll be out on Sunday,' says Rex.

'Sunday your big day, is it, Rex?' says Ed.

'I help out here and there,' says Rex.

'I'll do my best,' says Larry. 'How do I reach you?'

'You don't. I'll just show up here, noon Sunday. You produce Kitty. But no sticky fingers in the till. I saw her first.'

Next morning a pale sun rises as promised, and by eight o'clock a mist hangs over the water meadows. Larry rides his motor-bike the short distance to the big house with his helmet off, wanting to enjoy the arrival of summer at last. Soldiers in the camp, stripped to the waist, are playing a raucous game of volleyball. The pale stone towers of Edenfield Place gleam in the sun.

On such a day before the war he would have tramped off alone up the Downs, carrying an easel and a fresh canvas, a box of paints and a picnic, and painted till dusk: precious empty days, few enough but intense in memory, when the world simplified before him to the play of light on form. Now like everyone else his time is filled with the tedium and pettiness of war. The cause may be great, but the life is diminished.

He leaves his bike in front of the house and goes through to the galleried hall. The first person he meets coming down the sweeping staircase, taking the steps two at a time, is Johnny Parrish.

'We're running late,' says Parrish. 'CO's morning briefing's now at 0830.'

'Not like Woody to run late.'

'Bobby Parks is joining us. He's one of your lot, isn't he?'

Parks is in Intelligence at Combined Ops. Larry has not been told he's coming, but this is par for the course. Communication between the various branches of the organisation is erratic at best.

He checks his watch. He has a good fifteen minutes.

'I'll go and find the ATS drivers.'

'Motor Transport Office in A Block. Who are you after?'

'Corporal Kitty. I don't know the rest of her name.'

'Oh, Kitty.' Parrish raises his bushy eyebrows. 'We're all after her.'

'Just passing on a message for a friend.'

'Well, you can tell your friend,' says Parrish, 'that Kitty has a boyfriend in the navy, and if, God forbid, her sailor buys it one day, an orderly queue will form at her door, and your friend can go to the end.'

'Righto,' says Larry cheerfully.

Captain Parrish goes into the dining room where breakfast is laid out for senior staff. Larry makes his way down the passage past the organ room to the garden door. Outside there's a wide stone-paved terrace enclosed by a low stone balustrade. This terrace is raised above a second grass terrace, which in turn is raised above the extensive park. An avenue of lime trees crosses the park, leading to an ornamental lake. On either side of the avenue, laid out in grid formation between the lake and the house, lie row upon row of Nissen huts.

Larry pauses to admire the camp. The anonymous engineer who devised its plan has instinctively worked to counterpoise the neo-Gothic riot that is the big house. The camp is a modernist vision of order. Military discipline asserts control over the mess of life. What can be made straight is made straight.

He passes down the stone steps to camp level. A soldier heading for the ablutions huts gives him a grin and a wave. Larry is still new as liaison officer to the division, but the Royal Hamilton Light Infantry are a friendly crowd, and seem to have accepted him. Johnny Parrish calls him their 'native guide'.

The door to the transport office stands open. Inside, two ATS girls are drinking tea in their shirtsleeves. One is stocky and red-faced. The other is tall and blonde, with a long face that might be called 'horsey'.

Larry says, 'I'm looking for Kitty.'

'Who wants her?' says the horsey girl.

'Just delivering a message. Purely social. From a friend she met in the pub last night.'

'The commando?'

'Yes.'

The horsey girl's manner changes. She throws a glance at the red-faced girl.

'What did I say?' Then to Larry, 'She's in the lake house.'

'Thanks.'

He needs no directions to the lake house. It's a shingle-roofed hexagonal wooden structure built out over the water, linked to the shore by a jetty. The jetty is roped off, and a sign on the rope reads: *Out of bounds to all ranks*.

He steps over the rope and crosses the jetty to tap softly on the closed door. Getting no answer, he opens the door. There, seated on the floor with a book resting in her lap, is a very pretty young woman in uniform.

'Are you Kitty?' he says.

'For God's sake shut the door,' she says. 'I'm hiding.'

He comes in and shuts the door.

'Down,' she says. 'They can see you.'

He drops down to sit on the floor, below the level of the windows. All he has to do now is pass on his message and leave. Instead, he finds himself taking in every detail of this moment. The moving patterns on the walls thrown by sunlight reflected from the surface of the lake. The folds of her brown uniform jacket, discarded on the floor. The pebbled leather of her shoes. The way her body is curled, legs tucked beneath her and to one side. Her hand resting on the book.

The book is *Middlemarch*.

'That's a wonderful book.'

She looks at him in surprise. He realises that what has felt to him like a slow passage of time, within which he has come to know her well, has in reality been no more than a second or two, and he doesn't know her at all.

'Who told you I was here?' she says.

'The girls in the office.'

'What do you want?'

'I'm just passing on a message. You met a friend of mine in the pub, yesterday evening.'

'The commando?'

'He wants to ask you to lunch on Sunday.'

'Oh.' She wrinkles her brow. He watches her, but all he can think is how lovely she is. How he wants her to see him properly.

'Do you like it?' he says.

'What?'

'*Middlemarch*.'

'Yes,' she says. 'I didn't at first.'

'I suppose you find Dorothea a bit much.'

'Excuse me,' she says, 'but who exactly are you?'

'Larry Cornford. Liaison officer attached to Eighth Infantry.'

He holds out his hand. She shakes it, half-smiling at the formality. Smiling at the whole strange meeting.

'What on earth is she doing marrying Mr Casaubon?' she says. 'Anyone can see it's a really stupid idea.'

'Well, of course it is,' says Larry. 'But she's idealistic. She wants to do something noble and fine with her life.'

'She's a nincompoop,' says Kitty.

'Don't you want to do something noble and fine with your life?'

He can't help himself speaking as if they're on intimate terms. It just feels that way to him.

'Not particularly,' she says.

But her sweet face, those big brown eyes exploring him, puzzling over him, tell him otherwise.

'I don't expect you'll be an army driver for the rest of your life,' he says.

'Actually I love driving.' And then, briskly, aware that this is heading into uncharted waters, 'So what's this lunch?'

'Sunday. About twelve? The farm behind the church. It's where I'm billeted. Ed says bring your friend too. The blonde one.'

He manages not to say the 'horsey one'.

'If it's a farm, does that mean real food?'

'Absolutely.'

'Then we accept.'

'Right. Message delivered.' He rises. 'I shall leave you with Dorothea.'

Striding briskly back across the camp to the big house, anxious not to be late for the CO's morning meeting, Larry is aware of a new sensation. He feels light of body, light of heart. It seems to him that nothing really matters very much at all. Not his senior officers, not the war, not the turning of the whole great world. He tells himself it's the morning sunshine after weeks of rain. He tells himself it's no more than natural animal spirits inspired by the smile of a pretty girl. But he can still see that smile before him in his mind's eye. She's sharing with him the oddity that two strangers should be crouched on the floor of a lake house in wartime, discussing a nineteenth-century novel. She's trying to make him out. That wrinkle between her eyebrows asks: what sort of person are you? Her smile so much more than a smile.

As is his habit, his mind reaches for comparisons in art. Renoir's smudgy pink-cheeked girl reading a book, smiling to herself. But Kitty's smile wasn't private; nor was it provocative, like a hundred faux-innocent Venuses. She smiles to lay a courteous veil over an active curiosity. There's a painting like it by Ingres, of Louise de Broglie, gazing, head a little tilted, one finger to her cheek, daring the viewer to know her.

'Buck up,' says Johnny Parrish.

Larry hurries into the library, which is already noisy with the chatter of officers. Brigadier Wills arrives and the meeting begins. Most of it concerns the lessons to be learned from yesterday's exercise. Larry, perched on a window shelf at the back, allows his mind to drift.

He thinks of the library in his father's house in Kensington; far smaller than this grand open-roofed hall, but sharing the magic of all libraries, which is that the books on their shelves open onto infinite space. He came every evening in the school holidays to join his father in prayers in the library, which gave it something of the mystery of a church. He has almost no memory of his mother, who is in heaven, and therefore inescapably confused with the Mother of God. It came as a shock to him to discover when he was sent away to school that the Blessed Virgin cared for other children as well.

*Our Lady, hear my prayer. St Lawrence, hear my prayer.*

St Lawrence is his own saint, the third-century martyr who was roasted to death on a grid-iron, saying apocryphally, 'Turn me over, I'm cooked on this side.' There was fun with that at school.

Larry prays often, from long habit, inattentively. It has become the manner in which he expresses his desires. This despite the fact that at Downside the subtle monks taught him a wiser notion of prayer. Its object is not to seek God's intervention in our favour, but to align ourselves with God's will for us. Perhaps even – Larry has been especially drawn to this – to relieve us of self-will altogether. Dom Ambrose, the same monk who taught him to love George Eliot, was a devoted follower of Jean-Pierre de Caussade. The eighteenth-century Jesuit preached abandonment to the will of God within the sacrament of the present moment. Père de Caussade's prayer was 'Lord have pity on me. With you all things are possible.'

Lord have pity on me, prays Larry. Find me a girl like Kitty.

# 3

Ed Avenell shows up at River Farm early on Sunday morning, and by the time Larry gets up he finds Mary Funnell is eating out of his hands.

'Mary, sweet Mary,' he's saying to her, 'do you dance, Mary? Of course you do. I can always tell a girl who has dancing feet.'

He spins her round the kitchen table, bringing her back pink-faced and flustered to the draining board where she's been washing dishes.

'You'd dance the night away if you could.'

'What a terrible man your friend is,' Mary Funnell says to Larry. 'The things he says to me.'

'I'm buying your love, Mary,' says Ed. 'I'll say almost anything for a hard-boiled egg.'

Larry marvels to see Ed's charm operating at full throttle. The wonder of it is he tells nothing but the unvarnished truth, and yet he so manages it that the lonely and overworked farmer's wife feels he understands her and respects her.

The results are to be seen in the basket she is assembling for their lunch. Ed has decided it is to be a picnic. He now heads off to recce its location.

'You sort out the crockery, Larry. And don't forget glasses.'

By the time Kitty and Louisa come bicycling into the farmyard in their summer frocks, the war seems a thousand miles away. Ed reappears, and treats Kitty with an offhand friendliness, as if they have known each other for years.

'Larry, you take the basket. I'll take the box.'

'What am I to carry?' says Kitty.

'You can carry the rug if you like.'

Ed's plan is that they picnic in the copse above the nearby village of Glynde, on the flank of Mount Caburn. Kitty sits in the front of his jeep, with Larry and Louisa behind.

'You get your own jeep?' says Kitty.

'Not exactly,' says Ed. 'But in our outfit the idea is we use our initiative.'

'He's stolen it,' says Larry.

'What exactly is your outfit?' says Louisa.

'40 Royal Marine Commando,' says Ed.

'I've heard that name.' Kitty frowns, trying to recall where.

'Kitty drives the Brig,' says Louisa. 'She hears everything.'

'Is your CO called Phillips?'

'Joe Phillips, yes. How do you know that?'

'I must have had him in the back of the car. Does that mean your lot are part of the big show that's coming up?'

Ed laughs and glances back at Larry.

'What price security, eh?'

'Oh, save your breath,' says Louisa. 'Even the dumb Canucks know it's coming.'

Ed drives the jeep off the road up rising land into a wood,

and stops on the far side. Here a small clearing in the trees opens out to the east, giving a wide view of the Sussex plain. The fields, not yet harvested, lie brown and gold in the midday sun. Here and there the faded red of tiled roofs reveal a village.

Larry spreads the rug over the ground, and Kitty and Louisa unpack the picnic, exclaiming at the discovery of each new delight.

'Tomatoes! Hard-boiled eggs! Oh my God, I'm in heaven! Is this home-made bread? Look, Louisa! Real butter!'

Ed opens the flagon of cider and pours them all a glass. He proposes a toast.

'To luck,' he says.

Larry keeps looking at Kitty, and each time he looks he sees that her eyes are on Ed. He makes an effort to take control of his own foolishness. This entire picnic has been got up, after all, to give Ed a clear run at Kitty. As Ed's friend his duty is to pay attention to Louisa.

'Do you believe in luck?' he says to her.

'Not really,' she says. 'I'm not sure what I believe in. Does everyone have to believe in something?'

'You don't have to,' says Larry, 'but I think you do, whether you realise it or not. Even Ed.'

Ed has taken out a scary-looking long-bladed knife and starts cutting slices off the loaf.

'I believe in luck,' he says. 'And I believe in impulse. And I believe in glory.'

'What does that mean?' says Kitty.

'It means you do what you feel like, when you feel it. No fear, no shame, no hesitation. Live your life like an arrow in flight. Strike hard, strike deep.'

He strikes the loaf hard and deep.

'Good heavens!' says Kitty. 'How thrillingly single-minded.'

Her words are teasing, but her eyes shine.

'That is classic Ed tommyrot,' says Larry. 'Who wants to be an arrow?'

Louisa gathers up the chunks of bread as they fall.

'Do you mind if I start eating?' she says. 'I feel like I haven't eaten for at least a year.'

They all set to, getting their fingers messy with butter and tomato pulp, forming their bread into thick ragged sandwiches. Kitty takes on the job of peeling the hard-boiled eggs. Larry watches her, seeing the care with which she manages to remove the shell in large sections.

'You look as if you've done that before,' Ed says.

'I like peeling eggs,' says Kitty. 'I hate it when people take the shells off roughly, just smashing them into tiny pieces. How would you like to be undressed like that?'

She looks up and sees Ed's eyes on her, silently amused. She blushes. Ed takes one of the unpeeled eggs and says, 'Can anyone make this stand on one end?'

'Oh, that's Columbus's trick,' says Louisa. 'You just bash its bottom in.'

'No,' says Ed. 'No bashing.'

He scoops a little hollow in the earth and stands the egg upright in it.

'That's cheating,' says Kitty. 'You have to make it stand on a flat surface.'

'Only according to your rules,' says Ed. 'There's nothing about a flat surface in my rules.'

'Anyone can win if they make up their own rules.'

'So there's the moral,' says Ed. 'Always play by your own rules.'

Now he's looking at Kitty in a way that makes her shiver.

'I think you must be quite a ruthless person,' she says.

'Don't tell him that,' says Larry. 'You're just feeding his fantasy. He'll go on about impulse and glory again. Ed's always been rotten with romanticism. I expect that's why he joined the commandos. The lone warrior who kills without a sound and cares nothing for his own life.'

Ed laughs, not offended.

'More like a bunch of oddballs who can't fit in with the rest of the army,' he says.

'But don't you have to be tremendously tough?' says Louisa.

'Not really,' says Ed. 'Just a little crazy.'

Kitty looks at Ed most of the time because most of the time he seems not to be looking at her. She sees the small impatient movements he makes, the jerk of his head with which he flicks back the dark hair out of his eyes, the opening and closing of his hands as if he's grasping the air, or perhaps letting it go. He has long, delicate, almost feminine fingers. His complexion too is pale and girlish. And yet there's nothing soft about him, he feels as if he's made of taut wire; and every time those blue eyes turn on her his gaze hits her like a splash of cold water.

He says odd things in a straight way, his voice giving no clues. She can't tell when he's joking or serious. She feels out of her depth with him. She wants to touch the cool pale skin of his cheek. She wants to feel his arms pulling her towards him. She wants him to want her.

'That egg story,' Larry says. 'Columbus didn't make it up at all. Years before Columbus, Brunelleschi pulled the same trick, when asked to present a model for his design for the duomo in Florence. According to Vasari, at least.'

This is met by silence.

'Larry, as you can tell,' says Ed, 'was actually listening during class.'

Larry pulls a face to show he's a good sport, but in truth he's not having a good time. He's doing his best not to look at Kitty because every time he does so he's swept by a wave of longing. He watches Ed, so lean and debonair and at ease with himself, and he knows he has none of his effortless style. He can only look on in awe at the careless charm with which he is all too visibly fascinating Kitty. His own freckled face gives him away at every turn, wrinkling with earnest eagerness when he talks, smoothing out when understood into a grateful smile.

'I've always wanted to see Florence,' says Kitty.

'Rather you than me,' says Louisa. 'Art gives me a headache.'

'Don't say that to Larry,' says Ed. 'He wants to be an artist when he grows up.'

'And what do you want to be?' says Louisa.

'Oh, I shan't ever grow up.'

'Ed will succeed at whatever he turns his hand to,' says Larry. 'He can't help it. He's loved by the gods.'

Ed grins and tosses a fragment of bread at him.

'Those whom the gods love,' he says, 'die young.'

After they've eaten and drunk, Louisa takes out her box Brownie and makes them pose for a photograph.

'Kitty, you in the middle.'

'I hate being photographed,' says Kitty.

'That's because you're vain,' says Louisa. 'Be like Ed. He doesn't care.'

Ed is sitting by Kitty's side, his arms round his knees, his blue eyes gazing unseeingly into the distance. His shoulder touches Kitty's arm, but he seems not to be aware of it. Larry places himself on Kitty's other side, cross-legged, his hands on the rug behind him.

'Smile, Larry,' says Louisa.

Larry smiles. The shutter clicks. Louisa winds the film on.

'Oh, bother. That's the last one.'

'But we have to get you too,' says Kitty.

'There's no film left.'

'We'll make a memory instead,' says Ed.

They all look at him in surprise.

'What do you mean?' says Kitty.

'Oh, I don't know,' says Ed. 'Stand on our heads. Howl at the moon.'

'Kitty could sing for us,' says Louisa. 'She's got an amazing voice. She used to sing solos in her church choir.'

Ed fixes Kitty with a sudden intent gaze.

'Yes,' he says. 'Kitty can sing for us.'

Kitty blushes.

'You don't want to hear me sing.'

Ed raises one hand, as if it's a vote. He's still got his eyes fixed on Kitty. Larry raises his hand. So does Louisa.

'It's unanimous,' says Ed. 'Now you have to.'

'There's no accompaniment,' protests Kitty. 'I can't sing unaccompanied.'

'Yes, you can,' says Louisa. 'I've heard you.'

'Well, I can't sing with you all staring at me.'

'We'll close our eyes,' says Larry.

'I won't,' says Ed.

'It's all right,' says Kitty. 'I'll close mine.'

So she gets to her feet and stands there for a moment, collecting herself. The others watch her in silence, suddenly aware that for Kitty this is a serious matter.

Then she closes her eyes and sings.

The water is wide
I cannot cross o'er
And neither have I
The wings to fly.
Build me a boat
That can carry two
And both shall row,
My true love and I.

Her voice is high and pure and true. Larry looks from her to Ed and sees on his friend's face a look he's never seen before. So that's it, he tells himself. Ed's in love.

A ship there is
And she sails the seas.
She's laden deep
As deep can be;
But not so deep
As the love I'm in,
And I know not if
I sink or swim.

Then like one waking from a dream Kitty opens her eyes and takes in Ed's watching gaze. He holds her eyes and says nothing. She lifts her shoulders in a shrug of apology.

'That's all I can remember.'

'I think perhaps you're an angel,' says Ed.

'I'd just as soon not be,' says Kitty.

Later they lie on their backs on the rug, partly in sun and partly in shade, and gaze up at the summer sky. Isolated clouds go by, like sailing ships scudding slowly in the breeze. A single aircraft, high above, whines towards London.

'I'm sick of this war,' says Louisa. 'The world was so beautiful before. Now everything's so ugly.'

'What were you doing before the war, Louisa?'

'Oh, nothing. I came out in '39, the way you do. It was all very silly, I suppose. At the time I didn't like it really, being dressed up like a parcel and made to smile at dull little men. But now it seems to me it was heaven.'

'I'm grateful for the war,' says Larry. 'It's saved me from a life in bananas.'

That makes them laugh.

'It's not over yet,' says Ed. 'The bananas may get you yet.'

Kitty wants to know about the bananas. Larry tells her how his grandfather, the Lawrence Cornford after whom he's named, built up Elders & Fyffes, and invented the blue label stuck on bananas, and was the first to advertise fruit, and was known as the 'banana king'.

'When the Great War came along we had sixteen ships, and my grandfather was called in by the First Sea Lord to help with the war effort. He said, "My fleet is at the disposal of my country." The First Sea Lord was Prince Louis of Battenberg, Mountbatten's father. Which is why I'm in Combined Ops now.'

'The long arm of the banana,' says Ed.

'I think it sounds like a wonderful business,' says Kitty.

'Well, everyone laughs when you say it's bananas,' says Larry, 'but actually places like Jamaica depend on the banana trade. And this blue label thing really was quite revolutionary in its day. No one believed you could brand fruit until my grandfather did it. It was a tremendous struggle finding the right sort of gum, and persuading the packers to stick the labels on. But my grandfather said, "Our bananas are the best, and when people realise that, they'll look for the blue label." And they did.'

'Now his dad runs the company,' says Ed. 'Guess who's next.'

'Unfortunately I'm a bit of a disappointment to my father,' says Larry.

'Isn't there a banana called Cavendish?' says Louisa.

'Absolutely,' says Larry. 'The Duke of Devonshire grew it in Paxton's conservatory at Chatsworth.'

'I'm a sort of cousin,' says Louisa.

'Then you should be very proud. My grandfather began the business shipping Cavendishes from the Canaries.'

'Why are you a disappointment to your father, Larry?' Kitty asks.

'Oh, because I want to be an artist. Dad was rather hoping I'd follow him into the firm. But mostly he's just afraid I won't be able to make a living.'

'Larry's good,' says Ed.

'You haven't seen anything of mine since school.'

'So? You were good then. I say follow your dream.'

'Impulse and glory, eh, Ed?'

'Strike hard, strike deep.'

His words hang lazily in the air above them, softened by the laconic tone.

Because Ed has been kind about his art, and because he's his best friend, and because it's going to happen anyway, Larry decides to be a good sport. Anything to put a stop to this ridiculous hankering feeling.

'Why don't you show Kitty Mount Caburn, Ed? Me and Louisa can stay here and talk about Cavendishes.'

'I've seen Mount Caburn,' says Kitty.

'You have to climb up to the top,' says Larry. 'Then you'll see a whole lot more.'

Ed gets up.

'Come on, then,' he says to Kitty. 'Ours not to reason why.'

Kitty gets up obediently.

'Well, all right,' she says. 'If I must.'

They set off together across the rising flank of the Downs.

'What was that all about?' says Louisa when they're out of earshot.

'Ed's stuck on her,' says Larry. 'He needs a shot at her on his own.'

'So kind Uncle Larry arranges it for him.'

Larry can tell from Louisa's voice that she understands precisely what he's done and why.

'I'd rather be kind Uncle Larry than sulk in a corner,' he says.

'Good for you,' says Louisa. 'I hope he realises.'

Larry sighs.

'Yes. He knows.'

They lie in silence for a while. Then Louisa sits up and wraps her arms round her knees and looks down at Larry.

'You seem a good sort,' she says.

'I am,' says Larry. 'Worse luck.'

'So I suppose you're in love with Kitty too.'

'Should I be?'

'It's just that everyone else is. I don't see why you should be any different.'

'Well, then.'

'She's a good sort too, actually. It's not as if she can help it. She told me she's had seven proposals. Seven!'

'And she still hasn't said yes.'

'Not so far.'

'I wonder what she's waiting for.'

'God knows. If you ask me she wants someone to make up her mind for her. You could just carry her off.'

Larry laughs at that.

'Ed would kill me,' he says. 'He did see her first.'

'Oh God, so what? All's fair and so on. But let's not talk about Kitty. She gets so much attention sometimes it makes me feel quite ill. And anyway, I've got a question to ask you.'

'Ask away.'

'How can I get George Holland to marry me?'

Larry bursts into laughter.

'Have you tried just asking him?'

'Girls can't do that.'

'Do you think he'd say yes if you did?'

'Put it this way. I think I'd make a jolly good wife for him, and he should be jolly grateful. But I don't think he knows it yet.'

'Well,' says Larry after a moment's thought, 'you could pretend to think he's proposed to you. Then you could accept. And by the time you've done accepting he'll think he must have proposed.'

Louisa gazes at Larry with a new respect.

'That,' she says, 'is brilliant advice.'

'Not my idea,' says Larry. 'Tolstoy's, in *War and Peace*.'

★

Kitty follows Ed up the long grassy slope, picking her way through the piles of sheep droppings. He strides ahead of her, not looking back, leaving her to follow at her own pace. She doesn't mind. Watching his lean powerful body climb the hill, she understands that his single-mindedness is in his nature, and nothing to do with her. He sees a hill to be climbed and he climbs it. This leaves her free, unburdened by her habitual impulse to please.

When he reaches the long flat approach to the top he stops and waits for her. Ahead the circular ridges of the old Iron Age fort ring the summit.

'Bit of a scramble here,' he says. 'You might need some help.'

He holds her hand as they descend into the wide grassy ditch, and supports her on the steep climb up the other side. His hand is warm and dry and very strong. As they reach the shallow dome of the summit he lets go of her and spreads his arms at the view.

'There!' he says, as if the view is his gift to her.

That makes her laugh.

Southward below them the river winds past the sprawling village of Edenfield to the distant sea. Kitty gazes down as if from an aeroplane. She sees the Canadian Army camp drawn up in its ranked rows in the park, and the shine of the lake, and the spikes and towers of Edenfield Place. Seen from this distance her little world seems to dwindle into nothingness. There's a wind up here on the top of the Downs, it flurries her hair and makes her eyes water.

'You see over there,' says Ed, 'where the river meets the sea. That's a haven.'

'Newhaven,' says Kitty.

She gazes at the harbour of the little port, and the long embracing arm of its pier.

'I like the idea of a haven,' says Ed. 'The river always running, running. And then at last it meets the sea, and can rest.'

'I've never thought of the sea as restful,' says Kitty. She's touched by his words. 'But haven does rather sound like heaven, doesn't it?'

She looks up. The sky above is big and bare and frightening.

'Heaven's too far away,' he says.

'It makes me feel like I don't matter at all,' she says.

She looks down again. He's gazing at her with that perpetual half-smile.

'You don't matter. None of us matter. So what?'

'I don't know.' His smile confuses her. 'You want to feel you're some use, don't you?'

He doesn't answer this. Instead he reaches out one hand and gently pushes the hair away from her face.

'You're a lovely angel, Kitty,' he says.

'Am I?'

'I'm not what you think I am.'

'What do I think you are?'

'Single-minded. Ruthless.'

She's flattered that he's remembered her words. At the time he seemed hardly to hear.

'So it's all just an act, is it?'

'No,' he says. 'It's true enough. It's just not everything.'

'So what else are you?'

'Restless,' he says. 'Alone.'

Kitty has a sensation of falling. She wants to reach out to him. She's overwhelmed by the simple desire to hold him in her arms.

'Stupid thing to say,' he says. 'I don't know why I said it.'

'It's a terrible thing to say.'

'Yes, it is terrible. There are times when I feel terror. Doesn't everyone?'

'I expect so,' says Kitty.

'But we don't talk about it, do we?'

'No,' she says.

'In case it wins.'

'Yes.'

'Will you kiss me?'

He means, if you kiss me the terror won't win. If you kiss me, we won't be alone any more.

'If you want,' she says.

He draws her into his arms and they kiss, wind-blown on the top of Mount Caburn, beneath the infinite emptiness of the sky.

# 4

Opposite Downing Street, across Whitehall, a short but grand street named Richmond Terrace runs down to the river. The entrance to 1A Richmond Terrace, a handsome doorway into a ponderous stone building, is neither identified nor guarded. This is the headquarters of Combined Operations, a warren of overcrowded offices that are always bustling with activity. Officers from all three services stride purposefully down basement corridors, past unmarked doors where unnamed teams are at work on secret schemes to win the war. Combined Operations was formed to develop amphibious assaults, bringing together sections of Army, Navy and Air Force. The ethos is non-hierarchical. The head of Intelligence, a one-time racing driver, was until recently managing the Curzon Cinema in Mayfair. Organisations have a way of reflecting the personality of their leaders, and this is supremely so in this case. Its chief, appointed by Churchill personally, is Vice-Admiral Lord Louis Mountbatten, known to all as Dickie. When Churchill offered him the job, Mountbatten initially declined, wishing to stay in the navy. 'Have you no sense of glory?' Churchill thundered.

Dickie Mountbatten has a sense of glory. Direct in all his dealings, handsome, charming, with a strong streak of the maverick, he has set about building an organisation that is free-thinking, innovative, and above all, informal. He has brought in friends, and friends of friends, who are known collectively as the Dickie Birds. Staff numbers have grown from twenty-three on his appointment to over four hundred.

A chance encounter between Lord Mountbatten and William Cornford at a club led to an invitation to Larry to present himself at Richmond Terrace in early March. There, as is the way of these things, Larry was greeted by someone who had been in his house at school, in the year above him: a beak-nosed, prematurely balding young man called Rupert Blundell.

'Cornford, isn't it? You thinking of joining us?'

'That seems to be the general idea.'

'You know what they call this place? HMS Wimbledon. All rackets and balls. But don't let that put you off.'

The interview with Lord Mountbatten, which Larry supposed would explore his own very limited war record, was entirely taken up with memories of his grandfather.

'Lawrence Cornford was a fine man,' said Mountbatten. 'My father thought highly of him. My father was First Sea Lord at the time, but when the war came, the Great War, they pushed him out because he had a German name. Disgraceful business. Even the King had to scuttle about and bodge himself up an English name. If my father was German, so was the entire royal family. It was Asquith behind it, he was a total shit. Though Winston comes out of it pretty poorly, too. He was at the Admiralty back then, he could have stopped that nonsense. I was a naval cadet at Osborne when it happened, fourteen years old.

It was quite a blow, I can tell you. But anyway, your grandfather, the banana king, wrote a letter to *The Times* deploring the decision. "Have we so many great men," he wrote, "that we can afford to lose one because his name is not Smith or Jones? If Great Britain is to remain great, we need leaders of the stature of Prince Louis of Battenberg." My father appreciated that very much. So you're looking for a change of scenery, are you? Well, we're an odd bunch. The only lunatic asylum in the world run by its own inmates. But if I've got anything to do with it we should have some fun.'

This was the extent of it. Larry learned he was seconded to Combined Ops, and duly reported to Richmond Terrace. Rupert Blundell took him under his wing.

'Any idea what you're supposed to be doing?'

'None whatever,' said Larry.

'Something'll come up,' said Rupert. 'Inertia, crisis, panic, exhaustion. The four phases of military planning.'

He carried Larry off to a dungeon-like basement room which was fitted out as a canteen. Here over mugs of tea they swapped memories of schooldays.

'Of course I hated every minute of it,' said Rupert, the steam from his mug of tea misting his glasses. 'But as far as I can tell that's the point of school.'

'I rather liked it,' said Larry. 'It was more fun than life at home, I can tell you.'

'Fun?' Rupert shook his head, bemused. 'I expect it's me that's the problem. I've never been much of a one for fun.'

'You were a brainbox,' said Larry. 'We were all in awe of you.'

He could picture Rupert Blundell from those long-ago schooldays, moving rapidly down the long corridors, keeping close to the wall, books under one arm, murmuring to himself. Spindly, bespectacled, alone.

He found himself wondering what Rupert was doing in Combined Ops. He couldn't imagine this unworldly figure leading an amphibious assault.

'Oh, we're all cranks and Communists in COHQ,' Rupert told him. 'Solly Zuckerman roped me in to do what he calls thinking the unthinkable. I'm supposed to come up with wacky ideas that challenge the conventional military approach. Could it be done other ways? Is the price worth the cost? Keeping an eye on the bigger picture, and so forth.'

Larry's period of idleness did not last long. General Eisenhower arrived in London charged with planning the invasion of Europe, and began by calling for a probe of Nazi Europe's defences. No full-scale invasion could function without a port. A raid was planned that was designed to discover whether a major French port could be captured in working order.

At a meeting of the chiefs of staff Eisenhower emphasised the need to find the right commander for this 'reconnaissance in force'.

'I have heard,' he said, 'that Admiral Mountbatten is vigorous, intelligent and courageous. If the operation is to be staged with British forces predominating, I assume he could do the job.'

Mountbatten, who Eisenhower had not met before, was sitting across the table as he spoke. This was the beginning of an excellent working relationship. The planned raid was code-named Operation Rutter.

Mountbatten's intention was to use a combination of marines and commandos for Operation Rutter. However, the War Cabinet had become increasingly embarrassed over the Canadian troops stationed in England. For two years now an entire Canadian Army had been training and waiting. The Canadian press was agitating for their boys to be given some real fighting. So Mountbatten was ordered to expand the scale of Rutter, and make it a Canadian show.

The raid depended on absolute secrecy and surprise for its success. All information between Combined Ops in London and the Canadian forces encamped on the south coast had to be carried by hand. In this way, Larry found himself with a function.

On the last day of June 1942 Larry enters the main Ops Room as instructed, to find a heated discussion under way. The room is crowded, the key officers clustered round a table on which is spread a large map of the French coast. Rupert Blundell is making himself useful laying out a sequence of aerial photographs.

'I don't understand,' Mountbatten is saying. 'We asked for bomber strikes. Winston signed up for bomber strikes.'

'Scratched,' says the RAF man. 'Meeting of June the tenth. I've got the minutes somewhere.'

'Scratched?'

'Roberts didn't like it,' says the army man. 'Doesn't want bomb damage blocking the advance of his new tanks.'

'Leigh-Mallory said the target was too small,' says the RAF man.

Mountbatten looks disconcerted.

'Where was I when all this was decided?'

'You were in Washington, Dickie,' says Peter Murphy.

'How many battleships have we got? We have to soften them up somehow.'

'No battleships,' says the navy man. 'Dudley Pound vetoes battleships off the French coast in daylight. Says it's utter madness.'

'So what have we got?'

'Hunt-class destroyers.'

'Destroyers?'

'And,' says the army man, 'one hell of a lot of Canadians.'

Larry feels he shouldn't be hearing this. He moves forward just as Rupert Blundell moves back.

'I was told to pick up a packet for Div HQ,' he says in a whisper.

Blundell looks round his colleagues.

'Orders for Div HQ?' he says to no one in particular.

Bobby Casa Maury, Head of Intelligence, sees Larry by the doorway and frowns. He speaks low to Mountbatten. Mountbatten looks up and recognises Larry.

'One of ours,' he says. He returns to the map. 'What's the story on air support?'

'Full pack there,' says the RAF man. 'Should be the biggest show of the war.'

'Excellent,' says Mountbatten, cheering up. 'Control the air and the battle's half won.'

Bobby Casa Maury catches Larry's eye and waves one hand, palm downwards, fingers flicking forwards, in a gesture that means go away. Larry withdraws.

In the hallway outside a Wren called Joyce Wedderburn sits at a desk with a typewriter and two telephones, guarding entrance to the chief. She gives Larry a friendly smile as he sits himself down on one of the upright chairs that line the long wall.

'Back to waiting?' she says. 'Want a cup of tea?'

'No, thanks,' says Larry. 'Shouldn't be long.'

He finds himself thinking how much better it would be if there were pictures on the walls. So much of wartime consists of sitting, waiting, staring at blank walls. Why not get all the artists painting, and hang all their pictures on all the walls? Even if you don't like a picture you can stare at it and see everything that's wrong with it, which passes the time. All it would take would be for someone like Mountbatten to give the order, and all over the country armies of artists would set to work doing watercolours of sunsets, and army canteens and ministry corridors would take on a new eccentric character. Put a picture on a wall and you cut a window into another world.

From this he falls to thinking of all the paintings he knows which represent actual windows, and the view beyond. Leonardo's *Madonna of the Carnation*, which he saw once in Munich, with its view of mountains framed by arched openings. Or Magritte's strange broken windows, where the fragments of glass carry the same sunset sky as the view beyond, but fractured and displaced. The effect of the frame within the frame is potent, almost magical. What is it about windows? The comfort and safety of the known world set beside the promise and excitement of a world beyond.

'There you go.'

It's Rupert Blundell with a big brown envelope. Larry jumps up and takes the packet, pushes it into his satchel.

'Wish the boys luck from us,' says Blundell.

# 5

A sharp rat-a-tat at the bedroom door summons Kitty and Louisa from a deep sleep. Hurriedly they wake, wash, dress. Downstairs the great hall is abuzz with activity. Colonel Jevons is standing in the Oak Room lobby with a sheet of paper on which are lists of names.

'You've just got time for a bite of breakfast,' he tells Kitty. 'Have the Brig's car outside for 0330.'

She follows the stream of half-asleep men clustering round the tea urn in the dining room. At this hour she can't eat. The others coming and going round her seem to be taking care to make as little noise as possible. Then she realises they're all wearing soft-soled boots.

Her section leader, Sergeant Sissons, is pacing the yard by the garages, using her torch to direct the troop transport trucks.

'Got your orders?'

'All set,' says Kitty.

She opens the garage doors and feels her way down the side of the Humber to the driver's door.

'Early for you, Hum,' she tells the car. 'Be a darling and start first time.'

As she reverses out into the yard she sees the lines of soldiers filing into the transport trucks. They move silently, shadows in the deeper shadow of the night. The headquarters building is alive with purposeful activity, but all of it muffled and cloaked in darkness. She drives slowly out of the yard and round the chapel, finding her way to the front porch by the slot of light from the car's blackout masks.

Jevons comes out and sees that she's in place. Other cars begin to arrive. She no longer feels in the least sleepy. She hears the throb of truck engines in the yard, the crackle of boots on the gravel, the drone of a plane passing overhead. Not yet dawn, but the world is up and about its work.

A mass of officers now appear from the house. They stand close together, torchlight flickering over papers held open between them. The heavy lorries start rumbling past, away down the drive. Then the doors of the Humber are being opened from the outside and officers are climbing in. Shortly Kitty hears the brigadier's voice from behind her head.

'Let's go,' he says.

'Where to, sir?' says Kitty.

That causes a soft laugh from the officers. So much secrecy, no one has thought to tell the driver.

'Newhaven,' says the brigadier. 'The harbour.'

Kitty eases the Humber down the drive, following behind a long line of troop transports, their tail lights glowing softly in the night. At the junction with the road she takes her turn, waiting as vehicle after vehicle rolls past. A faint gleam is now appearing in the sky to the east. Behind her the voices of the officers murmur, and papers rustle. She hasn't been told what's going on, and knows better than to ask, but it doesn't take a genius to guess.

On the dark winding road now, and making for the coast. The light grows brighter on the horizon. The boys in the back of the truck ahead wave at her and grin. One of the officers behind lights up a cigarette, and the tang of smoke fills the car.

The harbour cranes come into view. The road runs alongside the railway. The column of trucks rolls into the port, and the Humber follows. The great marshalling yard by the quay is full of vehicles and disembarking men. Out on the water, lit now by the dawn, lies an immense fleet of craft of every size. Little boats are buzzing about, carrying men from craft to craft. A crane is hoisting an armoured vehicle onto a deck. The heavy throb of ship's engines fills the air.

'This'll do,' says the brigadier.

Kitty pulls up and the officers get out. Kitty too gets out, and stands by the car as she's been taught. No one pays her any attention. The brigadier strides away, trailed by his staff. All round, platoons of men are being marched across the concrete yard to the boarding ramps. They wear helmets and carry guns and kitbags. No one shouts or breaks into song, the way troops on the move usually do. The early morning is filled with a purposeful seriousness.

Kitty waits and watches, and the sun rises. The scale of the operation slowly becomes visible. There are ships at sea all the way from the pier to the horizon. As each craft fills up with men and vehicles, it churns out of the harbour to join the waiting fleet.

A train pulls into the quayside and more streams of men get out. Among them Kitty sees a group moving differently to the rest. Instead of forming up in marching order, they slope along in a disorderly straggle, wearing wool hats in place of tin helmets.

She hears one of the other drivers murmur, 'Commandos.' For the first time it occurs to her that Ed might be part of the operation.

She leaves her post and goes to one of the muster officers by the ramps.

'Is 40 Commando going?' she asks.

'Can't say,' he replies.

She tries to find Ed among the faces streaming by, but there are too many and it's still too dark. She returns to her post.

The endless flow of tramping men moves onto the boats. After a while Sergeant Sissons comes round, releasing the drivers.

'Return to HQ. Await orders.'

'Will it be long, Sarge?'

'Long enough.'

One by one the staff cars pull away from the quay. Kitty is reluctant to leave. She's still there, standing by her car, when the muster officer she approached comes over to her.

'Got a boyfriend in 40 RM, then?' he says.

She nods.

'They've embarked,' he says. 'Don't say I said so.'

He leaves her there, looking out to sea at the great fleet.

*Got a boyfriend in 40 RM, then?*

She hardly knows him. They've met twice, kissed once. And yet the memory of his pale face is before her, his mouth almost smiling, his blue eyes holding hers, his thoughts unreachable. She realises with a sudden ache that she wants more than anything to see him one more time. There's something she wants to say to him that he may not know. That she wants him to know.

We've only just begun. Don't leave me yet. I'm waiting for

you, here on the harbour side at Newhaven. Where the river meets the sea.

She gets back into the Humber and starts the engine. The great yard is almost empty now. Day has begun. A ridge of low cloud has gathered to hide the sun. It's the second day of July, and still this strange summer is keeping everyone guessing.

The journey back, alone in the car, alone on the road, has none of the electric anticipation of the journey out. The big house and the camp are empty and silent. She returns the car to its garage and crosses the yard to the inner courtyard, entering the house by the servants' door. The long dining room with its three bay windows and its heavy fake-leather wallpaper has been cleared of all signs of the early breakfast. Hungry now, she seeks out the kitchen.

Here, sitting at the scrubbed deal table, she finds George Holland. He's eating a bowl of porridge by himself. From the scullery beyond comes the clatter of washing up.

'Ah, Kitty,' he says, visibly cheered by her appearance. 'It's the strangest thing. I got up this morning and found the house empty.'

'Yes,' says Kitty. 'There's a big show on.'

'So when will they be back?'

'I don't know.'

'The real thing this time, is it?'

'Yes,' says Kitty.

George eats some more of his porridge.

'I expect you think it's a bit rich, me sitting here eating while men are risking their lives.'

'Not at all,' says Kitty.

'It's different for you,' he says. 'You're a girl. A man should fight.'

'We can't all be fighting. Someone's got to keep the country going.'

'I do have various official duties,' he says, frowning down at his bowl. 'Local defence, magistrate, that sort of thing. But I can't fight. Eyesight, you know.'

'I'd better be going,' says Kitty.

'Don't go. There's something I want to say.'

He takes his bowl and spoon into the scullery and returns empty-handed, nervous, avoiding her eyes.

'Odd to have your own house full of strangers,' he says. 'Have you seen the library?'

'It's the officers' mess,' says Kitty.

He leads her across the hall and into the Oak Room, the lobby to the library. He points to the lettering on the doors.

'*Litera scripta manet, verba locuta volant.* "The written word remains, the spoken word flies away." All very true, of course. But even so . . .'

His voice tails away. He leads her into the library itself.

The great arched window at the end floods the long room with light. Down the walls on both sides stand book-stacks numbered with Latin numerals, holding leather-bound volumes with gold titles. The floor is a pattern of inlaid marble, a tangle of leaves and flowers. Clusters of War Office-supply armchairs stand about on this shiny expanse. A table at the far end is crowded with bottles.

'It's not the way we had it before the war, of course,' says George, looking round. 'My father was a great traveller, you know. He collected maps and travel books. I do a bit in that way myself.'

'It's a beautiful room,' says Kitty. 'You must hate having your house messed up like this.'

'No, no. It's good to see it full of life. Houses need to be lived in.'

He crosses to the high window and stands looking out at the park and the distant rows of Nissen huts. Kitty understands that he's leading up to something.

'The world has changed so much, hasn't it?' he says.

'War does that,' says Kitty.

'People come and go. They live and die. You can't stand on ceremony any more. My father has left me a relatively wealthy man. That must be worth something, don't you think?'

'Oh, yes,' says Kitty.

'But this eyesight business isn't so good. Rather clips my wings. Cramps my style. No point in complaining. There are pros and cons to every venture you undertake. Are you a reader?'

'Yes,' says Kitty. 'I love reading.'

'I'm not so much of a reader myself. I find it tires me. Anyway, the thing is this. What do you say about it? Is it something you could contemplate? Or do you recoil in horror?'

Kitty's about to say he's not made himself clear, when she stops herself. Of course he's made himself clear. She's known from the moment he finished his porridge in the kitchen. He doesn't deserve to be forced into the humiliation of speaking the plain words.

'Earlier this morning,' she says, 'I was at Newhaven watching the men go into the boats. Wherever they're going, they're going into danger. And you see, among them is the man I love.'

Strange to be saying these words to someone she barely knows; words she has not yet said to Ed.

'The man you love,' says George. 'Yes. Of course.'

'I shall be there on the quayside when he returns.'

'Quite right. Quite right.'

He moves away down the long empty room. His arms hang loosely by his sides, as if he's lost the use of them.

'I should report back to my section leader,' says Kitty.

'Yes, of course.'

He's standing before the carved stone mantelpiece, gazing at the framed photographs arrayed there.

'My mother,' he says, indicating one of the photographs. 'If you go into the chapel, there's a plaque on the south wall. It says, "In memory of a faithful wife and a loving mother." I could have said much more, but in the end that seemed to cover it. A faithful wife. A loving mother. What more can a man ask?'

Kitty leaves him with his photographs and his memories. She wants to be out of this house. It's too full of sadness.

She finds Louisa in the Motor Transport Office in A Block.

'Let's get out of here,' says Kitty. 'No one'll miss us.'

They ride their bikes down the Eastbourne road as the clouds gather and the sky darkens. They've just reached the Cricketers in Berwick when the rain starts to fall. There, wet and panting and pink-cheeked, they beg the bar girl for something – anything – to eat, and she brings them cold boiled potatoes. Two farm workers come in to escape the rain and stare at them.

'Don't know why we bother,' they grumble to each other. 'Could have done with this back in April.'

By silent agreement Kitty and Louisa don't talk about the great military operation now under way. Kitty tells Louisa about George Holland.

'I knew it,' says Louisa. 'I could tell from the way he watched you like a dog waiting for his dinner.'

'Poor George. He always looks so lost.'

'Not all that poor. He's a millionaire, and a lord. There's a limit to how sorry you can feel for him.'

'Anyway, I told him my heart was pledged to another.'

'Even though that's a whopping lie.'

'Actually it isn't,' says Kitty. 'It turns out I'm in love with Ed.'

'Kitty! When did this happen?'

'I don't quite know. I only realised it this morning, when I was watching the boys going away. I just want him to come home safe.'

'Oh, Kitty.' Louisa is touched by Kitty's trembling voice. 'Have you really fallen in love at last?'

'I think so. I'm not sure.'

The rain passes, blown away by strong south-westerly winds. They bicycle home down the empty road, side by side, with the wind on their backs.

'So what's going to happen to poor George?' says Louisa.

'He'll be fine,' says Kitty. 'Some strong-minded female will gobble him up.'

'You make him sound like a canapé.'

'He's rich and titled. Someone'll have him.'

'What about poor Stephen?'

'I'll write to him. Oh, God. Isn't it all difficult?'

'You know what,' says Louisa, 'now that you're out of the running with George, I might have a go myself.'

Kitty wobbles wildly on her bike and regains control.

'Are you serious? You know he's practically blind?'

'I haven't had a single proposal, Kitty. My people have no money to speak of. God has billeted me in the house of a young unmarried man with a title and a fortune. It would be ungrateful to the Almighty not to give it a shot.'

Kitty pedals on without further comment.

'I expect you despise me for seeing things this way,' Louisa says.

'No, not at all,' says Kitty. 'I just want you to be happy.'

'Don't you think I'd be happy with George?'

'If you loved him you would.'

'If he marries me,' says Louisa simply, 'I shall love him.'

They bicycle down the back lane into the camp. A small crowd has gathered round the front of the NAAFI to share such news as there is. Everyone is asking if this is the start of the second front.

Kitty sees Larry Cornford come out of the big house onto the west terrace. He gives her a wave, and they meet up in the lime avenue. They too talk about the big show.

'I saw them go,' says Kitty.

'I don't like this wind,' says Larry. 'They need calm seas for the crossing.'

'Do you know where they're going?'

'I know,' says Larry, 'but I can't say.'

'Has to be somewhere in France.'

'Nothing we can do now till they come back.'

Kitty says, 'I think Ed's with them.'

'It's quite likely.'

'Will you promise to come and tell me if you hear anything?'

'Yes, of course.'

They walk on in silence to the lake. The lake house stands empty before them.

'How are you getting along with *Middlemarch*?' says Larry.

'I can't read,' says Kitty. 'I can't do anything.'

'He'll come back,' says Larry.

'You don't know that. He may not.'

Larry says nothing to that.

'At least you've not gone,' she says. 'You, and George.'

Larry looks away over the wind-ruffled lake.

'I expect my turn will come,' he says.

That night the winds grow stronger, and rattle the casement in the nursery window. Kitty sleeps fitfully, tormented by half-dreams in which Ed is reaching for her from a distance she can't cross.

In the morning word spreads round the camp that the fleet is still standing offshore, and has not yet sailed. The forecast is that the weather will worsen. In the way of such things, half-understood terms are passed from mouth to mouth. 'They'll miss the tide.' 'The RAF won't fly in this.' 'You need air cover for a big op.'

The day passes slowly. In the late afternoon rain begins to fall again. Larry rides over to Divisional HQ and takes part in a meeting with the Acting CO. When he comes out he goes looking for Kitty and finds her cleaning the Humber in the garage.

'You could eat your dinner off that,' he says.

'What's the news?'

'The show's off. Don't say I told you.'

'It's off?'

'All troops to be disembarked.'

'He'll come back?'

'Yes.'

Kitty feels a surge of relief beyond her power to control. There in front of Larry's kind concerned gaze she bursts into tears.

'Honestly,' she says, dabbing at her eyes, 'what have I got to cry about now?'

Larry smiles and offers her a handkerchief.

'He's a lucky sod,' he says. 'I hope he knows it.'

'You won't tell him, will you?'

'Not if you don't want.'

'It's too silly, crying like that.'

'If I was Ed,' says Larry, 'I'd be proud to know you cried for me.'

Just after six in the evening the order comes through for all drivers to muster at Newhaven harbour. Kitty makes the short journey with a light heart. No one has been wounded. No one has died. But as she sees the men file off the ships, all their former swagger gone, she realises that for them this is a kind of failure. Standing by her car, she scans the hundreds of moving figures for the group that will contain Ed, but she doesn't find him. The trucks fill with men and grind past on the way back to the camp. Brigadier Wills comes stamping out to find her.

'Good girl. I'll be with you when I've seen to the navy chaps.'

So she waits on. She's used to it. A staff driver spends more time waiting than driving. This is usually when she reads, but recent events have unsettled her. So she stays beside the car, watching the slow dispersal of an army.

Soldiers go by laughing, grumbling.

'That was a fucking waste of time. I'd like to meet the genius dreamed that one up.'

One Canadian soldier mimics a British officer: 'I say, you chaps! The colonials are getting restless. Let's shut them in the hold for twenty-four hours and spray them with vomit, eh, what?'

Their laughter recedes into the distance.

'What's a nice girl like you doing in a dump like this?'

'Ed!'

She spins round, eyes glowing, and there he is. He's wearing rumpled battledress and carrying all sorts of bundles and his face is smeared with black. But underneath he's just the same. The same cool gaze in those blue eyes.

'Oh, Eddy!'

She throws her arms round him and kisses him. He holds her for a moment, and then gently eases her away.

'There's a welcome,' he says.

'I thought you'd never come back.'

'No chance of that,' he says. 'We never even went away.'

'Oh, Ed. I'm so happy.'

She can't disguise how she feels, and makes no attempt to. He smiles to see her happiness.

'Seeing you almost makes it worth it,' he says.

'Was it horrible?'

'I'll tell you,' he says, 'I'd rather parachute naked behind enemy lines than do that again.'

Kitty sees the brigadier heading across the yard towards the cars, accompanied by two of his staff.

'When can I see you, Ed?'

'Soon,' he says. 'I can't give you a day. Very soon.'

His eyes rest on her, suddenly gentle in that wild black-smeared face.

'My lovely angel,' he says.

Then he's gone.

The brigadier reaches the car.

'Well, that was Operation Rutter,' he says. 'Now you see it, now you don't.'

# 6

William Cornford is not an old man, but his bald head, together with a slight stoop in his posture, makes him appear more than his fifty or so years. He stands now in the doorway of the company offices at 95 Aldwych, feeling for his hat, watching as his son climbs off his motorbike. He hasn't seen him for many weeks. He looks on as he removes his helmet and gloves, noting every remembered detail of the boy who is all his family, his only child, the one he loves more than himself.

Then his son is before him, reaching out one hand, and the old formality returns.

'Spot on time,' Larry says. 'That's what the army's done to me.'

'Good to see you.' The father shakes the son's hand. 'Good to see you.'

'So what's the plan?'

'Lunch at Rules, I thought. Give us a chance to catch up.'

They walk round Aldwych and up Catherine Street, talking as they go. Larry asks about the company, knowing that this is what occupies his father's waking hours.

'Difficult times,' says William Cornford. 'Very difficult. But we've managed to keep all our people on so far.'

This is a major achievement in itself, as Larry knows. Since November 1940 bananas have been a prohibited food.

'No signs of a change of heart at the Ministry?'

'No,' says William Cornford. 'Woolton has told me himself the ban is for the duration. At least I've managed to convince him to do something for the growers in Jamaica.'

'The war can't go on for ever.'

'That's what I tell our people. In the meantime, we've become the vegetable distribution arm of the Ministry of Food. When the war's over, we'll just have to start again from scratch.'

'And how's Cookie?'

Miss Cookson is his father's housekeeper, at the family home in Kensington.

'Same as ever. Asks after you. Do look her up some day.'

Larry realises they've walked on past their turning.

'We should go down Tavistock Street, surely?'

'I thought we might take a turn past the old building,' says his father.

'Isn't that rather depressing?' says Larry.

'I find it has some value. *Lacrimae rerum*, you know.'

They walk up Bow Street to the place where the company headquarters building once stood. A direct hit in January last year destroyed the entire six-storey structure, leaving the tall side of the adjoining building standing, fireplaces exposed, doors agape. The site is still filled with rubble.

'Fifty years,' says William Cornford. 'Almost my entire life. This is where my father built the company up from nothing.'

Larry too remembers it well. The dark panelled room where

his father worked. Where they had their one and only terrible quarrel.

'Why are we here?'

'Thirteen of our people died that night.'

'Yes, Dad. I know.'

'Eight company ships sunk since the start of hostilities. Over six hundred members of staff on active service. All still on the payroll.'

'Yes, Dad. I know.'

'This is the front line too, Larry. We're fighting this war too.'

Larry says nothing to this. He understands what his father would like to say, but will never say. How does his son serve his country any better by wearing a uniform and riding a motorbike?

William Cornford was and remains deeply hurt that his son has not chosen to enter the family firm. The company built by his father, the first Lawrence Cornford, and made great by himself in the second generation, should be passed on, its culture and traditions intact, to the third. But Larry dreams a different dream.

Father and son walk on to Rules. They take their usual table under the stairs.

'Not what it was, of course,' says William Cornford, glancing over the menu. 'But they've still got shepherd's pie.'

'So how's Bennett?' says Larry.

'At his desk every morning. You know he'll be seventy this year?'

'I don't believe he ever actually goes home.'

'He asks after you from time to time. Maybe you could stop by after lunch and give him five minutes.'

'Yes, of course.'

The long-serving employees of the company are Larry's greater family. Most of them still believe he'll take his proper place in the hierarchy in time.

William Cornford studies the wine list.

'Care to share a bottle of Côte Rôtie?'

Larry asks his father to tell him more about the trading conditions of the company, framing his questions to show he understands the current difficulties; aware there's no one else his father can speak to of his worries.

'The branch depots are actually all running at full capacity, believe it or not. But the truth is I've been turned into a sort of a civil servant. I have to take my orders from the Ministry, which goes against the grain a little. I've never been a man for committees.'

'My God! You must hate it.'

'I'm not as patient as perhaps I should be.'

He gives his son a quick shy smile.

'But I expect you have your frustrations too.'

'Soldiering is ninety-nine per cent frustration,' says Larry.

'And the other one per cent?'

'They say it's terror.'

'Ah, yes,' says William Cornford. 'Battle.'

He himself has never been a soldier. In the Great War he remained in the company, which was then the nation's sole importer of fruit. Larry fully understands his father's complex feelings about his son's war service. He represents the family on the sacrificial altar of war, even as he deserts the company in its hour of need.

'So is Mountbatten looking after you?' his father asks him.

'Oh, I'm just a glorified messenger boy.'

'Still, I don't want you to come to any harm.'

This is the war his father has arranged for him: if not safe in Fyffes, then safe in a headquarters building in London.

'As it happens,' Larry says, 'the division I'm attached to looks like it's going into action soon.'

He sees his father's face, and at once regrets his words. He feels ashamed of pretending to a coming military action that will give his father sleepless nights.

'Though I doubt if they'll be taking me along. I'm afraid I'm doomed to be a paper-pusher.'

The wine comes. His father thanks the waiter with his usual courtesy.

'An excellent Rhône,' he says. 'We shall drink to the liberation of France.'

'Do you have any news of the house?'

The family has a house in Normandy, in the Forêt d'Eawy.

'I believe it's been requisitioned by German officers,' says his father.

He meets his son's eyes over their raised glasses. They share a love of France. For William Cornford it's the land of the great cathedrals: Amiens, Chartres, Albi, Beauvais. For Larry it's the land of Courbet and Cézanne.

'To France,' says Larry.

With the cancellation of Operation Rutter an uneasy calm settles over the Sussex countryside. The thousands of troops encamped on the Downs resume the training exercises designed more to occupy them than to raise their fighting form. More beer is drunk in the long evenings, and more brawls break out in the warm nights. The storms of early July pass, leaving overcast skies and a heavy sunless heat by day. No one believes the operation will be off for good. Everyone is waiting.

On a rare bright day Larry gathers up his paints and his portable easel and goes down to the water meadows by Glynde Reach. He sets up his easel on the hay-strewn ground and starts work preparing the board he's using as a canvas. He has in mind to paint a view of Mount Caburn.

As he works away, a figure appears from the direction of the farm. It turns out to be Ed.

'Thank God someone's around,' he says. 'I come all the way from the other side of the country to see Kitty and she's not bloody there.'

'Did you tell her you were coming?'

'How could I? I didn't know myself.'

He stands behind Larry, looking at the sketch forming on the board.

'I really admire you for this,' he says.

'Good Lord! Why?'

'Because it's something you love to do.' He kicks moodily at the hay on the ground. 'There's nothing I really want to do. I feel like a spectator.'

'You want to see Kitty.'

'That's different. Anyway, she won't be back till this evening. What do I do till then?'

'You could always help Arthur get his hay in.'

This is not a serious suggestion, but rather to Larry's surprise his friend seizes on it eagerly. He goes back to the farmhouse and reappears a little later pulling a light hay cart.

'Arthur says I'll make a mess of it,' he says, 'but it doesn't matter as it's ruined already.'

'Rather you than me,' says Larry.

Ed strips to the waist, takes a long-handled rake out of the cart, and proceeds to gather the lying hay into mounds. Larry looks round from his painting from time to time, expecting to see his friend leaning on his rake, but Ed never stops. His lean, tight-muscled body gleams with sweat as he works, keeping up a pace no overseer would ever demand. As he forms the hay into knee-high piles he drags the cart alongside and hoists the hay into it. With each lift he emits a short low grunt of effort.

Larry's attention is on the line of trees before him, and the rise of land that culminates in the round prominence that is Mount Caburn. His brush, moving rapidly, is reducing the scene to its essential elements, in which land and sky are masses of equal weight, the one cupped into the other. The flanks of the hill meet the dull sunlight at different angles, forming elongated triangles of different tones. He works with browns and reds and yellows, applying paint in rough dabs, hurrying to capture the ever-changing light.

When he next pays attention to his friend, he finds the hay cart is piled high.

'My God!' he exclaims. 'You must be exhausted. Give yourself a break, for heaven's sake.'

'Just getting into my stride,' says Ed, tossing another forkful of hay over the high hurdle side of the cart.

Larry watches him for a few moments, awed by his relentless self-discipline. For a man who wants to do nothing he has a remarkable capacity for work.

'You know what it's called, doing what you're doing?'

'What?' says Ed, never ceasing in his work.

'It's called doing penance. You're paying for your sins.'

'Not me,' says Ed. 'That's for you believers. I don't have to pay for my sins. They come free.'

Larry laughs at that and goes back to his painting.

At midday Rex Dickinson appears, carrying a basket.

'The good Mary has taken pity on you,' he says.

The three of them settle down in the shadow of the hay cart and eat bread and cheese and drink cider. Larry looks at Ed sitting sprawled on the hay-strewn earth, breathing slow deep breaths, chewing the thick home-made bread, sweat drying on his face and shoulders.

'You look like a handsome healthy animal,' he says.

'That's all I want to be,' says Ed.

Rex goes over to look at Larry's painting.

'Very Cézanne,' he says.

'I don't know why I bother,' says Larry. 'It's all been done before, and better.'

Rex looks round the silent landscape.

'You'd hardly know there's a war on.'

'I love war,' says Ed.

'That's because you're a romantic,' says Larry. 'Half in love with easeful death.'

'That's rather good.'

'Not me. Keats.'

'As far as I'm concerned,' says Ed, 'I'll be dead by Christmas. And that's just fine. Once you make up your mind to it, everything tastes and smells so much better.'

Larry frowns, unsure whether or not to believe him.

'But what about Kitty?' he says.

'What about her?'

'I thought you loved her.'

'Oh, Lord, I don't know.' Ed stretches himself out full length on the ground. 'What kind of future can I offer a girl?'

'Have you told her you're planning on being dead by Christmas?'

'She doesn't believe me. She says that if she loves me enough I won't be killed.'

'She's right,' says Larry. 'When you love someone, you can't believe they'll ever die.'

'I believe we're all going to die,' says Ed. 'I suppose that means I don't love anyone.'

'Kitty thinks you love her.'

'Well, I do.'

'You just say the first thing that comes into your head, don't you?'

Ed rolls over and shades his eyes with one hand so he can gaze at Larry.

'We've known each other a long time,' he says. 'We don't have to piss about saying polite nothings, do we? We can be pretty straight with each other, I'd say.'

'I go along with that.'

'The thing is, Larry, I think you genuinely are a good chap. One of the very few I know. But I'm not a good chap. I live in what you might call the outer darkness. I really do. I'm not proud of it. What I see when I look ahead is darkness. I know you think I'm just being selfish. But I do love Kitty, and I ask myself if it's fair to drag her into that dark place.'

Larry realises now what it is his friend wants from him. He loves him for it, even as he feels the sad weight of it fall upon him.

'What is this, Ed? You want some kind of blessing from me?'

'Maybe I do.'

'All you owe her is your love,' he says.

'What about the darkness?'

'It's not your private darkness.'

He speaks so softly that Ed doesn't hear him.

'What's that?'

'It's not your private darkness,' he says again, louder.

Ed stares at him.

'We all have to face it,' says Larry. 'Kitty too. She's not a child.'

Ed goes on staring at him.

'The war won't go on for ever,' says Rex.

Larry returns to his painting. His brush moves more quickly now, applying paint in bolder strokes. Above the hill the sun is burning through the layer of cloud, and in his painting the sky becomes charged with amber and gold.

Ed has had enough of haymaking. He puts one hand on Larry's shoulder, squeezing it.

'Thanks.'

'What for?'

'You know.'

Rex stays on after Ed has left them, mooching about the stream bank looking for butterflies.

'You should study butterflies, Larry. Their colouring is just like a work of modern art. See there, that's a Meadow Brown. A really common species. But on each brown wing there's a patch of yellow, and in each patch of yellow there's a black spot, like an eye.'

Larry goes on painting, but he's grateful for Rex's presence. He wants to talk.

'What do you think about Ed and Kitty?' he says.

'Nothing, really,' says Rex.

'Do you think he's right for her?'

'I wouldn't know. That's rather up to her, isn't it?'

Larry changes brushes, and mixes up a blob of blue with a touch of black. He wants the sky to be more dangerous.

'Don't you think he sounds odd about it all?'

'He's an odd fellow,' says Rex.

He's found another butterfly worthy of remark.

'That's a Chalkhill Blue. Isn't he a beauty?'

Larry continues to pursue his line of thought.

'You say it's up to Kitty,' he says, 'which it is, of course. But she can only go on what's on offer. And right now, that's Ed.'

'Oh, I get it,' says Rex. 'You want to make a bid.'

'Do you think that's wrong?'

'It's not morally wrong,' says Rex. 'I suppose it might be considered bad form.'

'Well, that's just it,' says Larry. 'If one chap announces he's interested in a girl, does that mean he has some kind of rights over her? Does it mean everyone else has to keep off?'

Rex thinks about that.

'I think the general idea is you back off while the first fellow takes his shot. Then if he misses, you take a pot.'

'That's what I thought,' says Larry. 'But listening to Ed today I started thinking maybe I'm being a bit feeble. As you say, it's all up to Kitty.'

'Look, Larry,' says Rex. 'If you want to drop a hint to Kitty, I should just do it. I don't see what harm it can do.'

'Really?'

Larry works away on his thunderous sky.

'What about you, Rex? Don't you ever wish you had a girl?'

'Oh,' says Rex, 'I'm not very good at that sort of thing.'

Louisa Cavendish receives orders assigning her to new duties in central London, effective from the start of September. This has the effect of concentrating her mind.

'I'm taking the afternoon off,' she announces.

She touches up her lipstick, brushes out her corn-coloured hair, tightens her belt, and heads for the private quarters of the big house.

'George,' she says, finding the lord of the manor in the kitchen as usual, 'it's a warm day, and you should be outside. It's no good to be indoors all the time.'

George Holland looks at her in surprise.

'You sound like my mother,' he says.

'Did you like your mother?'

'I adored her.'

'Come on, then. Out for a walk.'

Not knowing how to refuse, George rises and follows.

'I know we've met,' he says politely, as they make their way through the outer courtyard, 'but I seem to have forgotten your name.'

'I expect I never told you. I'm Louisa Cavendish. Same family as the Devonshires. I'm a friend of Kitty's.'

'Oh, very well, then.'

'Why don't you take your glasses off?'

'I shouldn't be able to see very much if I did,' he says.

'Don't worry, I'll make sure you don't bump into things. Here, take my hand.'

She removes his glasses and he takes her hand. They walk out past the chapel. Louisa does not want to be seen by the camp.

'I expect you could do this walk with your eyes shut,' she says. 'We'll go up onto Edenfield Hill.'

She turns him towards the cart track that runs up the flank of the Downs.

'It's strange without my glasses,' he says. 'The world feels very different.'

'Different good or different bad?'

'Less alarming, somehow.' He turns to her with a shy smile. 'Rather a good idea of yours.'

'And what do I look like?' says Louisa.

'Somewhat indefinite,' says George.

'Describe what you see.'

He stares at her.

'White face. Eyes. Mouth.'

'Ten out of ten so far.'

'Sorry. I'm being dim.'

'What impression does my face make?'

'Rather impressive. Rather fine.'

'Okay. That'll do.'

They walk on to the top of the hill. A steady warm wind is blowing in off the sea, bringing with it flocks of gulls with their harsh cries.

'Can you see the view with your glasses off?' she asks him.

'Not exactly. I get the feeling of it, though.'

'What feeling?'

'Spacious,' he says. 'Roomy.'

'Liberating?'

'Yes. That's the one.'

'You see, I was right,' says Louisa. 'You should get out more.'

They walk a little way along the ridge.

'Don't you hate the war?' says Louisa.

'Yes,' he says. 'I think I do.'

'Having to give up your house. Having all those ghastly huts in your park. Having all the servants leave.'

'Yes,' he says with a sigh. 'It was all so different in my father's day.' Then he adds after a moment's thought, 'But I'm not the man my father was, of course.'

'He was a great man, I hear.'

'He was a giant,' says George. 'He made his fortune from nothing, you know. People think it was luck, that he stumbled on this little pill that everyone wanted, and that was that. But it wasn't luck at all. My father was the sort of man who could make the world do his bidding.'

'I'm not sure I'd like to have a giant for a father,' says Louisa.

'No,' says George. 'He did rather frighten me.'

He comes to a stop and peers at Louisa in his half-blind way. Then all at once his face crumples. To her dismay she realises he's about to cry. Without his glasses his face looks soft and helpless.

'I've never said that before,' he says.

'What you need is a hug,' says Louisa.

He comes awkwardly into her arms and lets her embrace him. Then pressing his face to her shoulder he begins to sob. She strokes his back gently, not speaking, letting him cry himself out like a child.

He takes out a handkerchief at last, and dries his eyes and blows his nose.

'You've been left alone too much, haven't you?' she says.

# 7

The conference room was built as a ballroom for the great London house, in the days when it belonged to the Duke of Buccleuch. Now, its tall windows bandaged with tape and blinded by blackout curtains, it exists in the perpetual gloom of underpowered electric lights. Here the commanding officers of the Canadian forces in southern England have gathered for a briefing by the chief of Combined Operations. Mountbatten, flanked by his service heads, wears the uniform of a vice-admiral of the fleet.

'Gentlemen,' he announces. 'We have been given the go-ahead. Your boys, weather permitting, will see action this summer after all. Naturally I can't give you a precise date today. But my message to you is: stand by!'

This is met with murmurs of approbation.

'The relaunched operation goes under the code name of Jubilee. Detailed orders for each sector are now being drawn up. My staff will issue them within a matter of days.'

He then invites questions. General Ham Roberts speaks first.

'Is there any concern, sir,' he says, 'that the element of surprise has been lost?'

'Because of Rutter, you mean?' says Mountbatten, nodding encouragingly.

'Yes, sir. The Germans can hardly have failed to notice something was afoot last time.'

'You're perfectly right,' says Mountbatten. 'So what are the Germans thinking? They're thinking that we couldn't possibly be so stupid as to lay on the same operation again.'

He pauses, and looks at the assembled commanders with his infectious boyish smile.

'So that's precisely what we're going to do!'

The last half of the drive back takes place in silence. The brigadier evidently has much on his mind. Kitty concentrates on her route, watching the road for the potholes caused by the endless convoys of heavy army vehicles. For much of the way she has the road to herself, and is able to maintain a steady fifty miles an hour. The petrol tank is on the low side. She makes a note to herself to fill it up tomorrow.

As they weave their way round the outskirts of Brighton the brigadier becomes conversational.

'I've been meaning to ask you, Kitty,' he says. 'Where do you come from? What do you call home?'

'Wiltshire, sir.'

'Is that a fine part of the world?'

'Yes, sir. Hills and woods.'

'I miss my home,' he says. 'I miss it real bad. My boys'll be turning ten soon. I haven't seen them for two years. Do you know Canada at all?'

'No, sir.'

'Why would you? I grew up in a little place on the shores of

Lake Huron called Grand Bend. Feels like a long way away now, I can tell you.'

He gazes out of the car window as they drive along the foothills of the Downs.

'This is pretty country,' he says, 'but it looks small to me.'

Kitty delivers the brigadier back to headquarters, and returns the Humber to its garage. She looks in on the Motor Transport Office to hand in her work docket and to request petrol for tomorrow. Louisa is there, and some of the other girls, and Sergeant Sissons.

'Don't forget the clocks go back on Saturday night,' says Sissons. 'End of double summer time.'

'Is that good or bad?'

'Another hour in bed, isn't it?'

'Anything on for this evening?' says Louisa.

'My night off,' says Kitty. 'I need it.'

'All right for some,' says Louisa.

She's looking at Kitty in an odd way.

'What?'

'Nothing,' says Louisa. 'Sweet dreams.'

Kitty climbs the terrace steps into the main house, suddenly feeling the strain of the long drive. She thinks maybe she'll just lie on her bed and read. She should be writing to Stephen, should have written to him days ago, it's not fair to leave him dangling. Except she never asked him to fall in love with her. How can you fall in love with someone you've only met twice? Then she thinks of Ed and blushes. But what can she say to Stephen? That she's met someone she likes better? Dear Stephen, I value your friendship but I don't want to tie you down. And so on.

She has no means of communicating with Ed, and no idea

when she'll see him again, but she thinks about him all the time. Not in a making-plans sort of way: it's more that the idea of him is a permanent presence in her life now, which causes her to feel differently about everything. Because of him the immediate future has become unpredictable and exciting.

She can hear her mother's warning voice: Don't get in too deep. What are his prospects? How's he going to provide for you? But her secret dreams of Ed have nothing to do with marriage. It's not about living happily ever after.

I want to get in too deep, Mummy. I want to be swept off my feet, and not be able to do anything about it. I want adventure.

She climbs the dark and narrow nursery stairs to the corridor in the eaves. As she goes she begins the process of unbuckling her belt, then undoing the four brass buttons of her uniform jacket. She loosens her tie and undoes the top button of her shirt. She's tugging the tie out of her collar as she enters the nursery bedroom.

Ed is lying on her bed.

He puts a finger to his lips.

'Shut the door,' he says softly.

She shuts the door.

He lies there in his shirtsleeves, his hands behind his head, his shoes kicked off his feet. His eyes hold her with that mocking gaze.

'How did you know this was my room?'

'Louisa told me,' he says.

'I'm going to kill her.'

'That would be an overreaction,' he says.

She stands there gazing down at him, confused but excited. She's not sure what he expects her to do.

'How about saying hello?' he says.

He makes no move to get up. She goes nearer to the bed. His arms reach up and draw her down. They kiss, in a polite, almost formal way.

'Hello,' she says.

Then he pulls her onto the bed, and she finds herself lying half across him. Now he's kissing her properly. She feels his lips on her lips, his hands on her back, his body warm beneath hers, the rise and fall of his chest. She lets him overwhelm her, saying to herself, I have no choice. From the moment she entered the room and saw him lying on her bed she ceased to take responsibility for her own actions.

He shifts to the edge of the narrow bed and arranges her beside him, now kissing her forehead, her ears, her neck. She closes her eyes, wanting to feel his lips on her eyelids. His fingers move down her throat. He starts to unbutton her shirt. When he reaches the third button she holds his hand with hers.

'Wait,' she whispers.

The room has two dormer windows and a corner tower window. On this summer early evening it's filled with light. Kitty is ashamed to be seen in her army-issue underwear.

She leaves the bed and pulls the blackout curtains closed. The room is plunged into darkness, but for a faint thread of light coming under the door.

She feels her way back into his arms. Liberated by the darkness, she lets his hands go where they will. He takes her shirt off, and her brassiere. She feels the light touch of his fingers on her bare breasts. Her skin tingles. Her entire body begins to tremble. She wants his touch. She wants to feel his body against hers.

'Not fair,' she whispers. 'You're still dressed.'

He pulls off his shirt and they lie together naked from the waist up, kissing eagerly. The more he touches her the more her body awakens, and the closer she wants to be to him. She knows now what will happen, and knows that she wants it. She's been wanting it since he kissed her on Mount Caburn. Since he came back to her on the quay at Newhaven, not killed after all.

Kitty has never been naked like this with a man before. She has never made love. She's not ignorant, there are girls in her unit who give graphic descriptions of their nights out, but every moment is new to her. She has no words for what she's doing now other than the crude slang of toilet walls, the laughing exchanges in the training camp dorm. *You should have seen his equipment! I screamed like a stuck pig. Takes a big hammer to drive a big nail.*

She feels it now, swelling against her body, this mystery that is his desire for her. She pushes against it and feels it grow hard. He takes her hand and places it on the ridge it makes. She moves her hand gently up and down, learning its form by touch in the darkness. Then his fingers are unbuckling his belt and opening his trousers. Her hand slips inside to touch his naked body *there*. It's warm and soft and strong and hard all at once. She holds it and strokes it, not knowing how tightly she should grip, and feels it give little twitches of response. All her body is hot now, her skin is burning. She wants him, she wants all of him. She wants him so close that he drowns her thoughts in the smell and touch and feel of him.

Now his hands are tugging gently at her skirt. Of course, she must be as naked as he is, it's obvious. She moves quickly to unbutton her skirt, and unpop the clips on her stockings. As she does so she feels his hand between her legs, moving right up inside her knickers, and she becomes still. She wants his touch so much that she's holding her breath. He strokes her *there*, and she shivers with nervous intensity. His touch makes her body new for her, as if *there* has never been discovered before. He explores her unknown land, he inhabits her. She lets her legs part so that his hand can move more freely over her and into her.

I'm all yours, Eddy. All of me is yours.

Now she's undoing the hooks and eyes of her suspender belt and letting it fall away. His hands slip inside the waistband of her army knickers, blessedly invisible in the dark, and pull them down over her buttocks and thighs. She helps him with twists of her legs to get them off. Now all she's wearing are her lisle stockings.

His hand is back between her legs, stroking, probing, burrowing. She feels for his erection, and holds it between her palms. Her eyes have become more accustomed to the dark, and the single thread of light lets her see a little. She looks up to his face and thinks she sees him smiling at her.

'Ah!'

She gives a gasp of surprise. His fingers have found a place to touch that sends shocks of pleasure all through her body.

'Oh, Eddy! Oh, Eddy!'

He kisses her breasts, lingering over the nipples, tweaking them with his lips. Kitty feels as if she has never had a body before, as if his touch creates it. She wants to hold him so close, so close that she ceases to exist. She wants to give herself to him and lose herself in him.

'Darling,' she whispers. 'Darling, darling.'

He moves his body over hers and she parts her legs, making herself open for him, longing for him. She feels the push, the soft head nuzzling at her crotch, seeking the way in. She wriggles her hips and it finds its place, and rests there.

He lowers his face to hers to kiss her. As his lips touch hers, he gives a little push, and it's in. Just the tip, but it's begun.

Kitty feels her heart pounding, scrambling all rational thought. Somewhere far away there are things she should be concerned about, but she doesn't want to know. She wants to possess him. She wants all of him in all of her.

He moves again, and penetrates a little deeper. She can tell from his breathing that he's excited. Then she feels a spasm of pain, and makes a sound. He stops. For a brief moment of terror she thinks, He can't do it. I'm too small for him. But all the time she can feel herself opening up. And now he's moving again, and it hurts but she doesn't make a sound, and he's deeper in.

This is his desire. His desire is hot and hard. The deeper into me he goes, the more he wants me.

Now he's all the way in. She can feel the weight of his body on hers. He lies still, letting her grow accustomed to the sensation. For Kitty this is the time, when he's inside her but neither of them are moving, this is the time she remembers for the rest of her life. Their haven of love.

He's mine. We'll never be parted now.

'Darling,' she whispers. 'Darling.'

He starts to move, drawing almost all the way out, then pushing back all the way in. Kitty feels the pain again.

'Slowly,' she whispers.

He moves slowly after that, and when he's all the way in he pauses. Then out, then in. The sweet pause.

'Oh, God!' he cries.

'What is it?'

A shudder goes through his body. His hips convulse in a series of sharp jerks. She feels him twitch inside her. Then he lies still.

So it's happened. She thinks she can feel it, a liquid warmth, but maybe she imagines it. This is what they do it for. This is the prize.

'Was it good?' she whispers.

He grunts. She realises that whatever it is he has just experienced, it has half-stunned him. All his limbs have gone slack. His weight is heavy on her. She doesn't mind, she wraps her arms round him, holds him tight. His moment of helplessness touches her deeply. Then all at once she has the strangest thought.

He has died for me.

She pushes the thought away, ashamed to compare what they've just done to the real death that waits in this real war. But the two are tangled up, even so. Had she not stood on the quay at Newhaven and thought of him dying in France, would she be naked in his arms now?

He's shrinking inside her. She feels a cool trickle between her thighs. He gives a long groaning sigh. Then he rolls off her, and lying beside her, takes her in his arms.

For a while they lie together in the dark room in silence. She thinks he might be sleeping, but she can't tell. He has become infinitely precious to her, she doesn't want to disturb him, doesn't need to disturb him. What they have just done together changes everything. They're together now.

Kitty wonders at this, wonders that her girlfriends have so much to say about the act and so little about the closeness. Perhaps it's just too ordinary. It happens to all couples. Except it's extraordinary, it's beyond anything she believed possible, that two people can lie together and become one.

'Kitty?'

His soft voice interrupts her thoughts. He's looking at her, smiling.

'Will you marry me?'

'Yes.'

She feels no sense of surprise. Of course she'll marry him. They're married already. But the way he asks, with a slight hesitation in his voice, floods her with a tender joy. She draws him close, kissing him.

'Of course I'll marry you, Eddy darling.'

'We seem to have done things the wrong way round.'

'What difference does it make?'

'And I'm sorry . . .'

She understands he feels bad because it was all over so quickly, but doesn't know how to say so.

'It was wonderful, Eddy. It was perfect.'

'No,' he says. 'But it will be.'

He gazes at her and there's no mockery any more. No distance.

'I do love you, Kitty,' he says. 'I'll do my best for you.'

# 8

The library at Wakehurst Place is packed with officers assembled for the operational briefing by General Harry Crerar, commander of the 2nd Canadian Infantry Division. Larry Cornford stands near the back, his hands clasped behind his back, his gaze roaming the room. The Elizabethan library has an embossed ceiling and an elaborately carved fireplace. As he listens to the general's steady tones, he finds himself studying the figures in the niches on either side of the fireplace. A curiously shaped female, naked from the waist up, holds a large naked child horizontally across her midriff, like a roll of carpet. The child reaches one hand up to tweak her left nipple, and with the other hand pats the head of a second smaller child at its mother's knee; if mother it is. What can it all signify?

'The forces chosen for Operation Jubilee are as follows. The RHLI, the Essex Scottish, the South Saskatchewans, the Camerons, the Royals, and the Fusiliers Mont-Royal. The 14th Armored, the Calgary regiment, will be in action for the first time with the new Churchill tanks. Number 3 Commando, Number 4 Commando, and 40 Royal Marine Commando will carry out designated tasks, as will a small unit of US Rangers, and Free French forces. Operation Jubilee will be a reconnaissance in force. Its object is to seize and hold a seaport for twenty-four hours, and then to withdraw. It is not an invasion. It is not the opening of a second front. I can't tell you our destination, or our planned date. But I can tell you that it will be very soon now.'

A murmur of satisfaction runs round the room.

'This is pretty much a Canadian show, boys,' says the general. 'Ham Roberts will be in overall charge. I'm very proud that we're being given the first real smack at the Hun on his own ground. I know you won't let me down.'

There's nothing in the general's briefing that hasn't been rumoured for weeks now, but the official confirmation creates a buzz of excitement. As the meeting breaks up, Larry sees Brigadier Wills go into a huddle with Crerar and Roberts. A trolley of tea and coffee is wheeled clanking into the room by two members of the kitchen staff. Officers crowd round, jostling each other to be first in line. Dick Lowell, Larry's Canadian opposite number, joins him by the doorway.

'Bigger show than I expected,' he says. 'But my God, are they ready for it! What do you reckon? Boulogne? I say Le Touquet.'

Larry, who has known the target port for weeks, says nothing to this. He looks out through the high windows to the handsome grounds beyond.

'Quite a place, isn't it?'

'Famous, too,' says Dick Lowell. 'Culpeper the herbalist lived here.'

'Do you think I've got time for a wander round the grounds?'

'Christ, we'll be here all morning. There's still the supply and logistic meetings to go.'

'Do me a favour, Dick? If Woody comes looking for me, give me a shout.'

Larry leaves the library, and passes down the wood-panelled corridor and out through the south-east door to the gravelled forecourt. Here the rows of staff cars are pulled up, waiting to convey the top brass back to their bases. Beyond the line of cars, in a bend of the drive, stand two tall sequoia trees. The staff drivers have gathered in the shade of the trees to gossip, or just to doze.

Larry shields his eyes from the glare and scans the shadowed figures. He locates Kitty at last, sitting a little apart from the rest, reading a book.

He goes to her.

'Still on *Middlemarch*?'

She looks up with a pleased smile.

'Almost at the end now. Poor, poor Lydgate.'

'I've got another book for you.' He takes a book out of his shoulder bag. 'You may have read it already.'

It's *The Warden* by Trollope.

'No, I haven't,' she says. 'How sweet of you.'

'There are so few good men in books,' says Larry. 'In good books, I mean. All the best characters are bad. But there's one in *The Warden*. It's the story of a good man.'

'That's just what I need,' says Kitty.

'Care for a walk in the park?'

She jumps up, slipping the books into her long-strap handbag.

'What if they come out?'

'We won't go far.'

They go round the house and down a path that runs south between unkempt lawns. The once-grand gardens are suffering from neglect. Yet another casualty of war.

'I think you must be a good man, Larry,' says Kitty.

'Why do you say that?'

'I don't know. Just a feeling I get.'

'Not half good enough,' says Larry. 'Sometimes I look at myself in the mirror and all I see is idleness and selfishness.'

'Oh, we all think that about ourselves. Me most of all.'

'So what's to be done?'

'We shall get better,' says Kitty.

'You're right. We shall get better.'

'I think loving people makes you a better person,' says Kitty. 'Don't you?'

'Yes, I do,' says Larry.

'But it has to not be selfish love. It has to be selfless love. And that's so hard.'

'That's because it's your self that does the loving,' says Larry.

'You love them for them, and then they love you back, and that makes you happy. So maybe it's all selfishness in the end.'

The path leads to a circular terrace with a small stone monument at its centre. Round the stone base is a brass plaque on which lines of poetry are engraved.

> Give fools their gold and knaves their power
> Let fortune's bubbles rise and fall
> Who sows a field or trains a flower
> Or plants a tree is more than all.

'Do you think that's true?' says Kitty.

'Well, I've never sown a field,' says Larry. 'Or trained a flower, or planted a tree.'

'Nor have I.'

'So I think it's tosh.'

'I think it's tosh too.'

They stand by the curving stone balustrade and look down into an overgrown pond, and return to talk of love.

'The thing is,' says Kitty, 'I can only love with all of myself. And if that makes me happy, well, I just have to lump it, don't I?'

'There is another side to it, you know? You have to accept love as well as give it.'

'Yes, but that's not up to me. That's up to the other person.'

'Well, you do have to let yourself be loved.'

'What an odd notion,' says Kitty. 'Let myself be loved? I don't understand that at all. That's like saying let myself be warmed by the sun. The sun shines and it warms me, whether I choose to let it or not.'

'You could go into the shade.'

'Oh, well, yes.'

She frowns, becoming confused.

'What I mean,' says Larry, 'is that some people don't let themselves be loved. Maybe they're frightened. Maybe they don't feel worthy.'

'Oh, I see. But you don't feel that, do you?'

'Sometimes. A little. You can call it shyness, if you like. People can be afraid to ask for love, even though they may want it very much.'

'Yes, I can see that.'

'After all, not everyone feels they're bound to be lovable. Most of us wonder why anyone would ever be remotely interested.'

Kitty is silent for a moment.

'It's funny about people loving people,' she says. 'I don't really know what it is makes you love one person and not another. I know it's supposed to be about looks, but I don't think it is at all.'

'So what is it?' says Larry.

'It's something that gets inside you,' she says. 'Suddenly it's inside you, and you know it can't ever be taken out. Not without tearing you apart.'

'What makes that something get inside you?' says Larry.

Kitty gives him a quick frowning look, and for a moment her sweet face is filled with sadness.

'Standing on the quay at Newhaven harbour,' she says, 'and knowing he's going to die.'

Larry looks back towards the house. He feels far away from everyone and everything. He nods slowly, wanting to show he's heard her, not trusting himself to speak.

'We're going to get married,' Kitty says. 'Do you think I'm a terrible fool?'

'No,' he says. 'Of course not. That's wonderful news.'

He forces lightness into his voice.

'Congratulations, and so on. Lucky old Ed.'

'I do love him, Larry. I love him so much it hurts.'

They walk back down the path. Larry is filled with an aching emptiness. Following some instinct of self-preservation he says all the good things he can think of about Ed.

'He was my best friend at school. I know him better than anyone. He's incredibly intelligent, and ruthlessly honest. And though he likes to make out he sees through everything, it's not true. He cares too much, really. That's where the sadness comes from.'

'The sadness,' she says. 'I think that's almost what makes me love him the most.'

'He'll make a fine husband,' says Larry. 'If Ed says he'll do a thing, he does it. But look here' – he suddenly remembers the morning's briefing – 'you'd better get a move on if you're to get married. He could be posted overseas any day now.'

Kitty takes his hand and squeezes it.

'What's that for?'

'For being a darling.'

They return in silence to the side of the house where the cars and drivers wait.

'I'll see how much longer they're going to be,' says Larry.

He goes into the house. In the central hallway, by the dark oak staircase, he meets Brigadier Wills coming out of his meeting with General Roberts.

'All done,' says the brigadier. 'Let's get on the road.'

Larry walks back through the house with the brigadier.

'This op, sir,' he says. 'I know it's a Canadian show. But I was wondering if you could find a berth for me.'

'It won't be a picnic, Lieutenant.'

'My war too, sir.'

'So it is, so it is.'

They come out onto the forecourt. The drivers are now all standing by their cars, waiting for their officers.

'I can use you, Lieutenant. But you'll have to clear it with Combined Ops.'

'Thank you, sir.'

The brigadier finds his car. Kitty opens the passenger door for him.

'Back to base, Corporal.'

Larry watches the Humber drive away past the giant trees and out of sight. Then he makes his way slowly across to the stable block, where he has left his motorbike. He stands for a long time, motionless, his helmet held in his hands, before at last he raises it to his head.

In the car driving south the brigadier says to Kitty, 'You know Lieutenant Cornford, don't you?'

'Yes, sir.'

'He just asked me if he can ride along when we go into action.'

He shakes his head as he thinks about it.

'That's war for you. A man leaves his home and his loved ones and puts himself in the line of fire, all of his own free will. Don't tell me he does that because he wants to free the world from tyranny. Don't tell me he does that for his country. He does it for his buddies. That's what war's about. If your buddies are fighting and dying, you want to fight and die alongside them.'

'Yes, sir,' says Kitty.

Larry knows by now how the system works. Rather than putting his request through the official channels, he goes to Joyce Wedderburn.

'I just need two minutes,' he says.

'He's not here right now,' says Joyce. 'But if you don't mind waiting.'

'Of course not.'

'They also serve who only stand and wait,' she says, smiling.

'Bet you don't know where that comes from,' says Larry.

'I've no idea.'

'Milton. His poem on his blindness. "Who best bears his mild yoke, they serve him best." Meaning God, of course.'

'How clever of you to know that.'

Larry sighs as he settles down to wait.

'Over-educated and under-employed,' he says.

Mountbatten shows up fifteen minutes or so later, striding along in a great hurry with Harold Wernher at his side. He sees Larry waiting and stops at his office door.

'You want me?'

'A very quick request, sir.'

In the office, Mountbatten hears him out, and turns to Wernher.

'This is why we're going to win the war,' he says. Then to Larry, 'Your father won't thank me if I say yes.'

'My father will be proud of me, sir,' says Larry, 'if you tell him I've done my duty.'

Mountbatten smacks his hands together.

'By George, that's right!' he says. 'I wish to God I could do the same. But surely, you've not been trained for this sort of command?'

'Not a command, sir. I'll go in the ranks.'

Mountbatten gazes at him, evidently moved.

'Bless you, my boy,' he says. 'If that's what you want, I'll not stand in your way.'

# 9

The cellars at Edenfield Place are kept locked these days, and George Holland has the only key. He unlocks the cellar door and leads Larry down the steep steps, bending his head as he goes.

'Watch out here. Low arch.'

Light filters into the cool vaults through dusty cobwebbed slots. Bay after bay is filled with bottles.

'Mostly from my father's time,' says George.

'Seriously, you don't have to do this,' says Larry.

'Someone has to drink it,' says George. 'You're his friend, aren't you?'

He moves down the bays, peering at the labels.

'St Émilion '38,' he says. 'That should be good.'

He pulls out two bottles and gives them to Larry.

'You must join us, George,' says Larry.

'No, no. It's for the two of them.'

On an impulse he pulls out two more bottles.

'There. Tell Kitty congratulations from me.'

Larry carries the bottles in the pannier of his motorbike,

wrapped in his pullover so they don't bang against each other. He transfers them to the kitchen table in the farmhouse and wipes them down. They're standing on the table, glowing deep purple in the evening sunlight, when the outer door opens, and Ed enters.

'Can't keep away, can I?' he says.

He sees the wine.

'Grand Cru Bordeaux! Where in God's name did you get this?'

'It's for you,' says Larry. 'For you and Kitty, from the lord of the manor. He says congratulations. And so do I.'

'Word travels fast. I came here to tell you myself.'

'I saw Kitty at the corps briefing.'

'She still happy about it?'

'She's crazy about you, Eddy. You know that.'

'And I'm crazy about her.' He picks up one of the bottles. 'Why such generosity from the lord of the manor?'

'He has a soft spot for Kitty. Or had, I should say.'

Ed goes out into the yard to empty his bladder. Rex shows up, in a subdued mood.

'I just heard,' he says, 'they're fitting out warehouses by the docks as field hospitals.'

'Won't be long now,' says Larry.

Rex touches the bottles of wine, one by one, clearly unaware that he's doing so.

'You want to hear a funny story?' he says. 'There's this fellow in the RAMC who faints at the sight of blood.'

'He's in the wrong job, I'd say.'

'I don't faint,' says Rex. 'I'm fine with blood. But sometimes I think, what if I don't know what to do? What if I do the wrong thing?'

'Has to happen sometimes,' says Larry.

'If I do the wrong thing, someone dies.'

He takes off his glasses and looks at Larry, blinking.

'Rex,' Larry says, 'you can't think that way. You'll go nuts. You're a medic, you do your job. That's all.'

Ed comes back in and tells Rex his news. Rex offers his congratulations, glancing at Larry as he does so. Ed proposes they open one of George's bottles of wine.

'So we can drink to Kitty,' he says.

'Not for me,' says Rex. 'I'm not a wine drinker.'

'I know you're teetotal,' says Ed. 'But this is Grand Cru Bordeaux!'

'I just don't like the taste,' says Rex.

'You'll have some, Larry.'

'You bet.'

The wine is good.

'You don't know what you're missing, Rex,' says Ed. 'See the smile on my face? That should give you some idea.'

He refills Larry's glass, then his own.

'Two smiles are better than one.'

Ed decides to stay for dinner. They finish the bottle between them. Rex excuses himself.

'Early night for me.'

Left on their own, Ed fixes Larry with his cool blue eyes.

'Now comes the big question,' he says. 'Do we open bottle number two?'

'It may not be as good as number one,' says Larry.

'That is true. That is very true.'

'We could be gravely disappointed,' says Larry.

'We could,' says Ed.

'But we bear up under disappointment, don't we?'

'Always,' says Ed. 'The show must go on.'

'So let's risk it.'

Ed opens the second bottle, and fills Larry's glass.

'Still good,' Larry says, drinking.

'So far,' says Ed.

'We live in hope,' says Larry.

'The other reason I came over this evening,' says Ed, 'was to ask you to be my best man.'

'Honoured,' says Larry.

'Kitty wants a church wedding. Not a grand do or anything. But she wants the full vows.'

'Then she shall have them.'

'All right for you. But I don't go in for all that stuff.'

'So what? You can go through the motions, can't you?'

Ed sits back in the deep old chair in the corner and stares at the ceiling.

'Yes. I can go through the motions. But I'm marrying the girl I love. I want it to be real. I want to mean every word I say. I don't want to tell lies.'

'You're not lying. You're just saying words that have no meaning for you.'

'Would you do that at your wedding?'

Larry says nothing to that. Ed follows his own thoughts.

'Kitty believes in God. I asked her why, and she said she didn't know.'

'You can't ask why someone believes in God,' says Larry. 'It's not rational. It's just something you know.'

'So how come I don't know it?'

'I don't know. You must have believed once.'

'I can see a thousand reasons for saying there's no God, and no reasons for saying there is a God. But just about everyone in the world believes there is a God.'

'So who's out of step here?'

Ed jumps up, suddenly restless. He fills up their glasses once more, and starts to pace the room.

'I want to be wrong, Larry. Believe me, I want to be wrong. I want to be on Kitty's side. I want to be on your side. But I don't know how to get there. I only have to look out of the window and I see what a shit-filled world we live in.'

'Why call it a shit-filled world? What about all the beauty?'

'And all the misery, and all the cruelty. The human race has a lot to answer for. Just look at this bloody war.'

'Yes,' says Larry. 'There are bad men out there. But there are good men too. For every Hitler there's a Francis of Assisi.'

'I notice your good man is long dead and your bad man is very much with us.'

'Gandhi, then.'

'Oh, I don't know about Gandhi. I don't trust vegetarians.'

'He lives the life he preaches. Simplicity. Non-violence. Self-sacrifice.'

'So why doesn't God make us all like Gandhi?'

'Oh, come on,' says Larry. 'You know the drill as well as I do. God made us free. If he made us so we couldn't go against his will, we'd be slaves, or machines. You know all this.'

'What I don't understand is why he couldn't at least make us so we're more good than bad.'

'He does. I believe we are more good than bad. I do. I believe people's deepest instinct is to love each other, not to hurt each other.'

'Do you?' Ed stops pacing to stare at Larry, as if unsure he can really mean what he says. 'Do you?'

'Yes. I do.'

'Any day now,' says Ed, 'I'm going to be sent into some god-forsaken corner of France to kill people who'll be doing their damnedest to kill me. Where's the love in that?'

'I'm coming too.'

'What!'

'I'm on loan to the RHLI. At my request.'

Ed seizes Larry by the shoulders and turns him so he can't avoid his gaze.

'What's going on?'

'I'm a soldier,' says Larry. 'Soldiers fight.'

Ed holds his gaze, his blue eyes searching for the truth Larry is withholding.

'Soldiers kill. Are you going to kill?'

'If I have to.'

'For your King and country?'

'Yes.'

Ed lets him go with a laugh.

'Well, there you are. Even you. What hope for humanity now?'

'If it's wrong for me to kill, it's wrong for you too.'

'Of course it's wrong! Everything's wrong!'

Larry is shaken by Ed's challenge. Will he kill? He can't imagine it. He's not going into action to kill, he's going into action to come under fire. It's all about self-respect. Or pride. Or Kitty.

'Anyway,' he says, 'war isn't the common human condition. Most of the time we're not trying to kill each other.'

'Fine!' says Ed. 'Forget war. Forget killing. How about plain old common-or-garden unhappiness? You can't deny that most people are unhappy most of the time. What's the point of that?'

Larry wants to say, Kitty loves you. You at least can be happy. He wants to say, What more do you want to be happy? But even as the thought forms in his mind he knows this talk of happiness is all beside the point.

'The fact is,' he says, 'you can't make sense of any of it if you believe this world is all there is. You have to see it in the light of eternity.'

'Ah, the light of eternity!'

'You think it all ends with death, as far as I can tell.'

'Yes. Lights out and that's it.'

'I see us as on a journey towards becoming gods.'

'Gods!' Ed laughs. 'We're to be gods!'

'That's the simplest way to put it.'

'All sitting on thrones together, up in the sky.'

'I'm doing my best here. You could at least try to take me seriously.'

'Yes. Yes, of course. You're right, my dear comrade-in-arms! What do you say to the third bottle?'

'That wine's for you and Kitty.'

'Mine is the greater need right now.'

He opens the third bottle.

'What we're going to do,' announces Ed as he extracts the cork, 'what we're going to do is we're going to go out in the cool night air, bringing this excellent bottle with us, and that way we'll stay sober, and you'll tell me why you and Kitty are right, and I'll take you seriously.'

They go out through the farmyard into the hay meadow beyond. They hand the bottle back and forth as they go, drinking from its neck. The night sky is clear, with a quarter moon low over the Downs.

'You know what, Ed,' says Larry. 'Neither of us knows the truth about this. All we've got is beliefs, and all our beliefs come from is our feelings. I can't imagine this life being all there is. I can't imagine death being extinction. There has to be more. And as it happens, Jesus says there is more. He says he came to give eternal life. He says he's the son of God. I don't understand what that means, but he says it, and he says that all that matters is love, and he says his kingdom is not of this earth. And all that just feels *likely* to me. I mean, what sort of a world would it be if I knew it all? It would be tiny. Existence has to be bigger than me. So the fact that I don't understand it doesn't make it unlikely, it makes it far more likely. I just know there has to be more than I know. More than you know, too. That's all you have to concede. Just accept that you don't know *everything*. Leave a bit of room in your philosophy for surprises. Leave a bit of room for hope.'

Larry becomes more and more expansive as he speaks, liberated by the wine and the darkness round him and the majesty of the star-filled sky.

'You know what,' says Ed laughing. 'I think I'd rather be you than me. All this love. All this hope. That's good stuff.'

He passes Larry the bottle. Reaching his arms out on either side he begins to make pirouettes over the grass. Larry puts the bottle to his lips and tips it back. The last of the wine runs down his throat and spills out over his chin. He tosses the bottle away with a fine disregard and it lands in the stream.

Ed comes spinning up to Larry and takes him by the hand.

'Come on, best man!' he says. 'If we're going to die, let's die together!'

They swoop about together, laughing out loud, until they lose their balance and tumble to the ground. There they lie, panting, smiling at the stars, still clasping hands.

On Saturday August 15th Ed and Kitty are married in the chapel of Edenfield Place. The wedding is small. Both bride and groom wear uniform. Kitty's parents, the Reverend Michael Teale and his wife Molly, come from Malmesbury. Ed's parents, Harry and Gillian Avenell, come from Hatton in Derbyshire. Larry Cornford is best man. Others present are Louisa Cavendish, George Holland, Brigadier Wills, and Ed's commanding officer, Colonel Joe Picton-Phillips. After the ceremony there's a wedding breakfast in the mess, hosted by George Holland and Brigadier Wills.

Everyone is smiling and cheerful, most of all Kitty's parents, but it's not an easy occasion. The two families are meeting for the first time. Harry Avenell is a tall distinguished man, a director of a brewing company, but Kitty's pink-cheeked father has far more of the look of a brewer about him. Ed's mother teasingly reprimands Ed for not marrying in a Catholic church.

'Why would I do that, Mummy?' Ed says. 'You know I'm through with all of that.'

'Oh, so you say,' says Gillian Avenell.

Kitty likes the way he calls his mother 'Mummy' so unselfconsciously, but wonders a little at the way he behaves with both his parents. There are no embraces, no kisses. Harry Avenell takes part in the ceremony with an oddly detached manner, as if standing in for the father of the groom before the real man arrives.

Kitty's mother talks in a ceaseless stream.

'If only Harold could be here, but even if he could get leave it would be no good. He's in North Africa, you know, with the Eleventh Hussars, they call them the Cherry Pickers, they were in the Charge of the Light Brigade, but they drive armoured cars now. I remember when my mother got the news about Timmy, he was behind the lines at Passchendaele, but there was a shell and that was that. Of course it was happening to everybody, but even so. And now here's Harold out in the desert when he should be here with us, and I can't help thinking it's just all wrong.'

'Now then, Molly,' says her husband. 'This is Kitty's day.'

The newly-weds have booked a week's leave for their honeymoon, which they take in Brighton.

The Old Ship Hotel is one of the few on the seafront that hasn't been requisitioned for war personnel. The hotel is very rundown, its paintwork cracking and its wallpaper peeling. The only porter is old and sick. A girl called Milly offers to carry their bags up to their room, but Ed says he can manage. The stairs creak as they climb.

The room has a double bed, and a window that looks out over the promenade. Outside they can see the beach with its concrete anti-tank blocks and its undulations of rolled barbed wire.

'The beach will be mined,' Ed says. 'We won't be going swimming.'

The Palace Pier is deserted, its walkway broken in the middle so that it can't be used as a landing stage. The seafront is under curfew by the time they arrive. The sea gleams in the light of a golden summer evening, but there's nobody about.

'Maybe we should have gone to a B&B in the countryside,' says Ed.

'I don't care where we are,' says Kitty.

Ed is quiet, looking round the shabby room. He seems to be almost at a loss.

'What is it, Ed?'

'I wanted everything to be perfect for you,' he says.

'And for you too.'

'Oh, I don't mind. So long as I've got you.'

'Well, you have got me. You'd better think of something to do with me.'

He takes her in his arms. She leans her body against his.

'I love you so much, Kitty.'

'Just as well.'

'I love you so much I can't think or move or hardly even breathe.'

'That's too much,' Kitty says. 'You'd better love me less and breathe more.'

He kisses her.

Later they lie in bed together, and every time they move the bed makes a pinging noise. They try to stay still but it isn't easy. They start moving again and the pinging returns. They try lying in different places on the bed, and find one position, right on the edge, that almost silences the noisy bed-spring, but it's hard not to fall off.

Ed stops moving, holding Kitty close in his arms.

'We have a choice,' he says. 'We lie doggo, or we jangle.'

'Let's jangle,' she says.

On Sunday morning they walk along the seafront as far as the big Bofors gun outside the Grand Hotel. A crowd of Canadian soldiers are playing football on the promenade, using kitbags for goalposts. Kitty holds Ed's arm and leans a little against him as they walk, and loves him so much it hurts. The sun shines on the sea, and on the patches of black tar on the pebbles under the barbed wire, and on the dull metal of the big gun. Ahead the West Pier has been severed like its sister. Across the water lies France.

I'm married, thinks Kitty. He belongs to me now. His body belongs to me.

She loves his body. She loves the feel of it pressed against hers all the way down. She wants to tell him so but there seem to be no words and she's shy. So instead she squeezes his arm and strokes the small of his back. They come to a stop by the Bofors gun and kiss. The soldiers playing soccer pause in their game to clap.

Later that Sunday afternoon all leave is cancelled and all personnel are recalled to their units. On Tuesday August 18th Admiral Lord Mountbatten, Commander-in-Chief Combined Operations, gives the order for Operation Jubilee, the largest military assault on mainland Europe since the disaster of Dunkirk.

# 10

It's a clear night, and the sea is calm. Larry is up on deck with Johnny Parrish to escape the thick fog of tobacco smoke below. He looks through a gap in the tarpaulin at the dark coast of England as it recedes. On either side of the troopship other craft reach as far as the eye can see, their low rumble filling the night. Bulbous transport ships carrying invasion barges; tank landing craft lying low in the water; the sleek forms of destroyers.

'Bloody big show,' says Johnny.

Over the lapping of the waves against the hull they hear the sound of a motorboat drawing alongside.

'That'll be the CO,' says Johnny. 'Better get below.'

The troop deck is packed and buzzing with excitement. Larry joins the crowd of officers by the companionway. Shortly after, the brigadier enters, with General Ham Roberts. Roberts wastes no time in preliminaries.

'We're on our way, men,' he says. 'You've been told this is another training exercise. Well, it isn't. This is the real thing.'

A great shout goes up from the mass of soldiers, followed by hoots and cheers. The officers look at each other and grin.

'Our destination is Dieppe. We will land at dawn, hold the port for a maximum of twelve hours, and withdraw. This is not an invasion. This will be the very first reconnaissance in force of the enemy mainland. The port of Dieppe is well defended. This isn't going to be a picnic. But it's our first chance in this war to get a poke at the Hun. So let's see we give him a poke he won't forget.'

The men cheer again. Roberts departs, to repeat his short speech on the next ship in the great armada.

Larry retreats to the wardroom, where he and the crowd of other officers are joined shortly by Brigadier Wills. Orders are now opened and given out, complete with maps, schedules, and aerial photographs. Jevons talks them through the plan.

'RAF air cover will be in place by dawn. Naval bombardment of the beaches will begin at 0510 hours. At 0520 hours our landing craft will hit Red Beach, here. Our mission is to seize and hold the Casino, which is here.'

Larry listens attentively. The plan is so detailed, so specific, that it has an air of inevitability. But what is it all for? Why are they to attack this fortified port, and then go home again? All round him, beneath the grave faces and the air of businesslike concentration, he feels wild pulsing excitement. They're going into battle. No one asks to measure the risk against the reward. All they require is the assurance that the cause is just.

'Just point us at 'em,' the men say, 'and leave us to do the rest.'

Larry feels it too, but he doesn't yet understand it. All he knows is it's nothing to do with love of England, or hatred of Germany. He isn't on this mission because he wants to die for his country. He's here because his whole world is on the march, and it has become impossible to stand on the margins and watch the parade go by. He sees on the faces of the men around him the same conviction that possesses him: we're on our way at last.

Shortly after midnight the fleet enters a minefield. The order goes out for all men to inflate their lifejackets. The command ship, the Hunt-class destroyer HMS *Calpe*, enters the minefield first, following the channel cleared by navy sweepers. The convoy falls in behind, guided by the faint green lights of marker buoys.

Larry stands at the ship's rail on the open deck, now packed tight with silent men. All watch the white froth of the ship's wake as the engines drive them fast through the danger zone.

'The old man's gone through first,' says a voice. 'He's got guts, give him that.'

'They lay these magnetic mines,' says another. 'You don't have to hit them. They come and hit you.'

'Just like me and the girls.'

'Me, I'm old-fashioned. I like to hit the girls first.'

Subdued laughter ripples outwards in the night. The ship veers suddenly to starboard and the men fall silent. Then the ship veers again, to port. A light on the water ahead comes nearer, and then passes away into the darkness.

A bell jangles. Voices and laughter break out again. The troopship is safely through the minefield. The tension lifts. Brigadier Wills, doing the rounds, finds Larry still leaning on the rail.

'Try to get some sleep,' he says.

'Yes, sir, I will,' says Larry.

'Good to have you along. The boys appreciate it.'

Larry finds a space to lie down below deck, but he knows he won't sleep. He's in a state he's not experienced before, a strange combination of stillness and intense inner excitement. He takes out a cigarette and lights it, noticing now that all round him glow the tips of other cigarettes. He inhales deeply, and feels a tingling sensation pass through his body, followed by a deep powerful languor. Unthinkingly he gives a sigh of pleasure. His neighbour says out of the darkness, 'Always fresh,' and Larry follows up with a laugh, 'And truly mild.' The slogan of the Sweet Caps he smokes these days, to show his solidarity with the Canadian forces. As he exhales he can see the cigarette smoke shivering in the air above him, shaken back and forth by the vibrations of the ship's engines.

The river gunboat *Locust* emerges from the minefield in its turn, following the long line of troopships and landing craft. Three hundred and seventy officers and men of 40 Commando are crowded onto the narrow deck, either asleep or sitting still and breathing evenly to conserve energy. The commanding officer, Colonel Phillips, is reviewing the maps and photographs of White Beach, and familiarising himself with the layout of the town beyond.

'You know what Dieppe's famous for?' says Ed Avenell. 'Dirty weekends.'

'You should know, Ed,' says Abercrombie.

Ed smiles and says nothing.

Breakfast is served early, just before two in the morning. Beef stew, bread and butter and marmalade, and coffee. The officers eat in silence.

At fleet rendezvous point new orders are received from Operational Command. Phillips announces that 40 Commando is to be held in reserve. A groan goes up from the men.

'What are we, fucking nursemaids?'

'We're to wait for the Canadians to clear the main beach.'

4 Commando's job is demolition. By the time they're through, not one port facility will be left operational. Joe Phillips doesn't like the new orders any more than his men. Commandos are raiders, trained to move fast and light. They're not assault troops.

'Try to get some sleep,' he tells the men.

Ed Avenell remains on deck, leaning on the stern rail, watching the long line of the fleet behind them. Here Phillips finds him, as he does his rounds.

'Biggest naval operation of the war,' he says.

'Looks like it,' says Ed.

'You've not told the boys you got hitched.'

'No,' says Ed.

'You don't want any special treatment.'

'That's about it, sir.'

Titch Houghton joins them.

'Lovat and his boys will be ready to go in about now,' he says.

4 Commando are to make a night landing on Orange Beach to the west, while Durnford-Slater's 3 Commando makes for Yellow Beach and the big guns of Berneval.

'Has Lovat taken his bloody piper?' says Phillips.

'Of course,' says Titch Houghton.

'I don't like this reserve bullshit. It means we go in by daylight.'

At three in the morning, as required by the complex timetable of the operation, the men of the RHLI form up below decks in their platoons to prepare for the transfer to landing craft. They wear their netted tin hats. The inflated Mae Wests beneath their tunics give them all powerful chests. They carry Brens, Stens and rifles over their shoulders, hand grenades on their belts, knives at their hips. Larry Cornford, armed like the rest, takes his place in the line for Number 6 boat, and waits for the man in front of him to move.

This is what his entire life has become: waiting, moving, waiting again, always in lines, carried along by the great machine of which he is one tiny part. Now the lines begin to move up onto deck, where the night is still dark. Ahead men are climbing ladders into the slung barges, great black masses against the starlit sky. Larry follows in his turn, jumping down onto the benches that run the length of the craft. Men are ahead of him, and all the time more men are piling on after him, and soon he finds himself pushed towards the back of the starboard bench. A voice hisses at him, 'Sit crossways! Face forward!' Shortly he is wedged tight on the bench between the packs and weapons of other men.

The barge lurches and swings. The davit gear emits its high-pitched whine. The side of the ship rises above them. Then comes the slap of the water as the long steel craft settles, and the throb of the engine starting up.

A voice from above calls, 'You're on your own now, boys! Give 'em hell!'

The landing craft chugs away from the mother ship, taking its place in a line of other assault craft. The coast of France is still fifteen miles to the south-east, two hours and more away.

Larry gazes at the steersman in his armoured box over the bow, and hears the ping-ping of the engine-room telegraph. These are navy boys, their job is to ferry the assault troops, not to take part in the attack.

I'll be in the attack. I will fight.

This extraordinary fact has filled his being since he left England. Every single moment since then, however tedious, however uncomfortable, has been charged with intensity. All this time is *before*. Nothing has prepared him for the feelings he now experiences. It's not fear, not yet. The danger he faces has no reality yet. Nor is it that state he's heard talk of, called battle exultation. He feels sharp, as if all his being has been sharpened to a single point. Gone are all the usual little complications of life. He has no thoughts of his family or friends, no memories of his life gone by. Nothing but this landing craft, the pressure of the man behind him, the juddering of the engine, the twinge of cramp in his leg, the smell of spray on the air, the stars above, and *it* – the battle to which they sail.

After this nothing will ever be the same again. I am about to be transformed. Out there in the darkness there waits for me an *enemy*, men who wish me harm, who will try to hurt me, even though they know nothing about me. And will I try to hurt them? Of course. And because of this, nothing will ever be the same again.

He settles down at last into a doze. All along the benches men grunt and mutter in their sleep, as the craft maintains its course straight ahead. The flotilla, no longer in single file, is spread out over the surface of the night sea, seeming almost not to be moving.

Suddenly there comes a streak of bright light to the north-east, and a flare explodes in the sky. It drops slowly down, illuminating the water's surface.

'What the fuck was that?'

Men jerk out of sleep to watch.

Brilliant green streaks arc up into the sky, followed by red streaks, rising, cresting a curve, falling and fading to nothing. There follow bright white silent shell bursts, and shooting stars of gold, and more lazy leaping arcs of dazzling red.

'Tracer! Some bugger's hit trouble!'

The landing craft has neither slowed nor deviated from its course. Now the men on board hear the bark of ack-ack guns from the French coast.

'Sounds like Jerry's woken up.'

'That'll be fun for us.'

The men of 40 Commando are halfway through transferring from the *Locust* to their landing craft when the tracer battle lights up the sky. Colonel Phillips is on the bridge with the navy team, trying to make out what's happening.

'Not good,' he says. 'There goes our surprise.'

Wireless traffic between HMS *Calpe* and HMS *Berkeley* reveals that the easternmost craft in the fleet, Number 3 Commando's boats, have run into a German tanker and its escort. Orders are to continue according to plan.

Phillips leaves the gunboat last of his men, jumping down into the fourth landing craft. The *Locust* is to accompany them all the way, short of the beach itself.

'Don't worry about it, boys!' says Phillips, standing in the craft so all can see him. 'It's only 3 Commando screwing up.'

Soft laughter ripples through the boats.

'Let's go.'

The four barges set course for the coast of France, joining almost two hundred others now spread over a line eight miles wide. Ed Avenell is in 2 Boat commanded by Titch Houghton. The diminutive major stands up in the bow as they pick up speed.

'Plenty of time yet, boys,' he says. 'We're to get into position offshore, then we wait for the order to go in.'

As the glow of dawn appears to the east, the naval barrage opens up, according to plan. The eight destroyers pound the coastal defences for ten minutes, filling the air with the scream and glare of high explosive. At the same time there comes a distant singing in the sky as the squadrons of Spitfires arrive, escorting the Boston bombers. At 0530 hours the barrage ceases, and the main assault on the beaches begins.

Larry waits in his landing craft a little way off the beach, dazed by the bombardment, unable to see anything ahead other than his fellow soldiers. The barge heaves and lurches on the tide. All round, the darkness is fading into light. Bostons rumble low overhead, laying a trail of thick white smoke along the beach. Tank landing craft come surging past, first in line for the assault. He hears the boom of guns open up, followed by the rattle of light weapons. On either side other assault craft wait for the signal to advance. The men in his boat are tensed, ready to go. The sound of gunfire grows louder all the time, a ceaseless refrain now, but nothing can be seen through the smoke. Then comes the deep hollow boom of a big gun.

'Howitzer!' murmurs a voice. 'Six-incher.'

Tracer bullets flash across the sky ahead. Somewhere in the dawn shadows, in the white smoke, the battle has already begun. Then at last, in response to some unheard command, the engines pick up speed and the barge surges forward. A loud cheer goes up from the men. A sergeant in the bows starts up a progress report.

'Five hundred yards . . . I can see the beach . . . Three hundred . . . Smoke's lifting . . .'

The smoke is being swept away in long streamers by a westerly wind. In the dawn light the beach appears before them, with the town beyond. All along the shore, landing craft stand beached on the shingle. Beyond, between the sea-line and the town, a dozen or so box-like objects are spread out, crawling slowly. Between them the pale grey beach is in constant eruption, like the surface of a heated pan of porridge. Each bursting bubble emits its small puff of smoke, which arises and disperses on the wind.

'Brace, lads! Here we go!'

The landing craft smashes into the sandbar and every man lurches forward. The ramp falls and the lead men are out, floundering in shallow water. Larry sees only the men ahead, and he follows in his turn, possessed by one passionate desire, to move, to be in action.

He jumps, sinks in the water, hits the pebble ridge, scrambles to find a footing, feels the shingle skid beneath his weight. Round him men flounder and fall, thrashing the water with their arms. A spout of seawater rises up before him, and a shockwave hits him in the face, stinging his eyes. His boots won't grip the seabed, he struggles to advance, but with each downward kick he feels himself slipping back. Then a wave comes in and lurches him forward, and all at once he's climbing, he's up onto the beach proper, and he's tramping over the spreadeagled body of a man.

Shocked more by the touch than the sight he stops and looks round, bewildered, unable to make sense of what he sees. A man nearby throws himself over on one side. Ahead a man is crawling, groaning as he goes. Beyond there are figures to be seen scattered here and there over the beach, crouched or toppled. The sounds round him are deafening, irregular, inescapable. Men come heaving past him, loaded down with packs and weapons, firing as they go.

Who are they shooting at? There's no sign of the enemy. Only these puffs of smoke, these eruptions in the pebbles.

Ahead a tank is thrashing its tracks, struggling to make way over the slippery beach. A shrill whine, a violent bang, and the tank kicks over onto its side, ripped apart by an artillery shell. There are men running past Larry again, as the next wave of troops streams out of the landing craft. A mortar lands in their midst, hurling them to the ground. Larry too, unbalanced by the blast, falls forward onto his arms. Somewhere nearby a man is screaming.

'Buddy! I need a hand here! Buddy!'

The rattle of machine-gun fire comes and goes. Bullets ping on stones. Larry lies still, thinking. Their orders are to take the Casino. He can see the Casino from where he lies. Much of the fire that pins them down is coming from its windows. It would be suicidal madness to charge across the open beach into those guns.

Between himself and the promenade wall he counts seven disabled tanks. As for men, there are too many to count, and more are falling all the time. What is the purpose of this? Why have they been sent ashore unprotected into heavy enemy fire, to capture a heavily defended Casino for which they have no use?

The men around him who've not been hit are up again and struggling forward. Larry too staggers to his feet and lurches forward, not because there's any sense to it, but because this is what the others are doing. He finds that his progress is slow and flailing, as if he's still running in water. I must be in shock, he thinks. Then the beach erupts before him, and he feels the sting of a thousand tiny pebbles. His ears ring, his skin trickles with wetness. Ahead of him stands a man with blood shooting out of his neck and shoulder, pierced by shell splinters, toppling slowly forward into the crater formed by the mortar.

There are hundreds of men advancing up the beach, but Larry has the sensation of being alone. Gone are the orderly ranks and lines of army life. Here there is only howling space, sudden danger, and the deep rolling surge of the sea.

He drives himself on up the beach, flinching with every screaming shell or whining bullet that passes, and so reaches one of the abandoned Churchill tanks. It's shed its tracks in its desperate efforts to claw its way over the pebbles, and now stands sideways on to the promenade. Larry crawls up close and sinks to the ground, resting his back against its steel flank, taking cover from the machine guns that strafe the beach. From this position he can see the waves of men still spilling from the assault landing craft, still charging the beach into the withering enemy fire.

Now for the first time he understands that he is almost paralysed by fear. Until this moment the shock of being under fire has driven out all other thoughts. Now in the comparative safety of his one-walled fortress he understands that he will certainly be injured, that he'll maybe die, and he feels his guts melt with terror. Fear turns out to be physical, a rebellion of the body, the refusal to do anything that will take him closer to danger. He would burrow himself into the ground if he could. He has become an animal who has nowhere left to run, and so has frozen into immobility.

Then after a little time the fear too passes. In its place comes a strange detachment. He watches the aircraft circling high above, like starlings turning to follow their leader. He sees the sun climb into the sky. He thinks how meaningless it all is, the explosions and the killing, the winning and losing. He thinks of his father, and how there's something he needs to tell him, but he can't remember what it is. He thinks of Kitty, and her sweet smile, and how he'd like to tell her how much he loves her. But it's too late now, because he's going to die. He finds he's not afraid of dying after all, it turns out just to be another thing that happens. You think you're in control of your life but really all you can do is accept what happens with a good grace.

I'm not fighting any more.

Not meaning fighting as a soldier, fighting in a war, God knows he's done little enough of that. He's no longer fighting for life. Whatever that instinct or passion is that chooses life at all costs has slipped away, overwhelmed by fatigue and fear. So the fear hasn't left him after all, it's merely taken this new form, of loss of will. Like a dog that accepts its master's blows in silence, hoping by lack of opposition to win reprieve.

I've surrendered, Larry thinks. Take me prisoner. Take me home. Let me sleep.

There comes a roar overhead and the shadow of low-flying bombers, and then the smoke rolls down the beach. Larry gazes at the veil of whiteness that curtains him in his refuge and pretends to himself that now he's safe after all.

General Roberts on the command ship HMS *Calpe* receives a steady stream of messages from the assault forces, many of which contradict each other. Some of the Calgary regiment's tanks are reported to have broken into the town itself. A platoon of the RHLI has fought its way up to the six-inch gun before the

Casino. 4 Commando are back on their mother ship after successfully destroying the coastal battery behind Varengeville. The Royals have suffered heavy losses on Blue Beach, which remains exposed to the Berneval guns, but the RAF still have air supremacy, and the Essex Scottish, following the RHLI, are ashore in the centre. Reports are coming in that the beaches have been cleared. With all the information the commander has at his disposal it makes sense to commit his reserve forces. The objective remains the outright capture of the port. Fresh troops, sweeping past the units who have done so much to break the enemy's resistance, will tip the balance of the day.

'Send in the reserves now.'

The order is transmitted to the landing craft standing offshore, holding seven hundred men of the Fusiliers Mont-Royal, and three hundred and seventy men of 40 Commando. The smokescreen hangs heavy over the sea and shore as the barges line up and make their approach.

On Ed Avenell's boat the order is received with a cheer.

'About fucking time!'

For three hours now they've sat helpless as shells from shore batteries have passed overhead, or into the water nearby, while from the distant beach has come the ceaseless chatter of gunfire. Now at last they can go about their business.

The four boats of the commando advance in line with each other, forming the last wave after the Fusiliers. They pass through the smokescreen and out into sunlight, and so get their first clear sight of the beach, barely a hundred yards ahead. They see the Fusiliers landing, scrambling onto the beach, falling, hit by the relentless crossfire. They see mortars plop down and blow men away like dolls. They see the shells of the big howitzers rip up the beach. And most of all they see the countless corpses that lie all the way from the water to the promenade.

Ed Avenell, rising to his feet, preparing to jump, sees all this and knows that he is participating in a cruel and bloody joke.

'This is fucking insane!'

Colonel Phillips understands that a terrible mistake has been made. He pulls on a pair of white gloves so that his signalling hands can be seen by the other boats, and standing tall in the bow he shouts and gestures the command to go back.

'Turn about! Turn about!'

As he signals his order a bullet strikes him in the forehead, killing him instantly. Number 2 Boat, running a little ahead, does not see the signal. The others turn back.

Titch Houghton, eyes on the beach, shouts to the men in Number 2 Boat, 'Stand by! This is it!'

The barge shudders to a stop and the commandos spring out, guns in firing position. Moving at speed they lope up the beach, spreading out as they go. Whatever plan there was has been overtaken by events. They're hunting enemy to kill.

Now there are silver Focke-Wulf 109s up in the sky as well as the Spitfires of the RAF. As the Spitfires run short on fuel and turn for home the Focke-Wulfs fly low, strafing the men on the beach. Ed Avenell, fuelled by a toxic mixture of frustration and rage, storms the promenade wall, firing from a Bren gun as he goes. The enemy are nowhere to be seen, but their shells and bullets are everywhere. Racing down an empty street, shooting as he goes, he shouts, 'Come on out, you bastards!' A sniper fires at him from a house, and catching a glimpse of him at an upper window, he swings back, spraying bullets.

The Fusiliers punch their way into the marketplace just as the

RHLI finally capture the Casino. But the mortars keep on coming, and the big guns on the clifftop emplacements keep on booming. An empty building on the promenade has been taken over as an assembly point for the wounded and the dead. A large contingent of Camerons has formed a defensive line against enemy forces massing in the woods on the west side of the town. There is no objective any more, no overall strategy. Men run with great urgency in opposite directions, each following some imperative of his own. In the midst of this random violence the inhabitants of the town go about their business seemingly indifferent to the danger. One man leads four cows into the shelter of a barn, and then goes back out again to fetch in hay. Another, in hat and jacket but no shirt, bicycles down the street with a baguette in his basket. Small boys stare with big eyes at the soldiers running past. Some buildings are burning, but not fiercely, issuing thin trails of smoke into the clear sky.

The tide is far out now. Between the pebble beach with its litter of corpses and the sea where the armada waits, shrouded in smoke, there lies a wide strip of shining sand. The hour is past ten. On HMS *Calpe* General Roberts knows the assault has failed. He gives the order to retreat.

Ed Avenell's rage has only grown as he has taken in the scale of the disaster. He rages at the enemy who won't come out to fight. But most of all he rages at the sheer folly of it all. Why would any sane military planner send men to storm a heavily defended beach in broad daylight? But there are no sane military planners. The world is run by fools and the outcome is and always will be chaos. So together with his rage goes a fierce gladness that his deepest instincts should be proved so visibly right. This battle, that has no structure and no objective, that takes place merely to cause men to die to no purpose, is for Ed a perfect model of existence stripped bare. His anger flows from him in a righteous stream, but he's laughing at himself even as he deals out his vengeance, because he knows his only true justification for killing is that he too is prepared to die.

By the time he gets the order to retreat he has entered an almost ecstatic state. He should have been hit countless times, but somehow the bullets have not found him, and the shell splinters have passed him by. Now he believes his luck is impregnable, and he takes no precautions at all. He has become invulnerable.

Larry remains crouched behind the abandoned tank as the retreat unfolds. He sees men running back down the beach towards the returning landing craft. He smells seaweed, and salt water, and blood. He has no desire to get up himself and go to the boats. The space between himself and the water is a killing zone, men fall repeatedly as they run, hit by the guns in the cliffs, or the strafing of planes, or the unending boom of the mortars. But Larry does not stay where he is because he's afraid of the danger on the open beach. He remains motionless because he has lost the will to act. He has become utterly resigned, even to his own destruction.

His dulled gaze is caught by a man who is striding down the beach with another man in his arms. Larry sees him deliver his burden to the group clustered round the landing craft. Then he returns, striding back up the beach, oblivious to the bullets flying all round him.

It's Ed Avenell. Larry watches him with a smile. He even

attempts to greet him, 'Eddy!', as if he's passing in a London street, but he makes no sound. Larry is pleased to have found a friend in this strange place. His eyes follow him.

He sees him pick up another wounded man and carry him down to the water's edge. Slowly it enters Larry's fuddled mind that the assault force is now withdrawing. He sees Ed return up the beach, still unharmed, and gather up a third wounded man.

It's the way he walks that strikes Larry. He walks with his head held high, in a straight line, briskly but with no sense of hurry. And he never stops. While others stream for the boats, and load them to the point of sinking in their desperation to escape that deadly beach, Ed simply delivers his load and walks back up again.

Well, then, thinks Larry. That's how it's done.

He stumbles to his feet, and looks down towards the waterline. Every hundred yards or so boats lie with their noses grounded in the sand. Beyond them dozens of boats are coming in or going out, some circling to pick up survivors in the water. The batteries on the cliffs maintain their relentless barrage, now directed at the landing craft, their shells sending up great showers of water as they land between the boats.

Better get going, thinks Larry.

He sets off down the beach, just as he has seen Ed do. A rattle of gunfire, the wind of passing bullets, and suddenly he's running. His boots feel heavy, he stumbles on the pebbles, wrenching one ankle. Careless of the pain, possessed by terror, he runs onto the strip of wet sand. Now he feels as if his boots don't even touch the ground, he's flying. He hears a man shout, it's a stretcher bearer standing there with a stretcher at his feet. His other stretcher bearer lies dead on the beach.

'Give me a hand here!'

Larry runs on, powerless to arrest his flight. He sees a landing craft ahead, its ramp raised for sailing. He runs into the water, feeling its sudden chill. He reaches the craft, clings to its side, pressing himself to the steel plates, sobbing. The craft moves, rocked by a wave, settles back onto the sand bar, and then rocks again. Larry crouches low in the water by its side, as if the bullets won't find him if they can't see him. He has hold of a rope dangling over the craft's side in a long loop. A young boy comes lurching through the water and grabs another loop of rope, but as he does so the boat swings away out to sea and the rope is jerked from his hand. He lowers his arms and stands still, waist deep in water, watching the craft move away.

Larry, clinging tight, is carried out into deep water. His hands are now numb with cold. He loops the rope round his arm so he won't be cast adrift. Others clinging to ropes like him now climb up the flat steel side and onto the deck. Larry tries to climb, but all he has is the rope, and he lacks the strength for the pull to the top. Then he feels his reaching hand clasped from above, and he begins to rise. At the same time a hand below locks onto one of his legs, and drags him down again. He kicks violently, and the hand lets him go. Up he rises again, and so at last is pulled floundering onto the deck.

He lies gasping, exhausted, his cheek pressed to the cold steel plates. He feels the juddering of the engine as the boat pulls away from the shore, away from the nightmare of the beach. His gaze takes in the hold below, which is packed tight with wounded men. They seem to be standing knee-deep in water. As he watches, the water rises, up to their waists. The water is red. And still the water rises.

Now he becomes aware of commotion all round him.

'Jump, lads! Jump in the water! Swim for it!'

The craft is sinking. The bow end of the boat is dipping lower and lower. The wounded men are scrambling out of the bloody water now filling the hold.

Larry jumps with the rest. Bobbing in the water, kept afloat by his Mae West, he looks towards the beach. It's barely yards away. He's still in the danger zone. A plop in the water nearby is followed by a gushing explosion that buries him in seawater, and leaves him choking. The men who had been bobbing on that spot are gone. Here and there tin hats float on the water.

Another landing craft is now circling towards the throng of men in the water. Larry paddles to its sides and takes his place in the crowd attempting to board. One by one they're hauled up onto the deck. When Larry's turn comes he hears a series of sharp pinging sounds and feels a sudden sting in his buttock. At the same time strong hands are hauling him up and over the side. Helpless to control his exhausted body he topples over the edge and slithers down into the hold seven feet below. He lands on men already packed there, and almost at once becomes himself a cushion for the next man to fall. The sharp pinging sounds continue above.

Voices are shouting. 'Lighten ship! We're too low in the water! Lighten ship!'

Men throw up their tin hats, out of the hold. They pull off boots, tunics, trousers. They throw out water bottles and webbing. The craft is under way now, its deck almost flush with the water.

Larry is in his underclothes, surrounded by men in their

underclothes. Someone passes him a cigarette, but his fingers are numb, and he hasn't enough breath left to smoke it.

'You take it.' He passes it on. 'I'll have one later.'

Half a mile out from shore the landing craft is made fast to a big ship and the wounded are taken aboard. Larry is limping as he follows the others across the main deck. A tap on his shoulder and a voice says, 'Wardroom's down the companionway, Lieutenant.' His legs buckle as he descends the ladder, and he feels himself helped to a chair. A blanket is wrapped round him, and a glass of brandy thrust into his hands.

'Rough out there,' says the steward.

Larry nods, and sips his brandy.

'The MO'll take a look at you when he can.'

'Nothing serious,' says Larry. 'What ship am I on?'

'You're on the *Calpe*,' says the steward. 'You're on the command ship.'

Another wounded man calls out, 'Say, could you send down a jug or something?'

'Right away,' says the steward.

The wardroom is packed with wounded officers, some on the couches, some on the floor, some seated at the mess table, their heads resting on their arms. No one speaks. A sickbay attendant appears with a white enamel jug. The wounded man pees into it, making a bell-like ringing sound. After that the jug makes the rounds.

A naval officer comes down to tell them the MO will be with them as soon as he can, but there are so many emergency cases in the sickbay.

'How long before we're home?' one man asks.

'Once we get under way,' says the officer, 'we'll be back in two hours. But I don't think we'll be leaving until every man's off the beach.'

'So where are we now?'

'Dieppe,' comes the reply.

Here below decks the battle feels far away, but for the ceaseless sound of the big guns. They know the ship's under attack from the air because they hear the heavy-calibre ack-acks followed by the clatter of the Oerlikons and then the roar of the bombers passing overhead. Then the guns reverse order, the light rattle chasing the retreating planes, and the heavy pom-pom-pom of the 4.7 guns taking the long shots.

The steward brings food: ship's biscuits and tins of sardines. The medical officer comes at last, blinking with exhaustion. His head sways from side to side as he speaks.

'Hey, doc, you need a drink.'

'Yes, I expect I do.'

But he doesn't drink, he makes his round of the wounded officers. When he gets to Larry, Larry says, 'Don't bother with me. It's nothing.' But he looks anyway.

'You've got a bullet in the bum,' he says. 'Can you cope for now?'

'Sure.'

'Go and get it sorted when you're home.'

Now that he's been told the wound is real, Larry becomes aware that it hurts. He tries to shift his position to ease the pain but only succeeds in making it worse. He accepts another glass of brandy in the hope that he might sleep.

HMS *Calpe* finally begins its journey home at three in the afternoon, the last ship to leave the scene. The return is slow, because there are heavily laden landing craft to escort. It's past midnight when the last of the fleet reaches Newhaven.

Larry files off the destroyer in his underwear, wrapped in a blanket. On the quayside there are hundreds of figures moving about with hurricane lamps, lighting up the ambulances, troop trucks and mobile canteens lined up along the dock. A soldier hands him a pack of cigarettes as he steps off the gangway. A nurse takes his arm and ask him questions.

'Can you walk? Do you need immediate assistance?'

'I'm okay for now. I could do with a cup of tea.'

She takes him directly to the canteen, and gets him a cup of tea.

'See to the others, Nurse,' Larry says. 'I'll be all right.'

He stands on the dark quay among the quiet bustle and drinks his tea. Now that he's out of danger the numb sensations of the last many hours are beginning to lift. Exhaustion and pain sweep through him in waves. And then at first in fragments, then in whole sequences like scenes from a film, he starts to recall his day under fire. He feels the pebbles slip under his boots. He sees the corpse-strewn beach. He tastes the memory of his fear. He sees the tall lean figure of his friend striding up and down the beach, saving the lives of others. And he sees himself, crouched under cover, thinking only of his own survival.

Where is Ed now?

As Larry sips the hot strong tea and feels strength return to his body, the shame in him grows and grows. He bows his head and starts to sob. He weeps for the horror and the weariness and the waste, but most of all for his own moral failure. He wants to ask forgiveness but doesn't know who to ask. He wants to be comforted but believes he doesn't deserve comfort.

'Larry?'

He looks up, face streaming with tears, and there's Kitty.

'Oh, Larry!' He sees the shock on her face. 'Are you wounded?'

'Nothing much,' he says.

He reaches up to rub the tears from his cheeks. His blanket slips. She holds it in place for him.

'Come on,' she says. 'There are beds right here.'

He lets her lead him to a nearby warehouse, which has been fitted out as a field hospital. She hands him over to the nurses. They take him in and get him into a bed. They examine his wound and dress it for the night and tell him he's going to be fine. Then Kitty comes back and sits by him and holds his hand.

'I saw Ed over there,' Larry says. 'He was a hero. A real hero.'

'He hasn't come back,' says Kitty.

'Why not?' Larry knows how stupid this is even as he speaks the words. Somehow it hasn't occurred to him that Ed wouldn't make it.

'Not accounted for,' says Kitty.

'But I saw him!'

Larry falls silent. He wants to say, Nothing can touch him. He was invulnerable. But as he forms the thought he realises the absurdity of it. The opposite is true. Ed took insane risks. How can he have survived?

'He hasn't come back,' says Kitty again, her voice shivering like glass about to break.

Larry closes his eyes and lets his head lie back on the pillow.

'A lot of men haven't come back,' says Kitty. 'But at least you have.'

# 11

'Amazing job! First class!'

Admiral Mountbatten paces up and down the room, flexing his upper arms, as if so moved by admiration that only his agitated limbs can express his feelings.

'I want to hear all about it.'

Larry Cornford is standing, using a walking stick to ease the weight on his right buttock, from which a bullet has been extracted. The only other person in the room with them is Rupert Blundell. Larry has no idea how to tell his supreme commander about the action at Dieppe. Two months and more have passed, but it feels like a hundred years.

'I don't really know what to say, sir.'

'I know, I know,' cries Mountbatten, turning on him his intent and seductive gaze. 'That's what we all say afterwards. When the *Kelly* sank under me, I thought, no one can ever know what this feels like. No one. But then I got talking to Noel, and you know what he's done? He's made a film of it! Bloody good film, too. I've seen it. It should be showing in a few weeks. Go and see it. I can fix tickets for you if you want.'

'Thank you, sir,' says Larry.

'You were on the beach at Dieppe, were you?'

'Yes, sir.'

'Good for you. That's what I want. The real unvarnished PBI view. They say the lessons we've learned from Jubilee are priceless. Shorten the war by years, they say. Plus the whole show finally lured the Luftwaffe out of their hidey-holes and let the RAF give them one hell of a spanking. I've had Winston patting me on the back, I've had Eisenhower like a kid in a candy store. But at the end of the day it's the Poor Bloody Infantry who did the job.'

Larry can think of nothing to say to this.

'Pretty bloody for real, eh?'

'Yes, sir.'

'That's war for you. You heard about Lovat's outfit? Copybook operation. So the Canadians did us proud, did they?'

'Yes, sir.'

'A hard, savage clash, as Winston says.'

'Yes, sir.'

'I shall tell your father when I next see him, Larry. You chose to go in the line of fire. You didn't have to be there. I don't forget things like that. Your name has been put forward.'

'No, sir.' Suddenly Larry becomes agitated. 'I did nothing, sir. I landed, I was on the beach for two or three hours, and I got away. I don't deserve to be noticed above the others, sir. Above any of the others.'

Mountbatten continues to eye him keenly.

'I understand,' he says. 'Good man.'

'If you're putting names forward, sir, there's one you should add to the list. Lieutenant Ed Avenell of 40 Royal Marine

Commando. I watched him carrying wounded men to the boats, while under constant fire himself. He must have saved ten lives at least.'

Mountbatten turns to Rupert Blundell.

'Make a note of that, Rupert.'

'Another one of ours, sir,' says Rupert.

Mountbatten turns back to Larry.

'What's become of him?'

'Missing in action, sir,' says Larry.

'Got that, Rupert?'

'Yes, sir.'

'And there's something else to note,' says Mountbatten, apparently still talking to Blundell, but with a nod towards Larry. 'Here's a man who volunteers for the front line, charges into the heart of battle, catches a bullet, and all he'll tell me is how some other fellow is the true hero. That's the sort of spirit that Noel understands.'

He turns to Larry and holds out his hand.

'It's an honour to have you on my staff.'

Rupert Blundell escorts Larry back down the corridor to the exit.

'He's not a complete chump,' he says. 'He knows it was an almighty balls-up. He asked me if I thought he should resign.'

'What did you tell him?'

'I told him it all depended on the nature of his failure. Was it extrinsic or intrinsic? Did he think he could learn from it?'

'Christ, Rupert, you sound like his father confessor.'

'It is an odd relationship. But he's a very unusual man. He's vain and childish, but at the same time he's humble and genuinely serious. Of course, Edwina makes an enormous difference. He depends on her approval more than anything, and she holds him to very high standards.'

'Edwina Mountbatten?' says Larry. 'Isn't she supposed to be a playgirl?'

'People are always so much more complicated than one thinks, aren't they?'

At the door, bidding Larry goodbye, he adds, 'Did you mean that about Ed Avenell?'

'Every word.'

'I'll see that it gets looked into.'

The army camp in the park of Edenfield Place is now a ghost town. Twelve hundred men left from here to join the assault on Dieppe. A little over five hundred returned. This rump has now departed, to combine with other units of the Canadian forces, in new quarters. The NAAFI shelves have been cleared, the mess huts stripped of their tables and chairs, the Canadian flag struck from the flagpole in the parade ground.

Larry walks slowly up the camp's main street, limping a little, using his walking stick. He is back in Edenfield to collect his few belongings from his farmhouse billet, and is making this last visit as a kind of homage. Too many men have died.

He turns away from the camp and down the avenue of lime trees to the lake. There is the lake house, where he first set eyes on Kitty. That sunlit day now seems to him to have slipped away into the distant past. He's been trying not to think of Kitty, because that leads to thoughts of Ed, and the possibility that he was killed on the beach at Dieppe. Thinking this causes such turmoil within him that he shakes his head from side to side, as if by doing so he can drive out the shameful hope that follows.

He makes his way back up the avenue to the big house, wondering if George Holland is at home, when he sees a figure coming towards him.

'Kitty?'

The figure breaks into a run.

'Larry!'

She comes to him and hugs him, laughing out loud.

'I thought it must be you!'

'Careful! I'm still wobbly.'

'Oh, Larry! How wonderful to see you!'

Her eyes so bright, her lovely face so filled with happiness.

'I didn't think you'd still be here,' Larry says. 'Haven't your mob been posted somewhere else?'

'I'm out,' she says. 'Para eleven.'

One of the few ways of being released from service, and available only to women.

'Kitty! You're going to have a baby!'

She nods, smiling.

'And even better – Ed's alive! He's a prisoner of war.'

'Oh! Thank God!'

He speaks quietly, but he means it. A deep sensation of relief flows through him. It's as if in loving Kitty, in hoping to benefit from Ed's death, he has wanted to kill him. But Ed is not dead. As soon as he understands this Larry knows that it's the right way for things to be. Ed, so gallant, so genuinely courageous, deserves to live. He deserves to be loved by Kitty. He deserves to be the father of her child.

Kitty feels the silent intensity of his relief, and is moved.

'You really are good friends, aren't you?' she says.

'Ed's part of my life,' says Larry.

She slips her arm through his, and they walk back together to the house.

'I'm glad Ed has you,' she says. 'It shows he has good taste in friends.'

'In wives, too.'

This reminds Kitty of her other news.

'Guess what? George is going to marry Louisa!'

'Is he, now?'

'Are you surprised?'

'Not entirely. Though I'd like to know how George ever got round to popping the question.'

'I don't think he did. I think Louisa did the popping.'

Oddly enough, this news leaves Larry feeling a little sad. Everyone round him is getting married. Life moves so fast in wartime.

'So where will you go to have the baby?'

'Back home. Mummy is going to look after me.'

'In deepest Wiltshire.'

'Malmesbury's the oldest borough in England, you know. We're very proud of that. Also the dullest. So you'll have to come and visit me.'

'And it.'

'Definitely. It must be visited.'

They enter the house through the garden porch.

'It's awful here now the Canadians have gone,' says Kitty. 'We all miss them frightfully. That whole Dieppe affair was pretty bad, wasn't it?'

'The rumour is seventy per cent casualties,' says Larry.

'I can't even imagine that. I know it's wrong, but all I can think is, Ed's alive, and you're alive.'

'It's not wrong. It's how we're made. There's only so many people we can care about.'

'You know what, Larry?' She clasps his hands and drops her voice, as if she's imparting a secret that's almost too precious to be spoken aloud. 'I shall love my baby so much.'

# 12

The first days of June bring rain and sunshine. The cornflowers at the wild end of the garden glow bright blue in the slanting early-morning light. The bedroom has no blackout curtains. In these long summer days there's no need for lights going to bed.

Kitty is woken early, as she is every morning, by the baby's sudden cry. For some reason the little thing is incapable of waking gently. She comes out of sleep with a sharp call of alarm, as if frightened to find herself alone in her cot. Kitty is out of bed at once, and has her baby in her arms.

'There, darling. Don't cry, darling. Mummy's here.'

She settles down in the high-backed armchair in the bay window, and opens up her nightdress. The baby's eager searching mouth finds the breast, and settles down to contented sucking. Kitty holds her close, stroking her fine hair, feeling the heat of her tiny body against hers. Her baby is not quite four weeks old.

It's just after five and the house is still, and the town is still. The baby makes regular snuffling noises as she sucks, and Kitty holds her close and loves her more than she ever knew it was humanly possible to love.

'You're my baby, my baby, my only baby. Mummy'll love you for ever and ever.'

These early mornings have become precious to her. She knows the two of them will never be as close again. This is their time of utter absorption in each other, when she is everything to her child, food and drink, warmth and love and protection. In return this tiny creature takes up her every waking moment, and half of her dreams.

Her name is Pamela, after Kitty's grandmother. When it came time to fix on a name her mother said to her, 'What are the girls' names in Ed's family?', and Kitty realised she didn't know. There's so much she doesn't know.

'Daddy'll come home to us one day, darling. And won't you be his princess? Won't he just love you more than anyone in all the world?'

Little Pamela finishes feeding at last, and slips back into sleep. Kitty watches her sleeping in her arms, her eyelids blue-shadowed, her cheeks radiant as the morning, her perfect little lips twitching as she dreams. She kisses her, knowing it won't wake her, and lowers her back into her cot.

Hungry herself now she pads barefoot down to the kitchen, and draws back the heavy blackout curtains. Brilliant light streams into the familiar room, making the white tiles on the walls glitter, throwing a stripe of gold over the scrubbed-wood kitchen table. She gets the iron hook and lifts the plug out of the Rayburn hotplate, and shakes a handful of coke into the furnace. Then she opens up the air vent below to get a good heat going, and puts the kettle on to boil.

She explores the larder, before the war always so crowded with good things to eat, now given over to jars of pickled cabbage and apple chutney and potatoes still clotted with the earth from which they were dug. Her mother has become a grower of vegetables. 'Life would not be bearable without onions.' At such a time before the war Kitty would cut herself a slice of leftover veal pie, or feast on some of her mother's famously moist and chewy gingerbread. Now there is a thin end of a loaf left, and no butter until the new week's ration is fetched.

She puts a small pan of porridge on the hob, wishing she'd remembered to set the oats to soak last night. The kettle boils. She scoops a spoon of tea leaves into the pot, and adds the steaming hot water. There's milk in the cold safe in the larder, put aside for her exclusive consumption, because she's a nursing mother.

By the time the porridge is cooked, and she's eating it sweetened with a precious spoonful of pre-war home-made blackberry jam, she can hear her mother rising in her bedroom overhead. The water pipes gurgle as she runs the taps. Soon now she'll be down, and Kitty's time of quiet will be over.

Kitty misses her life in the service. She misses driving. She would almost say she misses the war, since here in this ancient little town nothing seems to have changed, except for the food shortages. The main roads still pass to the east or west of the town, and the canals and railways miss it altogether.

It's not been easy being home again. Once her pregnancy was confirmed, and the news came through that Ed was a prisoner of war, she understood that her life was to change. Her job now is to raise little Pamela, and wait for the end of the war to bring Ed home. Then they can have their own house together, the three of them, and she won't have to be grateful to her mother any more.

A little later Mrs Teale comes down and joins her in the kitchen, and the stream of well-meaning anxious chatter begins.

'How are you this morning, darling? I heard Pamela grizzling in the night and I almost got up to tell you to make sure to lie her on her tummy or she won't sleep. I see you've not had the last of the bread which I left specially for you. It'll be good for nobody by tomorrow. Such a beautiful morning, really you could almost put Pamela outside in the pram now, fresh air makes such a difference when they're tiny. Harold used to love it so, he cried when I brought him back inside.'

There's been no word of Harold for several weeks now. This awareness floats briefly past Mrs Teale's eyes, causing her to look to one side and wince as if stung.

'You were so different, you didn't like being in your pram at all, I never could work out why,' she resumes. 'Sometimes I wonder where they all come from, the ideas you get. I still have no idea why you refused the Reynolds boy, I should have thought he was perfect for you, and he adored you. Of course, he is in the church, and you're set against that, though I can't imagine why, you sing so beautifully in the abbey choir, and Robert Reynolds is just the kind to do well, everyone says so. You ask your father.'

'Mummy, I'm married.'

'Yes, darling, of course you are.' Though truth to tell, Mrs Teale has temporarily forgotten this fact. Kitty's husband has made such a fleeting appearance in their lives, and who knows what new sorrows this terrible war will bring before it's over? 'Robert Reynolds hasn't married yet, as it happens, which many people find very strange, but I always did think he was such a serious boy, not the kind to chop and change once his mind is made up.'

'I hope you don't mean his mind is made up to marry me.'

'No, of course not, though as it happens I'm not perfectly sure he knows that you're married. After all, the wedding wasn't really done in the way people might have expected, was it? I mean, not from home and in the Abbey as would have been so natural, and all in such a rush, so that there was no time to tell people, and Harold not there, and Michael so disappointed not to be asked to conduct the service.'

'Daddy didn't mind a rap. You know that very well.'

'He tells you that so as not to hurt your feelings, but of course he minded, it's only natural.'

Kitty gets up from the table.

'I'd better go and see to Pammy.'

As usual her mother has managed to put her out of temper. She meets her father in the hall as he comes downstairs, dressed for the day in clerical suit and dog collar. His round pink face lights up as he sees her.

'Kitty, my dear!' he says, embracing her. 'You have no idea how the sight of you lifts my spirits each morning.'

'You didn't mind not doing our wedding, did you, Daddy?'

'Not one bit. Why would I mind? I spend my life doing weddings. It was pure pleasure to have nothing to do but admire you.'

A rustling in the letterbox announces that the paperboy has delivered the morning *Times*. Michael Teale draws it out of the wire basket and points it unopened at Kitty.

'You give that beautiful child of yours a kiss from her grandpa.'

He goes on into the kitchen. When Kitty is halfway up the stairs she comes to a stop. Her father is speaking to her mother in a cold clear voice.

'I told you never to tell Kitty I minded about her wedding.'

'But Michael . . .' Her mother's voice wheedling, placatory.

'You're a fool. What are you?'

'A fool, Michael.'

Kitty continues up the stairs, not wanting to hear, not wanting to feel. Little Pamela senses her coming into the room and is lying awake, big eyes gazing up at her from her cot.

'Did you have a lovely sleep, sweetheart? Would you like to have a nice clean nappy? Then we'll go out for a walk by the river and see the swans.'

Mrs Teale, though in many respects a fool, has undeniable skills when it comes to household management in wartime. As soon as she knew of Kitty's pregnancy she set about preparing for the baby. In this way, when Kitty arrived in the house in Malmesbury, heavily pregnant, she was presented with four cotton baby gowns, four vests, three matinée jackets, three pairs of knitted woollen bootees, and two knitted shawls. Most magnificently of all her mother had tracked down a reconditioned pre-war Marmet perambulator, for which her father paid £10.

This is the pram in which Kitty takes her baby out for walks along the River Avon; attracting as she goes admiring and envious glances from other young mothers. There are large concrete blocks all along the river bank to stop tanks, which people say are there to defend the secret factory at Cowbridge. No one knows what goes on at Cowbridge. The rumour is that rich people pay to send their sons there so they can get out of being called up.

Kitty no longer believes in the war. She never says so, that would be defeatism, but all she wants is for it to be over and Ed to come home. It's gone on too long and she no longer feels part of it. The world has become tired. She wants to start all over again.

The hardest part is that she's finding she can't remember Ed. Their time together was so brief. She remembers the feeling of him, the intense excitement she felt when he was with her; but his face has become hazy, little more than an expression, which is itself little more than a feeling. The way he looked at her, smiling with his mouth but not his eyes. That sense that he was always out of reach. She has his photograph, of course, but she has gazed at it for too long, and her gaze has drained it of life. His photograph no longer looks back at her.

She wheels the pram down the river path, and returns up the High Street. The queue outside Mallards is shorter than usual so she joins it, and smiles as the other women coo over her baby. One woman gives Kitty a shy smile and says, 'I was told your husband got the VC.'

'Yes,' says Kitty.

'You must be so proud.'

'Yes, I am.'

It's almost her turn now. She takes out her ration book and the baby's ration book.

'You make sure you get your share,' says the woman to little Pamela. 'Your dad's a hero.'

As Kitty arrives home again her mother is looking out for her.

'You've got a visitor,' she says.

Kitty gathers Pamela up from the pram, letting her mother take the shopping and the pram itself, which lives in the shed down the side path.

'Who is it?' she says.

'I didn't catch his name,' says Mrs Teale.

Kitty goes on into the house. The visitor is not in the parlour. She goes through to the kitchen, and finds the back door standing open. There's a man at the far end of the garden.

She goes out into the sunshine, Pamela wriggling in her arms. The visitor is in uniform. He hears her, and turns.

'Larry!'

A wave of joy passes through her. He too is grinning with delight as he comes towards her. He's taken his cap off and his curly hair is all golden in the sunlight, like a halo over his cherub face. A freckly cherub with a snub nose and a worried look, like a pug dog.

'Oh, Larry! How wonderful to see you!'

'Well, I promised I'd come and visit the little stranger, didn't I?'

He gazes intently at the baby. Unusually for her, Pamela stops wriggling and gazes just as steadily back.

'Hello,' he says softly. 'Aren't you a beauty.'

'You can hold her if you want.'

'Can I?'

She arranges the baby in his careful arms. He clasps her too tightly, like all men with babies, as if afraid she'll jump out. Then he paces back and forth over the small lawn, swaying slowly from side to side. It makes Kitty laugh to see him.

'Am I doing it wrong?'

'No, no. I think she's a bit surprised.'

Pamela starts to cry. Hastily, Larry gives her back.

'I'm afraid she does a lot of crying,' she says.

Once in Kitty's arms, the baby closes her eyes and goes to sleep.

'Luckily she does an awful lot of sleeping too,' Kitty says.

Larry beams at her.

'It really is good to see you, Kitty. I'd have come sooner. But you know how it is.'

'How's your wound?'

'Oh, that's all sorted. I get twinges, but as you see, I'm up on my pins. Desk jobs only, of course.'

'I'm glad.'

Kitty knows her mother will be looking out from the house, consumed with that strange greed for company that afflicts her; but she wants Larry to herself.

'Let's stay out here for a bit,' she says. 'It's such a beautiful day. Do you mind?'

They sit side by side on the iron bench by the wild garden and talk about the few short weeks when they were all together in Sussex.

'It seems like another life, doesn't it?' Kitty says. 'And one day it just ended.'

'Over three thousand men were killed or captured in that show,' says Larry. 'People don't talk about it much, but it was a pretty bloody mess.'

'Oh, Larry. Sometimes I think I just can't bear any more.'

He pulls a thin newspaper out of his satchel.

'I brought you this.'

It's a copy of the official publication, the *London Gazette*, that carries the citation for Ed's award. He's folded it open to the right page. Kitty reads it, only partly registering what she reads.

> The King has been graciously pleased to approve the award of the Victoria Cross to Lt Edward Avenell, 40 Commando Royal

Marine. At Dieppe on August 19th 1942 Lt Avenell landed under heavy fire . . . During a period of approximately five hours . . . carried wounded personnel across the open beach under fire . . . utter disregard for his personal safety . . . saved at least ten lives . . . refused a final opportunity to leave the shore . . . The calmness and courage of this heroic officer will never be forgotten . . .

Larry says, 'You have to have at least three witnesses for the VC. Ed had over twenty.'

She gives the *Gazette* back to him.

'No. It's for you. And for Pamela.'

Kitty looks at him with tears in her eyes.

'I know he's a hero, Larry. Everyone keeps telling me so.'

She wants to ask the question that haunts her: why didn't he get on that last boat and save himself?

'He'll come home,' says Larry, understanding what she doesn't say. 'You'll have him back.'

'He's in a camp near a place called Eichstätt. I looked it up on a map. It's north of Munich.'

'It could take another year. But he'll come home.'

'Another year,' she says, looking at her baby asleep in her arms.

'So how's motherhood? You look well on it, I must say.'

'It's like nothing else in the world,' says Kitty. 'It's utterly, utterly different. I keep on bursting into tears for no reason. My heart wants to explode with happiness. I feel like I'm a thousand years old. I want to scream with boredom. I long to be young and silly again. But if I lost her I'd die. It's as simple as that.'

'Very simple,' says Larry.

'Darling Larry. I'm so glad you came. How long can you stay?'

'I'll head back after lunch. I hitched a ride with a chap in MI who's visiting some facility near here.'

Kitty's face falls.

'So little time. Let's not talk about the war.'

'What do you want to talk about?'

'I finally got round to reading that book you gave me. *The Warden.*'

'How was it?'

'I wasn't all that gripped by it, to be honest. I think maybe I see enough of clergymen in ordinary life.'

'It's a bit plodding, I grant you. It's a sort of moral thriller, really. Everything hinges on the power of a good but weak man to find the courage to do the right thing.'

'Yes, I do see that,' says Kitty. 'I did read faster towards the end. But poor Mr Harding is so fearfully drippy, isn't he? And I do think Trollope could have done more in the way of punishing the archdeacon. I wanted to have him be publicly humiliated.'

'Ah, you're a harder judge than I am. I can find it in my heart to pity the archdeacon, with his secret drawer and his secret copy of Rabelais.'

'I do want to believe that goodness wins in the end,' says Kitty. 'But you have to admit, in real life it doesn't always seem that way.'

'That's why it's our duty to make it be that way,' says Larry.

'Oh, Larry.' She takes his hand with her free hand. 'I am so glad you came.'

Larry joins them for a simple lunch. Kitty's father returns

from the abbey promptly at one. He too is all smiles to see that they have a guest, and better still, a male guest.

'What do you make of the bombing of Pantelleria, eh? I've been saying for weeks the invasion will begin in the Med. Sicily is the open door.'

Kitty shows her father the *London Gazette* with Ed's citation. Both he and her mother read it, taking in every word.

'If ever a man deserved a VC, that's the man,' says her father.

'Larry was there,' says Kitty. 'He saw him.'

'Oh, my Lord!' exclaims her father. 'The tales you must have to tell! And here I am, worrying myself to death over the repairs to the abbey.'

'The war will be over one day,' says Larry, 'and when it's over we'll still want to see the grand old churches, and the cornflowers in bloom.'

'Larry is such a romantic,' says Kitty, smiling across the table at him. 'He's an artist, really.'

'An artist!' exclaims her mother.

'I like to paint,' says Larry.

'You should paint Kitty,' says Mr Teale. 'I'm always telling her we should have her portrait done.'

'I'm afraid I don't dare attempt portraits,' says Larry. 'That requires skills I have yet to acquire.'

'Larry paints like Cézanne,' says Kitty. 'All blotchy and wrong colours.'

'A very accurate description,' says Larry.

When it's time for him to leave Kitty walks with him to the road junction, leaving Pamela in her mother's care.

'You know I'm not really so silly about your painting, Larry. I'm only teasing.'

'Yes, I know.'

'Thank you for being so sweet to Daddy.'

Larry glances at her as they walk.

'You find it hard, don't you?' he says. 'Ed being away.'

'Yes, I suppose so. Oh, Larry. I'm so afraid I'm forgetting him.'

She feels she's about to cry and knows she mustn't. But then he puts his arms round her and it's so good to be held in a man's arms that she does cry, just a little.

'This time will pass,' he says.

'I know. I know it will. I have to be strong, for Pamela.'

He kisses her gently on the cheek.

'That's from Ed,' he says. 'He's thinking of you right now. He loves you so much.'

'Darling Larry,' she says. 'Can I kiss him back?'

She kisses Larry on the cheek, as he kissed her. They stand still for a moment, saying nothing. Then they part, and walk on to the junction.

Larry's friend is waiting in his car. As he climbs in the back Kitty says to him, 'I heard from Louisa the other day. She's turned into a lady of the manor. She's practically taking soup to villagers.'

'Hurrah for Lady Edenfield!' says Larry.

Then the car is driving away, down the road to Swindon, and Kitty turns to walk slowly back.

# 13

After the Dieppe raid, a number of German soldiers are found dead, shot in the head, with their hands tied behind their backs. This is believed to be the work of commandos. In reprisal, the German High Command orders that all commandos held in prisoner-of-war camps are to be shackled until further notice.

A later commando raid on the island of Sark leaves more German soldiers dead, also with their hands tied. Hitler, enraged, issues a secret order known as the *Kommandobefehl*. Only twelve copies are made. The order states:

> For a long time now our opponents have been employing in their conduct of war, methods which contravene the International Convention of Geneva. The members of the so-called Commandos behave in a particularly brutal and underhand manner . . . I order therefore: from now on all men operating against German troops in so-called Commando raids . . . are to be annihilated . . .

The *Kommandobefehl* does not go unchallenged. Field Marshal

Rommel refuses to issue the order to his troops, believing it to be a breach of the code of war. In prisoner-of-war camps its implementation varies with the character of individual commanders. In Oflag VII-B near Eichstätt captured members of commando units are shackled, but they are not handed over to the *Sicherheitsdienst*, the Security Service; more because of inter-service rivalry than out of any wish to save the men from execution.

However, when news reaches the camp authorities that Lieutenant Edward Avenell of 40 RM Commando has been awarded the Victoria Cross, there is a reaction of anger.

The prisoner is woken from his bunk in Block 5 before dawn by two camp orderlies who are themselves still half asleep. They march him out, handcuffed, into the parade ground. Here they order him to stand before the stony bank that rises to the Lagerstrasse and the kitchen block.

An *Obersturmführer* arrives from the *Kommandantur*. He opens a folder and shines a small electric torch on the typed order within. The light reflects off the paper onto his face as he reads the order aloud. Ed understands nothing of the German except that this is how the order for an execution is given. When the voice falls silent, the *Obersturmführer* draws a pistol and orders him to kneel. Not a firing squad, then.

Ed feels cold. His spirit is indifferent but his body cares. Dryness in his mouth and throat, a hot loosening in his bowels. He should close his eyes but they remain open, seeing nothing. There are rooks in the trees on the hillside across the parade ground, he hears their cries. Light seeping into the sky.

He's aware of the raw pain in his wrists from the handcuffs, and how any time now he's going to shit his pants. He'd kill for a cigarette, or at least die for one.

There comes a loud report. The pistol shot echoes down the valley. The rooks burst up in a swarm into the light of the coming day.

The pistol is lowered once more. The *Obersturmführer* departs. The orderlies march Ed back to his quarters.

'So what was that all about?' say the others in his block.

Ed has no answer.

The pantomime is repeated the next day. The pre-dawn summons, the reading of the order, the shot in the air. And then again the next day. The process of repetition brings no lessening of the fear. Each time the game could turn real. Each time his body betrays him. But the failure is secret. To outside eyes he remains indifferent, magnificent.

He understands that it's not his death they want, but his disintegration. Or perhaps it's all just a way for bored camp officers to pass the time. There's a rumour they're laying bets in the guardroom, so many days before he cracks, at such-and-such odds, paid out in cigarettes. You want your life to have value and your death to have meaning, but in the end it's all just a game.

The hero doesn't crack. At least not so you can see from the outside.

In December 1943, after he's been a prisoner for almost five hundred days, the handcuffs are removed.

In April 1945, after he's been a prisoner for almost a thousand days, the war stutters to its end.

The American Army is rumoured to be across the Rhine and advancing rapidly. The commandant of the camp calls an early-morning parade of all prisoners and announces that for their safety they will be moving east to Moosburg. The officer-prisoners are issued bulk rations and march out in good order down the road to Eichstätt. Five Thunderbolts of the US Air Force spot the marching column and mistaking them for German troops, dive-bomb the prisoners. For thirty minutes they strafe them with their cannon, oblivious to all the waving arms. Fourteen British officers are killed and forty-six are wounded. The survivors return to the camp.

Ed Avenell is among the party detailed to bury the dead.

'Fucking typical,' says one of his companions. 'Talk about giving your life for your country.'

Ed says nothing. He's been saying nothing for a long time now.

That night the column forms up again, and under cover of darkness they march south-east. At dawn they sleep in a barn. As dusk falls they resume their march. American planes can be heard high overhead day and night. A fine cold rain is falling as they march through Ernsgaden and Mainburg. The prisoners are growing weaker all the time. In the course of the next seven days and nights, four men die on the march. On the eighth day they reach Oflag V, the giant camp at Moosburg. Here over thirty thousand prisoners of all ranks and nationalities have been herded together. There are thunderstorms that evening, and rumours that Bavaria is suing for a separate peace. American guns can be heard. The Seventh Army is said to be as close as Ingolstadt. The prisoners are packed four hundred to a hut. Rations are pitifully low.

Next morning the commandant goes searching for an American officer of high enough rank to receive his surrender. By noon the camp is liberated. The liberators are C Company, 47th Tank Battalion, 14th Armored Division, 3rd Corps, Third US Army. They raise the US flag and tell the cheering prisoners they will be evacuated in Dakotas, taking twenty-five men at a time, starting as soon as a landing strip can be prepared.

Ed smiles when he hears this, and draws deeply on the American cigarette he's been given, and fixes his gaze on the far distance.

'We're not going anywhere in a hurry, boys,' he says.

On the first day of May snow falls over the camp. A rumour spreads that Hitler is dead. The men are too tired and hungry to care. All they want now is to go home.

On May 3rd they're transported in six-wheeler trucks to Landshut. The houses they pass on the way have white flags in their windows. At Landshut the former prisoners of war are billeted in empty flats, six to a room, and supplied with American K rations. Here the waiting begins again.

The snow turns to rain, and the winds are too strong for planes to take off. The American POWs who arrived earlier take precedence; also a batch of seven hundred Indians. Two hundred planes are promised, flying back from Prague, but only seventy arrive.

On the morning of May 7th, which is being celebrated at home as VE Day, Ed takes his turn at the aerodrome, and by mid-afternoon he is boarding. The Dakota lands at St Omer in northern France, where he is cleaned up and deloused. Next day RAF Lancasters fly the British contingent to Duxford air base near Cambridge. It is now twenty-five days since they were marched out of the camp; and two years, eight months and twenty days since Ed left England.

He sends two telegrams, one to his parents and one to his

wife. A repatriation orderly recognises his name on the manifest and tells the base commander, a young-looking squadron leader.

'I'm told you're a VC,' says the squadron leader.

'Yes,' says Ed. 'I've been told that too.'

'Honour to have you here. Anything I can do for you?'

'No, thank you, sir. I'm on my way first thing in the morning.'

'Good job,' says the squadron leader, shaking his hand. 'Damn good job.'

Kitty arrives early at King's Cross station, holding very tight to Pamela's hand. Pamela is just over two years old, and a sturdy walker, but the giant railway station overawes her. Kitty is wearing her prettiest pre-war frock beneath a dark grey wool coat. It's a chilly spring day.

'Daddy,' says Pamela, pointing to a man striding across the concourse.

'No, that's not Daddy,' says Kitty. 'I'll tell you when it's him.'

She's been training Pamela ever since the telegram came. She wants her to say, 'Hello, Daddy,' and give him a kiss.

There are other women waiting, staring anxiously down the long platforms. One holds a bunch of flowers. Kitty thinks Ed wouldn't want flowers, though the truth is she doesn't know. In her letters to him she's told him all her news, mostly about Pamela, and how pretty she is, and how forward. She's told Ed how they've left her parents' house and are now living in Edenfield Place, thanks to her friend Louisa. It's somewhere to be until he comes home, and they can set up house on their own.

Ed's letters from Germany have been strange. He writes about the absurdity of the life he leads, and the folly of human nature, but never about his own state of mind. Nor does he ask after his daughter. The letters always end, 'I love you.' But they have not brought him closer.

'You have to expect it,' Louisa says in their late-night talks. 'You had three weeks together, almost three years ago. It'll be like starting all over again.'

'I know you're right,' Kitty says. 'But he's the most important person in my life, apart from Pamela. The thought of him takes up almost all the space I have.'

'My advice is, don't get your hopes up.'

Kitty hardly knows what she feels as she waits at King's Cross. All she wants is for it to be over. She has longed for this moment for so long that now it's close, it frightens her.

'Hello, Daddy,' Pamela says to a young airman on the platform.

'No!' says Kitty a little too sharply. 'I'll tell you when it's Daddy.'

Pamela feels the rebuke. Her sweet face sets in a look Kitty knows well, eyes unfocused, lips pouting.

'Daddy,' she says, pointing to an elderly man sitting on a bench.

She calls out to a porter wheeling a trolley, 'Daddy! Daddy!'

A soldier appears, running, breathless.

'Hello, Daddy!' cries Pamela.

'Stop it!' says Kitty. 'Stop it!'

She controls an overwhelming urge to smack the child.

'Daddy,' says Pamela, very quietly now. 'Daddy, Daddy, Daddy.'

Only the arrival of the train silences her. The immense engine sighs slowly to a stop, thrilling her with its living breathing power. The carriage doors open and the passengers come streaming down the platform. Kitty looks without seeing, afraid he isn't on the train after all, afraid he isn't coming home, afraid he is coming home.

She remembers standing on the quay at Newhaven after the first aborted operation against Dieppe, and all the men filing off the boats in the night, and how she looked for him and couldn't see him. Then all at once he was there before her. Remembering that moment, her love for him bursts within her, and she wants so much, so much, to hold him in her arms again.

Pamela senses that she's lost her mother's attention. She tugs at the hand that holds hers, saying, 'Go home. Go home.'

The people from the train stream by, mostly men, mostly in uniform. There are too many, their faces hazy in the steamy air, the sound of boots tramping the platform dulling the nervous hugger-mugger of reunions.

Pamela starts to cry. She feels ignored and sorry for herself. At the same time she's intensely excited. As she maintains a steady low-level snivelling she holds tight to her mother's hand, knowing that she'll feel it in her mother's body when it happens, the mysterious and wonderful moment for which they've come.

Kitty catches her breath. He's there, she knows it, though she hasn't yet seen him. She searches the faces bobbing towards her, and finds him. He hasn't seen her yet. He looks so thin, so sad. He's bareheaded, wearing worn battledress, a kitbag over one shoulder. He looks like his photograph, except older, more real, wiser. There's a nobility about him she never knew he possessed.

Oh my darling, she says to herself. You've come back to me.

He sees her now, and a brightness lights up his face. He hurries faster towards her, one arm half raised, half waving. She lifts a timid hand in answer.

He comes to her and at once takes her in his arms. She holds him close, letting go of Pamela's hand to give all of herself to him. His body is so thin, she can feel all his bones. Then he kisses her, only lightly, as if he's afraid she's fragile, and she kisses him, nuzzling her face against his. Then he drops down onto his haunches to greet his unknown daughter.

'Hello,' he says.

Pamela gazes back at him in silence. Kitty strokes the top of her head.

'Say hello to Daddy, darling.'

Pamela still says nothing.

'Don't you say a word,' says Ed. 'Why should you?'

He reaches out one hand and lightly touches her cheek. Then he stands up.

'Let's go,' he says.

'I have it all planned,' says Kitty. 'We're going to take a taxi to Victoria.'

'A taxi! We must be rich.'

'Special occasion.'

Pamela trots along obediently by her mother's side, from time to time peeping up at the stranger. She has no notion of him being her father, and doesn't even know what that means. But from the very first moment she saw him take her mother in his arms, and felt her mother let go of her hand to embrace him, she surrendered to him. He has become in an instant the most powerful being in her universe. When he knelt before her, and fixed her with his grave blue eyes, she knew that all she desired in life from now on was the love and admiration of this magnificent stranger.

In the taxi Kitty stops trembling and becomes more talkative.

'You're so thin, my darling,' she says. 'I'm going to feed you and feed you.'

'I'm all for that.'

'I don't know what to ask you first. There's so much.'

'Let's not talk about it,' he says.

'Tell me what you want. Tell me what I should do.'

'Nothing at all,' he says. 'Just be my beautiful wife.'

Pamela leans across her mother and says to him in her clear high voice, 'Hello, Daddy.'

Louisa has scraped together a celebration dinner of some magnificence. There's an actual roast chicken and George contributes a bottle of Meursault, one of the few not consumed by the Canadians.

'We have to welcome home our hero,' Louisa says.

Ed retires to the rooms where Kitty and Pamela live, a bedroom, dressing room and bathroom above the dining room. He soaks in a deep warm bath, and then dresses in clothes lent him by his host. There is nothing here that belongs to him.

'I didn't know what else to do,' says Kitty.

'This is perfect,' says Ed. 'I shall be a new man.'

A bed is made up for Pamela in the dressing room. Kitty is surprised she accepts her expulsion from her mother's bedroom without protest. Ed comes and kisses her good night at her bedtime. He seems to expect nothing from her, which Pamela finds thrilling. After he's given her a kiss he touches her cheek with one forefinger, as he did when they met for the first time. As he does so, his gaze lingers on her, and he's almost smiling.

At dinner his homecoming is toasted with the mellow burgundy.

'There's some newspaperman wants to talk to you,' Kitty says. 'He wants the story of your VC.'

'Well, he won't get it,' says Ed mildly.

'But we're all so proud of you!' says Louisa.

'I'm afraid it's a lot of nonsense,' says Ed. 'Let's leave it at that, shall we?'

They eat by candlelight, in the dining room. The effects of the military occupation are everywhere in the house, but in the warm glow of the candles it's almost as if the war has never been. Ed, bathed and wearing a freshly laundered shirt that hangs loose on his spare frame, draws all their eyes. His face, hollowed out by his years in prison, has the austere beauty of a medieval saint. He seems to the others to be present only partly in their world. A part of him has gone on, to a place where they can't follow him.

That night he lies in Kitty's arms, but they don't make love.

'I need time,' he says.

'Of course you do, my darling. We have all the time in the world.'

In the night while Kitty is sleeping he gets out of their bed and lies down to sleep on the floor. In the morning, finding him there, Kitty asks him if he'd like a room of his own.

'Just for a night or two,' he says. 'It's been so long since I've been able to be alone.'

Kitty doesn't look at him as she answers, and she forces her voice to remain light.

'Of course,' she says.

*

After that Ed spends his nights in a bedroom across the passage. By day he goes for long solitary walks over the Downs.

Kitty has made plans for his return, for them to have a house of their own. The idea comes from Louisa, that they should rent one of the farmhouses on the estate. Since Arthur Funnell's death the land attached to River Farm has been worked by the tenant at the Home Farm, and the house is no longer occupied. The rent would be nominal. But for now she says nothing of this to Ed. It's as if he hasn't yet fully returned from the war.

When they're alone together, she tries to get him to talk about his time in the camps.

'What did they do to you over there, Ed?'

'Nothing much,' he says. 'Some of the other fellows had it far worse than me.'

Little by little she builds a picture of his time in captivity. He tells her about the hunger, and the cold, but not as if he was much troubled by either. He seems to have suffered most from restrictions on his movement.

'Do you mean being locked in a cell?'

'No, we weren't locked up. We were in blockhouses most of the time. But the handcuffs got me down rather.'

'Handcuffs?'

He shows her, holding out his wrists a foot or so apart.

'It's not like I was chained to a wall. But you'd be surprised how many things you can't do when you're cuffed. Makes it hard to sleep at night, too.'

'How long were you in handcuffs?'

'A little over a year.'

'A year!'

'Four hundred and eleven days.'

He delivers the number with a wry smile, as if ashamed to admit that he kept count.

'But handcuffs don't kill you,' he says.

One night Kitty is woken by a sudden cry. She knows it comes from Ed's room. She goes to him and finds him standing in the middle of the room, eyes staring, still half asleep. Her appearance wakes him fully.

'Sorry,' he says. 'God, I'm sorry.'

She sits him down on the bed and takes him in her arms. He huddles against her, trembling.

'Just a bad dream,' he says.

'Darling.' She kisses his damp cheek. 'Darling. You're safe home now.'

The more she learns of how much he's been hurt, the more she loves him. That cry in the night binds him to her more tightly than any words of love.

She watches him when he can't see her watching, wanting to be part of what's happening to him. There are so many stories these days about men coming home from war, and how difficult it is for them to adjust. Always the advice is the same: give them time. Kitty is willing to give him all the time in the world, so long as she can be sure he still loves her. Often when his faraway gaze falls upon her she sees his face light up with happiness. And once, kissing her before retiring to his solitary bed, he says, 'If it wasn't for you, I'd have let them kill me over there.'

One great consolation is that he loves Pamela, and she loves him. Often she'll sit on his lap for an hour at a time, clinging to him tightly, her face pressed to his chest. They never talk.

They just sit like that, his arms round the child's little body, in one or other of the empty echoing rooms of the great house, and let the world go by.

# PART TWO
# ART

1945–47

# 14

In early November of 1945 the painter William Coldstream, finally released from the army, accepts an invitation to teach at the Camberwell College of Art. His friends Victor Pasmore, Claude Rogers and Lawrence Gowing are already on the staff; and altogether it's as if the pre-war Euston Road school has been reborn and moved south of the river.

Coldstream takes his first evening class wearing his dark blue demob suit, looking more like a bank clerk than an artist. His class of twenty students covers a range of ages, from the very young, fresh from the Downs School or a foundation course in a provincial town, to ex-service men and women in their late twenties. Among them is Larry Cornford. The class takes place in one of the Life Rooms in the shabby Victorian building on the Peckham Road, where the roar of passing lorries outside competes with the shriek of tram wheels. A life model waits, fully dressed, sitting on an upright chair to one side.

The teacher begins by reading from Ruskin's *Elements of Drawing*.

'I believe that the excellence of an artist depends wholly upon refinement of perception, and that it is this which a master or a school can teach.'

Larry watches his teacher intently as he speaks. He's seen some of his paintings and he admires them. The man himself is a surprise: his voice unassertive, his face almost expressionless as he speaks. He tells the class that they must learn to judge the distance of objects from the eye. He calls the life model to stand in front of the class. He faces her, one arm outreached, holding a pencil vertically in his hand.

'The eye notes the length of the head, crown to chin, on the pencil. The hand transfers the same distance to the pad, making marks accordingly. Now looking again, note the distance from eyebrows to mouth. Make the marks. You see how, little by little, you build up a precise set of relationships between the elements of the face.'

Larry does as he is told. The model is young and has a thick fringe. Her straight brown hair falls to her shoulders, framing a pale face with sleepy eyes. She seems not to mind being looked at.

Coldstream moves among the students as they work, peering at their sketch pads, saying nothing. Larry finds the process of measuring and making marks an awkward business, far removed from the rapid freehand sketching with which he has always begun before. The student beside him, a very young man, almost a boy, evidently feels this too, judging by the way he scowls and mutters as he works. When the teacher is by him he vents his frustration.

'It's like painting by numbers, isn't it?' he says.

'What would you rather do?' says Coldstream, unoffended.

'I'd rather paint what I feel.'

'That comes later,' says Coldstream. 'First you must see.'

As the students work, the girl model's gaze roams the room and comes to rest on Larry. Her eyes linger on him with disarming directness, as if she supposes he doesn't see her. Larry realises with a shock that this face he's been so obediently mapping is, if not exactly beautiful, certainly very striking. Her nose is too strong, her mouth too full, her eyes too startling; but the overall effect is undeniably attractive. She looks both very young and very sure of herself, almost imperious.

When the class ends some of the students gather round Coldstream, who is pulling on a beige officer's topcoat against the night chill. The others pack up their sketch pads and drift out down the bare-board corridor to the street.

'Poor old Bill,' says a voice behind Larry.

It's the young model. Larry is vaguely aware that Coldstream's first name is Bill.

'Do you know him?' he says.

'No, not at all. But you just have to look at him to see he's unhappy.'

'Oh, do you think so?'

It hasn't occurred to Larry to consider the personal happiness of his teacher.

'I'm Nell,' she says. 'Who are you?'

'Lawrence Cornford. Larry, I mean.'

'I like Lawrence better. How old are you, Lawrence?'

Her command of the situation so surprises him that he doesn't think to object to such a sudden personal question.

'Twenty-seven,' he says.

'I suppose you had a harrowing war and now you're mature beyond your years. All I've been doing is going quietly mad in

Tunbridge Wells. It seems so unfair that just when I'm old enough to be harrowed they take the war away.'

'How old are you?'

'Nineteen. But if you count former lives, I'm about nine hundred.'

'Do you believe in former lives?'

'No, of course not,' she says. 'Do I look completely potty?' Then without waiting for an answer, 'So why are you here?'

'To learn,' says Larry. 'I want to be a better painter.'

By now they're out on the street. Coldstream and the group with him are walking down the road. Without thinking, Larry and Nell follow.

'So you have a private income, I suppose,' Nell says.

'My father is supporting me.' Larry blushes a little at the admission. 'But we have a strictly limited agreement. He's giving me a year.'

'To prove you're a genius?'

'To prove I'm in with a chance.'

'How do you prove that?'

'I'm to show my work. And we'll see if anyone buys anything.'

The group ahead turn into the pub on the corner, the Hermit's Rest.

'How about you buy me a drink?' says Nell.

They go into the pub, which is half full and noisy and smoky. The intense young student who was Larry's neighbour in the class leaves Coldstream's group and joins them.

'Old boys' reunion,' he says, nodding behind him. 'They were all at Euston Road. What do you make of all this Ruskin and taking measurements like a fucking tailor? I signed up to be inspired by an artist not trained by a draughtsman.'

'I suppose he could be both,' says Larry.

'Never!' The boy's eyes flash with contempt. 'An artist is an artist above everything. He may teach to earn his bread, but even when teaching he's an artist. Why should he care about us? We're impedimenta. I've seen his work. It's good. But there should be more of himself on the canvas. He should take more risks. There should be more danger.'

Having so delivered himself of this verdict, he departs.

'God, how the young bore me!' says Nell.

'You being so very old,' says Larry.

'Oh, I promise you, I bore myself. But I mean to grow older just as fast as I can.'

'Not too fast, I hope.'

'Why? Did you like being nineteen? Was it the best year of your life?'

'No,' says Larry.

'You know life models pose naked.'

'Yes.'

'Shall I tell you why I'm doing it?'

'If you want to.'

'No. I'm asking you if you want me to tell you.'

She fixes him with truth-demanding eyes. Confused by her nearness, Larry smiles and shakes his head.

'You don't want me to tell you?'

'Yes. Yes, I do.'

'Well, then,' she says. 'I've left home, and I'm not going back. I would have died if I'd stayed one day longer. I'm starting my whole life again, and this time I'm going to live it quite differently, among quite different people. I'm going to live a real life, not a show life. And I'm going to do it among people who live real lives. I know I'm not an artist myself, but I want to live among artists.'

'Sounds like you want danger, like that boy.'

'That's just silly play-acting. Who wants danger? I want truth.'

This is strong stuff, made all the stronger by her unrelenting gaze, and her pale sensual face. The more he looks at her the more fascinated he becomes.

'I think that's what I want too,' he says.

'Then shall we help each other find it? Shall we, Lawrence?'

'Why not?' he says.

'No, that's no good. We don't do things because we can't think of a reason not to. We do things we want to do. We act out of desire.'

She doesn't smile as she speaks, but nor is she as sure of herself as he first thought. Her intense gaze is asking for his support.

'Yes,' he says. 'Yes.'

'The rule is, we say what we want. We tell each other the truth.'

'Yes.'

'So I'll start. I want to be friends with you, Lawrence.' She holds out her hand. 'Do you want to be friends with me?'

'Yes. I do.'

He takes her hand and holds it, not shaking it. He feels her warmth.

'There,' she says. 'Now we're friends.'

# 15

'Golly, you were hard to find,' says Kitty, giving Larry a warm hug. 'You shouldn't just disappear and leave no forwarding address.'

'I thought I had.'

She ushers him out of Lewes station to a dark green Wolseley Hornet parked outside.

'George bought her in '32. Isn't she glorious?'

The December roads are icy. Driving slowly back to Edenfield, Kitty confides her worries.

'You'll find Ed's changed a lot.'

'I suppose it must be hard for him to adjust,' says Larry.

'See what you think when you meet him.'

Larry gazes out of the window at the familiar hump of the Downs.

'You remember that place where you were billeted?' Kitty says. 'George is offering it to us at a peppercorn rent.'

'Are you short of money?'

'We have no money at all. We're living off Ed's demob

payments. No, actually we're living off George and Louisa. Ed's looking round for some sort of job, but you wouldn't say his heart was in it.'

'He's a VC, for God's sake! Where's the nation's gratitude?'

'The nation awards VCs an annual sum of ten pounds. But only if you're non-commissioned. Officer class is assumed to have private means.'

She eases the car off the road and down the drive to Edenfield Place.

'Just wait till you see Pammy. She's turning into such a little madam.'

Louisa is there to greet Larry, and then George appears, nodding and blinking. Gareth, the indoor man, takes Larry's weekend bag and his satchel up to his allocated bedroom. There's tea laid out in the drawing-room.

'All a bit more civilised than when I was last here,' Larry says.

'I rather miss the Canadians,' says George. 'They made such a jolly noise.'

'Where's Pammy?' says Kitty.

'Out somewhere with Ed,' says Louisa. 'They'll be back soon.'

Ed doesn't appear, so after they've had a cup of tea Larry and Kitty go in search of him.

'He'll be in the wood beyond the lake,' says Kitty. 'If he's not up on the Downs.'

As they stroll past the lake house in the gathering dusk Larry says lightly, 'That's where I first met you.'

'Reading *Middlemarch*.'

Ed comes into view on the far side of the lake. He has Pamela on his shoulders, and he holds her fast by her ankles.

'My God!' says Larry softly. 'He's so thin!'

Ed sees them and breaks into a careful bounding run. The little girl squeals with fear and delight.

Eyes shining, chest heaving, Ed reaches them and swings Pamela down to the ground.

'Larry! Good man!'

He takes his hand and pumps it.

'I would have come sooner,' says Larry, 'but I didn't know what sort of a state you were in. And look at you! You look like a ghost!'

'I am a ghost.' Then his eyes meet Kitty's and he smiles. 'No, I'm not. Not a ghost at all. And will you look at this! I have a daughter!'

Pamela is gazing curiously up at Larry. Her father's joy at his friend's arrival causes her to give him serious attention.

'Hello, Pamela,' says Larry.

'Hello,' says the little girl.

'Come along, then,' says Kitty. 'There's still some tea left.'

Ed puts one arm over Larry's shoulders. He's more animated than he's been for days.

'Oh, Larry, Larry, Larry. I am so glad to see you.'

He beats with one fist on Larry's shoulder as they walk back to the house.

'Me too, old chap. For a while I wasn't sure I'd ever see you again.'

'I hope you trusted you'd meet me in heaven. Or wasn't I to be allowed in?'

'They'll serenade you with trumpets, Ed. You're a genuine hero.'

'No, no. Don't say that.'

'I was on that beach.'

'I don't want to talk about that,' says Ed, withdrawing his arm. 'Tell me about you. Is it art, or is it bananas?'

'It's art for now. I've enrolled in a course at Camberwell College. I'm having a go at taking it seriously.'

'And frivolously too, I hope. Art should be fun too.'

'It's more than fun, Ed. It's what gives me my deepest happiness.'

Ed stops and gazes into his friend's eyes.

'There, you see,' he says. 'I'd give anything to have that.'

Alone in his bedroom, a fine large room over the organ room with a west-facing window, Larry changes slowly for dinner, and thinks about Kitty. It frightens him how much he longs to be in her company, and how happy he is when her lovely face is turned towards him. But his part is to play the role of faithful friend, both to her and to Ed; and play it he will.

Over dinner he has an opportunity to observe the curious relationship between George and Louisa. Louisa has got into the habit of talking about George in his presence as if he doesn't hear her.

'Is George doing something about the wine?' she says. 'Oh, isn't he hopeless! Sometimes I wonder that he manages to get out of bed in the morning. You never saw a person with less get up and go.'

'The wine is on the table, my dear.'

'He hasn't got his napkin on. You'll see, he'll spill the sauce all down his tie.'

Obediently, George tucks his napkin into his collar. His eyes peep at Larry through the thick lenses of his glasses.

'She's quite something, isn't she?' he says.

Ed hardly touches his food. Larry sees how Kitty watches his plate with anxious eyes. Louisa complains bitterly about the petrol rations.

'They say they've increased the ration, but four gallons a month! That won't get anyone very far.'

'I think the truth is we're broke,' says Larry. 'The country, I mean.'

'Do let's not complain,' says Kitty. 'Think how frightening it was, not knowing day by day if people were still alive even.'

When dinner is over Ed slips away, not saying where he's going. Louisa and George settle down to a game of Pelmanism, which it turns out is their customary evening relaxation. Louisa spreads out the cards face down on the long table in the library.

'George has a surprisingly good memory for cards,' she says. 'I think it must come from all that peering at maps.'

Kitty and Larry leave them to their game. They retreat to the smallest of the family rooms, the West Parlour. Here family portraits hang on chains against a pale eau-de-nil wallpaper, and the chintz-covered armchairs are deep and comfortable. For a few moments Kitty looks at Larry in silence, and he too remains silent, not wanting to break the sweet intimacy.

'Well?' she says at last.

'He's not in a good way, is he?'

'He won't see a doctor. He won't see anyone.'

'How is he with you?' says Larry.

'He's kind, and gentle, and loving. And you see how he is with Pammy. But most of the time he just wants to be alone.'

'What does he do when he's alone?'

'I don't know. Nothing, as far as I can tell. He just thinks. Or maybe he doesn't think. Maybe he wants to be alone so he can switch himself off, or something.'

'Sounds like some sort of breakdown.'

'He had a terrible time in the camps. He was kept handcuffed for four hundred and eleven days.'

'Jesus! Poor bastard.'

'I just don't know what to do.'

She's clasping her hands together as she speaks, working them against each other, as if trying to rub out some invisible stain.

'Will you help us, Larry?'

Her lovely face is looking at him in mute appeal, admitting the unhappiness she can't name.

'I'll try talking to him,' says Larry. 'But he may not want to talk to me.'

'He'll talk to you if he talks to anyone.'

'You say he's looking round for a job.'

'He isn't really. He knows he must find some kind of income. But the way he is at present, I don't see that he's employable.'

Larry nods, frowning, pondering what best to do.

'I love him so much, Larry,' Kitty says. 'But we're sleeping in separate bedrooms for now. It's what he wants.' There's the glisten of tears in her eyes as she speaks. 'I wish I knew why.'

'Oh, Kitty.'

'Do you think it's me?'

'No. It's not you.'

'We've been apart so long. You'd think at least he'd want that.'

'I'll try and talk to him,' Larry says.

'Now,' says Kitty. 'Go to him now.'

'Do you know where he is?'

'Yes, I know.' She looks down, suddenly ashamed. 'I follow him sometimes, just so I know where he goes. He'll be in the chapel.'

'The chapel!'

'We were married there, remember?'

'Of course I remember.'

'He goes and sits there by himself. Sometimes for hours.'

Larry gets up out of his armchair.

'I'll see what I can do.'

A first floor corridor leads past bedrooms to a bridge across the courtyard entrance. This is the family's private way to the chapel. The vaulted space is in darkness but for a single light over the altar. When Larry first enters, it appears to be empty.

'Anyone here?'

A voice answers from the darkness.

'Is that Larry?'

'Yes, it's me.'

Ed uncoils himself from where he's been lying, stretched out on a row of dark oak chairs. Larry walks down the aisle to him.

'I suppose Kitty sent you.'

'Yes.'

'Dear Kitty. She does her best with me.'

Larry is on the point of saying something noncommittal and sympathetic when he changes his mind.

'Why don't you just sort yourself out, Ed?'

Ed raises his eyebrows, smiling.

'There speaks the voice of reason.'

'Sorry. Stupid thing to say.'

'No, you're right. But the thing is, I'm not sure I can sort myself out. And even if I could, who'd sort out the world?'

'Oh, honestly,' says Larry.

'All the rottenness and mess.'

Larry thinks of Kitty gazing at him in the parlour with tears in her eyes.

'It won't do, Ed,' he says. 'What right do you have to indulge yourself in the luxury of despair? You have a wife. You have a child.'

'Well, well.' He's not smiling any more. 'Did Kitty ask you to tell me that?'

'This isn't from Kitty. This is from me. We've known each other for almost fifteen years. You're my best friend. You're the man I admire most in the world. Compared to you, I'm nothing.'

'Oh, don't talk such rot.'

'You think I don't mean it? I was on that beach, Ed. I was in such a total funk I couldn't move. I would have sat there on those bloody pebbles for all eternity. I was sick with fear, helpless with fear. And then I saw you.'

Only now does Larry realise he is here for his own reasons too. There's something he must say to his friend: a tribute and a confession.

'Don't do this, Larry,' says Ed.

But Larry can't be stopped now.

'It was like seeing an angel,' he says. 'I saw this man come walking up the beach where the bullets were flying and the shells were landing, like he was taking a stroll in the park. Up and down that beach he went, saving life after life, and every time he turned back from the boats he threw his own life away. And as I watched him, the fear went out of me. You were my angel, Ed. Because of you I got up and I walked to the boat, and I lived. I'll never forget that to the day I die. Mine was one of the lives you saved that day. By Christ, you earned that VC. You earned a hundred VCs. Do you have any idea what that means?

God was with you that day, Ed. I know you don't believe in God, but I swear to you he was by your side on that beach. I'm supposed to be the believer, but God wasn't with me. God abandoned me the moment I stepped off the boat into that sea of dead men. But God was with you, Ed. Why? I'll tell you why. Because you gave yourself up to God and God knows his own. I didn't. I clung to my wretched little life. I thought only of myself. You walked with angels, and God saw you, and God loved you. And because God loved you and protected you, you have *lost the right to despair*. You have to love yourself, whether you want to or not. That's the choice you made on the beach at Dieppe. That's your life now. So wake up, and live it.'

He stands before his friend, pink in the cheeks, breathing fast, furiously pushing his hands through his curly hair. Ed looks back at him, his blue eyes bright.

'Quite a speech.'

'Have you heard a single word I've been saying?'

'I heard every word.'

'I'm right, aren't I? You know I'm right.'

Ed gets up and stretches, reaching his arms high up into the shadowed air. Then he starts to prowl, up as far as the altar and back.

'You say I've lost the right to despair,' he says. 'But you live in a different world to me. I'm somewhere else, far away, beyond despair.'

'Why should you live in a different world to me?'

'I don't know. Maybe we all live in different worlds. You have God in your world. You say God was with me on that beach. Why wasn't he with all the other poor bastards?'

'I told you. God knows his own.'

'You say I gave myself up to God. You have no idea. No idea at all.'

'Then tell me,' says Larry.

'Why?'

'Because I'm your friend.'

Ed doesn't speak for a few moments, pacing the aisle of the chapel like a ghost in the night.

'Well, then,' he says at last. 'I'll tell you how Lieutenant Ed Avenell of 40 Royal Marine Commando won his Victoria Cross.'

He comes to a stop in the aisle and stands facing the altar. His voice is quiet as a prayer.

'I'm in the landing craft. In the smoke. And there ahead of me is Red Beach. The Fusiliers have gone in just before us. I stand up in the boat and see bodies in the water, and bodies on the beach. I see shell craters and I hear the big guns booming out of the cliffs. And I know, beyond a shadow of a doubt, that it's all a colossal mistake. It's a stupidity. It's a joke. All these men are being sent to die for no reason. A bunch of fools in London have dreamed up this adventure without the first idea of the price to be paid. And here am I in the middle of it, and I'm going to die. The folly of it, the wickedness of it, just took my breath away. My CO saw it too, he's no fool. He gave the order to turn back, and then a bullet got him. A fine man went down, just like that, for no reason. That made me angry, I can tell you. Jesus, I was angry. I wasn't angry at the Germans, I was angry at Mountbatten, and the chiefs of staff. And then I got angry at all the world, this stupid wicked world that hurts people for no reason. So after that I went a little crazy. I thought, I've had enough, time to go. Time to say goodbye. So I waded ashore and the mortars were dropping in front of me and behind me and the bullets were humming over my head and nothing touched me. Not a blind thing. I wasn't being a hero, Larry. I was being a fool. I wanted to die. I was going up that beach shouting, Here I am! Come and get me! And nothing touched me. So I thought to myself, while I'm waiting for my number to come up, why don't I help some poor bastard lying on the beach? So I went from body to body and rolled them over until one moved, and I picked him up. Not his fault he was smashed up. He never asked for this. So I took him down to the boats, and went back up the beach, waiting for my turn. Here I am! Come and get me! You hear what I'm saying, Larry? It wasn't courage. It was rage. I didn't want to stick around to see the whole sick joke told to the end. I wanted to get out, all the way out, finished, dead. But nothing touched me. You say God was with me. God was nowhere on that beach. God was absent without leave. God knows the way the joke ends and he's gone off to get pissed and forget all about it. Why didn't any of those bullets get me? Luck, that's all. There's nothing unusual about that. Half the men who landed on that beach were killed or wounded. That leaves half the men who never got a scratch. I was one of those men, one among thousands. That's all. The only way I was maybe different to them is I wanted to die. So it wasn't an angel you saw, Larry. It was a dead man walking. I never saved your life. You did that yourself. And I'll tell you something for free. The guns didn't get me on Red Beach, but I died anyway. I don't belong in the world of the living any more.'

He puts his hands on Larry's shoulders and holds him with those bright eyes.

'Do you understand a single word of all that? Because I'm

never going to say it again, and I'm never going to say it to anyone else.'

'Yes,' says Larry. 'I understand.'

'Then in the camps – did you ever hear of something called the Commando Order?'

'Yes,' says Larry. 'A lot of our best men were shot in captivity.'

'Well, I wasn't shot.' Ed laughs as if it's all a joke. 'They just pretended to shoot me. But it's not as different as you might think. When a German reads out an order and then puts a gun to your head, you think that's pretty much it.'

'Is that what they did to you?'

'Three times. Just their little game.'

'Jesus!'

'You know how you survive? You stop caring. You want to die. Anything to escape the long slow horror of life.'

'But you didn't die, Ed. You came home.'

'Home, yes. I come home and they give me a medal, and I'm supposed to be proud. These arrogant halfwits who play their war games with other men's lives think *they* can honour *me*? I don't want them anywhere near me. Let them go crawling up the beach at Dieppe and try to wash away the blood.'

'It was a terrible, terrible mistake,' says Larry.

'The world is a terrible mistake,' says Ed. 'Life is a terrible mistake.'

'But you're in it.'

'I wish to God I wasn't.'

'And you have a wife and child.'

Ed turns away abruptly, as if stung.

'Why do you think I go on? Don't you think I'd have got out before this if it wasn't for Kitty?'

'Just going on isn't enough, Ed.'

'Don't tell me that!' He's shouting suddenly, the tension breaking through. 'I'm doing all I can! What more do you want of me?'

'You know as well as I do.'

'You want me to pretend? You want me to smile and say I'm happy and isn't the world a beautiful place?'

'No,' says Larry. 'Just let her near you.'

'You want me to drag her down to the hell I live in?'

'She loves you, Ed. She can take it.'

'That's what you said to me before.' He points an accusing finger at Larry. 'You and me in that hayfield. It's not your private darkness, you said. That's why I went to her, Larry. Because of you.'

'You went to her because you loved her.'

'Yes. Yes, God knows I do love her.'

'Then why do you hide yourself away from her?'

'Because I must.'

Now he's pacing again. Away down the mosaic-floored aisle and back.

'You ask me to let her near me,' he says. 'You have no idea how much I long to do just that. To me, Kitty is the only pure good thing in a bad world. And Pammy, too. Those two are all that's precious and holy to me. You can keep your Jesus and your Virgin Mary. The only gods I worship are my wife and child. I don't want the rottenness of the world to touch them. But here's the devil of it. I'm part of that rottenness. Of course I want to let her near me. Of course I want to touch her. I'm a man, aren't I?'

Larry begins to understand.

'Kitty says you sleep in your own room.'

'For her sake.'

'You leave her alone, letting her think you can't really love her, for her sake?'

'God damn it! What am I supposed to do? What do you want me to tell you, Larry? I'm not a good man, do you hear? Think of me as sick. Tell yourself poor old Ed's got leprosy or something. Kitty doesn't need my attentions, I can promise you that.'

'But she does.'

Ed shouts out of the darkness.

'You think she'd like it if I raped her?'

Larry is silent.

'Yes, she's my wife. A man can't rape his wife, can he? But what if he's a bad man? What if something happens inside him that makes him want to hurt and crush and destroy? Sex is a monster, Larry! I don't want Kitty to meet that monster.'

He swings away from him, all the way up to the altar.

'How long has it been like this?' says Larry.

'I don't know. Maybe it's what the war's done to me. Maybe I was always this way.'

'You could at least talk to Kitty about it.'

'How would she ever understand? You're a man, you know how it is.'

'Yes,' says Larry.

'Kitty's a girl. Girls have no idea at all. For them it's all a part of loving. How can I talk to her the way I talk to you?'

'I think you have to tell her something.'

'I know, I know.' The old despairing tone returns. 'Every day I think, I'll talk to her today. But the moment comes, and I let it pass. I don't want to lose her, you see. She's all I've got.'

'You think if she knew the truth about you she'd stop loving you?'

'Oh, yes! Without a doubt! Look at me!'

'I can't see a thing,' says Larry with a laugh.

'Just as well. Thank God for darkness. I wouldn't have been able to say any of this in daylight.'

Footsteps sound, approaching the chapel across the bridge.

'Time's up,' says Ed.

'Please talk to her,' says Larry.

'Oh, we'll muddle along somehow,' says Ed.

Louisa enters the chapel.

'Heavens, it's all dark! Are you in here, you bad-mannered men?'

'We're here,' says Ed.

'Everyone's on their way to bed. Are you proposing an all-night vigil?'

'No, we're coming too,' says Ed.

Kitty is in the library with George, helping him put away the cards. She looks up first at Ed as they enter, then at Larry.

'Had a good talk?' she says.

'Larry's been giving me a good wigging,' says Ed. 'I'm to stop being so bloody antisocial.'

Larry has changed into his pyjamas and washed and is ready for bed when there comes a tap on his bedroom door. It's Kitty, in her nightgown.

'Sorry,' she says. 'I just know I won't sleep.'

She comes in and closes the door behind her.

'Please tell me.'

She sits herself down in the single armchair and fixes him with her eyes.

'It's not easy to explain,' Larry says.

'But you'll try.'

He tells her about Ed's anger and how he wanted to die on the beach at Dieppe, and again in the camps. She nods as he speaks, doing her best to understand.

'What did he say about me?'

'He said he loves you more than anyone or anything.'

'So why does he keep away from me?'

Larry hesitates.

'It's still all very recent, Kitty. This nightmare he's been through.'

She shakes her head impatiently.

'Tell me, Larry.'

'The thing is, he almost worships you. He sees you as the only good there is in the world.'

'He worships me? He said that?'

'Yes.'

'Is that why . . . why he won't touch me?'

Larry doesn't answer.

'Don't protect me, please,' she says. 'I have to understand this or I shall go mad.'

Larry sits himself down on the side of the bed and fixes his gaze on the rug on the floor between them.

'I think,' he says slowly, 'Ed feels there's a part of him that's bad, and he doesn't want that to . . . to hurt you.'

'Because I'm good.'

'Yes.'

'You're talking about sex, aren't you?'

Larry keeps his eyes on the rug.

'Yes,' he says.

'Sorry, Larry, but I don't know any other way to get to the

truth of this. You mustn't be afraid of upsetting me. Up to now I've been thinking he no longer finds me . . . he's stopped being attracted to me. Almost anything's better than that.'

'No, it's not that.'

'He feels that sex is bad, and I'm good.'

'Something like that.'

'But it's so silly, isn't it?'

Larry looks up and finds her attempting a smile. But she's trembling at the same time.

'Yes, it is.'

'Do lots of men think sex is bad? Do you?'

'No, not exactly. But there is a kind of sex that can feel bad.'

'What kind? Tell me about it.'

'Oh, Kitty. This isn't easy.'

'Just shut your eyes and pretend you're talking to a man. What's this bad kind of sex?'

Larry shuts his eyes.

'It's a feeling you get,' he says, 'that's quite aggressive, and urgent, and entirely selfish. You want a girl, any girl. Not to be sweet to, or to love. Just for the one thing. You don't want to ask, you just want to take. It's a kind of conquering, I suppose. It's very primitive. You don't like it about yourself. But it's there in you.'

'Yes,' says Kitty. 'Yes, I can understand that.'

'Does it disgust you?'

'No. Not at all. Now tell me more. This bad feeling, is it there all the time?'

'Oh, no.'

'So what's there the rest of the time? Is there a good feeling?'

'Yes, there is. There's real love, where you want to be loved back. The opposite of taking what you want, and conquering, and selfishness.'

'And this real love – is that part of sex too?'

'Yes. I think so.' He hesitates, and then gives up the effort of pretence. 'Actually, I don't know. I don't have enough experience.'

'Does Ed have experience? Apart from me, I mean?'

'I don't know. Not that I know of. Probably.'

'It doesn't matter. I don't mind about that, really I don't. I just want so much to understand what it is men are thinking and feeling. It's hard for us girls, you know. We're told such stories all the time. Then you come up against the reality, and nothing makes any sense.'

'It's the same for us. We don't really know anything about girls. I don't, at least.'

'You can forget about worshipping us, for a start.'

She gets up out of her chair.

'Now I'm going to let you get some sleep.'

She reaches out for him, and gives his hand a little squeeze.

'Thank you, Larry. You're a good friend.'

# 16

One afternoon Larry's class is set to work on a life drawing of a female nude. The model is Nell. She takes off her clothes without hesitation, and places herself as the teacher instructs her, sitting on an upright chair, one leg tucked a little back. She asks him how she should hold her head, and he tells her to make herself comfortable. She chooses to bend her head a little forward, gazing over her knees at the bare boards of the floor.

The students set to work on a pencil sketch, following the measuring technique Coldstream has taught them. The teacher moves among them, checking to see they are marking what he calls the 'fixed points'.

'It's all about touch,' he says. 'Your own feelings about what you see are unimportant. See accurately, and the touch will come.'

Larry doesn't fully understand this, but he works away as best he can, and a passable sketch begins to emerge. At the same time he can't deny the presence of other feelings. Nell's naked body becomes more beautiful to him, and more desirable, as his pencil traces the curves of her thigh. He glances round the other students, almost all of them male, and sees them all intent on their work, and wonders if they're feeling the same.

When the class finishes Nell puts her clothes back on, and lingers in the Life Room as the students pack up their sketches. Larry, watching furtively, sees the effect she has on the others, how they stand up straighter when talking to her, and laugh more loudly. He hears her asking Leonard Fairlie if she can see his sketch, and hears Fairlie say, 'I'm useless at figures.'

'It's not figures,' Nell says. 'It's me.'

Fairlie laughs at that, his baby face going pink beneath his month-old beard. Larry wants Nell to come over and talk to him, but instead now she's talking to Tony Armitage, the wild boy who's become something of a friend. Larry can tell at once from Armitage's agitated arm movements that he's trying to impress Nell.

'What are you thinking when you're drawing?' she says.

'I don't think,' Armitage replies. 'Artists never think. I look.' He gives Nell a ferocious glare. 'I look.'

'And what do you see?'

'I see *you*,' says Armitage.

Then evidently aware that he can't improve on this, he sweeps himself out of the room, following the others.

Larry has lingered. Now he gets his reward.

'I think they're all shy,' Nell says to him.

'Well, they have been staring at you with no clothes on.'

'You wouldn't know it. No one's mentioned it.'

'What do you expect them to say?' says Larry.

'Oh, you know. Ooh, I can see your titties! Ooh, I can see your bum!'

Larry laughs. She slips one arm through his.

'Buy me a drink, Lawrence.'

The Hermit's Cave has survived the war unscathed, protected, say the locals, by the hermit himself, who gazes philosophically into the distance on the pub sign, wearing what seems to be a nightdress. Inside, beneath the smoke-grimed mustard-coloured ceilings, the students from the art college lunch on Scotch eggs and Murphy's stout and argue about art and politics and religion. Leonard Fairlie takes the orthodox Marxist line on Christianity.

'How else are the ruling classes to persuade the masses to be content with their pitiful share of the nation's wealth? Obviously you have to create a compensation mechanism for them. You have to tell them the less jam they have today, the more jam they'll have tomorrow.'

'So who are these people, Leonard? Who are these cynical liars who've fabricated this monstrous perversion for their own evil ends?'

Peter Prout is a big smiley young man who may or may not be homosexual.

'You want me to tell you who rules the country?' says Leonard.

'Somehow I don't think Churchill dreamed up Christianity,' says Peter. 'Or Attlee or Bevin, for that matter.'

'Beveridge, more like,' says Larry.

'Listen,' says Peter. 'I'm not saying any of it's *true*. I don't believe in Jesus being the son of God and all that. But it doesn't have to be a conspiracy. It's a folk myth. It's a kind of communal dream.'

Larry then says, almost apologetically, 'Actually I do believe Jesus was the son of God.'

This causes general amazement. Nell, sitting by Larry's side, grins to see the looks on their faces.

'You can't!' says Tony Armitage.

'And I believe in heaven and hell,' says Larry. 'And the Last Judgement. And I think I believe in the virgin birth. And I'm trying hard to believe in papal infallibility.'

'Oh, God!' says Leonard. 'You're a Catholic.'

'Born and bred,' says Larry.

'But Larry,' says Tony Armitage, 'you can't believe all that rubbish. You just can't.'

'I suppose it may be rubbish,' says Larry, 'some of it, anyway. But it's the rubbish I grew up with. And it does make a sort of sense, you know. You belong to a church because you believe the wisdom of an institution is greater than the wisdom of one man. We have rather overdone the cult of the individual, don't you think?'

'The cult of the individual!' Peter Prout mocks shock. 'Next you'll be doubting the romance of the lone artist!'

'But Larry!' exclaims Armitage. 'Virgin birth! Papal infallibility!'

'Well, to be honest,' says Larry, 'I don't really follow some of that. But then, why would I? I don't know everything. It's like falling in love. You don't go down a checklist of all the girl's opinions, making sure you agree with each one. You just love her, and you take what you get.'

'I can understand that,' says Nell.

'It's theatre,' says Peter Prout. 'The Catholic Church is all about theatre.'

'But where's the intellectual honesty?' says Leonard.

'Who needs intellectual honesty?' says Nell. 'Who needs intellectual anything? That's just another way for people to bully people. Larry grew up believing in a religion that really matters to him, and it's got power and beauty and so on to him, so why not let him get on with it?'

'But Nell,' says Armitage, 'we're not talking about art, or poetry. We're talking about so-called eternal truths.'

'It is art and poetry for me,' says Larry. 'It's just like that. Once you decide your brain is too small to know everything, you look at things differently. You say, all right, I might as well stick with my traditions until I run into a good reason not to. I'm not saying the Catholic Church has the only truth. It's just the faith I've grown up with. So for me, it's faith itself. It's the part of me that believes there's more than this life, and that goodness wins in the end, and that there's a purpose to existence. I expect if I'd been born in Cairo I'd get all that from being a Muslim, but I wasn't. I was taken to the Carmelite church in Kensington every Sunday, and I was sent to a school run by Benedictine monks, and so it's all just part of who I am.'

'You're allowed to grow up,' says Leonard. 'You're not obliged to stay a child for ever. You can break out on your own.'

'What did you grow up believing, Leonard?' says Nell.

'My parents have always been free-thinkers,' says Leonard. 'I've been allowed to grow up in my own way.'

'Do they believe in God?'

'Not at all.'

'So you've been raised by atheists,' says Nell, 'and you're an atheist. When do you break out on your own?'

The others laugh at that. Larry grins and holds out his hand. Nell shakes it.

Nell walks down Camberwell Grove with Larry later that afternoon, heading for the room Larry rents in McNeil Road.

'I love it that you're a Catholic,' she says. 'It's just so wacky and different. I've never known anyone who's a Catholic.'

'What are your family, then?'

'Oh, nothing, of course. You know, Anglican. They never talk about religion. I think it's supposed to be bad manners, like talking about sex.'

'God and sex. Big secrets. Not in front of the children.'

'What I like about you, Lawrence,' she goes on, 'is the way you're not afraid to be who you are. Actually I'm quite impressed that you know who you are at all. I've no idea who I am.'

'Well, I am older than you.'

'Yes, I like that too.'

When they get to the door of his digs she says, 'Are you going to ask me in?'

'Would you like to come in, Nell?'

'Yes, thank you, Lawrence. I would.'

His room has a bed, a table, a small high-backed armchair, and a washbasin. A gas fire has been crammed into the small fireplace. Larry lights the gas. Nell sits on the bed, crossing her legs.

'It's funny to think,' Nell says, 'that I was sitting naked in front of you and you were staring at me, and there were all the others there too, and now we're alone and I'm all dressed, and you can't even look at me.'

'Yes, it is funny,' says Larry.

'Is it because you'd rather I wasn't here?'

'No. No, not at all.'

'Do you think it's wrong for me to be a life model?'

'Of course I don't.'

'But you must think it's a bit strange. I mean, most people are shy about taking their clothes off.'

'Well, I'm glad you're not.'

'I am shy, really. But I make myself do it. I'm determined to get away.'

He understands what she means. This is her equivalent of his impulse to paint.

'You know we agreed we should always tell each other what we want?' says Nell.

'Yes.'

'I want to kiss you.'

'Oh,' says Larry, taken by surprise.

'Do you want to kiss me?'

'Yes.'

'Then come over here. That way we'll warm up quicker, too.'

Larry goes to sit beside her on the bed. She reaches up to cup one hand round his head.

'Do you think it's wrong for me to be so forward?'

'No,' he says.

He leans close and they kiss. Then she lies down full length on the bed and he lies down with her and they kiss holding each other in their arms. He feels her slight body warm against his, and her lips soft and secret on his, and he's overwhelmed by the sweet rush of desire.

She feels him growing hard against her.

'What's this?' she says.

'Sorry,' he says. 'Nothing I can do about it.'

'Of course there is,' she says.

She slips her hand down between them and strokes the ridge in his trousers.

'Does the Catholic Church say it's wrong for me to do this?' she says.

'No,' he whispers.

She feels for the buckle of his belt and undoes it. Then she unbuttons his flies. He lies still, grateful and amazed. She pushes her hands inside his pants and touches his cock, gently stroking it.

'How about this?' she says. 'Is this a sin?'

'No,' he whispers.

'Do you think maybe we should draw the curtains?'

'Yes,' he says.

He gets up off the bed and his trousers fall down. He stoops and pulls them up, but Nell says, 'Take them off, silly.' He goes to the window and pulls the thin curtains closed. Now the room is filled with a green shade, in the midst of which the gas fire glows orange.

Nell is sitting up on his bed pulling her dress over her head. Larry stands there in shirt and underpants and socks, shaking with confused excitement. Beneath the dress she wears a brassiere and knickers. She tosses the dress to the floor and unhooks the brassiere.

'It's not as if you haven't seen it all before,' she says.

Larry takes off his shirt and socks, but not his pants. His erection pushes out all too visibly. Nell poses for him on the bed, as she did in the life class.

'Remember?'

'Yes,' he says. 'Yes.'

'Come here, then.'

He goes into her arms, and holds her naked body close.

'My God, Nell,' he whispers. 'My God, you're lovely.'

'Have we started doing anything wrong yet?'

'No, not yet. But we're very close.'

'I want to do something wrong with you, Lawrence. I want you to want to do it with me.'

'I do. I do.'

Her hand is back feeling his cock, stroking it, making the desire in him go crazy. Then she takes his hand and puts it between her legs.

'Feel me there, Lawrence. I want you there.'

He feels the tickly mound of pubic hair, and the yielding softness below. She moves her hips, pushing her crotch against his hand.

'All yours,' she says.

'Oh, God, Nell,' he says, feeling his blood race. The wonder of her touch wipes his mind clean of all other thoughts. He knows only that he is entirely possessed by his desire, and that she is wonderfully, generously, inexplicably granting it.

'God, you're beautiful,' he says.

She rubs her body against his, exciting him to near-frenzy.

'Are we going to do it, Lawrence?' she says. 'Are we?'

'I'm not prepared,' he says. 'I haven't got— '

'Don't worry about that,' she says. 'I've dealt with that.'

She has his cock in her hand now, and she's rubbing the tip against her slit. Larry feels tremors of dangerous delight run down his cock.

'So are we going to do it, Lawrence?'

'Yes,' he whispers. 'Yes.'

'Doesn't the Catholic Church say it's wrong?'

'Yes,' he says.

'Fucking me is wrong.'

'Yes.'

'But you want to fuck me even so, Lawrence.'

'Yes,' he groans, feeling the tip of his cock pushing into her a little way.

'If you fuck me, will God punish you, Lawrence?'

'I don't care,' he says.

'God won't punish you,' she says, 'if you love me.'

'I love you, Nell. I love you. I love you.'

He feels the intensity of his love for her with each repetition, along with the tingling in his cock, and the profound shock of joy with which he has heard each utterance by her of the word *fuck*. She seems to know how much this electrifies him. She moves her hips, pushing him deeper into her all the time, and as she does so she whispers, 'Fuck me now, Lawrence. Fuck me now.'

His cock is in her now, gripped by sweet warmth, and he knows he can't restrain himself any longer. His desire is in total control of his being, and it seeks its explosive release.

'I can't,' he says, 'I can't— '

'Do it, Lawrence,' she says. 'Do it. Do it.'

He thrusts deep into her, and pulls back, and thrusts again, and the moment comes, and he half-faints with the intense pleasure of it. He feels the pulsing release spread from his cock to every part of his body.

She strokes his back with warm hands.

'There,' she says. 'There.'

'Oh, Nell.'

'Was that nice?'

'Oh, God! It was heaven!'

'I'm glad,' she says. 'I wanted it to be nice for you.'

He lies over her, still helpless, his entire being disintegrated, his muscles powerless to move. Then his frantic heart begins to regain its usual rhythm, and his senses return. He kisses her eagerly, gratefully, adoringly.

'You're wonderful, you're amazing, you're perfect.'

'Darling Lawrence.'

'I've never known anything like that before.'

'That's because you're a good Catholic boy.'

'Not any more.'

'Yes, you are. It doesn't change anything. And anyway, all you have to do is go to confession.'

'But I want to do it again,' says Larry.

'Of course we'll do it again,' says Nell. 'This is only the beginning.'

She puts on his dressing gown and pads upstairs to the shared bathroom to clean herself up. Larry dresses slowly in the green light. Then she's back and he watches her lithe naked body as she too puts her clothes on.

'You've had boyfriends before, haven't you?' he says.

'Would you mind if I had?'

'No, not at all. It makes me feel proud.'

He feels no jealousy at all of her past. Only this gigantic gratitude that she grants him the same supreme privilege.

'I had a boyfriend when I was sixteen,' she says. 'Not a boy, a man. He taught me things. He liked me to say the dirty words. He was kind.'

'What happened to him?'

'The war,' says Nell. 'He died.'

Larry feels both shocked and elated. She's so young, it's cruel that she should have had to experience love and loss. But now she belongs entirely to him.

'I'm sorry,' he says.

'I was sorry then,' she says. 'But now there's you.'

'I don't understand,' says Larry. 'Why me? You're so beautiful you could have any man you wanted.'

'I'm not really beautiful,' she says. 'But it's true, if I want a man, I can have him. Men aren't that hard to get. But a good man – that's another matter. I think you may be a good man, Lawrence.'

'Because I'm a Catholic?'

'Because you're kind. Most people are mean. You're not mean.'

'You are beautiful, Nell.'

'You say that because I let you fuck me.'

'I love it the way you say that word.'

'That word.' She grins at him mischievously. 'What word would that be, Lawrence?'

'Fuck,' he says, blushing.

# 17

Harry Avenell's club is the Travellers in Pall Mall. Like so much in his life this is a second-best, but he has neither the connections nor the income to put up for White's. For all that, the Travellers, in its handsome Barry building, provides the civilised surroundings that he appreciates. By profession a director of Marston's Brewery, Burton-upon-Trent, by taste he is a country gentleman, the master of a small estate that overlooks the river Dove. The Queen Anne house is furnished with what might be called modest excellence. Every item, from the umbrella stand in the hall to the cut-glass decanter on the dining-room sideboard, is the best of its kind. The high standards of Hatton House have always exceeded the actual income of the family, but only by so much as to make living correctly demand a life of austerity that comes naturally to both Harry and his wife. Harry's philosophy is declared by his tailoring. His suits are of the best cloth, made by Gieves & Hawkes of Savile Row, and are expected to last his lifetime. Gillian Avenell, by contrast, though always immaculately dressed, has no real care for her appearance at all. Where Harry is anxious about money, she is frugal, happier on her knees in prayer than before a dressing-table mirror. She is the devout Roman Catholic of the family. Her husband has no religion. He calls himself a stoic, meaning he is an admirer of Marcus Aurelius, and values self-mastery above all.

Harry Avenell has come to town to make some arrangements for his son. Ed has distinguished himself on the field of battle, he has a wife and child, but he has no employment and no income. By the age of twenty-eight a man needs to have fixed on a career, but Ed shows no signs of even so much as looking about him. Harry has therefore looked about him on his son's behalf. A business acquaintance, Jock Caulder, turns out to have a son also in need of a parental push into the world of work. Caulder is a wealthy man, and proposes to set his boy up with a business of his own, importing French wine. The boy is willing enough, but being only just twenty years old, he's understandably nervous at the prospect of being solely responsible for the enterprise. A partner is required. Harry Avenell has proposed his son, who is older, can be said to be battle-tested, and is looking for a career. It's true he knows nothing about wine, but that can be learned. And his Victoria Cross, without being flaunted in any vulgar way, will surely add prestige to the infant business.

Jock Caulder is minded to agree. His son Hugo declares himself willing to give it a go. It remains only to sound out the war hero himself.

Harry is ensconced on a blue sofa at the far end of the Outer Morning Room of his club, a pot of Earl Grey tea before him, when Ed comes in and greets him with a raised hand. Harry has only seen his son once since his return, when he came up to Hatton and stayed for a single night. He feels shy in his son's company.

He waves him to the sofa opposite and offers him tea.

'How's Kitty? How's our granddaughter?'

'Flourishing,' says Ed. 'Pamela turns out to be tremendously strong-minded.'

'You're still living in the big house?'

'For now, yes. How's Mummy?'

'Very well. Do drop her a line sometime. Or better still, pay us a visit. You know she'd never dream of asking anything for herself, but it would mean a lot to her.'

'Yes, of course,' says Ed, his gaze drifting to the trees in the Mall outside. 'So tell me the news of Hatton.'

'Life goes on in its quiet way,' says Harry. 'But now, here's what I want to talk to you about, Ed. Something's come up that might suit you.'

He lays out the proposal. Ed listens, his handsome face revealing nothing. When he's done, his father expects some questions about the partnership terms and the anticipated income. Instead Ed gives a slight shrug and looks away again, out of the window.

'I suppose I have to do something.'

'It's quite a chance, Ed,' his father says. 'You'd be going in as a full partner without having to invest a penny.'

'Yes, I suppose I would.'

'Obviously everything would depend on how you and Hugo hit it off.'

'I'm sure he's a decent enough chap.'

'Well, yes, he is. He went to Harrow. Not the university type, his father tells me. Clever in his way, but a bit inclined to rest on his oars.'

'Not like me, then.'

He meets his father's eyes and smiles, and for a brief second they share the secret of how far life falls short of dreams.

'I've no doubts about you, Ed. Once you make up your mind to do something, I know you'll do it with all your heart.'

'French wine,' says Ed. 'Well, after all, why not?'

Kitty waits until Pamela is well settled for her afternoon nap and then turns to Louisa for advice. She doesn't expect Louisa to know anything more than herself, but her friend has a knack of seeing the obvious that Kitty has learned to value. She passes on some of what Larry has told her, ending up with what has become for her the simplest expression of her dilemma.

'Ed thinks I'm good, and sex is bad.'

'Bloody Catholics,' says Louisa.

'No, Ed isn't a Catholic any more,' says Kitty. 'He lost all of that ages ago.'

'Like hell,' says Louisa. 'Honestly! What a heap of nonsense! You're his wife! What's bad about it?'

'I think it's just something men feel.'

'It's that damn Virgin Mary of theirs,' says Louisa. 'All the good women have to be virgins, which means they can only do it with whores.'

'From what Larry said to me,' Kitty says, 'it's such a strong thing for them that it almost frightens them.'

'Can't be that strong, darling.'

'That's what I don't understand. If it's so strong, what's he doing about it?'

'Don't ask.'

'Oh,' says Kitty, going red. 'Do you think so?'

'I'll tell you something I've never told anyone,' says Louisa. 'About five years ago I found out my father has affairs with other women. He visits those houses men go to. A friend told me, Oh yes, your father's famous for it. I went to my mother to tell me it wasn't true, but she said, Yes, it's all true. So then I wanted to know why and she sat me down and she said to me, Darling, do you know the facts of life? I said yes, I thought so. She said, You know how men have seed in them, that makes babies? I said, Yes. She said, Well, there's a lot of it, and it has to come out at least once a day, and that's not always convenient for me, so he goes elsewhere.'

'Louisa!'

'Yes, I know. Quite an eye-opener, I can tell you.'

'Once a day!'

'At least. Some men have to do it three times a day.'

'I had no idea,' says Kitty faintly.

'Once you know, it makes sense of a lot of things.'

'Doesn't your mother mind?'

'Well, yes, I think so. But the funny thing is, they seem to get on really well.'

Kitty ponders in silence.

'So what am I to do about Ed?' she says at last. 'I can't make him come to me if he doesn't want to.'

'Why don't you go to him?'

'I wouldn't know what to say.'

'Don't say anything,' says Louisa. 'Just do it.'

'I couldn't! Suppose he got angry? Suppose it made him think I was . . . I was . . .'

'What? You're his wife, Kitty.'

'Yes, but if he doesn't want me . . .'

'Of course he wants you! And anyway, how's he going to stop himself? Men can't. Crank the starter handle and they're off.'

Kitty starts to laugh, and that sets Louisa off laughing.

'What about George?'

'Well, no. Obviously not George.'

They both laugh until they have tears in their eyes.

'Oh, Lord, Louisa!' says Kitty. 'What a mess it all is.'

'Would you mind me giving you a little tip?' says Louisa.

'Tell me anything,' says Kitty. 'I'm done with blushing.'

'How long has it been?'

Kitty hangs her head and answers in a low voice.

'Not since he came home. Not since he went away. Three years.'

'So if you're going to go to him, it might be a good idea to go prepared.'

'Prepared?'

Louisa leaves the West Parlour where they've gone for their tête-à-tête and runs upstairs. She returns shortly with a small embroidered drawstring bag, which she gives to Kitty. Inside is a tin of Vaseline.

Ed comes back from town full of brittle nervous energy. When Pamela comes running to greet him he sweeps her up in his arms and tosses her into the air, again and again, until she's screaming with excitement.

'Your daddy's going to get a job!' he says to her. 'Your daddy's going to make money so you can have pretty frocks!'

'What is this, Ed?' says Kitty, laughing, watching the flying child anxiously.

'My father, my esteemed father,' says Ed, 'having sacrificed his life to a job in which he has no interest whatsoever, in order to earn enough money to keep us all in the style he believes to be our birthright, has done me the great kindness of finding me a sacrificial job all of my own.'

'What are you talking about? What job?'

'I'm to become a partner in a business that imports wine at low prices from France, and sells at high prices in England. Apparently a child of three could do it. Would you like to be a wine importer, Pammy? You could be a partner too.'

'I can do it!' squeals the little girl, wriggling in his arms.

'Is this serious, Ed?' says Kitty.

'I have to do something, darling. Would you mind very much?'

'Not if it's what you want to do.'

'Oh, that's asking too much! I don't *want* to do it. But I dare say I'll get into the way of it. I like wine, and I like France. It's just the buying and selling that fails to excite me.'

Over dinner more details of the plan emerge. Ed explains about his father's rich friend, and the rich friend's son.

'So you see, I'm to be a species of babysitter. If he has tantrums I'm to give him my VC to play with.'

'Well, it all sounds grand to me,' says George. 'You can help me restock my white burgundy.'

'You haven't even met this boy yet,' says Kitty.

'My father's met his father. That's how this sort of thing's done, you know. Like an arranged marriage.'

'Ed, promise me,' says Kitty, 'you won't do this unless it really feels right. I don't want you sacrificing yourself for us.'

He reaches across the table and takes her hand.

'Darling Kitty,' he says, smiling. 'You mustn't pay any attention to all the rot I talk. There isn't any sacrifice. All I care about in the world is you and Pammy.'

That night Kitty goes to bed as usual, but she lies awake until she's sure that all the rest of the house is asleep. Then she leaves her bedroom and passes softly down the passage to the room where Ed is sleeping. She enters without knocking.

The window curtains are wide open, and the light of a full moon fills the room. The bed is empty. Ed is lying asleep on the floor beside the bed, covered by a sheet and a blanket. He lies on his side, one arm tucked beneath him, the other arm thrown out. He looks peaceful, and beautiful.

Kitty lies down on the floor beside him, making as little sound as possible, and he doesn't wake. Slowly she moves her body up against his, and still he doesn't wake. Then he stirs in his sleep, and straightens out his legs, and rolls onto his back.

Very gently, she draws the sheet and the blanket down, until they're no longer covering him. He lies in the moonlight, in his pyjamas, the pyjama top buttoned up, the trouser cord tied in a bow.

Kitty undoes the buttons one by one, and she loosens the bow and draws apart the cords. She folds back the flaps of his pyjama trousers, and lays her warm hand between his thighs. Very slowly, back and forth, she strokes his cock, and feels it start to grow. She looks up at his face, but his eyes are closed, and his breathing is steady. She goes on stroking until the cock has grown big and hard. She can feel her own heart beating, and wonders that he can sleep on.

'What?'

He starts out of sleep, raising his arms to defend himself.

'What are you doing?'

'Hush,' she says. 'Hush.'

She goes on stroking him, moving her hand faster now.

'No, Kitty!' he says.

'It's all right,' she says. 'Don't talk.'

She leans close and kisses him, her hand moving all the time up and down his cock. His arms reach round her, pull her close. She hears him groan.

Then his hands are tugging at her nightdress, pulling it up, and she moves to free it, wanting to be naked for him. His whole body begins to turn now, his hips thrust upwards, his head thrown back, his eyes closed. His hands pull her onto him. She lets him do as he wants, moving her hand away so that he can press her body to his.

Now she feels his hard cock against her belly, and his chest against her breasts, and he's groaning loudly as if in pain. Then with a rough and powerful movement he rolls her over and now he's on top of her and he's forcing her legs apart and his cock is pushing between her thighs. She lifts her hips, wanting it to be easy for him, and feels his cock drive into her.

'You want it? You want it?'

His voice harsh and distant.

'Yes,' she says. 'I want it.'

He starts to ram into her, making wordless sounds with each thrust.

'I want it,' she whispers. 'I want it!'

Then all at once she realises she does want it. Her body awakens, she wraps herself round him, pulling him deep into her, hungry for sensation, rubbing herself against him, rocking with his angry thrusts.

'Ah!' he cries. 'Ah! Ah!'

He hammers at her, shouts at her, a creature possessed. Then there comes a gasping moan, and she feels his convulsion and feels the pumping inside her. Now he's sinking down onto her, moving still, but slowly now. She feels his body come to rest, heavy on hers, and she lies still, holding him in her arms. She kisses the sweat on his brow.

For a long moment he doesn't move. Then she realises he's weeping.

'No, darling. No.'

She kisses the tears on his cheeks.

'Sorry,' he says. 'Sorry. Sorry.'

'No, darling,' she says, kissing him. 'I wanted you. I came to you because I wanted you.'

'Not like that.'

'Yes,' she says. 'Like that.'

They lie in each other's arms until they become cold. Then she moves him off her, and he climbs shakily to his feet.

'Lie down now, darling.'

He lies on the bed and she covers him with the bedclothes. He holds her hand, doesn't want her to go.

'Kitty, I'm sorry. I didn't want to be like that with you.'

'I'm yours,' she says. 'You can be anything you want with me.'

'I didn't know. I thought . . . I don't know what I thought.'

'You thought I was too good for you.'

'You are good.'

'I'm yours,' she says again.

'Is it going to be all right?' he says.

'Yes, my darling,' she says. 'It's going to be all right.'

⋆

The next day Ed moves back into Kitty's room. Pamela expresses her disapproval.

'That's not your room. That's Mummy's room.'

'I want to be with Mummy,' he says.

'So do I want to be with Mummy,' says Pamela. 'But we have to sleep in our own rooms.'

Kitty points out that George and Louisa share a bedroom. Pamela becomes puzzled.

'Who can I share with?' she says.

'When you're grown up, you can share with your husband.'

'My husband!'

This enchanting idea distracts her entirely.

'What's his name?'

'Augustus,' says Ed.

'Augustus? Yech!'

That night Kitty lies in Ed's arms, and it's both strange and familiar at the same time. She thinks she won't sleep but she does sleep, and when she wakes in the morning he's still there.

She gives him a kiss and he too wakes.

'Good morning,' she says.

# 18

Larry Cornford kneels beside his father in the Carmelite church on Kensington Church Street, murmuring the familiar Latin words. All round him he hears the soft voices of the others in the packed pews. Before him the priest stands, his back to them, green-robed at the altar.

'*Beato Michaeli Archangelo, beato Joanni Baptistae, Sanctis Apostolis Petro et Paulo, omnibus Sanctis et tibi, Pater . . .*'

The names are friends Larry has known all his life. At the appropriate moment in the prayer his hand forms a fist and taps his breast in the sign of contrition.

'*Mea culpa, mea culpa, mea maxima culpa.*'

He feels no sense of blame, only deep and comforting familiarity. The shape of the Mass never varies, its mystery has embraced him since childhood. The buildings may change, priests may come and go, but the ritual unfolds always in the same way. When the time comes for the consecration – '*Haec dona, haec munera, haec sancta sacrificia illibata*' – and the priest bends in holy secrecy over the altar, making the sign of the cross over the bread and wine – '*Benedixit, fregit, deditque discip-*

*ulis suis dicens, Accipite et manducate ex hoc omnes, hoc est enim corpus meum*' – and kneels, and raises the host, and the altar boy tinkles the bell – at this time the wonder always returns, and he feels himself to be in the presence of the supernatural. The child who was taught to see in the Mass a true ever-repeated miracle, the real presence, the coming of God among them – that same child lives still in Larry today, as the priest elevates the host, and the smell of incense rolls over the pews.

Later he takes his place following his father in the line of communicants, and receives the papery biscuit on his tongue. He feels the living God melt in his mouth. He knows that by the letter of the law he has committed mortal sin and should not take communion, but his God and his Church are merciful. Larry is a very modern Catholic, taught by enlightened monks that God loves the generous heart and the truthful mind more than a petty conformity to rules. He returns to his place in the pews, and kneeling with his head in his hands he prays that he may learn to serve God with his chosen work.

After Mass he walks home with his father to the tall house on Camden Grove and shares a late breakfast with him. His father talks to him about the company and its present difficulties. He is to make a trip to Jamaica very shortly, to attend to problems on the ground.

'I'm afraid we're facing a serious supply shortage,' he says. 'Partly it's the hurricane season. But we also have a bad outbreak of leaf-spot disease.'

'I thought the *Tilapa* came into Avonmouth with a full cargo.'

'So she did, God bless her.' His father sips at his coffee and sighs. 'But there's not much more where that came from. We're looking seriously at the Cameroons. Also I think it's time now to come to a new arrangement with the Ministry.'

'Are you still managing the Ministry depots?'

'One hundred and twenty, all told. It's far too much, of course. But the truth is the Ministry is still operating on a wartime footing.'

'Will you see Joe Kiefer when you're in Kingston?'

'Joe's retired now. I'm glad you remember him, Larry. I shall tell him so.'

William Cornford gazes wistfully across the breakfast table at his son.

'You know we've got the house in Normandy habitable now,' he says. 'Why not join me there this summer? It should be a good place for your painting.'

'I'd like that,' says Larry.

'How's it coming along?' He wipes his mouth with his napkin. 'The painting and so forth.'

'I can't exactly say how I'm getting on,' says Larry, 'but I'm hard at work. I'm afraid I've no accounts to show you. No figures to prove my progress.'

'Of course not. But are you happy?'

'Yes, Dad. I'm very happy.'

His father smiles.

'Well, then. That's the point, isn't it?'

Larry tells his father he's happy because his father is subsidising him and he wishes to give some return on his investment. The truth is more complex. He is finding that the work he has chosen – he calls it 'work' following his teacher's example, shy of grander terms – causes him almost constant unease. Somehow, however steadily he applies himself, he always ends up dissatisfied with the end result. The process itself never fails to absorb him, even to obsess him. But he remains unconvinced of his talent.

He has chosen in recent weeks to limit himself to landscapes. Noticing that artists he admires have a way of repeating motifs in their work, or of working in defined geographical areas, he has decided to choose landscapes that feature a church. This is mostly a formal preference: the spire of the church, breaking the skyline like a knife, delivers a visual pivot for his composition. But it's also an emotional choice. The church acts as a lightning conductor, a conduit for the supernatural into his scene. This is not something he talks about with his fellow students. More and more of them are coming under the influence of Victor Pasmore, drawn towards pictorial geometry, if not full-blown abstract painting. Among the hold-outs is Tony Armitage, the farouche boy who is showing an extraordinary talent for portraiture.

'Geometry!' exclaims Armitage with disgust. 'It's pure funk. They can't face the world. They're running away from life.'

Larry is inclined to agree. The Pasmore school strikes him as a form of Puritanism.

'They're visual Calvinists,' he says. 'All this reduction to pure form.'

Nevertheless his own work is highly formal. He is painting a view of St Giles's church seen from an upper window of the college. The grey and white tower is built in three diminishing stages, two square, the last a hexagonal spire. On two sides of the tower project steep-pitched grey-tiled roofs. The church is the work of Gilbert Scott and has a window reputedly designed by Ruskin, but to Larry it has become a series of lines to be projected outward and upward as he forms his composition. He is painting both the actual church, and a diagram of sacred space. It's not something he fully understands, but as he works he knows very quickly which lines have significance and which are trivial. As he begins to overlay the lines with tones of grey and brown and white, he struggles to let the various colours convey the light he wants in the picture, the instinct he has that it's not stone walls he's painting so much as the space they enclose.

There are moments as he works when he feels so near to capturing this simple truth that all he needs to do is let his brush go free. The thing is there before him. Rather than painting it into existence he is uncovering it, his brush the instrument of exposure. At such times his excitement is so intense that he loses all awareness of time and place, and works on long into the evening.

'You know something,' says Armitage, pausing to look. 'That's not as bad as your usual stuff.'

Larry stands back to see for himself.

'No,' he says. 'It's not there yet.'

'Of course it's not *there*!' exclaims Armitage. 'It's never *there*! But it's not bad. And take it from me, not bad is as good as it gets.'

Larry has grown to like Tony Armitage very much, for all his startling outbursts and lack of personal hygiene. He has painted a head and shoulders of Nell that is to Larry's mind quite extraordinary. Somehow he has managed to capture both her directness and her evasiveness. Nell of course hates the portrait.

The more Larry now looks at his St Giles, the less he likes it. But at this point Bill Coldstream appears.

'Just the men I wanted to see,' he says.

He stands still for a moment, examining Larry's picture.

'Yes,' he says. 'Good. Do you know the Leicester Galleries?'

'Of course,' says Larry. 'I saw the John Piper show there.'

'They're putting together a summer show. Artists of Promise and so on. Phillips has asked me to suggest some of our people. I'd like to put you and Armitage up for it.'

Larry is speechless. Armitage takes it in his stride.

'How long have we got?'

'They want to open in early July,' says Coldstream. 'So the selection will have to be done by the end of April, I should think.'

With this he departs.

'That's one in the eye for Fairlie,' says Armitage.

'I had no idea,' says Larry.

He means he had no idea their teacher rated him so highly.

'I told you you were good.'

'No, you didn't. You said I wasn't bad.'

'What you need, Larry,' says Armitage, 'is faith in yourself.'

'Any idea where I'm to get it?'

'The great thing you have to keep in mind,' says Armitage, 'is that everyone else is clueless. They're all stumbling about in the dark. They've no idea what's good and what isn't. They're waiting to be told. So all you have to do is tell them, loudly and often.'

Larry sighs.

'Not my style, I'm afraid.'

Larry tells Nell the news that evening. She throws her arms round him and kisses him.

'I knew it! You're going to be famous!'

Nell no longer works as a life model at the school. She's got herself a job as receptionist to an art dealer in Cork Street. Julius Weingard, according to Nell, is both queer and crooked, but by her account so is everyone else. She tells Larry hair-raising stories of how Weingard cheats his clients. Everyone knows, she says, it's just how the art world works. No one believes in any artist's actual worth, only in reputation and the degree to which that can be converted into sales.

'I shall make Julius come to your show,' Nell says. 'Maybe he'll decide to take you on. He'll tell you to use brighter colours, darling. Everyone is tired of khaki.'

Nell continues to fascinate Larry, but their relationship is not simple. They sleep together but they don't live together. Nell has her own digs, which Larry has never entered. She is often away, carrying out assignments for Weingard, or visiting friends about whom she tells him nothing. This other life, which she keeps from him with a teasing secrecy, should trouble him, and occasionally does. But the truth is that much of the time it suits him.

Larry's feelings for Nell are forever catching him by surprise. The volatility of their relationship both disturbs and excites him. When she's away he can build up a longing for her that almost paralyses him. But when she's been with him for a few days, he begins to withdraw into himself, and want to be alone.

'You're getting so middle-aged, Lawrence,' she tells him. 'You should let yourself go more.'

He knows she's right, and he loves her for being a true Bohemian, a free spirit, a wild creature. But then there are the moments when he catches a glimpse of the other side of this freedom, and sees in her a lost child. Her youth and her powerful attractiveness disguise this inner core of fear, but every now and again it breaks through. Once, after making love, she began to cry.

'Nell! What is it?'

'Doesn't matter. You don't want to know.'

'Yes, I do. Tell me.'

'You'll say I'm just being silly. I am being silly.'

'No, tell me.'

'Sometimes I think I'll never be married and have children.'

'Of course you will. We'll be married tomorrow if you like. We'll have hundreds of children.'

'Oh, Lawrence, you are sweet. Maybe one day. I'm still only twenty.'

Then just as he's beginning to think they should get a flat together somewhere, she'll disappear for days on end. On her return she gives him no real answers to his questions about where she's been. She holds fiercely to her right to live her own life in her own way.

'Don't try to tie me down, Lawrence. That's what my father did. It drives me crazy.'

And yet she can erupt with sudden explosions of jealousy. Once after a party where he talked with another girl, she turns on him in fury.

'Don't ever do that to me again! I don't care what you do and who you do it with, but don't do it while I'm in the same room.'

'What have I done?'

'And don't gape at me like you don't know exactly what I'm talking about. I'm not a complete idiot.'

'Nell, this is all some fantasy of yours.'

'I'm not asking for fidelity. I'm asking you to show me some respect in public.'

'All I was doing was talking to her. Am I not to talk to other girls?'

'Fine,' she says. 'Have it your own way. Call it what you like.'

'For God's sake, Nell. It's not as if you don't talk to other men. Do I ever ask you not to talk to other men?'

'If you don't want me to go out with other men, Lawrence, all you have to do is say so.'

'I don't want to lock you up. You know I don't.'

'So what do you want, Lawrence?'

'I want us to trust each other.'

He tells himself her behaviour has no consistency, but at a deeper unacknowledged level he knows well enough what she's asking of him. She wants unconditional love. She wants to be told that he will be her lover and her protector and her friend for ever, however badly she behaves. There are times when his own need is strong in him and he wants to make all the promises in the world; but an instinctive caution in him prevents him from saying the words. So long as she's wild and free and desired by other men she's all that he wants. But the closer they come to each other the more clearly he sees her fragility and neediness, and in self-protection he pulls back once more.

He tries to understand what's happening to him, and why he swings so wildly between extremes. Is it just sex? Is it as simple as that? She takes it for granted that he wants and needs sex, and makes herself readily available to him, and for this alone he adores her. But it's not just sex. After a few days without her what haunts him is not just her naked body and the gratifications it brings, but her teasing laughter, her unpredictable turns of phrase, the vitality with which she floods his life. It's Nell who takes him swimming at night in Hampstead pond, or who goes out on an impulse to get crumpets to toast on the gas fire. It's Nell who knows the all-night cab-drivers' hut by Albert Bridge where a cup of tea can be had in the small hours. How can he not love her for the adventure she makes of his life? It seems to him then that this must be the fundamental shape of love, this cycle of craving and satiety and withdrawal.

Unless somewhere there's another kind of love, where you and your lover want never to be parted.

At such times he thinks of Kitty. He allows these thoughts with shame, knowing they're foolish. After all, what does he really know of Kitty? He's spent a few hours in her company, nothing more. It would be ridiculous to claim to be in love with her. Worse than ridiculous, it would condemn him to a life of loneliness. She's married to a man she loves, who is also his own best friend. Why then does it persist, this secret conviction? Sometimes, when he's alone, he feels a kind of terror at the thought of Kitty. What if it's given to every man to fall in love truly only once, and he has fallen for a girl he can never have?

'You know your trouble, Lawrence?' Nell tells him. 'You've got this thing about being good, but really you want to be bad.'

What does it mean, to be bad? It means to pursue your own desires at the expense of other people's. It means to live according to your own will, not the will of God. It means the pursuit of selfishness.

If I were to be bad, what would I do? I would paint, and I would love Kitty. That's all I want in life. And what value is that to others?

At such times he prays the prayer of Père de Caussade.

'Lord have pity on me. With you all things are possible.'

*

On the day of the private view Larry stands silent, smoking ceaselessly, white-faced, in the back of the room in which his three paintings hang. All three now seem to him to be lifeless and without merit. The guests move through the rooms exclaiming over the varied works, never pausing long over his paintings. No red spots appear beneath them to indicate a sale. Bill Coldstream is here, talking with his old Euston Road crowd. Leonard Fairlie is here, and while not being directly rude about Larry's work he makes it all too clear that he is unimpressed with the show.

'Of course it's a commercial show,' he says. 'One shouldn't be surprised. It's all about opening wallets. These days the kind of people who can afford to buy want to be reassured that the old world is with them still, in all its bourgeois glory. One has to expect to have one's mouth stuffed with bonbons.'

Tony Armitage is present, being one of the 'artists of promise'. He is as nervous as Larry, but shows it in a different way.

'Don't you hate the shits who come to these private views?' he growls. 'They wouldn't know real art if it was stuck up their bums with a poker.'

Despite this, Armitage's striking portraits are among the first to achieve the coveted red spot. Larry moves away, unable to bear the sight of his own unloved works. He sees Nell come in with her employer Julius Weingard, and another man who is small and prosperous and in his forties, if not older. He has his arm looped through Nell's in a proprietorial way, and is smiling at her as they go by. Two well-dressed middle-aged women pass near him, one saying to the other, 'Why are English artists so dreary compared to the French?'

This is hell, thinks Larry to himself. The glory of having been selected is all forgotten. He feels only the humiliation of looking on as his works are ignored. His distress is not wounded vanity. He has no conviction that his works deserve more attention. It's the gap between what he felt as he painted them and what he feels seeing them now that is so unbearable. These three all gave him such joy in the making. He can recall the heart-stopping excitement of realising the work was going to emerge at last, whole, living and harmonious, from the marks and daubs that went into their making. Impossible to describe to someone who hasn't attempted it. There's a magic to it, like being present at the birth of new life. And now these perfect creations, these gifts of wonder, are dying before his eyes. They hang on crowded walls, denied the love and attention which alone caused them to shine, revealed as commonplace efforts by a painter of no more than average ability.

'Larry!'

He looks round. There stands Kitty, her eyes bright, her pale face lit up by a smile.

'I'm so proud of you!'

She takes him in her arms for a warm hug.

'Kitty!' he exclaims. 'I didn't think you'd come.'

'Of course I've come. Your first exhibition! The others are still in front of your paintings, bathed in reflected glory. And I've come to find you.'

'Oh, Kitty. I just hate it here.'

'Do you, darling?'

Her eyes at once fill with sympathy, gazing at him intently, wanting to understand.

'It's all too much,' he says. 'Too many works. Too many people. I feel like an impostor. Any minute now someone's going to tap me on the shoulder and say, I'm afraid there's been a mistake, please take down your miserable daubs and leave.'

'Oh, Larry. How silly you are.'

But her eyes show she feels for him.

'No one will buy them, Kitty. I'm sure of that.'

'Louisa has George under orders to buy one,' says Kitty.

'Are George and Louisa here?'

'Of course. We want to take you out to dinner afterwards. Can you come? Or will you be going off with your smart art crowd?'

'I haven't got a smart art crowd. I'd far rather be with you.'

'Your paintings are wonderful, Larry. Really. I mean it.'

'Oh, Kitty.'

He doesn't care if she means it, he feels so grateful that she wants him to be happy. Now that she's here, before him, everything is transformed. He could stand in this corner for ever, gazing at her, filled with the sweet sensation of how much he loves her. It seems to him that she understands this, because she too stands there, saying nothing.

When he speaks again it's as if they've moved into a different and private space.

'How are you, Kitty?'

'Same as ever,' she says. 'Only older.'

'How is it with Ed?'

'Same as ever.'

Then he hears his name hallooed across the room, and Louisa is heading for him, with George in tow.

'Larry, you genius!' Louisa cries. 'We're all so excited! We know a real live famous artist!'

'Hello, Louisa.'

'We love your work. George loves your work. He's going to buy the big one with all the roofs. Go on, George. Go and tell them you're buying it.'

George shambles away to do as he's told. Ed now joins them.

'Larry, you old bastard,' he says.

His eyes glow with friendly warmth as he pumps Larry's hand. His face has grown even thinner.

'Hello, Ed,' says Larry.

'Next time you have a do, why don't you lay on some wine? You'll sell a whole lot more pictures. We're offering a very decent white right now. Between you and me it's made of peasants' pee, but only peasants who've drunk the best Grand Cru.'

Larry is taken unawares by just how pleased he is to be surrounded by his old friends.

'This is very decent of you all, I must say,' he says. 'Coming all this way.'

Nell comes over, bringing Julius Weingard. Larry makes introductions all round.

'Julius thinks he may have a buyer for you,' says Nell to Larry.

'No promises,' says Weingard. 'But this is a collector who likes to encourage new talent.'

'New talent is so much cheaper, isn't it?' says Louisa.

'That is so,' says Weingard with a smile.

'Lawrence darling,' says Nell, 'did you know you've sold one already?'

'That would be my husband,' says Louisa. 'He likes to encourage new talent too.'

Weingard at once produces his card.

'Send your husband to me,' he says. 'This is a circus.' He glances round in contempt. 'In Cork Street we are more civilised.'

He gives an old-fashioned bow and leaves the group of friends.

'What a repellent little man,' says Louisa.

'Louisa!' says Kitty, with a glance at Nell. 'Behave yourself.'

'He is a bit creepy,' says Nell, 'but he's terrifically good at what he does, and he knows everybody.'

Ed is looking at Nell with interest.

'So you're a friend of Larry's,' he says.

'A sort of a friend,' says Nell, glancing at Larry.

At once they all realise that she sleeps with Larry.

'Why don't you join us?' says Kitty. 'We're taking Larry out to dinner to celebrate. We've booked a table at Wilton's.'

George has a car outside, but they can't all fit in. Larry says he'd rather walk anyway, and Kitty says she would too, so in the end they all walk.

Larry walks with Ed. They fall at once into the real conversation that's only possible between old friends.

'She's interesting,' Ed says. 'Is she a serious proposition?'

'Maybe,' says Larry. Then realising Nell is not far behind, walking with Kitty, he says, 'How's the wine trade coming along?'

'Slow,' says Ed. 'The English seem to think drinking wine is like committing adultery, something you do rarely and abroad. What I really like is all the driving down empty roads in France.'

'Haven't you had enough of being away from home?'

'I've had enough of just about everything, if you really want to know. Do you ever get that feeling that nothing tastes of anything any more? Nothing excites you. Nothing hurts you.'

'Not good, Ed.'

'Sometimes I think what I need is another war.'

Outside the restaurant Nell says she won't come in with them after all. She has made other arrangements. She gives Larry a quick almost shy kiss as she goes, saying, 'Nice friends.'

'Why wouldn't she join us?' says Ed.

'Nell's like that,' says Larry. 'She likes to go her own way.'

Dinner turns out to be rather grand.

'Have whatever you want,' Louisa says. 'George is paying.'

Kitty is intrigued by this notion that Nell goes her own way.

'But what does she do?' she keeps saying.

Larry does his best to explain, but in the telling even he has to admit that Nell's life sounds as if it's going nowhere in particular.

'I don't see why she has to go anywhere in particular,' says Ed.

'Because otherwise what's the point?' says Kitty. 'We all want to feel our life has some sort of point.'

'I don't understand this,' says Ed. 'A point for who? A point when? Right now we're celebrating Larry and his paintings. We're eating good food, surrounded by good friends. Doesn't that give our lives a point?'

'You're deliberately misunderstanding me,' says Kitty.

Larry, watching and listening, sees that Kitty is unhappy. He wonders a little at the edge in Ed's voice.

'Well, I think Larry's friend is rather wonderful,' says Louisa. 'And she is very young. I'm sure she'll find her way soon enough.'

'And I say Larry's a great artist,' says Ed. 'I say he's had the guts to stick to doing what he loves, and now it's paying off. Here's to you, Larry. You're a great man. I salute you.'

'Thank you, Ed,' says Larry. 'All I have to do now is sell more than one painting.'

# 19

'Look what I found,' Nell says to Larry.

Her bicycle basket holds six small empty clear-glass bottles, of the kind used for medicines.

'You know what you do with bottles?' she says. 'You put messages in them.'

'Of course you do,' says Larry.

'Come along, then,' she says.

Larry heaves his own bike out onto the street, and together they cycle up the Walworth Road, round the Elephant and Castle, past Waterloo station, to the wide expanse of the new Waterloo Bridge. Here Nell comes to a stop, more or less in the middle of the bridge, and leans her bike against the parapet. Larry does the same. It's a fine sunny day, and for a few moments he stands admiring the view. To the east, the dome of St Paul's stands clear of the bomb-damaged buildings of the City; to the south, round the bend in the river, the Houses of Parliament.

Nell has one of the bottles out, together with a pad of paper and a pencil.

'So what's our first message to be?' she says.

'We really are sending messages in bottles?'

'Of course. I'll do the first one.'

She writes on the pad, tears off the sheet of paper, shows it to Larry. She has written: *If you find this message you will have good luck for the rest of your life.*

'You don't think that's going to end in disappointment?' he says.

'Not at all. If you believe in your luck, it comes.'

She screws the cap on the little bottle and drops it from the parapet of the bridge into the river below. They see it hit the water and sink and then come bobbing up again, to swirl away downstream.

They cycle across to the north bank of the river, and along the Victoria Embankment to Westminster Bridge. Once again, Nell parks her bike in the middle of the bridge.

'We're on a bridge crawl,' says Larry.

'I want this to be a day you'll never forget,' says Nell.

She takes out the pad and pencil.

'Earth has not anything to show more fair,' says Larry.

'What?'

'Wordsworth's poem. On Westminster Bridge.'

'Next message. Here. It's your turn.'

She hands him the pad. Larry is remembering the poem.

> 'The beauty of the morning, silent, bare,
> Ships, towers, something something lie
> Open unto the fields and to the sky,
> All bright and glittering in the smokeless air.'

'No fields now,' says Nell.

'No smokeless air, either.' He looks at the Houses of Parliament on the riverbank. 'You think all this has been here for ever, but Wordsworth never saw this. This isn't even a hundred years old. There were other buildings here, that have just vanished.'

'Send the next message.'

Larry thinks for a moment and then writes: *If you find this message, look around you and enjoy what you see, because one day it will all be gone.*

'That's a bit glum, isn't it?' says Nell.

'It'll make them appreciate what they've got.'

He rolls up the paper and pushes it into the bottle. He gives the bottle to Nell but she says, 'Your message, your throw.' So he drops it from the bridge into the river below, and watches it bob away out of sight.

They mount their bikes once more and ride round Big Ben and down Millbank to Lambeth Bridge. The obelisks on either side have pineapples on top, according to Nell. Larry claims they're pinecones.

'Why would anyone carve a giant stone pinecone?' says Nell. 'Why pineapples?'

'Pineapples are thrilling. All hard and scratchy on the outside, and sweet and juicy on the inside.'

She's pushing her bike up onto the pavement, sunlight gleaming on her hair. Larry gazes at her in admiration.

'How did you ever get to be you, Nell?' he says.

'What do you mean?'

'You're so open, so uncorrupted, so . . . I don't know. You just go on surprising me.'

'Is that good?'

'It's very good.'

She writes her message and shows him.

*If you find this message, go out and do the one thing you've been wanting to do all your life, but have been afraid to do.*

'What if he wants to rob a bank?'

'Who says it'll be a he? It might be a girl. She might want to kiss the boy she's secretly in love with.'

She kisses Larry, there on Lambeth Bridge.

'Now it's not a secret any more,' says Larry.

He feels light-hearted, happy in a way he's not been happy for a long time. Nell's game makes everything good seem possible, and everything bad seem far away.

She drops her bottle into the water.

They ride on past the Tate, past Vauxhall Bridge – 'Too ugly' – along the embankment to Chelsea Bridge. Here on the guardian lamp-posts in place of pineapples or pinecones there are golden galleons. Across the river looms the immense block of Battersea Power Station. Two of its four chimneys are streaming black smoke into the summer sky.

Nell gives Larry the pad.

'Your turn.'

*If you find this message*, writes Larry, *believe that happiness exists, because I am happy now*.

'That's beautiful, Larry,' says Nell. 'I want you so much to be happy.'

He drops the bottle into the river on the downstream side and watches it swirl away under the railway bridge.

Nell has taken the pad back and is writing on it.

'Where next?' says Larry. 'Albert Bridge?'

'No more bridges.'

She puts her message into its bottle without showing it to Larry, pushing it deep inside.

'I have to go now, darling,' she says.

'Go? Where?'

'Just go.'

She gives him the little bottle.

'The last one's for you.'

She gives him a kiss, climbs onto her bike, and pedals away up Chelsea Bridge Road.

Larry unscrews the bottle cap and tries to get the roll of paper out, but the neck is too narrow. Baffled, mildly irritated, he gazes at the bottle, wondering what to do. The paper inside has partially unrolled itself, so even if he were able to grip it through the neck it would tear as he pulled it out. The only solution is to break the bottle.

He holds it by its neck and taps it against the kerb. Then he taps it more briskly. Finally he hits it a sharp blow, and it shatters. He picks the paper out from among the glittering fragments of glass, and unrolls it, and reads.

*If you find this message please believe that I expect nothing from you and only want you to go on being happy. I am going to have a baby. I love you.*

Larry stands up, blood draining from his face. His first instinct is to ride after Nell at once. But he realises he has no idea where she's gone, and will never find her. So instead he wheels his bike slowly off the bridge, fighting a confusion of emotions.

Most of all, he feels frightened. It's not a specific fear, it's a kind of panic. Events are exploding beyond his control, unknown forces are bearing down upon him. Then through the panic, like a mist burned off by the sun, he feels a hot shining pride.

I'm going to be a father.

The thought is so immense it overwhelms him. It exhilarates him and fills him with dread at the same time. The responsibility is too great. It changes everything.

I'm to have a wife and child.

A wife! It's almost impossible to see Nell in this role. And yet of course they must marry.

So is this it? Is this my life already laid out before me?

He knows even as he forms the thought that this is not the life he meant to lead. But if not this, then what? What is this dream of a future that even now he sees being lost to him for ever?

Dazed, he mounts his bike and sets off pedalling up Chelsea Bridge Road, in the direction Nell took. He realises then that she must have planned it all to happen this way. She must have dreamed up her game with the messages in bottles as a way to give him time alone to form his response. He feels a sudden flood of love. What an extraordinary girl she is! Old beyond her years, she understands all he is now going through. She knows he'll have doubts about committing himself to a future with her. So she bicycles away. This touches him deeply. Adrift in the great world, she cares enough for him not to lay on him a greater burden than he can carry.

In this moment, pedalling behind a bus as it lumbers up Sloane Street, he feels only love for her, and gratitude. But as he swings left onto Knightsbridge and rides along the south side of the park, other concerns begin to present themselves. How is he to support a wife and child? Where are they to live? What will happen to his painting?

At this point he realises where he's going. This is the way

home. Guided by instincts deeper than conscious thought, in this time of crisis he is returning to the house where he grew up. There's no purpose to this, he can't expect his father to resolve his dilemma for him. He is going home as to a refuge.

So he turns into Kensington Church Street and climbs the rise to Campden Grove. His father will be in his office now, of course, on the other side of town; but Larry has a key. He lets himself in, heaving the old bike after him, and stands it in the front hall. Miss Cookham, the housekeeper, comes up from the basement to see who it can be.

'Hello, Cookie,' says Larry. 'I thought I'd look in.'

'Mr Lawrence!' She actually goes pink with delight. 'There's a sight for sore eyes! Look at you! I hear you're a famous artist now.'

'Not so famous,' says Larry.

He's shocked at how much it pleases him to be welcomed in this way; and at how comforted he is by the gloomy house.

'Shall I get you a pot of tea, and maybe a slice of cake?'

'That would be wonderful. How are you, Cookie?'

'Quiet, as you might say. Your father won't be long now.'

Larry settles himself down in the third-floor back room that was once the nursery, and then became his study room. Here, home from school in the holidays, he would retreat to read or sketch or just gaze into the fire. Here he hid himself on the day his father told him his mother had gone to heaven. He was five years old.

Cookie knocks on the door, and comes in with a tray.

'It's only seed cake,' she says, 'and plainer than I'd like it, but you know how it is. You'd never guess we won the war.'

'Thank you, Cookie. You're an angel.'

She stands there, looking at him in his old armchair by the bookcase.

'It's a pleasure to have you home again, Mr Lawrence.'

Left alone, Larry drinks his tea and eats his cake and finds he can't persuade himself to address his situation. Each time he sets out to discover what he should do, his thoughts veer away to one side, and he finds himself remembering his schooldays. Ed Avenell, whose family lived in the north, would always stay with him here at the beginning and end of the holidays, as he travelled back and forth to school. He can see him now, hunched up on the floor in front of the fire, poking things into the coals, watching them burn. Ed was a great one for burning things, pencils, toy soldiers, matchboxes. He burned himself too, in an experimental sort of way, passing his hand through the flames until it was coated with soot.

He hears the shudder of the front door closing, and hears his father's voice in the hall. He hears Cookie's excited twitter. His father will be tired. He'll want to wash and change after his day in the office; and then to enjoy a whisky in the library while he glances over the evening paper.

Larry comes downstairs to greet him. He hasn't seen his father since his return from Jamaica.

'Larry! This is a happy surprise!'

His eyes show his real pleasure. As always on coming home, Larry is struck by how much he's still part of this world, which in his own mind he has left behind.

'Will you stay and eat with me?'

'I'd like a drink,' says Larry. 'And a chat. But then I'd better be back on my bike.'

'Ah, the artist's life!' says his father, smiling. 'Give me ten minutes.'

Larry goes into the library and picks up the evening paper his father has brought in. He reads a little about the Paris peace conference, then puts the paper down. This room is so filled with his father's presence that he feels like a child again. Here, every evening in the long school holidays, he sat in what was always his special chair, a low tub chair upholstered in deep red velvet, and his father read to him. They read *King Solomon's Mines*, and *The Lost World*, and *Treasure Island*, which his father was fond of saying was the best tale ever spun.

And am I to be a father too?

William Cornford joins him and pours them both a shot of Scotch. They talk for a little about Jamaica, and the difficulties caused by the requisition of the fleet during the war.

'We've got the *Ariguani* and the *Bayano* back, but for now only the *Ariguani* is operating a regular schedule. We're badly short of capacity. I'm in negotiations to buy four ships from the Ministry. This government is doing all it can to increase non-dollar food imports. It's just going to take time. The great thing is we've managed to hold onto almost all our staff.'

'As far as I can see,' says Larry, 'no one ever leaves.'

'Not if I can help it,' says his father. 'People grow into jobs. They start off as little slips and they turn into oak trees.'

Larry knows he too should have been a little slip, should now be an oak tree in the family firm. His father, realising his words may be construed as a criticism, turns the conversation.

'So tell me,' he says, 'how is your art exhibition going?'

'Only two more days to go,' says Larry. 'Then I can have the dubious pleasure of reclaiming my works.'

'And what then?'

'That's something of a question.'

'Oh?' The single syllable spoken quietly, neutrally.

'There's been a new development. I'm not quite sure what to do.'

Until this moment Larry hasn't realised he wants his father's advice. He believes he knows what his father will say: his strong religious convictions give him very little choice. So why raise the matter?

Because whatever I do, Dad must approve.

This too is a surprise. Apparently, in order to feel that he has done the right thing he must obtain his father's blessing. This weary man sitting drinking Scotch, with his lined tanned face gazing so thoughtfully back at him, represents all that is just and right and good. This is what it is to be a father.

How can I ever live up to that?

'I've had a girlfriend for quite some time now,' he says. 'Her name's Nell. She works for an art dealer. She's a very unconventional sort of girl, very free-thinking, very independent.'

He pauses, and wonders whether his father can tell where this is going. As he speaks, he loses confidence. It seems to him that what he is about to say shows him to have been ridiculously irresponsible.

Why did I take no precautions to prevent this happening? Because Nell told me she had dealt with it. But I never asked more. I have no idea what method she used. I was too embarrassed, and too selfish, to pursue the question. Look at it rationally, as my father must look at it: my behaviour has been a kind of insanity.

'Anyway,' he says, 'I've run into a spot of difficulty with her. I expect you can guess.'

He finds he can't speak the actual words. He's too ashamed. And yet here he is, by his own choice, telling his father enough for him to draw his own conclusions.

'I see,' says his father.

'I know what I've done is wrong,' Larry says. 'I mean, I know you'll tell me the Church will say I've sinned. And I have.'

'Do you love her?' his father says.

This is not what Larry has been braced for. He takes a moment before he answers.

'Yes,' he says.

'Do you want to marry her?'

'I think so,' says Larry. 'It's all so new. I'm confused about it all.'

'How old is she?'

'Twenty. Nearly twenty-one.'

'What have you told her?'

'Nothing. She gave me the news and then ran off. I think she wants me to have time to think about it before I make any decision. She's not the kind of girl who'd want me to marry her just for the sake of appearances.'

'She'd want to know you loved her?'

'Yes.'

'And you're not sure.'

He throws his father a quick glance. Is it so obvious?

'I don't know. I might be. I'm not sure I'm not sure, if you see what I mean.'

William Cornford nods. Yes, he sees what Larry means. He's watching his son closely.

'You're right about the Church,' he says. 'The Church's position is perfectly clear. What you've done is wrong. But it's done. And your duty now, as far as the Church is concerned, is also perfectly clear.'

'Yes,' says Larry. 'I realise that.'

'But marriage is for ever. It's till death.'

'Yes,' says Larry.

His father was married till death. Nine years, and then death. Those nine years have crystallised into a sacred monument. The perfect marriage.

'Can you do that, Larry?'

'I don't know,' says Larry. 'How do you know? Did you know?'

His father gives a slow emphatic nod. No words. He has never spoken about his dead wife. Never mentioned her name since her death, except in their prayers. *God bless Mummy and watch over us from heaven and keep us safe till we meet again.*

Watch over me now, Larry thinks, wanting to cry.

'I'm not your priest,' says his father. 'I'm your father. I want to say something the Church can't say to you. If you don't really love this girl, you would be doing a wicked thing if you married her. You would be condemning both of you, and your children, to a life of unhappiness. From what you tell me, she understands this very well. She doesn't want a husband who is merely doing his duty. Of course, whatever happens, you must support her. But if you marry, marry of your own free will. Marry for love.'

Larry is unable to speak. In every word his father utters, he feels the powerful force of his love for him. He may use the language of moral imperatives, but his underlying concern is for his son's happiness. This is what it is to be a father. He's willing to set aside even his most deeply cherished beliefs for the sake of his child.

'Don't ruin your life, Larry.'

'No,' says Larry. 'That is, if I haven't already.'

'But if you think you really can love her – well then.'

Larry meets his father's eyes. He wants so much to hug him,

and feel his father's arms holding tight. But it's years since they hugged.

'There's the practical side of things,' he says. 'You say I must support her, and of course I must. But it's not so simple.'

'I take it,' says his father, 'that art has not proved to be remunerative so far.'

'Not so far.'

Now his father will tell him that this is just as he predicted in their one great row before the war. That he's wasted his youth on a foolish dream. That now he must face up to his responsibilities.

'But you love it?'

'I'm sorry?'

'Your painting. Your art. You love it.'

'Oh, yes.'

'You sound very certain about that.'

'You're asking me if I love to paint, Dad. I am certain of that. It's all I want to do. But I'm not certain about anything else. I'm not certain that I'm good enough. I'm not certain I'll ever be able to make my living at it.'

'But you love it.'

'Yes.'

'That's a rare thing, Larry. That's a gift from God.'

Abruptly he gets up from his chair and goes to the desk where he keeps his private papers. For a few moments he fiddles about, consulting the pages of his ledgers.

'Here is what I propose,' he says. 'I will increase your allowance by an additional £100 a year. I will pay for the rental of an appropriate flat for this young lady. Whether you live there with her, and upon what terms, is entirely your own business. How will that do?'

'Oh, Dad!'

'I'm trying to be practical about this, Larry. It's not for me to judge you.'

'I thought you'd tell me to take a job in the company.'

'What, as a punishment? The company isn't a penal colony. If you ever join the company, it must be of your own free will.'

'Like marriage.'

'Yes. Very like.'

He holds out his hand. Larry takes it and grasps it.

'Let me know what you decide.'

Bicycling back across London, Larry finds himself once more tossed this way and that by conflicting emotions. His father's generosity awes him and leaves him floundering. Without realising it, he now knows he had gone home to receive instruction in his duty. Unable to take the decision himself, he looks to the institutions that frame his life, family, school, church, to force his hand. Instead he leaves his father's house freer and more empowered than when he arrived; and therefore more solitary and more burdened.

How is it that others make this decision so easily? Do they feel absolute certainty? He thinks then of Ed and Kitty. They met twice – twice! – before deciding to marry. At the time he felt no surprise: why should love require more than an instant? And in wartime there was always too little time, and only a very uncertain future. But let peace break out, let the future stretch before you for its full span of years, and who can know for certain what they want?

So maybe, he thinks, it's this very demand for certainty that's the stumbling block. If certainty is impossible, then why expect it? Perhaps the decision to marry is a provisional one, made on best information at the time, and it takes years to grow into certainty. If this is the case, all that's needed to kick-start the process is some outside pressure. And what could be a more traditional outside pressure than a baby on the way? In some countries it's understood that no engagement takes place until the girl is pregnant; that, and not sex, being the purpose of marriage.

But what about love?

Still debating within himself, he turns into the road where he lives, and there's Nell, sitting on the steps, looking out for him. She jumps up, her face grinning from side to side.

'Guess what?' she says. 'I've been at Julius's. He says your pictures are all sold!'

'Sold! Who to?'

'Some anonymous buyer. Isn't that wonderful? You're being collected! Like a real artist!'

'I'm amazed.'

'It's good, isn't it?'

He feels a sudden exultation as the news sinks in. His paintings are wanted. Money has been paid for them. There's no endorsement quite as gratifying as this. Words cost the speaker nothing. But no one pays out real money unless they mean it.

He props his bike against the wall and takes Nell in his arms. Her excitement is all for him. In this time of crisis for herself, she thinks only of him.

'I couldn't wait to tell you. I've been sitting on the steps hugging myself.'

'It's brilliant,' he says. 'I can't believe it.'

He kisses her, there on the steps.

'We have to celebrate,' she says.

'Yes, but what about your message?'

'Oh, that,' she says. 'Did you manage to get it out of the bottle without breaking it?'

'No. I had to smash it.'

'I thought you might.'

'You shouldn't have run away.'

'Shouldn't I?'

She's in his arms, and she's smiling up at him, and she's so funny and beautiful, and his paintings have sold and the sun is shining, and suddenly it seems easy.

'Marry me, Nell.'

She goes on smiling at him, but says nothing at all. This isn't how it's supposed to be.

'Nell? I asked you a question.'

'Oh, it was a question, was it?'

'I want you to marry me.'

'Maybe,' she says. 'I'll think about it.'

'Don't you want to?'

'Maybe,' she says. 'I'm not sure.'

'You're not sure!'

'Well, I am only twenty.'

'Almost twenty-one.'

'But I do love you, Lawrence.'

'There you are, then,' he says.

'I just don't know that I'd be good for you.'

'Of course you would!' Hearing her express her doubts frees him of his own. 'You're perfect for me. You're good to me, and you never stop surprising me, and you make me happy. How am I to live without you?'

She gives him such an odd look then, as if that secret part of herself is revealing itself to him for the first time, the fearful, vulnerable part of herself. Her look says to him: promise me you won't hurt me.

'You see,' she says, 'it's different for girls.'

'What do you mean?'

'You've got your painting, and being important in the world, and doing the things men do. But for us it's just the husband and the children. There isn't anything else. So we have to get it right.'

She sits back down on the step, and he sits down beside her and takes her hand in his.

'So let's get it right together,' he says.

'We don't have to decide anything today, do we?'

'Not if you don't want to,' he says.

'I don't really know what I want,' she says.

Larry is nonplussed.

'But I thought . . .'

He doesn't complete the thought. Suddenly it seems foolish.

'You thought all girls want to be married, and it's the men who have to be pushed.'

'You said you want to be married.'

'I do,' says Nell. 'But only in the right way.'

'What's the right way?'

'My parents are married,' she says. 'But they're not happy. Sometimes I think they hate each other. I don't want to end up like that.'

'But if two people love each other,' Larry says.

'I suppose they thought they loved each other. In the beginning. You never really know, it seems to me. Not for absolute sure.'

She's looking at him earnestly now, stroking his hand as she speaks. He feels as if the world is spinning round him. Her words and her touch contradict each other. Does she love him or not?

'But Nell,' he says helplessly. 'What about the baby?'

'You mean we should get married because of the baby?'

'Well, it's part of it, isn't it?'

'And if there hadn't been a baby, you wouldn't have wanted to?'

Larry is caught. He wants to answer her, 'I might not have asked you so soon, but I would have proposed later.' Is that true? He feels the blazing force of her honesty, and is ashamed.

'Darling Lawrence,' she says, squeezing his hand. 'I love you so much. Let's not build ourselves any cages. I couldn't bear it if I thought you were trapped where you didn't want to be. Let's just love each other the way we do now, and let the days go by, and not ever have to lie to each other.'

In that moment he loves her more than he's ever done. This sweet child of truth, he thinks. Where does she come by such instinctive purity? An odd word to apply to a girl who gives her body freely to him, but he feels it deep in her, an innocence that is not a lack of experience, nor a childlikeness. Sometimes when she's looking at him with her solemn eyes he feels she's far older, certainly more mature, than he can ever be, for all his eight years longer in the world. Somehow Nell has been born true.

'If that's what you want,' he says.

'And if it's what you want,' she says softly.

## 20

Pamela makes her way slowly, deliberately, from rock pool to rock pool, in her ruched bathing costume and little wellington boots, carrying a plastic cup from a thermos flask. Her chubby three-year-old body moves gracefully. Reaching a miniature chasm between the rocks, she crouches and springs across to the other side, and in the same movement bends down to peer into the new pool. The tide is out, and the great expanse of shining rock and seaweed reaches almost to the horizon. She's exploring, seeking tiny crabs and transparent fishes, moving ever further from the narrow pebble beach beneath the cliffs. What if she were to fall?

'Don't go too far, darling,' Kitty calls, sitting at the bottom of the concrete steps.

Pamela pays her no attention as always. Silly to call out, really. This is a child who asserts her independent will so fiercely that she'll do the opposite of what she's told to do, just to make a point.

Hugo, who has gone hunting along the beach for treasure, now returns to the steps. He's a sweet-faced youth, a boy really, though as he likes to tell her, there's only five years between them. He was called up, but it was near the end of the war, and he never saw active service.

'No chance of a VC for me,' he says.

He's pink-faced, bright-eyed, eager to learn. He admires Ed above all men, and without realising it, has picked up many of Ed's ways of thinking and talking.

'Look what I found,' he says. 'Jewels.'

He shows Kitty a handful of shiny translucent pebbles, dark green, milky white, amber, ruby red. Fragments of glass that were once bottles or jars, ground smooth by the action of the waves.

'Pammy'll love those,' says Kitty. And looking out at the distant figure of her daughter, 'Do you think she's gone too far?'

'She is quite a long way out.'

'She takes no notice of me when I call.'

'I'll go and get her, shall I?'

He lopes off over the rocks, eager to be of service. Kitty is well aware that Hugo likes her company more than he should, but she sees no harm in it. Somehow the division of labour in his partnership with Ed calls for Ed to be away, touring the humbler vineyards of France, while Hugo stays home and manages the delivery of the orders as they come in. The business is not yet established enough to have its own premises, so the barn beside their farmhouse is used for storage, stacked high with cases of wine. Hugo is forever building up or depleting the stacks as the shipments come and go. His Bedford van has become a familiar sight in the yard, and he himself almost another member of the family.

She watches him now, silhouetted against the bright horizon, as he reaches Pamela. He stands between the rock pools reasoning with her. Kitty sees how the little girl turns her back on him and hops further away from the shore; and how he circles round to block her venturing any further. Then come sharp cries of frustration, and she's hitting his legs. Finally he's bent down and picked her up by the waist, and he's carrying her back.

She kicks her feet and beats with her fists and screams at him, but he holds on tight. By the time he deposits her before Kitty, the little girl is scarlet in the face and seriously insulted.

'I hate you!' she says. 'I hate you!'

'You went too far,' says Kitty. 'What if you'd hurt yourself?'

Pamela kicks Hugo's shin hard with her little boots. He lets out an exclamation of pain.

'Pammy!' says Kitty. 'Stop that!'

'I hate you!' says the child.

With a mother's instinct, Kitty understands the source of her daughter's rage. It's the being picked up, the being rendered powerless. Nevertheless she can't be allowed to kick people.

'Pammy,' she says. 'You hurt Hugo. Look, he's crying.'

Hugo takes the hint, and starts to whimper.

'Poor Hugo,' says Kitty.

Pamela looks at Hugo suspiciously. Hugo is kneeling on the pebbles, rubbing his shin, crying.

'Kiss it better for him,' says Kitty.

Pamela crouches down and gives Hugo's knee a quick rough kiss.

'Thank you,' says Hugo in a small voice.

'There,' says Kitty, trusting the balance of power has been restored. 'Now say sorry.'

'Sorry,' says Pamela, scowling at the cliffs.

Kitty then shows her the jewels Hugo has found for her, and she becomes silent, absorbed in wonder. Kitty looks up to find Hugo gazing at her.

'You're amazing,' he says.

Kitty pretends she hasn't heard him. He's becoming more and more open in his manner with her, no longer even pretending to hide his admiration. Kitty treats it as a game, which allows him, in playing along, to say more than he should. One day soon, she thinks, she must have a quiet but firm word with him, before he does something he regrets. But in the meantime, with Ed away so much, she sees no harm in letting herself enjoy his company.

There was a time when Kitty found the attentions of men oppressive, with their furtive looks, their veiled suggestions, their endless importunities. But since marriage and motherhood it has all ceased, and she finds to her surprise that she sometimes misses it. So Hugo and his absurd puppy-love is not as unwelcome as she pretends.

The three of them climb the steep flight of concrete steps up the cliff. She holds Pamela's hand tight all the way, even though Pamela pulls crossly to be released. At the top of the steps a wide grass avenue, grazed close by rabbits, runs between banks of gorse over the brow of the hill. This is Hope Gap, a notch in the great chalk cliffs that lies between Seaford Head and the Cuckmere valley.

Pamela, let go at last, runs on ahead. Hugo carries the basket that contains the thermos flask and what's left of their cheese and apple sandwiches.

'She's going to be a heartbreaker, that one,' he says. 'Like her mother.'

'What does that mean, heartbreak?' says Kitty. 'I've never understood that. I don't see how anyone can be properly in love with someone unless they know they're loved back. And if they're loved back, nothing's broken.'

'You don't think it's possible to love all on your own?'

'I suppose in the very beginning. You can get excited, and build up your hopes, and so on. But if it all goes nowhere, then what's the point? You're just wasting your time.'

'You may not be able to help it,' says Hugo.

'Rubbish,' says Kitty firmly. Then seeing Pamela disappear out of sight, 'Don't go too far, Pammy!'

They reach the brow of the hill. From here they can see the coastline curving away for miles. Kitty looks as she always does for the long pier reaching out from Newhaven harbour. She remembers how she waited on the quayside for Ed to return, and how the first time he came back, and the second time he didn't.

When they reach the sheep barn by the road, Pamela has already climbed into the back of Kitty's ten-year-old Austin. She has the shiny pebbles in her open hands and is studying them intently.

'Put on a jersey, darling,' says Kitty. 'It'll be blowy driving home.'

Pamela shakes her head. Kitty gets into the driver's seat, with Hugo beside her.

'Feels strange being driven by a girl,' he says.

'I'm a trained driver,' says Kitty. 'And I'm not a girl any more.'

The shiny black open-topped Bantam is her car, and she maintains it in perfect condition. Now that Pamela is getting bigger Kitty is rediscovering the self that existed before motherhood. She recalls her days as an army driver wistfully, almost envying her past. Of course she's a wife as well as a mother, but Ed is away so much. The business is proving very slow to get up on its feet. The top end of the market is dominated by the old-established firms, and the bottom end, where Caulder & Avenell aim to carve their niche, is virtually non-existent. They are having to create the demand that they hope to serve.

So Ed works hard, seeking out bargain wines from remote vineyards, building up a stock of such value for money that even the wine-averse English might be tempted to try a bottle.

'Reliable quality plus a visible name,' Larry tells him, offering his knowledge of the banana business. 'What you need is little blue labels.'

'I'm not sticking little blue labels on our bottles,' says Ed. 'You don't stick little blue labels on your pictures.'

'I expect I should,' says Larry. 'Then maybe I'd sell more.'

Kitty finds Ed's trips abroad hard. When he's home, when he's in her bed, in her arms, her life makes sense to her. But then he goes away again, and the bed is empty once more.

'You don't have to go so soon, do you, darling?'

'It'll only be like this for a year or so,' he says. 'Once we're properly up and running, I'll be able to be a gentleman of leisure.'

'I just miss you so,' she says.

'And I miss you, darling. But I'm doing it for you. And for Pammy. You know that.'

Pamela doesn't know it.

'Don't go, Daddy,' she says, clinging to him.

But he goes.

At the end of August Larry Cornford takes a train to Lewes and from there walks down the long and winding road to Edenfield.

He carries a change of clothes and his paints and brushes in an old army kitbag. He keeps to the high grass verge, clear of the lorries rumbling to Newhaven. Once round the flank of the Downs he can see the village in the river valley below, and the church with its square tower, and the red roofs of the farmhouse behind it. He has not announced his coming and is not expected, but he has the sensation that the valley welcomes him back.

The farmyard looks much the same as when he was billeted here, except that the barn doors are open, and within he can make out stacks of wooden crates. A young man appears, carrying a crate out to the open back of a big van. Seeing Larry he gives a friendly nod and loads the crate into the van.

'Hello,' he says. 'Can I help?'

'I'm a friend of Ed's,' says Larry.

'Ed's away,' says the young man. 'Kitty's here.'

Larry turns to the house, and there in the doorway stands Kitty, looking towards him. For a moment as their eyes meet neither speaks. Then Pamela appears, pushing past her mother, and stares at Larry.

'Who's that?' she says.

'That's Larry,' says Kitty. 'He's Daddy's best friend. He came to see us when we lived in the big house. You said he was nice.'

'I don't remember,' says the little girl.

'He is nice,' says Kitty.

All this time her eyes hold Larry's, telling him how deeply quietly pleased she is to see him.

'Hello, Pamela,' says Larry.

'Hello,' says the little girl, looking from him to her mother and back.

'Did you walk from Lewes?' says Kitty.

'Yes,' says Larry. 'It's only an hour or so.'

'Come on in.'

She looks the same and different. A little older, a little wearier. She's wearing a cotton summer frock that makes her slight figure seem vulnerable. Her wide mouth unsmiling, her deep brown eyes steady beneath those strongly-defined eyebrows. A pale face framed in dark waves of hair. What is it that makes one face so much more beautiful than all others? Seeing her standing there in the farmhouse kitchen doorway, her little girl tugging at her skirt, Larry abandons what remains of his defences. He knows he will never love anyone as he loves her.

Hugo Caulder joins them over a pot of tea in the kitchen. He talks about the wine trade, and remote French vineyards still recovering from the war years where extraordinary deals are to be done, and his dream of having his own premises in London.

'In Bury Street, or maybe even in St James's Street. Then we'd start selling the fine wines as well.'

'When does Ed get back?' Larry asks.

'He'll be away at least another two weeks,' Kitty says.

Hugo returns to loading his van.

'So will you stay?' says Kitty.

'If I may,' says Larry. 'This is no weather for stewing in town.'

Hugo drives away in his loaded van. Kitty makes a potato omelette for their supper, and gives Larry a bottle of Vin de Pays d'Oc to open.

'Ed's best,' she says. 'To celebrate your visit.'

She waits until Pamela is asleep to ask the waiting questions.

'So how's Nell?'

'Nell's thriving. She's away right now. A buying trip, with her boss.'

'You can bring her down here any time, you know. She'd be very welcome.'

'Yes, of course. Thank you.'

He lets a silence fall between them. As always, these silences act as gear changes, moments in neutral before the shift to a slower speed.

'She's an unusual girl, Nell.' He wants very much to tell Kitty about the baby, but something holds him back. 'She always had a thing about being independent. She has her job at the gallery, she earns far more money than I do. She knows I like to spend a lot of my time alone. So it works out quite well, really.'

'It sounds like you're leading separate lives.'

'No, not separate. We're very close.' He realises he sounds as if he's making excuses for her. 'It's hard to explain. She hates to make demands on me.'

He can see Kitty's lovely face puzzling over what he tells her, unable to make sense of it. He wants so much to touch her. But things are as they are, and he must make the best of it.

'She sounds a bit like Ed,' she says.

'You mustn't think I'm complaining,' he says. 'She's warm, and loving.'

'Maybe she's waiting for you to propose.'

'I've done that.'

'You've proposed!'

'She says she's thinking about it.'

'Well!' Now Kitty is awestruck. 'She must be a fool.'

But her tone of voice says otherwise. Her tone of voice shows Nell has risen sharply in her estimation.

'She's not a fool,' says Larry. 'She just doesn't want to compromise. Her parents have a bad marriage. She wants to be sure.'

'And she's not sure about you.'

'Apparently not.'

'How do you feel about that?'

'A bit odd, to be honest.'

'You're a good man, Larry. A rare man. What more does she want?'

'Who knows? It's not as if I'm such a terrific catch.'

'You know that's not true. But who am I to talk? We all play that game.'

'What game?' says Larry.

She gets up and starts clearing the table, speaking lightly as she works, to make out it's no more than idle chatter.

'Doing yourself down. Feeling you're not really worth very much at all. Thinking you haven't much to offer anybody. And there's the one person you're supposed to make happy, and you can't even do that.'

Larry understands then that she's telling him about herself.

'So what are we supposed to do about it?' he says.

'Try harder. Be more loving.' Stacking plates in the sink. 'Stop minding about our own happiness.'

So she's unhappy. He feels a sharp pang, both painful and sweet.

'He's away too much, isn't he?' he says.

'He works so hard.' Now she's standing still, her hands on the draining board, her head bent. 'He's doing it for us, so we don't have to live on George and Louisa's charity. So we can have a house of our own. He's thinking of Pammy and schools and all the things that need money. But I'd rather have him than the money.'

'Of course you would,' says Larry.

She looks up then, searching his face for clues.

'Why doesn't he know that?'

'That's how Ed is,' says Larry. 'He never does anything halfway. He's decided this is what he has to do, and he's doing it as well as he can.'

'What if it's because he doesn't love me any more?'

'No!' Larry's denial is immediate, urgent. Too urgent. 'Ed adores you. You know that.'

'Do I? I don't see why he should.'

'Kitty! What nonsense is this? Everyone adores you. You'd have to be blind not to see it.'

'Oh, that.' She passes one hand across her face, as if waving away a buzzing fly. 'That's just how you look. That's nothing.'

'But that's only the start of it! You're so much more than just a pretty girl.'

'I don't see how.'

She seems to mean it. There's a sadness in her voice that shocks him. How can she not know her own value?

'Ed loves you because you're beautiful and loyal and kind-hearted. He loves you because you're strong and don't weigh him down. He loves you because you understand things without having to be told them. He loves you because you don't ask him to be someone he isn't. Most of all, he loves you because you love him.'

He's looking at her as he speaks, and he can't help it, his eyes are giving him away. But what is there to give away? Kitty has known his feelings for her for a long time.

'Does he talk to you about me?' she says.

'Sometimes.'

'Does he say he loves me?'

'Many times.'

'All he says to me is that he doesn't deserve me.'

'Yes,' says Larry. 'He says that too.'

'You know what?' she says. 'I think it's because of that damned beach at Dieppe. That's where it all started.'

'Why do you say that?'

'I think that day did something to Ed. I don't know what. He won't talk about it. He hates it when anyone asks him about his VC. Why's he like that, Larry? So many people saw what he did on that beach. Why won't he talk about it? What happened to him there?'

'Something happened to all of us,' says Larry. 'It's hard to explain. You'd have to have been there. It was like the end of the world.'

'Is that what Ed thought? It was the end of the world?'

'It was all so stupid and pointless. Just a gigantic mistake, really. We all saw that. But Ed – he just went crazy. He was so angry he didn't care if he lived or died. He didn't even try to protect himself. He kept thinking it'd be his turn next, but his turn never came. He says it was just luck. And I think he feels he doesn't deserve his luck. I think some part of him feels he should have died on that beach.'

Kitty listens in silence. Larry is picking his words carefully, protecting her from the single most devastating cry that burst from Ed that night they talked in the chapel: *I wanted to die*. How can he say this to Kitty? Did he not want to live for her?

'Thank you,' Kitty says. 'That helps me.'

'But he should talk to you about all this himself.'

'People don't always talk about things.'

But you and I talk, Larry wants to say. You and I talk about everything and anything. There's nothing I can't say to you.

'It was different for me on that beach.' Suddenly he realises he's going to tell her what he's told nobody except Ed. 'I was a coward on that beach.'

'Oh, Larry. Everyone must have been terrified.'

'All I did was take cover. All I could think about was saving myself.'

'Anyone would've been the same.'

'No. There were a lot of brave men that day. I just wasn't one of them.'

She smiles at him.

'That damned beach,' she says.

Larry feels a weight roll off him, a weight he's been carrying for four years. He has told Kitty his shameful secret, and she doesn't mind. It seems to make no difference. He's flooded with love and gratitude; but this, unlike his shame, must remain unspoken.

There's something else he isn't telling Kitty, too. He isn't telling her about Nell and the baby.

Larry spends the next day painting. He sets up a board in the farmyard, using the split-chestnut rails as an easel. For a while Pamela watches him at work, saying nothing.

So long as he's absorbed in his painting he has no dreams and no regrets. This is the joy of it, the way it allows him to escape his own uncertain self, and live in another space. There, within the frame of his chosen image, the complexities are limitless, the challenges insurmountable, but he himself almost ceases to exist.

Kitty comes out to tell him George and Louisa will join them for supper. She looks at the work in progress.

'Caburn again,' she says.

At supper Louisa is eager to hear news of the artist's model who poses naked.

'She doesn't do that any more,' says Larry.

'But is she still your girlfriend? Isn't it time you settled down? How old are you, Larry?'

'I'm twenty-eight.'

'Leave the poor man alone, Louisa,' says Kitty.

'Well, you know what they say,' says Louisa. 'You're not a man until you've planted a tree, had a son, and something else I forget.'

Louisa is desperate to have a baby, and makes no attempt to conceal it.

'A woman, a dog and a walnut tree,' says George, 'the more you beat them the better they be.'

'What on earth is he talking about?' says Louisa.

'Old English proverb,' says George.

'How extraordinary! The things he comes up with!'

Lying in bed that night, back in the room he occupied in the summer of '42, Larry thinks to himself of the baby waiting to be born, who might indeed be a son. It seems to him that Louisa is right. He isn't yet a man.

# 21

'So how were your friends in Sussex?' says Nell. 'Did you tell them about me?'

'We talked about you a bit,' says Larry. 'But I didn't give away any secrets.'

He means about the baby.

Nell has returned from her trip looking tired and behaving restlessly. Larry shows her the paintings he's been working on during his time away, but she only looks at them for a moment before moving on again. She makes funny little dance steps round the room, lights a cigarette, traces circles in the air with one hand.

'Don't you sometimes think there's too much art in the world?' she says.

'Far too much,' says Larry.

'So what *bit* did you talk about?'

'Oh, Louisa had a go at me for not settling down.'

'Like a Labrador.'

'Is that what Labradors do?'

'My parents have one. He goes round and round in his basket, pawing at his blanket, and then he settles down.'

She acts it out, with such vivid mimicry that Larry laughs.

'I can't see myself doing that,' he says.

'So what excuse did you give?'

'Oh, you know those sorts of dinner conversations. No one expects a serious answer.'

'No, I suppose not.'

She stops pirouetting and stands looking out of the window, her back to Larry.

'But you have more serious conversations with Kitty, I expect.'

'Sometimes,' says Larry.

'What do you talk about?'

'Ed, mostly.'

'You talk to Kitty about Ed?'

'Yes,' says Larry. Nell's voice has gone quiet and she's become very still, as if she doesn't want to miss a sound. 'I've known Ed for ever. He can be a strange chap sometimes.'

'What sort of strange?'

'He goes off on walks by himself. Spends a lot of time away. He's a bit of a brooder.'

'He seemed rather interesting to me.'

'He is. He's remarkable, actually.'

'I suppose all that going on walks by himself is hard for Kitty,' says Nell.

'Yes, it is a bit.'

'And you talk to her about that.'

Larry goes and stands behind her, taking her in his arms.

'What's all this about?' he says. 'You're not jealous of Kitty, are you?'

'Should I be?' says Nell.

'No. Of course not.'

'Why of course not? She's very pretty. Beautiful, really.'

'Because she's married to my best friend.'

Nell holds herself stiff and upright, not yielding to his embrace.

'I'm not blind, Larry,' she says. 'I saw how you looked at her.'

'For God's sake!' He moves away. 'What's that supposed to mean? You do talk nonsense sometimes, Nell.'

'There, you see,' she says, as if he's proved her point.

'No, I don't see. What am I supposed to see? That I enjoy looking at Kitty? Why wouldn't I? She's an old friend. What am I supposed to do? Glower at her?'

'Why are you getting so worked up about this?'

'Because it's ridiculous! Because it annoys me that you even raise such silliness. You of all people! I thought you'd escaped all that conventional claptrap. You go off with Julius for two weeks and I don't cross-question you about who you've been looking at or who you've been talking to.'

'You can if you want.'

'I don't want. What I love about us is that we trust each other. You said it yourself. We don't put each other in cages.'

Nell says nothing. Larry feels he's proved his point, and is demonstrably right, while at the same time knowing he's in the wrong. As a result he's far more disturbed than he cares to admit.

Nell moves away and lights another cigarette. She stands by the window, smoking, looking out.

'Good old fags,' she says. 'Something to do while we're not talking.'

'Oh, Nell,' says Larry.

'Do you feel hurt?' she says. 'Do you think I'm being unfair to you?'

'Yes, I do,' says Larry.

'You know how I am,' she says. 'I've been the same from the start, haven't I? All I've ever said to you is, don't lie to me.'

'How am I lying to you?'

'I've never asked for promises. I've never tried to tie you down. We're with each other because we love each other. There's no other reason. If you don't want to be with me all you have to do is say so.'

'But I do want to be with you.'

'More than you want to be with Kitty?'

'Yes!' Larry feels helpless rage growing within him. 'Why do you keep going on about Kitty? She's my friend, just like Ed's my friend. Am I not to have friends now? Nothing has ever happened between me and Kitty. First she was Ed's girl, and now she's Ed's wife. That's all there is to it.'

'Why do you keep going on about Kitty, Larry?'

'Me!' He waves his hands in the air with frustration. 'Me! It's you who's been going on about Kitty, not me.'

'Can you guess why?'

'Of course I can guess why. You're jealous of her. But I keep telling you there is nothing between me and Kitty.'

'Still all about Kitty,' says Nell.

'All right! Forget Kitty! No more Kitty! She's not important.'

His chest feels tight. He wants to hit something.

'So what's important, Larry?'

He gets it then, the thing that's driving him wild. It's the soft relentless tone, as if he's a child who's been set a puzzle, and she's the teacher who wants to get him to work out the answer for himself. This has the perverse effect of making him not want to give the approved answer. He's supposed to say, 'You and me, that's what's important.' But it won't come out.

Instead he says, 'It doesn't matter. I've had enough of this conversation. I don't think it's getting us anywhere.'

'So what do you want to do instead?' she says.

'I don't know. Relax. Enjoy being with you. I haven't seen you for two weeks.'

'You want to go to bed?'

'No, I don't mean that. Well, yes, I do. But I mean just relax. Feel good together.'

'I want that too,' says Nell.

'Come over here, then. Give me a kiss.'

She comes to him and they kiss, but he can feel her holding back from him. This, and the kiss, and having her in his arms, fills him with a sudden rush of desire.

'We could go to bed,' he says.

'Would you mind if we didn't?' she says.

'No, of course not.'

But his body minds. The more he knows he can't have her, the more he wants her. The code of good manners sustains him. You don't grab. You wait to be served.

'I'm supposed to be having dinner with somebody,' she says.

'Who?'

'A friend of Julius's called Peter Beaumont. He came to your private view. He's rich.'

'Oh, well then. You'd better have dinner with him.'

'Why don't you come too?'

'Me!'

'I bet you could do with a square meal. I know I could.'

Suddenly it all seems too ridiculous for words. Larry feels the tension melting away.

'You just want the dinner?'

'Of course. He's bound to take us somewhere swish.'

'But he won't want me.'

'If I tell him to, he will.'

Peter Beaumont greets Larry with a soft handshake, a sweet sad smile.

'Nell's told me all about you. I did so admire your work. It's a pleasure to meet you.'

'I do hope you don't mind me tagging along,' says Larry.

'Of course he doesn't mind,' says Nell. 'I've told him you're a starving artist and it's the duty of the wealthy man to support the arts.'

Peter takes them to the Savoy Grill. It's immediately clear that he's a familiar figure here. Larry feels under-dressed and out of place. Nell behaves as though she owns the restaurant.

'I want heaps and heaps of red meat,' she says.

Peter is all too obviously smitten with Nell. From time to time he meets Larry's eyes with a look that says, Isn't she extraordinary! It doesn't seem to occur to him that Larry might be a rival. He orders two bottles of excellent wine, and Larry, not really knowing what's going on, decides to drink as much as possible.

'Lawrence is a genius,' Nell tells Peter. 'You must buy his paintings.'

'Perhaps I could visit your studio,' Peter says to Larry, as if seeking a rare favour.

'I'm afraid Nell is too kind,' says Larry.

She's certainly kind to Peter. She smiles at him, and reaches across the table to touch his hand when wanting to hold his attention, and takes care to turn the conversation towards his concerns.

'Peter has this terrible wife,' she says. 'She treats him in the most vile manner. If he ever touches her, even by accident, she shudders.'

Peter gives Larry his sad smile.

'One of those mistakes one makes,' he says.

'Poor Peter,' says Nell, stroking his hand.

Larry is lost. He has only joined them because it seemed Nell wanted him to be there, to witness that her evening with this male friend is innocent. And yet here she is, acting as if they're lovers.

'Isn't Nell amazing?' Peter says to Larry. 'I tell her she's like a princess in a fairy tale.'

'I'm the prize you get after all that nasty questing,' says Nell.

By the end of the evening Peter is holding Nell's hand in his and Larry is thoroughly miserable.

'Now you must come back to my place for a nightcap,' says Peter.

Even Larry knows when the time has come to go.

'I'll be on my way,' he says. 'Excellent dinner. Do me good to walk it off.'

Nell barely notices that he's leaving.

The walk back to Camberwell through night streets takes a good hour, long enough in the cool air to sober Larry up and leave him hurt and angry. He has no idea what Nell was thinking of when she included him in the dinner, and he has no idea what her relationship is with Peter Beaumont. All he knows is that he has been made to look like a fool.

He half expects Nell to show up at his door later that night, but she never comes. Nor does she make contact the following day. His hurt and anger, feeding on itself, turns into a crazy obsession which stops him from working or thinking about anything else. Then in the evening, there she is.

'Nell! Where have you been?'

'That's not much of a welcome,' she replies.

'I've been going insane!'

'Why? Am I supposed to report to you daily?'

Her blank pretence of not understanding him drives Larry into open rage. He shouts at her, there on the doorstep.

'I don't know what the hell you're doing! I don't know what you want of me! I don't know why you treat me like this! But I'm sick of it. I don't want any more!'

She lets him shout, looking away down the street until he's finished. Then she turns back to him as if everything he's just said is an embarrassing body noise to be overlooked.

'May I come in?'

In his room she turns on him with cold anger.

'Never do that again. Never shout at me in public. What right have you to talk to me like that? You don't own me.'

'Oh, for God's sake, Nell!'

'If you have something to say to me, say it right now.'

'You know I have.'

'I only know what you tell me, Lawrence. I'm not a mind reader.'

'Last night,' says Larry. 'That was humiliating.'

'Humiliating? You ate a very good dinner, if I recall. Peter was extremely pleasant to you. Why was it humiliating?'

'You went off with him at the end.'

'Did you stop me?'

'No, of course not.'

'Why not? Apparently you minded.'

'Of course I minded!' he cries.

'Then why didn't you say so?'

'Oh, come on, Nell. I have my dignity. I'm not going to throw my weight about when a man has just bought me an expensive dinner.'

'So I'm the one who's supposed to throw his generosity back in his face, am I? I'm supposed to say, Sorry, Peter, I'm going home with Lawrence because he's sulking.'

'Why did you ask me last night? What was the point of that? Anybody can see he's in love with you. Why rub my face in that?'

'Maybe I wanted to show you you don't own me.'

'Of course I don't bloody own you!'

'Then what's all this fuss about, Lawrence?'

She's staring at him with those big truth-demanding eyes, and he knows now he's going to have to say something he really means.

'You're going to have my baby,' he says.

'Ah,' she says. 'So that's it.'

'Of course that's it. That's everything.'

She takes out her cigarettes and offers him one, but he shakes his head. Her hands are steady as he lights her cigarette, but his are shaking. She draws the smoke in deep and exhales, turning her face away.

'So if there wasn't a baby, you wouldn't mind about any of it?'

'I don't know,' he says. 'Yes, I'd mind.'

'Do you know something I've realised about you, Lawrence? You never take the physical initiative. You never touch me unless I touch you.'

Larry feels the tightness in his chest returning. Somehow he's got caught in a trap from which there's no escape. Perhaps she means him to touch her now. He feels paralysed.

'Do you realise that?' she says.

'That doesn't matter,' he says. 'That's not the point.'

'Oh,' she says, 'is there a point? Do tell.'

'The point is the baby.'

'What baby?' she says.

'The baby you're going to have. Our baby.'

'There is no baby,' she says. 'Not any more.'

She goes on smoking, barely looking at him.

'What?' he says.

'I had a miscarriage,' says Nell. 'I wasn't going to tell you yet.'

He stares at her, unable to take in what he's just heard.

'You weren't going to tell me?'

'But I have now.'

He struggles to make sense of what's happening.

'Why not tell me?'

'I thought if I didn't tell you,' she says simply, devastatingly, 'you'd go on loving me.'

He gives a sudden gasp.

'Oh, Nell!'

He takes her in his arms and holds her close, tears rising to his eyes.

'Oh, Nell!'

He's overwhelmed by pity and relief and guilt. Once again the future has changed before him, swinging abruptly to send him off in a new direction. Nell reaches out from within his embrace to stub out her cigarette.

'I'm so sorry, Nell. I'm so, so sorry.'

'Are you, darling?'

Her gentle voice is back.

'What happened? When did it happen?'

'Almost two weeks ago now.'

'What about your trip?'

'There wasn't any trip. Don't keep asking me questions, darling. It's been beastly, but I just tell myself it's over now.'

'You poor, poor sweetheart. And there I've been, making it all worse. You should have told me.'

'Well, I've told you now.'

They retreat to the bed, not for sex, but for mutual comfort. They lie there, curled in each other's arms, like babes in the wood. The child that existed for so short a time seems to lie in their arms with them like a ghost, uniting them.

'We can have another,' says Larry, whispering.

'Do you want to?'

'Of course I want to,' he says. 'Don't you?'

'I'm not sure I'm ready yet,' she says. 'Do you mind?'

'No, I don't mind.'

She's wiser than him. When he talks of another baby it's no more than his way of consoling her, and showing her he loves her. For him 'another baby' is an idea, not a reality. But she is the one whose body will carry the child. For her it's more than an emotional gesture.

'I want you so much to be free,' she tells him.

It amazes him how instinctively she understands his workings. Of course the baby placed him under a certain obligation. Hadn't he asked her to marry him? But she knew better than him that this was not a free choice. Now she gives him back his freedom. Her truthfulness and her generosity humble him.

Then he remembers the way she reached across the table at the Savoy Grill to stroke Peter Beaumont's hand, and confusion overtakes him once more. He feels he's being manipulated, but has no idea to what end.

'Sometimes I don't understand what's happening to us,' he says to her.

'It doesn't need to be understood,' she says. 'People either love each other or they don't.'

'I do love you, Nell. I'm sure of that.'

In this moment, lying with her in his arms, released by her promise of freedom, he can say the simple words.

'And I do love you, darling,' she replies.

For a while they stay like this, warmed by each other, silent. The immensity of the information they have exchanged has exhausted them. Then Nell pulls herself up into a sitting position and straightens her clothes.

'I'm going to go now,' she says.

'When will I see you again?'

She gets up off the bed and stretches like a cat. Then she turns to him with a smile.

'Darling Lawrence,' she says. 'You can see me any time you want. But do you know what I think? You're not to be cross with me. I think what you need to do now is have a real, truthful talk with your friend Kitty. Tell her whatever it is you've got to tell her, and hear what she has to say to you. Because until you've done that, I don't think you're really going to be able to love anyone else, not with all of your heart.'

'That's not true,' protests Larry, going pink. 'No, that's wrong. That's not how it is at all. And anyway, even if it was, what's the point? She's married to Ed.'

'Is she happy with Ed?'

Larry stares at Nell in consternation. It's like hearing his own secret thoughts out loud.

'I can't do that, Nell.'

'You're quite a one for not doing things, aren't you, Lawrence? But if you want something, you have to do something about it. It's no good just waiting for it to fall in your lap. If you want Kitty, tell her so, and see what happens. And if it doesn't work out, and you decide it's me you want after all, tell me so, and see what happens.'

She gives him a soft lingering kiss on the mouth before she leaves.

'Don't be such a scaredy-cat, darling. Those that don't ask don't get.'

## 22

Towards the end of January 1947 snow begins to fall over south-east England, and it continues to fall until the land is thickly blanketed. Within two days the roads and railways have become impassable. Larry, visiting River Farm for the weekend, finds himself obliged to stay longer than he intended.

On that first weekend they go out sledging. Heavily wrapped in warm clothes, they cross the silent main road and climb the long diagonal track to the top of Mount Caburn. Ed carries the sledge. Larry holds Pamela's hand, so that he can swing her up out of the deep drifts. Kitty follows behind, only her nose and eyes visible in the bundle of scarves and woolly hats.

The sky is clear as ice. From the top of the ridge they look out over a white world. Their breath makes clouds as they stand, panting from the climb through shin-deep snow, marvelling at the view.

'It's like the whole world is starting again,' says Kitty. 'All young and unwrinkled.'

'Are we to go right to the top?' says Ed. 'I have a tremendous urge to ride the sledge down the front of Caburn.'

'You'll do no such thing,' says Kitty.

The south face of Caburn drops steeply down to the valley, too steep for the shepherds and their sheep to climb. The tracks are all up the gentler sides of the Down.

'Want to sledge!' cries Pammy. 'Want to sledge!'

Even here the slope is of some concern.

'It'll be all right if we run sideways,' says Ed, volunteering to test the ground.

He lays the sledge on the snow and sits on it. He rocks his upper body back and forth, and away he goes. For a few minutes he proceeds sedately across the hillside. Then the sledge tips on a snow-covered ridge and he topples off to one side. The onlookers cheer.

Ed comes trudging back, caked with snow, dragging the sledge. Kitty brushes snow off his hair and eyebrows.

'Why aren't you wearing a hat, you foolish man?'

'Me, me, me!' cries Pammy.

The little girl has her turn, squealing with excitement, Ed loping along beside the sledge on the downhill side, holding the rope. When she in her turn tumbles off he scoops her up out of the snow and sits her back on the sledge and tows it up to the others. The collar of her coat is thick with snow, and there's snow all down her neck, but she's jumping with the excitement of it.

'Your turn, Larry,' says Ed, giving him the rope.

'Me, me, me!' cries Pammy.

'I'll share,' says Larry.

He sits on the sledge, and Pammy sits between his knees, little arms gripping his thighs. Ed gives them a push off. All the way down Pammy carols with joy, and Larry tries with outstretched gloved hands to control their direction and speed. The cold wind on his face stings his cheeks and makes his eyes water. The eager child wriggles and shouts between his legs. The sledge lurches and sways, steadily gathering speed. There are no brakes, no way of stopping, other than tumbling off into the snow.

Then Pammy isn't shouting any more and he realises they're going too fast. The sledge is plunging directly down the slope. The speed is thrilling and frightening. The child's arms cling ever tighter to his thighs. The hill stretches far below, to the snow-covered roofs of the village of Glynde and the carpet of farmland beyond. Larry knows he must bring the sledge ride to a stop, but he lets them ride on for a few moments longer, captivated by the sensation of being out of control. Pammy twists her head round then and he sees the same look in her bright eyes: her first taste of the addictive drug that is danger.

Then he holds her thin body in his arms and tips them both off to one side, to tumble over and over in the deep snow. They come to a stop, dazed and snow-covered but unhurt. He brushes her face clear, and she does the same to him. The sledge too has turned over onto its side and lies just below them.

'You all right, Pammy?'

'More!' she says. 'More!'

He fetches the sledge and they climb back up the hill.

'Don't do that again, Larry,' says Kitty, brushing snow off Pamela. 'You scared me half to death.'

'No, no!' cries the child. 'I want more!'

'You wild man,' says Ed to Larry.

Pamela is allowed to go on the sledge again, but this time with her mother, very slowly, and escorted by Ed and Larry.

'Faster!' she cries. 'I want to go faster!'

This time there's no tumbling off. Descending in a series of hairpin bends they make their way back down to the valley. Once on the road again they walk, and Ed tows the sledge behind him.

Larry walks with Pamela, holding hands.

'Mummy is married to Daddy,' says Pamela. 'So I can be married to you.'

'All right,' says Larry.

'So we can do more fast sledging,' says Pamela.

'Of course.'

'An excellent basis for marriage,' says Ed from behind them.

That night the temperature drops again, and more snow falls. The next day Larry and Ed take shovels and dig a path from the house to the road, hard labour which takes them the whole morning. A tractor has been down the Newhaven road driving a snowplough, but there are no cars or lorries to be seen.

'If this goes on we're going to have to stock up with coal,' says Ed.

The hours shovelling snow warm them and give them an appetite. They head back down the path they've cleared, the shovels shouldered.

'So how's Nell?' says Ed. 'Is she still on the scene?'

'In a way,' says Larry. 'It's been a bit up and down lately. I was supposed to be seeing her when I got back today.'

'This weather's messed up everyone's plans.'

'The annoying thing is she's not on the phone. I suppose I could always ring the gallery.'

'I shouldn't worry. Everything's in chaos. She'll understand.'

'I wish I did,' says Larry.

'Oh,' says Ed with a smile. 'It's like that?'

'Not so long ago I was asking her to marry me. Now I'm not even sure if I'm ever going to see her again.'

'Why wouldn't you see her again?'

'I hardly even know myself,' says Larry. 'She's not like anyone else I've ever known. She lives entirely by her own truth. And that's what she wants me to do.'

'Whatever that means,' says Ed.

'It should be so simple. Say only what you mean. Do only what you want. No games, no pretence, no polite little lies. But what if you don't know what you want?'

'You can't tell people the truth,' says Ed. 'Being civilised is all about covering that stuff up.'

'Do you really think that?' says Larry.

'Don't you?'

'I suppose I think that if you really love someone, and they really love you, you can tell them everything.'

'That's because deep down you believe that people are good.'

'And you believe people are bad.'

'Not exactly,' says Ed. 'I believe we're alone.'

He gives a laugh, and punches Larry on the arm.

'Here you are, my oldest friend, and I'm telling you I'm alone. What an ungrateful dog of a fellow I must be.'

'You may be right even so,' says Larry quietly.

'Your Nell sounds to me like she's a bit of a handful.'

'But Ed,' says Larry, pursuing his own thoughts, 'you don't feel alone with Kitty, do you?'

'Now there's a question.'

'Sorry. Forget I said it.'

'No,' says Ed. 'It's a fair question. She's my wife, and I love her.'

He thinks it over as they come to a stop in the snowy farmyard.

'There are moments when I'm with Kitty, when I'm holding her in my arms, or when I'm watching her sleeping, when I go quiet. Very still moments. I don't feel alone then.'

Larry kicks the snow, making furrows in the virgin whiteness.

'But they don't last.'

'No. They don't last.'

'You shouldn't be away so much, Ed. It's hard on Kitty. And on Pammy.'

'I know.' He speaks humbly, accepting the rebuke. 'Unlikely as it may seem, I do my best.'

'Well,' says Larry, 'there'll be no trips to France in this.'

They go into the house, stamping the snow off their boots. Kitty and Pamela are making lunch.

'Daddy's back,' says Kitty. 'We can eat.'

'And Larry,' says Pamela. 'He's back too.'

The early excitement of the snow soon wears off, as the bitter cold grips the land. The electricity cuts out for hours at a time, without warning, plunging the house into a blackout as complete as any in wartime. For three nights running they eat their supper and go to bed by candlelight. Then the water pipes freeze, and it's no longer possible to wash, or go to the lavatory. They take to using potties, which Ed removes and empties in some secret place onto the hard snow. The wireless news tells them of the crisis that has overtaken the nation. Railway wagons can't move. Ships can't bring in supplies. Food rations are cut lower even than the worst years of the war. In early February the government announces there will be five hours of planned electricity cuts a day, three in the morning and two in the afternoon.

When the farmhouse supply of both coal and firewood runs out, Kitty turns for help to Louisa. Ed and Larry plot various ways of moving loads of fuel across the village, but in the end come up with a simpler solution. They move themselves. Edenfield Place is well stocked with coal, and by shutting up two-thirds of the house George reckons they can last a good six weeks. This terrible weather can't possibly go on to the end of March.

So Ed and Kitty return to the room in Edenfield Place in which they began their married life, and Pamela to her little bed in the adjoining dressing room, and Larry to the guest room down the corridor. Fires are kept burning in the Oak Room and the morning room, while the far larger drawing room and library are left to the winter cold. The butler's pantry, the domain of Mr Lott the butler, and the kitchen, the domain of his wife, Mrs Lott the cook, are also kept warm. Three of the four great boilers are switched off. Oil lamps stand in readiness for the hours when the electricity cuts out.

Due to the more modern heating system of the house, the water pipes are still running in the family quarters, and three lavatories are usable. Ed's potty-emptying duties are suspended.

'I'm rather sorry, really,' he says. 'I was looking forward to the day the snow melts, and all round the houses there'd be revealed the waste matter of the mid-twentieth century.'

The hard winter locks them all in the big house on top of one another, and Larry finds no opportunity to talk to Kitty alone. He originally expected to visit for a weekend only, and so has not brought his paints and brushes. Now as his stay enters its third week and there's no sign of a thaw, he passes much of his time huddled by the Oak Room fire, rereading *War and Peace*. When he finishes the first volume, Kitty picks it up, and begins to read behind him. This reignites their old conversation about good characters in books, and whether they can ever be attractive. The character in question is Pierre Bezukhov.

'But he's so fat,' says Kitty, 'and he's so clumsy, and he's so naive.' She's especially outraged by his marriage to the beautiful but cold Helene. 'All because of her bosom. It's ridiculous.'

'I promise you he gets better,' says Larry. 'You'll learn to love him.'

'I love Prince André.'

'Of course you do.'

'And you love Natasha.'

'I adore Natasha. From the moment she runs into the grown-ups' party and can't stop laughing. But do you know an odd thing? Tolstoy quite clearly tells us that she's not specially pretty. But when I imagine her, she's tremendously attractive.'

'Of course she's pretty!'

'Look.' He takes the volume from her and finds the page in question. '"This black-eyed, wide-mouthed girl, *not pretty* but full of life".'

'Oh, but she's still only a child,' says Kitty. 'She's only thirteen. She grows up to be beautiful.'

February is half gone, and the wireless news is that the miners in South Wales are to work full shifts even on Sundays. Ships have finally been able to dock with cargoes of coal. There are no signs of a thaw, but the trains are running once more, and everyone is telling everyone else that the thaw must come soon.

Kitty and Larry find themselves alone on either side of the Oak Room fire. Larry puts his bookmark in his place, closes his book, and lays it down.

'I shall go back to London tomorrow,' he says. 'I've been gone too long.'

'But we haven't had a chance to talk,' Kitty says. 'Not properly.'

She too lays down her book.

'I like having you here so much, Larry,' she says. 'I shall hate it when you go.'

'You know I'll always come back.'

'Will you? Always?'

'That's what friends do.'

Kitty looks at him, only half smiling.

'It's not much of a word, is it?' she says. '*Friend*. There should be a better word. *Friend* sounds so unimportant, someone you chat to at parties. You're more than that for me.'

'You too,' says Larry.

'I shan't like it when you marry, you know. Whoever it is. But of course you must. I'm not so selfish as not to see that.'

'The trouble is,' says Larry, 'I can't help comparing every girl I meet to you.'

'Oh, well. That shouldn't be too much of a problem. There are so many girls who are far more thrilling than me.'

'I have yet to meet one.'

She holds his gaze, not pretending she doesn't understand.

'Just tell me you're happy,' he says.

'Why ask me that? You know I'm not happy.'

'Can't anything be done?'

'No,' she says. 'I've thought about it so much. I've decided this is my task in life. Yes, I know how terrible that sounds, like some grim duty. I don't mean it that way. Do you remember saying to me once, Don't you want to do something noble and fine with your life? Well, I do. I love Ed, I'll never hurt him or be disloyal to him. This is just the thing I have to do. Being happy or unhappy doesn't matter any more.'

'Oh, Kitty.'

'Please don't pity me. I can't bear it.'

'It's not pity. I don't know what it is. Regret. Anger. It's all such a waste. You don't deserve this.'

'Why should I get a happier life than anyone else?'

'It could have been so different. That's what I can't bear.'

'Why think that way?' she says gently. 'I made my choice. I chose Ed. I chose him knowing there was a sadness in him. Maybe I chose him because of that. And I do love him.'

'Isn't there room in our lives to love more than one person?'

'Of course. But why think that way? There's nothing to be done.'

'Kitty— '

'No, please. Don't make me say anything more. I mustn't be selfish and greedy. You're more than a friend to me, Larry. But I mustn't hold on to you. What I want more than anything is for you to find someone who makes you happy. Then all I ask is that she lets you go on being my friend. I couldn't bear to lose you altogether. Promise me you'll always be my friend.'

'Even though it's not much of a word.'

'Even though.'

'Do friends love each other, Kitty?'

'Yes,' she says, her eyes on him. 'They love each other very much.'

'Then I promise.'

That same day Kitty sings to them, accompanying herself on the piano in the morning room. She sings 'The Ash Grove' and 'Drink To Me Only With Thine Eyes'.

> The thirst that from the soul doth rise
> Doth ask a drink divine . . .

Larry's eyes never leave her face as she sings. She plays by ear, and sings from memory, a slight frown of concentration on her face.

Then at Ed's request she sings 'The Water is Wide'.

> A ship there is
> And she sails the seas.
> She's laden deep
> As deep can be;
> But not so deep
> As the love I'm in,
> And I know not if
> I sink or swim.

Little Pamela is unimpressed by the sad songs and agitates for 'Little Brown Jug'.

> Ha ha ha!
> You and me
> Little brown jug
> Don't I love thee!

The following morning Larry walks the snowy road into Lewes, her sweet voice still sounding in his memory, her bright eyes reaching towards him across the piano.

# 23

London is quiet and mostly empty, the snow that lines the streets now a dirty shade of grey-brown. Occasional taxis clatter by over the lumps of ice. People passing on the pavements, heavily wrapped in overcoats, hats pulled low over their ears, keep their heads down to avoid stumbling on the ridged snow. All business seems to have closed down. Every day now like a Sunday in winter.

Larry returns to his room in Camberwell and lights the gas fire. It burns at low pressure, taking a long time to warm the chill air. Everything is cold to his touch, the covers on his bed, his books, his paints. He looks at the canvas he had begun before going to Sussex, and sees at once that it has no life in it. His room too, despite his return, has no life in it.

Suddenly he wants very much to see Nell.

He phones Weingard's gallery and a female voice answers. The gallery is closed. No, she doesn't know where Nell is. He writes a note to her, telling her he's back, and walks up the road to the post office on Church Street to send it. From there he goes on to the pub on the corner. It's a Monday and early for the evening crowd. The Hermit's Rest is eerily quiet. He sits at a table close to the meagre fire and works away slowly at a pint of stout. He thinks about Nell.

Ever since his last talk with Kitty he's been thinking new thoughts about his future. His feelings haven't changed. But he sees more clearly now that he must take active steps to make a life without Kitty, or he'll doom himself to live a life alone. Once again he marvels at Nell's insight. It seems she knows him better than he knows himself. She accuses him of never taking the initiative, and she's right. For too long he's allowed events outside his control to determine his course. The time has come to take charge of his own life.

He interrogates himself, sitting alone in the pub. Do I want to marry Nell? He recalls her elusiveness, her moodiness, her unpredictability, and he trembles. What sort of life would that be? But then he thinks of never seeing her again and he almost cries out loud, 'No! Don't leave me!', so powerful is the longing to hold her in his arms.

What is the gravest charge he has to bring against her? That she spends time with other men. That she leads them on to love her. In other words, that he does not possess her exclusive love. But what right has he to her exclusive love, when he makes no promise on his side? See it from her point of view: she has made herself over to him, body and soul, while he has kept much of himself apart.

But I asked her to marry me.

Ah, she saw through that. She knows me better than I know myself. She saw that I was doing my duty because of the baby. She puts no trust in duty. She requires true love.

Thinking this makes him admire her, and admiring her he

feels he does love her after all. It's just a matter of letting go whatever last inhibition holds him back. Offer her all the love of which he's capable and she'll give him back love fourfold, and his fears will melt away.

What a rare creature she is! A child of truth. With her in his life there'll be no complacency, and no idling. His days will be vivid and his nights will be warm. He can see her naked body now, rosy in the gaslight, and feels his body's gratitude to her tingling in his veins. Is this such a small thing? Some would say it's the basis of everything. Find happiness with each other in bed and love will never die.

His beer finished, his spirits excited by his train of thought, he feels the need of companionship. With luck Nell will get his note tomorrow and be with him by the end of the day. He has much to say to her. But between now and then he does not want to be alone. He could walk into Kensington and call on his father. Then he has a better idea. He will call on Tony Armitage.

Armitage has a studio in Valmar Road, on the other side of Denmark Hill. There's a fair chance he'll be in. Larry buttons his overcoat up to his chin and sets out into the snowy streets once more. Valmar Road isn't far, but it's an awkward place to find. A distant church clock is chiming seven as he rings the top bell at the street door.

A window opens above. Armitage's head pokes out.

'Who's that?'

'Larry,' says Larry.

'Bloody hell!' exclaims Armitage. Then, 'I'll come down.'

He lets Larry in the front door.

'I've not been outside for a week,' he says. 'Too bloody cold.'

Larry follows him up several flights of bare stairs to the rooms in the roof.

'I've got nothing to eat,' says Armitage. 'There may be some brandy left.'

His living quarters consist of one sizeable room with a big north-facing window, which is his studio, his kitchen, and his washroom, a single butler sink serving all these purposes; beyond, a closed door leads to a small bedroom. The electric light bulb that illuminates the studio is either very low-powered or the electricity is weak. In its grudging light Larry sees a chaotic array of paintings, most of them unfinished.

'I lose heart,' says Armitage. 'I know exactly what it is I mean to do, and then I see what I've actually done, and I lose heart.'

He doesn't ask Larry why he's come. He offers him brandy in a teacup. Larry looks round the canvases.

'But your work is so good,' he says.

He means it. Even in this poor light he can see that his friend's paintings are exploding with life. As he admires them, he feels with deep shock the contrast with his own work. Somehow this has never been as apparent to him before. Over the last two years his work has become accomplished, but looking at Armitage's pictures, he knows with a terrible certainty that he will never be a true artist. He has enough understanding of technique to see how Armitage achieves his effects, while at the same time knowing that this is so much more than technique. In his portraits particularly, he has the gift of expressing the fine complexity of life itself.

'This is so good,' he says again. 'You're good, Tony.'

'I'm better than good,' says Armitage. 'I'm the real thing. Which is why I drive myself crazy. All this' – he gestures round the studio – 'this is nothing. One day I'll show you what I can do.'

Larry comes upon two quite small sketches of Nell.

'There's Nell,' he says. In one of them she's looking towards the artist but past him, playing her unreachable game. 'That's so Nell.'

He realises now why he's come. He wants to talk to someone about Nell.

'She never sits still for long enough,' says Armitage. 'Also her skin's too smooth. I like wrinkles.'

'I think I might be in love with her,' says Larry.

'Oh, everyone's in love with Nell,' says Armitage. 'That's her function in life. She's a muse.'

'I don't think she wants to be a muse.'

'Of course she does. Why else does she hang around artists? You get girls like that.'

Larry laughs. Tony Armitage, barely twenty-one years old, his wild curls serving only to emphasise his boyish face, makes an unconvincing bohemian roué.

'How on earth do you know? You've only just left school.'

'It's nothing to do with age. I was seven when I found out I had talent. I was fifteen when I knew I would be one of the greats. Oh, don't get me wrong. I know all this is poor prentice work. But give me five more years, and you won't be laughing.'

'I'm not laughing at your work, Tony,' Larry says. 'I'm in awe of your work. But I'm not sure I'm quite ready to see you as a fount of wisdom on the opposite sex.'

'Oh, girls.' He speaks dismissively, evidently not very interested.

'Don't you care for girls?'

'Yes, in their way. Up to a point. One has to eat and so forth.'

Larry can't help laughing again. But he's impressed by the young man's invincible conviction of his own worth. It could be the groundless arrogance of youth, but on the whole Larry is inclined to take it at face value; all too aware that he lacks such self-belief himself.

'I'm afraid I get myself into much more of a mess with girls than you seem to,' he says. 'With Nell, anyway.' Then on an impulse he reveals more. 'Did she tell you I asked her to marry me?'

'No.' He seems surprised. 'Why?'

'Because I wanted to marry her. And also because she was pregnant.'

'Nell told you she was pregnant?'

'She isn't any more. She had a miscarriage. I expect I shouldn't be telling you this. But she's fine now.'

'Nell told you she had a miscarriage?'

'Yes.'

It strikes Larry now that Armitage is looking at him in an odd way.

'And you believed her?' he says.

'Yes,' says Larry. 'I know Nell's got her own strange ways, but the one thing she'd never do is tell a lie. She's got an obsession with truthfulness.'

Armitage stares at Larry. Then he lets out a harsh cackle of laughter. Larry frowns, annoyed.

'Nell never tell a lie!' says Armitage. 'She does nothing but lie.'

'I'm sorry,' says Larry. 'I don't think you know her as I do.'

'But Larry,' says Armitage. 'Telling you she's pregnant! It's the oldest trick in the book.'

He falls to laughing again.

'A trick to achieve what, precisely?'

Larry's voice has gone cold.

'To get you to marry her, of course.'

'I offered. She declined.'

This seems to Larry to be conclusive proof of Nell's integrity. To his surprise Armitage takes it in his stride.

'Oh, she's not stupid, our Nell. She must've picked up that you weren't a solid enough bet.'

'I'm sorry, Tony. I don't see things your way, that's all. I shouldn't have spoken about private matters.'

'Private? She tried the pregnancy trick on Peter Beaumont too, you know?'

Now it's Larry's turn to stare.

'Peter fell for it hook, line and sinker. But she decided to keep him in reserve. For a rainy day, as she puts it.'

'I don't understand.'

Larry's voice has become quiet. Armitage realises for the first time that this is no laughing matter.

'Didn't you know?' he says.

'Apparently not.'

'She's not a bad girl. She's a wonderful girl, really. But she's penniless. She has to look out for herself.'

'She told Peter Beaumont it was his baby?'

'Well, yes.'

Larry feels tired and confused. He passes one hand over his brow. He finds he's sweating.

'So whose baby was it?'

Armitage pours Larry the last of the brandy, and presses the teacup on him.

'There was no baby, Larry.'

'No baby?'

'No pregnancy. No miscarriage.'

'Are you sure?'

'Well, no one can ever be sure of anything with Nell. But I'm pretty sure. She tried it on me, but I just laughed.'

'You?'

Larry drinks the brandy, draining the cup.

'Look, old man,' says Armitage, 'I can see this has all rather hit you for six. Were you really serious about Nell?'

'Yes,' says Larry. 'I think I was.'

'I begin to see I've struck a bit of a wrong note.'

Larry can't reply. He's experiencing hot flushes of shame, beneath which far deeper griefs are waiting their turn.

'I'm very fond of Nell too,' says Armitage, trying clumsily to make amends. 'I suppose I don't mind her looking out for herself, because I do it too. We're all getting by as best we can.'

'But to lie to me.' Larry is still scarcely able to believe it. 'The first thing she ever said to me was, We tell each other the truth. She was always going on about the truth.'

'That's how it works, isn't it?' says Armitage. 'Thieves lock up their valuables. Cheats tell you the rules of the game.'

'Dear God,' says Larry. 'I feel so stupid.'

'Did you have a good time with her?'

'Yes,' says Larry with a sigh.

'Nothing stupid about that.'

Larry shakes his head, and looks round the room. There are all Armitage's works. There are the two sketches of Nell.

'You see more clearly than me, Tony,' he says. 'That's why you're a better artist.'

'Oh, come on. Don't start doing yourself down.'

'No, it's true. People talk about talent as if it's a gift of the gods, like being beautiful. But I think it's just as much to do with character. You've got the right character, Tony, and I haven't. You see clearly, and you believe in yourself. You're right, you will be one of the greats.'

'And you too, Larry. Why not?'

Larry turns from the power of the paintings to the boy who has painted them.

'You've seen my work,' he says. 'You know I'll never be like you.'

'Why shouldn't you be?' says Armitage. But Larry sees it in his eyes. He's not Nell. He can't look you in the face and lie.

'Thanks for the brandy,' Larry says. 'And thanks for the home truths. Not much fun, but I needed to know. Now I'm going to go off and sort myself out.'

Armitage sees him down to the street. Outside the street lights have gone off, and the only light on the icy pavements is the soft spill from curtained windows. Larry walks back to his room, oblivious to the cold. He's ashamed, and hurt, and angry, and lost.

When he gets back to his room he collects up all his paintings and bundles them in a blanket from his bed. There are over thirty works, mostly quite small, but one or two are an awkward size. He carries the bundle out into the street, and up the Grove to Church Street. He has some dim notion of walking all the way to the river, but a cab passes, and he hails it. The cab drops him at the southern end of Waterloo Bridge. He carries his bundle to the middle of the bridge, and unwraps it by the railings. Then one by one he throws his paintings into the river, and watches them slowly carried away downstream.

# 24

Larry lies awake in bed, cold even beneath all the blankets he possesses, and both his outer coats. He expects to pass the long night without sleep, dulled by dread, not wanting the new day to come, bringing with it the empty failure that is now his life. But in the small hours his body surrenders, and when he next opens his eyes there is light at his curtains.

Curtains he drew closed on that first afternoon Nell came to his room and undressed for him and lay in his arms. Light that has fallen on canvases that have held him breathless with concentration for hours on end. All this now gone: all this a stupidity, a vanity, a mistake. How is it possible to lose so much and still go on? Go on where?

At such times Larry has only one recourse. Just as he prayed when his mother died; just as he prayed when some small crisis at boarding school, great to him, left him friendless and alone; so now he turns to the familiar God of his childhood for kindness, and the comfort that lies in the prospect of eternity.

God, my God, God of my fathers, he prays. Show me what it is you want of me. Tell me where I'm to go, and what I'm to do. I have no will of my own any more. Your will be done, if only I can know it. Save me from myself. Teach me how to forget myself. I will serve only you.

How little, how ridiculous, his own existence now seems to him. Like a spoiled child he has strutted about, imagining that all eyes are on him, that the world has been made to gratify his desires. And all the time he has been a little squeaking nothing.

Driven from his bitter room by the need to escape himself and the memory of himself, he walks the dirty snow of London's streets, on and on, wanting only to wear himself out. In this way he trudges down the bombed canyon of Victoria Street to Westminster Cathedral. He has been here before, of course, with his father, to see the new mosaics in the Lady Chapel, and once, when he was ten, to Easter midnight Mass. He remembers the immensity of the nave, and its darkness. It's this darkness he now seeks, where he can become invisible, and his shame be forgotten.

On this winter Tuesday, approaching midday, the cathedral is virtually empty. Candles burn before the high altar, on the votive rack, but the electric lights are turned off. The massive walls of bare brick, one day to be made glorious with golden mosaic, reach up into the vaulted darkness on either side, as stern as a prison. He remains near the back of the nave, feeling neither the wish nor the right to approach the high altar. When some others enter from the street he withdraws into a side chapel, preferring not to be seen even by strangers.

In the side chapel he kneels, and rests his elbows on the chair back in front, and stares unseeingly at the small chapel altar and the decorated panel above it. Two saints gaze back at him, both unsmilingly secure in the truth they have to offer. One is a pope, signified by the triple golden crown; the other a monk, with tonsure and humble robe. Like generals of a victorious army, they admit no doubt in the justice of their war. The pope has one hand raised, one finger pointing skyward, invoking the Almighty God he represents, whose power and authority flow through him.

Such massive certainty. And yet popes and saints must have known what he, Larry, now knows. How little we are, how ridiculous, how lost, in the eye of eternity.

To his irritation the strangers now follow him into the side chapel. A man of his own age and a younger woman. The woman is slender, dressed simply but elegantly. Looking up he catches a glimpse of her face, and it seems to him he's seen it before: the pure line of the cheek, the mouth that curves without smiling, the blue-grey eyes. They stand before the altar, speaking in whispers so as not to disturb him in his prayers.

'There he is,' says the man. 'That's Gregory the Great.'

Larry realises then that the pope in the altarpiece is the same St Gregory who presides over Downside Abbey and School; and that the tall balding man in the chapel is his old schoolfellow Rupert Blundell.

'Rupert, is that you?'

The man turns round and peers at him over his bony nose.

'Good God! Larry!'

Larry rises and they shake hands. Rupert introduces the girl, who turns out to be his sister Geraldine. Looking at her directly now, Larry remembers where he has seen her before. She has a little of the look of Primavera, the goddess of spring, in the Botticelli painting.

'Larry and I were at Downside together,' Rupert tells her,

'and then we were both in Combined Ops.' To Larry he says, 'We've been on a buying spree at the army and navy stores. Fancy bumping into you here. Though I suppose it's not so odd, given that we're both Old Gregorians.'

'That's enough, Rupert,' says Geraldine. 'Can't you see we're interrupting your friend's prayers?'

'Oh, I'm done,' says Larry. 'If prayers can ever be said to be done.'

'Do you make a habit of this?' says Rupert, gesturing round the chapel.

'Not at all,' says Larry. 'I've not been in here for years.'

'Me neither,' says Rupert. 'It's hideous, isn't it? Of course I know it's not finished. But it seems all wrong to me, building a cathedral out of red brick.'

'And all stripy, like a cake,' says Larry.

Geraldine smiles at that.

'To be fair, I think it's supposed to be Byzantine,' says Rupert. 'Do you approve of it, as an artist?'

'Oh, are you an artist?' says Geraldine, opening her eyes wide.

'I was,' says Larry. 'Not any more.'

Rupert is surprised to hear this.

'I'd got the idea you were pretty set on it.'

'You know how it goes,' says Larry. 'Time goes by. You move on.'

'So what line are you in now?' says Rupert.

'Just looking about,' says Larry.

'Nothing fixed?'

'Not as yet.'

They walk out of the chapel and across the nave to the exit. The light beyond the doors is a bright pearl-grey.

'Guess where I'm off to,' says Rupert. 'India.'

'Oh?' says Larry politely, not interested.

'I'm back with Dickie Mountbatten. He's been given the viceroy job. He's being sent out there to wind up the Empire.'

'At least it'll get you away from this winter,' says Larry.

'You know Dickie thinks the world of you,' says Rupert. 'Ever since you volunteered for the Dieppe show.'

'Not very bright of me, as it turned out.'

'Look here, Larry. Why don't you come with us?'

He's come to a standstill in the narthex. The cold air from the outer doors ruffles their coats. He's looking at Larry as if he's serious.

'To India?'

'Yes. Dickie's been told he can hire all the staff he likes. Alan Campbell-Johnson's coming, and Ronnie Brockman, and George Nicholls. There'll be a lot of the old crowd there.'

'But why would he want me? What would I do?'

'Oh, it's going to be a devil of a posting, don't you worry about that. More work than any of us can handle. The great thing is, Dickie says, to surround yourself with good men. And you know what, Larry? We'll see history in the making. It may not be what you call glorious, but it'll be unforgettable.'

The proposal is so far-fetched that Larry wants to laugh. But at the same time the prospect Rupert conjures up fills him with excitement. To go far away, to a new world, with new concerns. To learn fast and work hard and forget the past. To leave behind in the endless winter that is England the fool who thought he was an artist, and thought he was loved by Nell. To start again, and be someone new.

'Do you really think Dickie would have me?'

'Yes, I do. It's chaos, to be honest, the whole shooting match. We're scheduled to go east in a month, and they're still arguing over the timetable for independence, or even if it's to be called independence. Winston and the Tories won't hear of anything with that name, and of course the nationalist leaders out there won't accept anything less.'

'I'm getting cold, Rupert,' says Geraldine.

'Yes, right, we're on our way.' To Larry, 'Do you want me to put in a word?'

'How long would it be for?'

'Six months minimum. Current target is to get us out by June next year.'

'Sounds like it would be quite an experience.'

'Good for you. Let me have your number, and stand by for a call.'

They exchange phone numbers, and Rupert and Geraldine hurry out into the street. Larry lingers for a little while in the big dark church, so that he can say thank you. It seems to him his prayer has been answered.

Two days later Larry presents himself in his only good suit at Brook House on Park Lane, the mansion that became Mountbatten's London base on his marriage to the heiress Edwina Ashley. Rupert Blundell is waiting for him in the immense lobby.

'Looking good,' he says. 'He's got someone with him, but he says you're to hang on.'

He leads Larry up the wide curving staircase to a first-floor reception room.

'Do you mind if I abandon you? We've got a sort of staff pow-wow coming up. The old man knows you're here.'

'No, no. Off you go.'

Left to himself, Larry feels out of place in the grandeur and the aura of power of his surroundings. He goes to the wide window and stands gazing out at the bare trees and grey snow of Hyde Park. He tries to imagine India, a muddle of images from Kipling's stories and models of the Taj Mahal and newsreels of Gandhi in his loincloth. Strange to think that this little frozen island should govern a faraway continent where the hot sun is, presumably, shining even now.

Rapid footsteps outside and in bursts Mountbatten, bringing with him a wave of energy and goodwill.

'Cornford!' he cries. 'This is marvellous news! Will you join us?'

'If you'll have me, sir.'

'I need all the good men I can find. It's going to be what they call a challenge.'

He sits Larry down before him and pins him with his handsome boyish gaze.

'Probably best to get you back into uniform,' he says. 'They go for that sort of thing out there. What rank did you end on?'

'Captain, sir.'

'Pity it has to be army. There, the terrible snobbery of a navy man. You'll just have to forgive me.'

He runs through the team he's assembling, and the nature of the challenges they face, speaking briskly, even bluntly.

'Our job is to get us out without it looking like a scuttle, and without leaving too unholy a mess behind. Not a pretty job, when you look at it in the cold light of day. Not a job I wanted at all, to be honest. But one does one's duty. And I think both Edwina and I need to get out of London.'

At this point Lady Mountbatten herself looks into the room.

'Just on my way out, darling,' she says.

Mountbatten introduces Larry.

'His grandfather was the banana king,' he says. 'Larry was in Combined Ops with me.'

Edwina Mountbatten gives Larry a sharp appraising look, and a quick smile.

'That was a shambles, as far as I can tell.'

She goes again.

'The most remarkable woman in the world,' says Mountbatten. 'I'll tell you what. Let me show you something.'

He strides out of the room and up the stairs. Larry hurries to keep up.

'My wife knows all I've ever really wanted is to be at sea. I worship the navy. You can keep all this viceroy nonsense. Just give me command of a capital ship and I'm a happy man.'

He leads Larry through a door into a suite at the back of the fourth floor. The walls and ceilings are white enamel, criss-crossed by pipes and cables. At one end is a ship's bunk, with a brass rail. On one side there are three portholes. The entire illusion is that they have entered the captain's cabin on a man-of-war.

Mountbatten looks happily at Larry's amazed face.

'Edwina had this made for me.'

On one side there stands a dressmaker's dummy wearing an admiral's uniform, complete with decorations.

'My father's uniform,' says Mountbatten. 'Prince Louis, who your grandfather wrote to *The Times* about. So you see, I don't forget.'

As they descend the stairs again he says, 'Speaking of not forgetting, and of what my wife calls a shambles, I've not forgotten Dieppe. I don't expect you have, either.'

'I'll never forget that day, sir.'

'Nor I. We did all we could, but I shall always have it on my conscience. What's done is done. All any of us can do is try to do better next time.'

At the bottom of the stairs an anxious group of staff members wait for him.

'Oh, Lord,' says Mountbatten. 'Is it time already?'

He turns and shakes Larry's hand.

'Welcome aboard,' he says. And with that he strides away, followed by his staff.

In the short period between his interview with Mountbatten and his departure for India, Larry sees no one. He writes his father a short letter to say he's leaving, implying that his trip to India is a chance opportunity too good to be missed. He says nothing about his abandoned ambition to be an artist. His father's support and generosity are now a reproach to him. He writes a second short letter, similarly reticent, to Ed and Kitty. He has heard nothing from Nell. He presumes that by now she's been alerted by Tony Armitage, and is keeping out of his way. He makes no attempt to contact her.

# 25

'It's like being back in the bloody Oflag,' says Ed, staring out at the falling snow. 'This winter's gone on longer than the bloody war.'

Kitty, still in bed, does not reply. She doesn't want to get up because the bedroom is so cold. She doesn't reply because she knows there's no point. These days Ed is always in a foul mood until he's got some breakfast inside him. Until he's got a drink or two inside him, to be precise.

Pamela comes in and scampers across the cold floor to jump into bed beside her mother.

'You're frozen!' exclaims Kitty, hugging her close.

'Snowing again,' says Pamela. 'Let's stay in bed.'

'See you downstairs,' says Ed, and off he goes.

Kitty lies in bed with her child in her arms, struggling with feelings of hurt and anger. At night in bed he can be so loving, but each day, when morning comes, it's as if she loses him all over again. Why must life be so hard for him? Can't he at least greet his own daughter? Why does he say it's like being in the prisoner-of-war camp when he's got her and Pammy with him?

The winter has been endless, but it's the same for all of them. He behaves as if he's been specially singled out by fate.

By the time she and Pamela are downstairs he's outside, fetching in firewood from the stack by the gun room. There's no need for him to do this, old John Hunter is kept on for jobs like this, or one of the outside men can do it. But Ed needs reasons to be up and out. He needs reasons to be away.

This is what hurts Kitty most. Yes, this is a hard time, but it's also a time when they're together. This could be such a precious time. And the worst of it is, it feels like it must be her fault. She's not making him happy.

'What are we going to do today, Mummy?' says Pamela.

'I don't know, darling. Shall we do some more reading?'

'I hate reading.'

She's not yet four years old, there's no hurry. And you can't really call it lessons. All Kitty has been doing is reading her *The Tale of Tom Kitten*, following the words on the page with her finger. And however much Pamela pretends not to like it, she has clearly been listening. The other day Kitty heard her say to Mrs Lott the cook, 'I am affronted,' just like Mrs Tabitha Twitchit in the book.

Pamela is an outdoors creature, like her father. But outdoors has become such hard work. So many clothes to put on, and just walking to the lake is such a labour in the snow, and the lake itself is frozen over and dangerous. Pamela wants to go on it because it looks just like the rest of the park now, all flat and smooth and white. She refuses to believe there's ice under the snow, and water under the ice, and she might fall through and freeze and drown. Or maybe she does believe it but still wants to go on the ice, because she sees how it frightens and angers her mother. Why is she like that?

Louisa comes down, blinking and yawning.

'Why is Ed doing the logs?' she says. 'That's John Hunter's job.'

'I've no idea,' says Kitty. 'I suppose he just wants to keep busy.'

'George has decided to rearrange all the books in the library,' says Louisa. 'Maybe Ed could help him with that.'

'Daddy hates reading,' says Pamela.

'That's nonsense, darling,' says Kitty.

'I wouldn't say George exactly *reads* his books,' says Louisa. 'But he loves collecting them. And he loves rearranging them.'

Later Ed takes Pamela out into the park and they draw patterns in the snow with sticks, and the falling snow obliterates them, along with the prints of their footsteps.

At lunch Ed calls for beer.

'A good bracing bitter,' he says.

Mr Lott taps the barrel in the cellar. Ed drinks all of a pint tankard and calls for more, and then retreats to the billiard room.

'I wish he wouldn't drink so much,' says Kitty. 'Can't you tell Lott not to serve him?'

'Awkward,' says George. 'One doesn't want to appear to be telling a fellow how to live his life.'

'You have to do it, Kitty,' says Louisa.

The problem is that Ed's drinking is in its way quite controlled. He never becomes loud and abusive. He just becomes more remote. By the end of the evening, when he's moved on to Scotch, it's as if he isn't there at all. He goes about slowly, and looks without seeing. At such times Kitty is possessed by a frightening rage that makes her want to hit him, and hurt him, so that he cries out in pain. Anything to make him see her.

Pamela has gone out with Betsy the scullery maid to search for eggs. The hens have taken to laying in odd places, in the storerooms and the workshop, which being close to the boilers share some of their heat. Pamela likes Betsy and always does whatever Betsy tells her, which puzzled Kitty until she asked about it.

'Why are you so good with Betsy?'

'Because I don't have to be,' said Pamela.

Sometimes she frightens Kitty, she seems so grown-up. How can a four-year-old be so self-possessed?

Kitty goes to the billiard room to talk to Ed. The room is unheated, with a handsome west-facing window opposite the great but empty fireplace, and dormer windows in the high beamed roof. Ed is leaning over the billiard table, his cue reached out to attempt a tricky shot. A half-empty glass of Scotch stands on the shelf beside the scoreboard.

'You should have a fire if you're going to be in here,' Kitty says.

'Waste of fuel,' says Ed, not turning to look at her.

He takes his shot and misses.

'Damn.'

She watches him shamble round the billiard table, eyes on the balls, and realises he's already very drunk.

'I wish you wouldn't, Ed,' she says softly.

'Wouldn't what?'

'Drink so much.'

'No harm in it,' he says. 'Keeps me quiet.'

'I don't want you to be quiet,' she says. 'Not like this.'

'Well, I'm very sorry to hear that,' he says, speaking slowly and heavily. 'But there's not much I can do about it.'

He lines up his next shot.

'Of course there is.' She can feel herself digging her fingernails into the palms of her hands. 'You could if you tried.'

'Ah, if I tried. Yes, I could do anything if I tried.'

This is what maddens her when he's drunk. This slow hazy way he has of not taking anything in.

'Please, Eddy.' She's aware her voice has risen. 'For me.'

He takes his shot. The billiard balls crack sharply in the chill air.

'Please will you do it for me,' she says again.

He straightens himself up and turns to look at her.

'I'd do anything for you,' he says. 'What is it I'm to do?'

'I just want you not to drink so much.'

'Right, then,' he says. 'That's easy. I won't drink so much. What else?'

'That's all.'

'You wouldn't like me to be a better husband? A better father? A better human being?'

'No— '

But something has come over him that she's never seen before: a darkness contorts his face, and all at once he's raising his voice, speaking sharply.

'I am what I am, Kitty. I can't change. It's no good. I always knew it would be no good.'

'But Ed, what are you talking about? What's no good?'

'I can't be what you want me to be. I can't do it.'

He's shaking, almost shouting, but not at her. She watches him in terror. He's acting as if some invisible force is binding him, and he's fighting to set himself free.

'I don't want you to be anything,' she says. 'Truly, truly.'

She tries to touch him, to soothe him, but he throws her off with a violent gesture that shocks her.

'No! Get off! Get away from me!'

'Eddy! Please!'

She feels the tears rising to her eyes. But the worst of it is, she still feels angry with him. Why is he behaving like this? Why has it somehow become her fault?

He picks up his half-full glass of Scotch and drinks it, gulping it down. Then he holds out the empty glass for her to see.

'You want to know why I drink too much? Because it's better for you if I'm drunk.'

'No!' she says. 'No! It isn't better for me!'

Suddenly her anger comes flooding out.

'I hate the way you tell me you're doing it for me. You're not doing it for me. You're doing it for yourself. You're doing it to run away. That's just taking the coward's way out. You've no right to do that. Why should you run away and leave the rest of us to clean up the mess? It's not fair. It's not right. We're all worn out by this vile winter, it's not just you. Stop being so sorry for yourself, for God's sake! Make a bit of an effort for once, can't you?'

He stares at her in silence. Kitty feels the anger drain away.

'Please,' she says in a gentler voice.

'Right,' he says. 'You know what I need? I need some fresh air.'

With that, he walks briskly out of the room.

Kitty sits down in the armchair in the corner and wraps her arms round her body and shakes. This is where Pamela finds her.

'Look,' she says, holding out her basket. 'Four eggs.' Then aware of the masculine nature of the room, 'Where's Daddy?'

'He's gone out.'

'But it's still snowing.'

'I don't think Daddy minds the snow.'

Ed returns later, and makes himself busy building a fire in the big drawing room, one of the rooms that has been closed off to save heat. He says nothing to Kitty about their argument. He comes and goes with the manner of one who has too many tasks to do to stop and talk. Kitty feels sick and miserable and doesn't know what to do.

Louisa comes to her as she sits by the fire in the Oak Room.

'What on earth is Ed up to?' she says. 'He's pushing the furniture about in the drawing room.'

'I've no idea,' says Kitty. 'We had a bit of a row earlier.'

'Oh, I'm always having rows with George,' says Louisa. 'You're allowed to have rows when you're married.'

'I don't like it,' says Kitty. 'It frightens me.'

Then Ed himself appears.

'I've got something to show you,' he says to Kitty.

She follows him across the hall and through the anteroom to the drawing room. Here a cheerful fire is blazing, and there are candles glowing on all the side tables, throwing their soft light onto the red damask walls. He has moved the sofas and chairs to one end, and rolled up the carpet. A gramophone stands ready on the table by the door.

'What's this, Ed?' says Kitty, looking round. The shutters are open on the tall windows, and outside the white light of afternoon makes a strange contrast with the amber light of the fire and the candles within.

'Our ballroom,' says Ed.

He pulls the lever on the gramophone that starts the turntable spinning, and lowers the arm with the needle onto the disc. The sound of a dance band fills the room.

'Would you care to dance?' he says, holding out his hand.

Kitty takes his hand, and he draws her into his arms. The high clear voice of the singer begins, and Ed and Kitty dance together, holding each other close.

> If I didn't care
> More than words can say
> If I didn't care
> Would I feel this way?

They dance in a slow wide circle over the bared floor, from the windows to the fire. Kitty rests her head on his shoulder and feels his breath on her cheek and wants to cry.

> If this isn't love
> Then why do I thrill?
> And what makes my head go round and round
> While my heart stands still?

He lowers his head to hers and they kiss as they dance. When she looks up again she sees Louisa standing smiling in the doorway, with Pamela beside her.

> If I didn't care
> Would it be the same?
> Would my every prayer
> Begin and end with just your name?

And would I be sure
That this is love beyond compare?
Would all this be true
If I didn't care
For you?

When the song finishes they come to a stop and stand by the fire in each other's arms.

'My Ink Spots record,' says Louisa. 'I love that.'

'Why are you dancing?' says Pamela.

'Because Daddy wanted to,' says Kitty.

'I want to dance,' says Pamela.

So Ed puts the song on again and dances with Pamela while Kitty and Louisa watch. The little girl frowns with concentration as they dance, trying to make sure she moves in time. Ed dances with his daughter, one arm on her shoulder, one hand holding her hand, looking down to make sure he's not treading on her toes, handling her with grave gentleness. Kitty feels almost more full of love watching him dance with Pamela than when she was in his arms herself. He has said nothing about their row, and nothing needs to be said.

The heaviest snowfall of that long hard winter comes near the end, on the first Tuesday of March. The blizzard rages all that day and night, and into Wednesday. Once again the men of the village set out with their tractors and shovels to clear the roads, grumbling to each other that the bad weather will never end. But as the next week begins, suddenly the thaw sets in. The air turns mild, and the snow that has lain so stubbornly for so long over the land starts at last to melt.

Ed travels up to London as soon as the trains are able to run again after the blizzard. There is still snow on the Downs as he leaves. Then comes several days of heavy rain, and the last of the snow disappears, leaving the land grey and waterlogged.

The postman returns to his rounds, bringing a letter from Larry.

> I've accepted a place on Mountbatten's staff and am off to India! By the time you get this I'll be gone. I'm not at all sure what I'm to do, but it feels like a good time to be out of England. I'll write and tell you all about it when I'm settled in. I hope you've all survived this foul winter and when we meet again there'll be sun over Sussex.

PART THREE

# INDEPENDENCE

1947–48

# 26

Two York aircraft carry the viceroy-designate and his team to India. The second plane containing chief-of-staff Lord Ismay and most of the new appointments, including Larry Cornford, takes a slower route, stopping overnight at Malta, Fayid and Karachi. On the way Ismay and Eric Miéville, the chief diplomat on the mission, speak openly of the difficulties ahead.

'Dickie doesn't want to go,' Pug Ismay says. 'The Indians don't want him. And we'll probably all get shot.' Then seeing that this isn't going down so well, he adds, 'Don't worry. Dickie's one of those chaps who was born with luck on his side. I like working for lucky men.'

The three-day journey to Karachi leaves them exhausted.

'Beginning to wish you hadn't come?' says Rupert Blundell to Larry as they emerge into the heat of RAF Mauripur.

'Not at all,' says Larry. 'I'm excited.'

Alan Campbell-Johnson, the press attaché, overhears him.

'This is my seventh flight between England and India,' he says. 'Believe me, the thrill wears off.'

They bunk for the night in the club house on the airfield,

Larry doubling with Rupert. The ceiling fan makes little impact on the humid night air. They lie on top of the sheets, stripped to their underpants, sweating, unable to sleep.

'Apparently one adjusts,' says Rupert.

'God, I hope so,' says Larry.

'I fixed up for my sister to come out and join us. I'm beginning to think that was a mistake.'

'When's she due to come?'

'Three weeks' time. There's a flight laid on for family members.'

Larry is cheered by this news. He likes the idea of meeting Rupert's sister again.

'Is she coming on the staff?'

'No, no. More of a jolly, really. But I'm sure she'll be given something to do.' He drops his voice in the darkness. 'Between you and me, she's been let down rather badly by a chap. Bit of a case of broken heart and so on. Nothing like a change of scene.'

'There's been a bit of that for me too,' says Larry.

'Sorry to hear it. Rather goes with the human condition, I fear.'

'Except for you, Rupert. I refuse to believe you've ever done anything as worldly as allow your heart to be broken.'

'You think I'm too high-minded for love?' says Rupert.

Larry realises how foolish this sounds.

'No,' he says. 'Of course not. It's just that you've always struck me as being' – he reaches for the right word – 'self-contained.'

'Yes,' says Rupert. 'I accept that. I've become selfish, I suppose. I value what I choose to call my freedom.' Then, after a slight pause, 'There was a moment, once. Right at the end of the war. But it didn't work out.'

He falls silent. Larry doesn't press him. He's learning to respect this awkward subtle man, who is so easy to mock, and yet who, for all his absurdity, seems to remain untouched by the world.

'What happened to your friend Ed Avenell? The one who got the VC.'

'He's married. Working in the wine trade.'

'I think of him from time to time. I remember him from school, of course. I bet he's married a pretty girl.'

'Very pretty.'

'I suppose I think of him because he's the opposite of me in every way. Good-looking, confident, gets the girls. I'd give a lot to have his life for just one day.'

'Ed's got his troubles too.'

After that they fall silent, lying in the hot darkness, listening to the clicking of the fan overhead.

The next day the party boards the York for the final leg of the journey, over the deserts of Sindh and Rajputana to Delhi.

'When you see how much of the world is desert,' says Alan Campbell-Johnson, 'it makes you appreciate our green little island a bit more.'

They land at Palam airfield on schedule. The heat and glare on coming out of the plane hit Larry like a blow, punishing his travel-weary body. A convoy of viceregal cars waits on the runway to drive them into the city. He follows the others across the cracking tarmac, breathing air that smells of petrol and burns his throat.

The drive into Delhi carries them in a short half hour across a desert, through a teeming shanty-town, and into the ghostly grandeur of imperial New Delhi. Alan Campbell-Johnson is watching Larry's face as their destination comes into view at the end of Kingsway, the broad ceremonial avenue that links India Gate to the Viceroy's House. Larry is duly astounded. The official home of the ruler of India is absurdly immense, a long, columned façade topped by a giant dome, with a flagpole from which the Union flag is flying. The flight of steps leading up to the main entrance is so wide that the sentries standing on either side look like toy soldiers.

'My God!' Larry exclaims.

'It's the biggest residence of any chief of state in the world,' says Alan. 'The house has three hundred and forty rooms. There are more than seven thousand people on the state payroll.'

'*Sic transit gloria mundi*,' says Rupert.

'When I was here before, in '43,' says Alan, 'we had all the high command of Congress locked up in prison. Now we're about to hand over the country to them.'

The cars pull up, and the new arrivals are escorted up the giant steps and into the cool of the building. The outgoing viceroy, Lord Wavell, is there to greet them, along with his staff. Mountbatten himself is due to arrive later in the afternoon. Everyone seems to be greeting everyone else as old friends. Larry feels both worn out and exhilarated.

As he stands gazing round the great entrance hall he is approached by a young Indian in the uniform of a naval officer. He holds a typed list of names.

'Captain Cornford?'

'Yes, that's me.'

Lieutenant Syed Tarkhan is himself a recent appointment to the incoming viceroy's staff. He has a handsome intelligent face, and the slightly stiff bearing of a well-trained navy man.

'We've all been asked to muck in,' he says. 'Show the new team around. Viceroy's House is quite a maze.'

He offers to guide Larry to his allocated room so that he can wash and rest after his journey. As they go down the long corridors Larry tells him of his time under Mountbatten at Combined Operations, and Tarkhan tells of his time under Mountbatten when he was in charge of South East Asia Command.

'He's a great man,' says Tarkhan. 'But I'm afraid that's not how he's seen here. They think he's a playboy who knows nothing about India, and is bringing in a staff who know nothing about India.'

'Some truth in that,' says Larry. 'Not the playboy bit. But I know nothing about India.'

'If I may tell you the truth, Captain,' says Tarkhan, 'the less you know the better. India will make you weep.'

They come to a stop outside a door. Tarkhan checks the number on the door against the list in his hand.

'You're to bunk here,' he says. 'If you need anything just shout for your *khidmutgar*, your servant.'

'I'm to have a servant? I thought I was the servant.'

'We all serve,' says Tarkhan with a smile, 'and we are all served. I'm afraid there's no air cooling in this wing. Your luggage will arrive shortly. Do you think you can find your way back? The new viceroy is due to arrive at three forty-five p.m.'

With that, Larry is left alone in his new quarters. The room is small, high-ceilinged, with a recessed window. The shutters are closed, leaving the room in semi-darkness. He goes to the window and opens the shutters onto blinding light, and a wave of heat. Outside across a broad empty courtyard are more grand buildings, or perhaps a further wing of this same unending house.

A servant in a turban is slowly sweeping the courtyard with a broom of sticks, making a mournful scritch-scritch sound. A heavy early afternoon stillness hangs over the scene. Larry feels briefly dizzy. He lies down on the narrow bed to rest.

What am I doing here? He thinks. And back comes the answer, I'm here to start again. I'm here to become someone else.

He oversleeps. When his *khidmutgar* wakes him it's past five.

'Why didn't you wake me before?'

'You did not so order me, Captain Sahib.'

He splashes water onto his face, brushes his hair, straightens the uniform that he has slept in, and hurries back through the great house. There seem to be more turns in the corridors than he remembers, and no clear indication of which way to go. All he can think to do is keep walking until he finds someone to ask.

He's hurrying down a broader corridor than the others when a door opens and a voice says, 'Could you help?'

It's Lady Mountbatten, thin, elegant, careworn.

'It's my little dog,' she says. 'He's done his business on the floor here, and my *khidmutgar* says he won't touch it. I don't want to step on it myself. So I wonder if you could hunt me out a servant of low enough caste to deal with it?'

Larry can't help smiling, and seeing him smile Lady Mountbatten smiles too.

'Yes, I know,' she says. 'It's all too ridiculous for words.'

'Why don't I deal with it,' says Larry.

He takes some lavatory paper from the viceregal bathroom and picks up the dog mess and flushes it away.

'Now you bad boy,' says Lady Mountbatten to her little Sealyham. 'You are so kind,' she says to Larry. 'Who are you?'

Larry introduces himself.

'Oh, yes. Dickie did tell me. Something about bananas.'

'Is there anything else I can do, your ladyship?'

'You can get me out of here. I can't bear this house. It's a mausoleum. I feel like a corpse. Don't you? I know it's supposed to be Lutyens's masterpiece, but I can't imagine what he thought he was doing, putting up such a monstrosity.'

'Intimidating the natives, I think,' says Larry.

Lady Mountbatten gives Larry a sharp look of surprise.

'Just so,' she says.

The next two days are taken up with organising the swearing-in ceremony of the new viceroy. Alan Campbell-Johnson has discovered that the press were badly handled at the airfield when the Mountbattens arrived, and are making complaints. The Sunday edition of *Dawn* shows a photograph of Ronnie Brockman and Elizabeth Ward described as 'Lord and Lady Louis arriving'. Campbell-Johnson asks for an extra pair of hands in the press room, and is given Larry. He takes him into the Durbar Hall. A high platform is being built in the dome.

'The idea is we put the newsreel boys and the cameramen up there,' says Alan. 'There's going to be twenty-two of them. I want you to get them up there, and then down again.'

'Is it safe?' says Larry, gazing up.

'God knows,' says Alan. 'It's Dickie's idea. They won't like it, I can tell you now.'

Larry is kept too busy in Viceroy's House to venture into the old city, but reports come through of a riot in the main shopping street of Chandni Chowk. Apparently a meeting of Muslims at the great mosque of Jama Masjid has been attacked by lorry-loads of Sikhs brandishing kirpans, and several people are dead. Syed Tarkhan tells Larry over a hurried lunch, 'You see, this is why we must have Pakistan. We must have a homeland.'

When the time for the ceremony arrives, Larry shepherds his flock of cameramen. They grumble openly about being made to go on the high platform, but once up there they realise the advantage of the viewpoint. Larry takes up a place on the platform also. The hall below fills with Indian princes arrayed in jewelled robes, and English gentlemen in tailcoats, and politicians of the Hindu nationalist Congress party proudly wearing homespun kurtas, in the tradition of Gandhi. Two red and gold thrones stand beneath the scarlet-draped canopy, illuminated by concealed lights.

'It's like a bloody movie set!' exclaims an American newsreel cameraman.

The ceremony begins with a startlingly loud fanfare from trumpeters placed in the roof. Then the ADCs in their dress uniforms come stalking slowly down the centre aisle, between the crush of dignitaries. After them, side by side, come Lord and Lady Mountbatten, both in white. Mountbatten wears a mass of medals and decorations, a ceremonial sword at his side. Lady Mountbatten wears an ivory brocade dress of inspired simplicity, and long white gloves above the elbow, and a dark blue sash. The cameramen go crazy, popping their flashbulbs at the grandeur of the moment. Larry, looking on, is more struck by how plainly Lady Mountbatten presents herself. No tiara, no necklace, just the grave dignity of her slender figure.

The Lord Chief Justice of India, Sir Patrick Spens, administers the oath of office. The new viceroy then makes a short address. Up on the platform Larry is unable to hear his words;

and he sees from their postures that the politicians below are straining to hear. Later, when the short ceremony is over, Alan thrusts a number of stencilled copies into Larry's hands, saying, 'Make sure they all get this. No one heard a bloody word.'

It turns out Mountbatten has asked India to help him in the difficult task ahead. This seems natural enough to Larry, but from the reaction of the press it's unprecedented. Eric Britter of *The Times* says it's as good as admitting the British have made mistakes in India, and if so, it'll win Mountbatten a lot of friends.

Rupert Blundell and Larry escape the marbled halls of Viceroy's House that afternoon, and Larry gets his first taste of the real India. They drive into old Delhi, which is now under curfew following the riot. There are no signs of the recent violence. The alleyways and bazaars are bursting with life and noise and colour. Everywhere Larry looks he sees, with his painter's eye, thrilling and jarring juxtapositions of scarlets and ambers and deep greens. The air smells rich with perfume and tobacco, dung and sweat. On foot now, moving through the bazaar, the crowd surges past them on either side, parting before them without touching them. Larry remembers Lady Mountbatten saying, 'I feel like a corpse.' It seems to him then that his people, the British, are dead, and only the Indian people are alive.

'What are we doing here?' he says to Rupert. 'I mean here, ruling India.'

'Not for much longer,' says Rupert.

'This isn't our country. This is another world.'

'Does it frighten you?'

'Frighten me?' Larry hasn't thought of it this way, but now that Rupert says it he realises it's true. 'Yes, in a way.'

'We English set such a high value on moderation. It strikes me that India is not moderate.'

An ox-cart passes, its driver shouting at the crowds in his way. Several voices shout back, hands raised in the air. The cart is piled high with manure and clouded with flies. There are children everywhere, their big solemn eyes tracking the Englishmen as they go by.

'The sooner we get out the better,' says Larry.

'If only it were as simple as that,' says Rupert. 'I'm part of the policy planning group. Our options are very limited. You could say the pot is boiling, and we're the lid.'

Over the next week the leaders of India take their turns in talks with Mountbatten. Larry, officially appointed assistant press attaché, is initiated into the complexities of the independence process. Syed Tarkhan shows him on the map of India how the Muslims are concentrated in what is called the 'ears of the elephant', Punjab in the north-west and Bengal in the north-east.

'This will be Pakistan,' he says. 'Jinnah will accept nothing less. There must be partition. We Muslims cannot live in a Hindu-controlled nation.'

'But you've lived in a British-controlled nation.'

'That is different.'

The difficulty with partition is that the 'ears' are not exclusively Muslim, and the rest of the elephant far from exclusively Hindu. What is to happen to the many who will find themselves in a fearful minority? Syed Tarkhan shakes his head over this.

'Nothing good,' he says.

'What does Gandhi say?' Larry asks.

'Ah, Gandhi. He of course wants a united India.'

'I've always had the idea that Gandhi is one of the few men alive who truly believes in the power of goodness.'

'The power of goodness?' says Tarkhan, raising his eyebrows. 'The mahatma is a very holy man. But whether goodness will prove to be powerful enough in the end, who is to say?'

Larry gets his own chance to see the mahatma when he makes a call at last on the new viceroy. A large gathering of newspapermen assembles to report on the meeting. Larry is on duty with Alan to attempt to control the story.

'You have to remember,' Alan tells Larry, 'that although Gandhi is the father of the nation and so forth, he's a Hindu, not a Muslim. So Jinnah and his lot are naturally suspicious of us getting too close to him.'

The press gather in the Mughal Gardens outside Mountbatten's study, where the meeting takes place. While they wait the *Times* man tells Larry, 'This little old fellow's the only one that can stop the violence. They listen to him.'

When at last the French windows open, and Gandhi comes out with Mountbatten to face the photographers, Larry is unexpectedly moved by the sight. Gandhi is so small and frail, with his bare legs and bald brown head and white khaddar robe and little round glasses. It seems inconceivable that such a tiny figure can have held the mighty British Empire to ransom, without the backing of an army, without the threat of violence, solely through the moral force of his character.

It's plain that he doesn't enjoy being photographed, but he puts up with it with smiling good grace. Lady Mountbatten joins them, and more photographs are taken. Then as they turn to go back into the house, Gandhi rests one hand on Lady Mountbatten's shoulder for support. Max Desfor, the AP man, still has his camera out, and at once he takes a shot.

'That's the one,' he says.

After Gandhi has departed, Mountbatten calls Alan and Larry into the staff meeting to discuss the communiqué that is to be issued to the press. This turns out to be far from straightforward. Gandhi has proposed a radical solution to avoid partition, with all of the bloodshed that it's feared will follow.

'He proposes,' says Mountbatten, reading from the notes he dictated after the meeting, 'that the Congress cabinet be dismissed, and Jinnah invited to form an all-Muslim administration.'

This causes consternation in the room.

'Out of the question,' says Miéville. 'Nehru won't stand for it.'

'His reasoning is,' says Mountbatten, 'that with a Muslim leadership of a united India, the Muslims need not fear Hindu persecution. The alternative, he believes, that is to say, partition, will lead to a bloodbath.'

'He's senile,' says George Abell.

'It's a trick,' says Syed Tarkhan. 'It's a trap to catch Jinnah out.'

'Oh, I think he's sincere,' says Mountbatten. 'But I'm not sure he's realistic.'

'He tried this on Wavell before,' says Miéville. 'He tried it on Willingdon. It's the only shot he's got in his locker. Claim the moral high ground through self-sacrifice. That sort of stunt works on us British because we know we don't belong here. But just you try it on the Hindus.'

A communiqué of sorts is fudged for the press that leaves all options open. Mountbatten sighs and rubs his forehead.

'I'm beginning to think this is one of those cock-ups where there just isn't a way out,' he says.

After dinner Larry finds himself beside Lady Mountbatten. She has been friendly to him ever since the episode of the dog mess.

'What do you make of Gandhi?' Larry asks her.

'I worship at his feet,' says Lady Mountbatten. 'The man is a saint. But the one who's going to save India is Nehru.'

Larry writes a letter to Kitty and Ed, wanting the chance to get his unruly crowd of new experiences into some sort of order.

> I feel as if I've tumbled into a different world, where all the rules no longer function. Nothing is simple. Whatever we do leaving India we will be blamed and hated. There is no great act of statesmanship that will resolve the crisis. Poor Mountbatten just looks done in. We've already said we're quitting India. The only thing left seems to be to go, but then there will be civil war. Gandhi says we must go anyway and 'accept the bloodbath'. So in the midst of all this you can imagine how unimportant my personal cares appear. I didn't tell you before I left that Nell and I have parted. Also that I'm no longer thinking that my future lies in art. Today there has been a story in the paper of riots in Calcutta and Bombay. Stabbings, bombings, throwing of acid. A car ambushed and set alight, four passengers burned alive, screaming for mercy. How can I even consider my own troubles worth one second's attention in the face of such suffering? Ed will read this and say, Where is your loving God now? But you, Kitty, will back me up when I say that there is good in us as well as evil, and we must believe in its power, and work for its victory. Otherwise what are our lives for?

# 27

The letter is addressed to Edenfield Place, but by the time it arrives Kitty and Pamela are back at River Farm. Louisa walks over to bring Kitty the letter and they read it together, sitting in the April sunshine on the seat in the yard.

'Heavens!' says Louisa. 'What dramas!'

Kitty realises with a shock that the news of Larry's parting from Nell pleases her more than it should.

'I wasn't ever sure that girl was right for him,' she says.

'Of course she wasn't,' says Louisa. 'Larry's far too good for her.'

'Doesn't it seem odd to think of him all the way over there and us still here?'

Still here. Kitty doesn't say so, but nothing has got any easier. The long hard winter is over, and her life is back in its usual pattern. Her days pass making modest meals, tidying up the old house so that Mrs Willis can clean it, repairing Pamela's torn clothing, helping out at the village church, driving into the shops in Lewes, listening to the wireless, reading to Pamela, reading to herself. There always seems to be just a little more to do than there's time to do it, and yet she has the feeling that she does nothing at all. She envies Larry his Indian adventure.

Louisa has her own reasons for being dissatisfied with her life. She's been trying for a long time now to get pregnant.

'Did I tell you,' she says, 'I'm going to see a quack? Mummy's persuaded me to go. George has to see him too.'

'Well, I suppose there's no harm,' says Kitty.

'I expect he'll tell me to eat raw eggs and lay off the booze or something. Just so long as he doesn't tell me to rest. Nothing gets me quite so worked up as being told to rest.'

'Maybe you should go up to town for a few weeks,' says Kitty.

'I don't see how that would get me a baby,' says Louisa. 'Unless, of course . . .' She gives Kitty a wicked look, like the old Louisa. 'Remember the girls who used to stand outside the barracks at night shouting "Para Eleven"?'

'Oh, God!' says Kitty, giggling. 'I do miss the war.'

'All we wanted at the time was for it to be over.'

Kitty sighs as she remembers.

'All I wanted was my own house, and my own husband, and my own little baby. I used to daydream about making curtains, and baking bread, and waking up in a sunny bedroom in my very own little home.'

'I don't see why it all had to be so little,' says Louisa.

'I think I was playing at dolls' houses,' says Kitty. 'Now it's real, and I'm turning into my mother.'

She doesn't tell Louisa the worst of it, which is that sometimes she sits in a chair for an hour or more, seized by a strange heavy torpor, doing nothing. She feels tired all the time these days. Her mind goes blank, and she can't think what she's meant to be doing. Then Pamela will appear, demanding to be fed or entertained, and so she'll stir herself; but even as she boils an egg, and toasts a slice of bread, she has this numb feeling that it's all pointless and going nowhere.

She can't share this with Louisa because Louisa believes having a baby will solve all her problems. She can't tell her that there are times when Pamela makes her want to scream. Of course she adores her daughter and would die for her if need be, but what's proving harder is the enterprise of living for her. It turns out a child is not enough. But not enough for what?

She wishes Larry were here. She could talk to Larry about all this. That's what's so good about people with faith, even if you don't share their faith. They know what you mean when you talk about meaning. They understand that there has to be some sort of greater purpose. She's never forgotten how he said to her, the very first time they met, 'Don't you want to do something noble and fine with your life?'

Sometimes, sitting doing nothing in the kitchen chair, Kitty thinks ahead to the time when Pamela will be grown-up, and will no longer need her. She asks herself, What will I do then?

I'll have Ed, of course.

Then her mind slides away from these thoughts, not liking where they lead her, and her head fills with grey vapour like a cloud.

Hugo comes, more than is justified by the demands of the business. He sits with her, and plays with Pammy, and acts the part of the dear old family friend, except for the looks he gives her. She reprimands him, always in light, easy terms, as if he's an over-eager child.

'That's enough, Hugo. Stop it.'

Then when she's expecting him one day and he doesn't come,

she finds she misses his attentions. That frightens her.

She has a dream. In her dream she's wearing a bathing costume and all the boys are looking at her. She feels youthful and desirable. She's on a beach, and the waves that come rolling in are frothing and churning on the shore. The ocean beyond is infinitely big. She starts to run, and runs over the sand and the pebbles towards the sea. She runs faster and faster, filled with gladness, because she knows she's going to hurl herself into those great crashing waves. The waves are going to embrace her and sweep her away.

She wakes before she reaches the water, but her heart is thundering, and her whole body is glowing. It's not a death dream at all, this isn't a desire to drown. It's a longing to use all of herself, to hold nothing back, to experience an overwhelming desire. And instead of the explosive urgency of her dream, all she feels in her waking life is fatigue.

'You know what I think we should do for Easter?' she tells Pamela. 'I think we should go and visit Grandma and Grandpa.'

Pamela thinks about this.

'I am affronted,' she says.

Kitty's parents always make a great fuss of Pamela, and there's nothing the little girl appreciates as much as attention. As for Kitty herself, she's aware that she doesn't visit her parents nearly as much as they'd like. Her mother has a way of getting on the wrong side of her, and so Kitty always ends up behaving badly, and being what her mother calls 'moody'. Still, they didn't visit at Christmas time, and tired and restless as she is, Kitty would rather go than stay.

'Hello, little stranger,' says Mrs Teale to Pamela. 'I expect you've entirely forgotten who I am.'

'You're Grandma,' says Pamela.

'Guess what I've got for the most beautiful little girl in the world?'

'A present,' says Pamela.

'I wonder whether you want it now, or whether you'd rather keep it for Easter Day?'

'Now,' says Pamela.

Kitty follows this exchange with helpless irritation. It's been a long slow journey and all she wants is a comfortable chair and a cup of tea. Why must her mother go in for this ludicrous arch teasing tone of voice, as if she and Pamela are engaged in some conspiracy?

The present is a small chocolate egg, wrapped in silver paper. Pamela unwraps it at once and puts it whole into her mouth.

'Who's a hungry girl?' says Mrs Teale.

'Say thank you, Pammy,' says Kitty.

'Thank you,' says the child, her mouth full.

Mrs Teale turns to her daughter.

'No handsome young husband, then?'

Kitty wants to scream. She's been in the house five minutes and already her mother has managed to enrage her.

'I told you, Mummy. Ed's in France.'

'Well, I don't know, darling. No one ever tells me anything. It would just be nice if he visited us once in a while. Michael was saying only the other day that he's never heard the story of how he got his Victoria Cross.'

'You know Ed doesn't like to talk about that.'

'I can't think why not. You'd think he'd be proud. Did I tell you Robert Reynolds has been made a canon of Wells? He still asks after you, you know?'

'I thought he was married.'

'Is he?' says Mrs Teale vaguely. 'Maybe he is. I can't keep up these days. We all thought Harold would marry the Stanley girl, but he says it's off, and there was never anything in it in the first place. I don't understand young people. It seems you can go about together and it all means nothing at all. Pamela is looking a bit peaky, isn't she? We'll do our best to feed her up and give her lots of good country air.'

'We live in the country too, Mummy.'

'Somehow I never think of Sussex as being the real country. I suppose because it's on the way to France.'

Kitty's father's return puts a stop to the stream of barbed prattle that issues from her mother's mouth. In his presence she becomes timid, clumsy, awkward. Michael Teale, by contrast, is all smiles and hugs.

'My two best girls!' he cries. 'My word, Pamela! You smell chocolatey enough to eat.' And turning to Kitty, 'Guess who's been filling my ear with your praises? Jonathan Saxon!'

'Dear Mr Saxon,' says Kitty. 'Is he still bossing the poor little choirboys about?'

'He asked me to ask you if you'd sing in the abbey on Sunday. You know he always says you were the best soprano he ever had.'

Kitty hasn't sung in public for years, and she was never properly trained. But this request pleases her more than she would have expected.

'Oh, I couldn't,' she says. 'I'm far too rusty.'

'Well, you tell Jonathan yourself. All I can say is, he seems dead set on it.'

When Mrs Teale hears of the proposal she manages to turn it around and make it a source of disappointment.

'Oh, do sing, darling. It's such a waste, the way you do nothing with your beautiful voice.'

'I've no intention of making a fool of myself in front of a full congregation,' says Kitty sharply.

'You could sing "Little Brown Jug",' says Pamela.

Mr Saxon calls round to make his request in person. Charmed by the sweet old gentleman's pink smiling face and flattered by his praise, Kitty agrees to sing, on condition that they can go through the piece at least once beforehand. He wants her to sing César Franck's *Panis Angelicus*.

Pamela's greatest pleasure on these visits is playing with the dolls her own mother played with when she was little. This notion, that her mother was a little girl once, both puzzles and fascinates her. She wants to know the names of every doll, and which ones were her mother's special favourites, and what they all did together. Then once told she repeats the pattern as faithfully as she can.

'Rosie, you're the birthday girl today. You can sit on the birthday chair. And Ethel, you're Rosie's best friend. Droopy, you can be by Rosie's feet. Oh, Rosie, I forgot your flower hat. You have to wear the flower hat on your birthday.'

Kitty watches her child's grave re-creation of her past with a smile. But along with the fond memories comes another more shadowed picture. She sees her daughter growing up and having a daughter of her own, and that little child playing the same game. And is this all? whispers a voice in her head. Are we never to leave the nursery?

Her father brings out the sherry before dinner, in Kitty's honour, and her mother drinks her entire glassful. It's clear from Michael Teale's frown that this is not what he wants, though having poured his wife the sherry it seems odd that she should not be supposed to drink it. However, he says nothing.

His smiles are all for his daughter.

'So have you had any trouble with these terrible floods?' he says.

'The river burst its banks,' says Kitty, 'but our house has never been in danger. I'm just so happy not to be freezing any more.'

'What a winter it's been! Here's Easter at last, the feast of the Resurrection, and I'm telling everyone the worst is over.'

'But Michael,' says Mrs Teale, 'winter will come round again.'

'Yes, yes,' he says, his eyes still on Kitty. 'So how's that famous husband of yours getting along?'

'He's in France,' says Kitty. 'He works so hard.'

'Jesus rises from the dead on Easter Day,' says Mrs Teale, her cheeks now a little flushed. 'And the year goes round, and then he's crucified all over again.'

'Be quiet!' says Mr Teale. 'You're a fool.'

Silence falls over the table. This is the first time Kitty has known her father reprimand her mother in the presence of others. It frightens her. She looks down at her plate. But her father resumes the conversation as if nothing has happened.

'I respect a man who works hard,' he says.

'It does mean he's away from home a great deal,' says Kitty, avoiding looking at her mother.

'We all have to make sacrifices,' says her father. 'When I was a young man I had a great dream. I was going to go round the world, working my passage on cargo ships. Then the war came along, of course, and that was that.'

Kitty has never heard of this dream before.

'Maybe you could go now,' she says.

'Impossible.' He beams at her, as if this impossibility somehow suits him. 'Here I am, nearly sixty years old. And there's your mother. No, I shall stick by the old abbey now, and be buried beside it. The abbey and I will crumble away together.'

She sees then, for the merest instant, a flicker of horror in his eyes, not at the coming of death but at the losing of life; at the life he might have lived, and knows he never will.

Lying awake that night in the bed she slept in as a child, Kitty tells herself her life will be different, that it is already different. She will not grow old in a loveless angry marriage. And yet her mother could never have anticipated such a fate. How is it to be avoided? The years go by, and the shadows lengthen. For a while you live for your children, and then the children leave home, and what do you do then? Turn slowly sour, like undrunk milk.

On Easter Day, at the big mid-morning service, Kitty sings *Panis Angelicus*. The abbey is full. Her father stands robed and beaming at the altar behind her. Her mother sits with Pamela in the front pew before her. Old Mr Saxon plays the gently falling chords of the introduction on the big organ. And the melody rises up from within her like the sweet breath of life itself.

*Panis Angelicus, fit panis hominum*
*Dat panis coelicus figuris terminum . . .*

She has sung it many times in her younger years, and the words flow effortlessly. She has no nervousness before the congregation: she hardly sees them. She is surrendering herself to the music, her body an instrument beyond her own control. She hears the throbbing hum of the organ notes as if the same keys and pedals press the clear high song from her throat, and she need do nothing. As she sings she can hear herself make mistakes, but somehow even her wrong notes sound right. So, self-forgetting, she reaches out for the high note, and gets it and loses it, and comes stepping down the melody, singing with a purity and a wholeheartedness she has rediscovered from her youth.

Pamela watches and hears with her lips parted, enraptured. It's not only the voice that astonishes her this Easter morning, a voice she never knew her mother had. It's the shining eyes of all the others round her, eyes fixed in admiration on her mother. From this moment the child knows that this is what she wants for herself: to be the object of such looks of love.

There's no applause as Kitty finishes. This is a religious service. But a kind of collective sigh goes up from the pews. Afterwards there are many old friends and neighbours pressing forward with their congratulations, and Kitty smiles and thanks them for their kind words, and Pamela clings tight to one arm wherever she goes so that everyone knows it's her mother who is the star of Easter Day. But inside herself Kitty has gone far away, and wishes she could be alone, because something big has happened. She's found a place where she can give all of herself. She has entered the wave.

Then comes the reaction, a sudden exhaustion so powerful she can no longer stand, accompanied by a bad taste in her mouth. Her mother sees her stumble, and coming to her side, takes her away from the crowd.

'You're worn out, darling. Go and lie down. Pammy, you stay here with me. Just go, darling. I'll explain.'

Kitty throws her a grateful look and runs upstairs to her room. There she lies full length on the bed and hears the buzz of voices below and attempts to find again the extraordinary joy she felt while singing. She can do no more than catch a faint echo; and even that is slipping fast away from her.

For a while she rests, half-sleeping. Then, wanting not to lose the precious moment for ever, she gets up and goes to her old desk. She will write it down, in a letter. There's only one person to whom she can send such confused thoughts. She writes to Larry.

I do so envy you your great adventure. Here life goes on the same old way, and sometimes I find myself wondering how it will be in a few years' time, when Pamela no longer needs me. I expect I shall turn into one of those good women who do good works, and then you, who believe in goodness, can come and praise me. I shall be duly grateful, I assure you, but I can't promise that it will be enough. I may grow restless and bad-tempered, and what is far worse, disappointed. I don't think you'll praise me for that.

Today has turned out to be a special day. It's Easter Day, but that's not what's special. As my mother says, it comes round every year. What happened is this. When I was younger I used to sing in the choir, I sang the soprano solos, and the very same choirmaster is still here. He begged me to sing in the abbey and I did, and Larry, for three or four minutes I was what Ed called me once, I was an angel in heaven. Actually I've no idea what it's like to be an angel or what heaven is like but I was let go – I don't know how else to write it – I escaped and got away and I was so happy. Is this what happens to you when you paint? You say you're not thinking of art any more, but how can that be? If it's the same for you with art as it is for me when I sing, at least as I sang today, then you can't give it up. It would be to give up the only time when you're fully alive. Do you feel that? How most of the time we're only half alive, or even half asleep? I've been so tired lately, I don't know why, it's not as if I have to do such hard work. I think people need something more than just food and shelter, they need a mission in life, and without a mission they go slower and slower until they can hardly move at all. I think Ed feels this most strongly of all of us, and that's why he drives himself so hard. I don't feel as if I want to drive myself, it's more that I want to jump, or fall, or fly away. I wish you had been here to hear me sing. You would have been so proud. I do miss you a lot. When things happen to me it's you I want to tell. Come home soon, please.

She folds the letter up and puts it in her suitcase to send when she gets home. Then as she straightens up again she feels a tightness in her chest, and a tingling of the skin of her breasts. All at once it comes to her.

I'm pregnant.

This simple immense fact drops into her mind like a key into a lock. Suddenly everything makes sense. The constant fatigue, the mild nausea, the metallic taste in her mouth.

I'm going to have another baby.

Of course there'll be doctors to visit, tests to endure, but she knows it beyond any possibility of a doubt. Her body is telling her. And as for all her questions about the future, they are already melting away. There is no future. She is to have another baby. With a baby there is only today, and today, and today.

# 28

The camp followers, as Pug Ismay calls them, arrive in the viceregal aeroplane in early May, just as the temperature in Delhi is rising to unbearable levels. A crowd of exhausted children come tumbling down the steps: three Brockman girls, a Nicholls boy, two little Campbell-Johnsons shepherded by Alan's wife Fay. Ismay's grown-up daughters Susan and Sarah follow, with Rupert Blundell's sister Geraldine.

That evening Larry is invited to join the Campbell-Johnsons and Rupert and his sister for a drink at the Imperial hotel in honour of the new arrivals.

They sit in the gardens, in low basket chairs, drinking gin and lemonade. After sundown the air is cool and pleasant. The perfectly kept lawns are lit by soft lamps. The tinkling of tonga bells sounds from the street beyond the walls. Turbaned servants stand discreetly by the open doors to the hotel, waiting to fulfil the guests' needs.

'Rupert, this is heavenly,' says Geraldine. 'And to think you've been making such a fuss.'

'I got cold feet about her coming out,' Rupert says to the others.

'This isn't the real India, I'm afraid,' says Alan.

'I suppose you mean it isn't the India of the poor,' says Geraldine. 'But at home I don't live in the England of the poor either. Perhaps I'm simply not real.'

She speaks with a smile in her voice, and they laugh as if she has made a joke, but Larry senses from the first that, like Rupert, she's someone who knows her own mind. To look at she's delicate, even fragile, with her pale perfect skin and her slender figure. The way she moves her head or her small hands is economical and precise, performing just enough of an action to achieve her object. She seems to be quite unaware how pretty she is, and entirely lacks the little tricks of flirtation that others take for granted. Modest, then, but also proud.

The men smoke, but both the ladies decline. Geraldine barely touches her drink. Alan catches sight of Colin Reid of the London *Daily Telegraph*, and beckons him over to join them.

'Colin's a real expert,' he says. 'He's studied Muslim culture in the Middle East. He's even read the Koran in Arabic. Am I right, Colin?'

'More than once,' says Colin. 'Don't quote me on this, but I know my Koran rather better than Muhammad Ali Jinnah.'

'Which one's Jinnah?' says Geraldine.

'He's the leader of the Muslim League,' says Larry.

'So tell us,' says Alan to the *Telegraph* man. 'Is this Muslim–Hindu division really about religion, or is it something else?'

'That's rather a broad question,' says Colin Reid.

'Religion is always something else, surely,' says Rupert. 'I mean, religion is not just about what you do on the holy days. It's how you see your life.'

'I should explain,' says Alan. 'We're surrounded by believers.

Rupert and Larry both went to the same Catholic school. I expect Geraldine is one of them too.'

'Certainly,' says Geraldine with a pretty smile. 'Like all the best people.'

'But Rupert's perfectly right,' says Colin Reid. 'Religion is more about identity and community than creed. And I'm afraid the different communities here are moving further apart every day.'

He and Alan and Rupert then get into a discussion about the nationalist leaders and whether they can ever find common ground. Geraldine, who is sitting near Larry, turns to him and asks him in a low voice, 'Did Rupert always know best at school?'

'I'm sure he did,' says Larry, smiling. 'But I didn't really know him. He pretty much kept himself to himself. He was in my house, but in the year above me.'

'I expect you've lost your faith too.'

'No, not yet. Is that what I'm supposed to do?'

'I rather got the impression that Downside has that effect,' says Geraldine. 'You either come out a monk or an atheist.'

'No, I'm still a muddled but willing believer.'

'Me too. I expect it's very dull of me, but I like there being rules. Fish on Friday. Mass on Sunday. Prayers at bedtime.'

'It's because it's what we're used to,' says Larry.

'No,' says Geraldine. 'It's what Rupert said. It's about how you see your life. Once you decide there's a right way to live your life, then that's what you want to do.' She stops, putting one hand to her pretty mouth, as if suddenly afraid she's said the wrong thing. 'I'm so sorry. I'm being serious. How bad-mannered of me.'

At the same time her eyes are laughing.

'I led you on,' says Larry. 'We're equally guilty.'

'It's because those rude men are talking Indian politics. Fay,' she says, turning to Alan Campbell-Johnson's wife, who is all too visibly falling asleep, 'Where have you hidden the children?'

'The children?' says Fay, blinking back to wakefulness. 'I'm taking them up to Simla, to get away from the heat.'

'They're such darlings,' Geraldine says to Larry. 'They were so good in that beastly plane. Fay, you need to be in bed. And so do I, to tell the truth.'

Larry is charmed by the graceful way Geraldine handles herself. He realises how much he misses feminine company; and in particular this way of speaking lightly while touching on serious matters. There's something else, too. He has the sense that Geraldine likes him.

As the party breaks up she says to him, 'I'm so glad you're out here. Rupert simply refuses to go to Mass any more. He's supposed to be a philosopher, but as far as I can tell he believes in nothing at all.'

That Sunday Larry accompanies Geraldine to the Sacred Heart on Connaught Place, a curious Italian-style church built only a few years before the war. Inside, with its rounded arches and long nave, its smell of burning candles and wood polish, it could be any Catholic church in the world. Geraldine kneels beside him, her face partly obscured by a black lace mantilla, and murmurs the responses in that absent but familiar way that is common to all Catholics. The words they speak are after all in Latin, and essentially meaningless incantations. And yet to Larry this itself is comforting. The mass in Delhi is identical to the mass at home. The raised hands of the robed celebrant, the tang of incense in the air, the tinkle of the consecration bell: he could be in the Carmelite church in Kensington, or Downside Abbey, or St Martin in Bellencombre, and it would all be the same.

After Mass they find their driver waiting in the hot sun, and drive back along the broad new roads of the imperial capital. New Delhi has the look of a city built for giants who have not yet got around to moving in.

'Or perhaps,' Larry says, elaborating his thought, 'they built it and then abandoned it, like Fatehpur Sikri.'

Geraldine hasn't heard of Fatehpur Sikri.

'It was the first Mughal city, built by Akbar the Great. But it turned out there wasn't enough water there, so they abandoned it after only fourteen years. It took fifteen years to build. It's been left to the sun and the wind for almost four hundred years now.'

'Is it still there?'

'Oh, yes, it's still there. There's no one living there, but people visit.'

'I'd like to go there.'

'I think it's quite a drive.'

Geraldine looks out of the open car windows at the bleak grandeur of the new city.

'I expect this took fifteen years to build,' she says.

'More or less,' says Larry. 'And here we are, getting ready to abandon it.'

'At least it won't be deserted when we leave.'

'Not at all. It'll come to life.'

They drive in silence for a few moments. Then Geraldine says, 'Why did you come out here, Larry?'

'Oh, you know how it is,' says Larry. 'Life has these turning points, doesn't it? I suppose it was just chance, bumping into Rupert when I did.'

'You think it was chance?'

'Why, don't you believe in chance?'

'I don't know that I do,' she says. 'After all— ' She breaks off, not out of nervousness, but with a kind of old-fashioned courtesy, to say, 'Do you mind if I talk about God?'

'Not at all,' he says. 'It is Sunday.'

'Well,' she says, 'if you believe God has a plan for you, then nothing happens by chance. Even the bad things have their purpose, however hard it is to see what that might be at the time.'

'Yes,' says Larry, wondering how far he agrees with this. 'But that doesn't mean we never have to make any decisions for ourselves, does it?'

'I think our duty is to do the right thing, as far as we know it. And beyond that, to submit to the will of God. If that means we are to suffer, then so be it.'

She speaks in a low voice that makes it all too plain she speaks from recent personal experience.

'I'm sorry if you've suffered,' says Larry.

She looks round, meeting his eyes with a searching gaze. Her look says to him, Don't play with me.

'I've been unhappy,' she says. 'I can't claim any more than that.'

The car pulls up by the north entrance to Viceroy's House, and they go inside. Larry hears Geraldine pausing to thank their driver. Breakfast is still being served in the staff mess.

'Here they are!' cries Rupert Blundell, halfway through eating a soft-boiled egg. 'Are you suitably shriven?'

'You will go to hell,' says Geraldine calmly. 'Pour me some coffee.'

Freddie Burnaby-Atkins, one of the ADCs, points a butter knife at Geraldine.

'Why only Rupert?' he complains. 'I've not been to church either.'

'You're one of the innocents, Freddie,' says Geraldine. 'You'll go to limbo. But Rupert knows better, so he goes to hell.'

There are several single young men on the staff, and Geraldine's arrival among them has created something of a flutter. As Rupert predicted, she is soon put to work assisting the hard-pressed team. She has no training in shorthand or typing, but she has a natural talent for organisation. Within a few days she has taken charge of the circulation of notes. Mountbatten has instituted a system where each hour of meetings is followed by fifteen minutes of dictation, in which he makes a résumé of the discussion. The resulting notes are then typed, stencilled, and distributed. Geraldine draws up a chart with the names of all key members of staff, and the date and issue number of each note, and ticks them off as they are sent out.

The workload grows heavier as the temperature of the capital rises. The thermometer in the entrance hall is now reading 110° in the shade. Mountbatten has been closeted in Simla with Nehru, and in London with Attlee and Churchill. Jinnah has made his demand for a 'corridor' between the two parts of what will become Pakistan. Baldev Singh has issued ominous warnings about the Sikhs, who will be the biggest losers in partition. The Indian states representatives have met and failed to agree. Lord and Lady Mountbatten are rumoured to be barely on speaking terms. No one has the least idea what Gandhi thinks.

In this atmosphere of confusion and mistrust, the viceroy calls a meeting of the five leaders: Nehru and Patel for the Congress party, Jinnah and Liaquat Ali Khan for the Muslim League, and Baldev Singh for the Sikhs. Nehru asks that Acharya Kripalani be included, as Congress President. Jinnah counters with a demand that Rab Nishtar be included for the League. So the five becomes seven.

Larry is on duty controlling the press photographers. When it emerges that no photographs are to be permitted, he finds himself with a rebellion on his hands. Max Desfor leads a walkout by the foreign press men, saying as he goes, 'You'll get a signed protest on this one, Larry. You tell your people, this is no way to get yourselves a good press.'

Larry does his best.

'The viceroy wants as little distraction as possible. We'll get you in there later, I promise you.'

The purpose of the meeting is to win all the leaders' consent to a carefully drafted plan for the transfer of power. Because different aspects of the plan are unacceptable to each one of the leaders, this is no easy task. Mountbatten's object is to make them realise that poor though the plan is, every alternative is worse. If the British are to quit India, somebody must take over the running of the country. If Jinnah will not work with Congress, there must be partition. If there is to be partition, there must be boundaries, and many people will find themselves on the wrong side of whatever lines are drawn.

Mountbatten explains carefully that he understands he cannot expect to win *agreement*. Instead he asks for *acceptance*, which means that the leaders believe the plan to be a fair and sincere attempt to solve the problems, for the good of all. He asks for their goodwill in the attempt to make the plan work. Nehru, for Congress, says he is willing on balance to accept the plan. Jinnah says he must consult further with his working committee.

The meeting then breaks up, to be resumed next day. Mountbatten calls a staff meeting to report progress.

'Bloody Jinnah,' he says wearily. 'I shall have to see him alone.'

The other hold-out is Gandhi, who is due at Viceroy's House shortly.

'He's never going to buy partition,' says V.P. Menon.

'He doesn't have to buy it,' says Mountbatten. 'Just so long as he doesn't speak against it.'

Gandhi comes, and says nothing at all. It turns out that he is observing one of his periodic days of silence. Instead of speaking he scribbles notes on scraps of paper.

> I know you don't want me to break my silence. Have
> I said one word against you during my speeches?

No one knows what this means. Mountbatten, incurably optimistic, deeply relieved not to have run into the stone wall that is Gandhi's conscience, says, 'He's letting out rope. He's giving me some space to try to pull it off.'

Jinnah then returns for his private session. He continues to insist that he can make no decision on his own.

'Delay now,' Mountbatten tells him, 'and Congress will withhold their acceptance of the plan too. Chaos will follow, and you'll lose your Pakistan.'

'What must be, must be,' says Jinnah.

Mountbatten gazes into Jinnah's implacable eyes.

'Mr Jinnah,' he says, 'this is what I'm going to do. Tomorrow, when we all meet again, I will ask the others formally if they accept the plan. They will say yes. I will then turn to you. I will say that I am satisfied with the assurances you have given me. I require you to say nothing. By that means, if your council so requires, you can deny later that you gave your acceptance. However, I have one condition. When I say, "Mr Jinnah has given me assurances which I have accepted and which satisfy me," you will not contradict me, and when I look towards you, you will nod your head.'

Jinnah gives this a moment of careful thought, then he nods his head.

The next day the conference resumes. The frustrated press photographers are allowed in, to record the historic meeting. The room is then cleared, and Mountbatten asks for formal acceptance of the plan. One by one the leaders accept. Jinnah gives his agreed nod of the head. Mountbatten then produces a thirty-four-page staff paper, raises it high above his head, and bangs it down on the table.

'This paper,' he says, 'is headed "The Administrative Consequences of Partition". You will find when you read it that time is of the essence. The longer we delay, the more the uncertainty will translate into unrest. I have therefore determined that the transfer of power will take place on August the fifteenth of this year. In ten weeks' time.'

The leaders are silent with shock.

Immediately after this bombshell the press staff go into battle stations, to distribute the right texts to the right people at the right time, and to avoid news leaking out in a manner that might provoke riots on the streets. Larry goes with Alan, accompanying Mountbatten in the viceregal Rolls-Royce, to All-India Radio. A group of orange-capped sadhus shout out slogans as they enter the building, protesting against any possible betrayal of the Hindu cause. Larry sees to the newsreel men while Alan attends Mountbatten in his broadcast. When the speech is done, Mountbatten comes through to the studio to repeat it for the cameras. A recording of the radio broadcast is played, and Mountbatten moves his lips to fit the words as the cameras run.

As the filming is completed, Nehru begins his own radio address. They stop to listen.

'We are little men serving great causes,' says Nehru. 'But because the cause is great, something of that greatness falls upon us also.'

Returning in the Rolls, Mountbatten, utterly exhausted, says, 'I never want to go through all that again.' Then he adds, 'I do truly believe that Pandit Nehru is a very great man.'

After the shock announcement of the date for Indian independence, Mountbatten has calendars printed and distributed to all staff. On each day is printed a number indicating the days left to transfer of power. The viceroy and his senior staff, including Alan Campbell-Johnson, then fly to London for consultations while the India Independence Bill passes through Parliament.

For those left behind, the pressure of work eases. Geraldine Blundell announces her intention to do some sightseeing, and reminds Larry of his promise to show her Fatehpur Sikri. Syed Tarkhan, hearing them speaking, reveals that he is knowledgeable on Mughal history, and would be happy to show them the sights. Rupert Blundell agrees to join them, but when he learns the trip involves four hours in a car each way, with no facilities for guests at the destination, he changes his mind.

'Too damn hot,' he says. 'You'll regret it.'

But Geraldine is smilingly stubborn.

'I want to see the deserted city,' she says. 'I may not get another chance.'

On Tarkhan's advice they set off early, leaving Delhi at seven in the morning. They take with them a picnic lunch, a canteen of water, and a bottle of Lebanese wine. Tarkhan, in his capacity as guide and leader, sits in the front beside the driver. Larry and Geraldine sit in the back.

In anticipation of the great heat, Geraldine wears a light cotton dress that leaves her arms and her lower legs bare. Larry, sitting beside her, is acutely aware of the nearness of her golden skin. He finds himself remembering Nell, naked in the Life Room at Camberwell, and later naked in his arms in the green light of his digs. Geraldine looks out of the window as they drive, and asks Tarkhan constant questions about what she sees, but Larry has the feeling that she senses the physicality of his thoughts. There's something in the way she moves her hands, from time to time smoothing her dress over her knees, that seems to be a response to his nearness.

'Those women with baskets on their heads,' she says to Tarkhan, 'how far will they walk?'

'For miles,' says Tarkhan. 'Perhaps all day. They're taking fruit to sell. They go on until they sell it.'

At one point a young man on a bicycle dashes out from behind a house right into the road before them, and the car hits him, sending him flying. The driver stops at once and jumps out.

'The poor boy!' says Geraldine. 'Is he all right?'

They see the driver haul the bike rider off the road and proceed to cuff him sharply about the head.

'No!' cries Geraldine.

'Don't interfere,' says Tarkhan.

The driver returns, shaking his head.

'Bloody fool should look where he's going,' he says. 'My apologies, Sahibs.'

'But is the boy hurt?' says Geraldine as they drive on.

They see him climbing back on his bicycle.

'This is India,' says Tarkhan.

Geraldine says nothing for a while. When she speaks at last it's clear she's been pondering the meaning of this minor accident.

'I wonder if we've really been all that good for India,' she says. 'I wonder what sort of a country it would be now if we'd never come.'

'That is a question we can never answer,' says Tarkhan from the front seat.

'You think we should be quitting India, don't you, Syed?' says Larry.

'Without a doubt,' says Tarkhan. 'But you know, for many of us it will also be a sad day. I am a navy man. I've been raised in a family that has deep respect for the motherland. It's not so easy to throw off such things overnight. Then again, when I hear the British saying they are graciously giving us our freedom, I want to say, Excuse me, sir, by what right did you take our freedom in the first place?'

'There was never any right,' says Larry. 'Only power.'

They are driving now between sunburned fields of brown earth, broken here and there by clusters of small green trees. The temperature has risen, and the air that rushes in at the open window is dusty and hot.

'I don't understand about power,' says Geraldine. 'I don't understand about war, either. Isn't there enough suffering in the world already?'

'You will see, when we get to Fatehpur Sikri,' says Tarkhan, 'there's a saying of Jesus inscribed on the victory arch: "The world is a bridge. Pass over it, but build no houses on it."'

'Where does Jesus say that?' says Geraldine.

'I thought Akbar the Great was a Muslim,' says Larry.

'So he was.'

He says no more. Geraldine falls into a doze, and as the car lurches on over the rough road her bare right arm comes to rest against Larry's left side. He feels its slight pressure there, and from time to time glances at Geraldine's face. Her eyes are closed, her lips very slightly parted. Somehow even in the heat of the car she manages to look fresh and lovely.

The last part of the journey is over a road that is cracked and fissured by the sun. The sharp jolting of the car wakes Geraldine.

'Almost there,' says Larry.

The car comes to a stop in the shade of a sheltering ashoka tree. Tarkhan, Larry and Geraldine step out into the burning noon. Geraldine puts on her straw hat and sunglasses and looks like a film star. Before them the track leads on to a gap in a ruined wall. An elderly man in a faded khaki shirt comes hobbling towards them and speaks with Tarkhan, bobbing his head repeatedly. Then he goes again.

'We're the only ones here,' says Tarkhan. 'We're the brave ones, he says.'

He leads them up the rising track through the gap in the wall, and there before them, quite suddenly, is the abandoned city. Its palaces are built of the same red sandstone on which it stands, and stripped of all life as they are, seem to be sculpted from the land. Domes and turrets reach skywards on spindly pillars, atop vast structures that are themselves so pierced and open to the sky that they seem to be light and insubstantial.

Tarkhan sees with gratification the astonishment on the faces of his guests.

'In its day the city was bigger than London,' he says, 'and far more magnificent. Akbar the Great ruled over a hundred million subjects, at a time when your Queen Elizabeth had barely three million.'

He leads them across the dusty square, in the centre of which is a paved cross, made of panels of red stone between bands of cream.

'This is a pachisi court,' he says. 'You know the game? It's like what you call Ludo. In Akbar's day it was played with people serving as the playing pieces.'

'This is extraordinary, Syed,' says Larry. 'How can it all still be here?'

'The dryness, I suppose. That building there is the Diwan-i-Am, the Hall of Public Audience. The five-storey structure is the Panch Mahal, where the ladies of the court lived.'

'How big is the city?'

'About four square miles. But come over here. This is what I want to show you.'

He leads them to a square building with four turrets on its corners, each one holding, on four slender pillars, an ornate dome.

'Come inside, into the shade.'

Each side of the building is pierced by a wide central door. Within there is a single space, dominated by an immense and intricately carved central pillar.

'This is the Diwan-i-Khas,' says Tarkhan. 'The Hall of Private Audience. This is where Akbar held his meetings.'

Larry is studying the complex carvings at the top of the pillar. It branches out into four stone overhead walkways sustained by a cluster of snakelike brackets.

'Remarkable,' he murmurs.

'I must now confess to an ulterior motive in bringing you here,' says Tarkhan. 'As you know, my country faces a great crisis, caused by the fears Muslims and Hindus have of each other. The terrible communal violence shows that the different faiths cannot live together. This is why there must be Pakistan. And yet, look more closely at this pillar.'

He guides their eyes with his hands.

'The designs at the base are Muslim. A little higher, and we have Hindu symbols. The third tier is Christian. And here at the top, the designs are Buddhist. And if you look higher up still, you will see the secret place behind the pierced screen where Akbar would sit, every Thursday evening, and listen to the discussions below. Hindus, Buddhists, Roman Catholics, atheists, he invited them all to come here and talk to each other.'

'Roman Catholics came here too?' says Geraldine.

'From Portugal, I believe,' says Tarkhan. 'Akbar wanted to formulate what he called the Din-i-Ilahi, the ultimate faith that would bring all religions together. According to the Din-i-Ilahi, there were to be no sacred scriptures or rituals, but all would take an oath to do good to all. And in his day, and for many years after, there was no hatred between the faiths.'

'And then the British came,' says Larry, 'and all the toleration came to an end.'

'No,' says Tarkhan gently. 'That would be too harsh. Though

as you know, there are those who believe you kept control of your great empire by the policy of divide and rule. For whatever reason, now to our shame and suffering, we are divided.'

'How difficult it all is,' murmurs Geraldine.

'Did you know,' says Tarkhan, 'that Tennyson wrote a poem about Akbar the Great? It's called "Akbar's Dream". It's rather long, but I remember two lines he gave to Akbar. "I can but lift the torch of reason, In the dusty cave of life."'

The three walk the deserted courts of the ghost city, made thoughtful by all that Tarkhan has said. Round them rise the skeletons of past glory, as if to mock the pretensions of the present imperial race. Larry thinks of the cold grey bankrupt homeland he has left behind.

'You say you were raised to respect the motherland,' he says to Tarkhan. 'How can we pretend to be the mother of any other peoples?'

'Perhaps we all have many mothers,' says Tarkhan.

They return to the car and take their picnic in the shade of the tree. The heat and the walking have wearied them. The Lebanese wine makes them sleepy.

'I think it would be good to return soon,' says Tarkhan.

On the drive back Geraldine abandons formality and falls asleep with her head in Larry's lap. Larry himself does not sleep. His head is buzzing with new thoughts. He thinks about the claims of the different religions to ultimate truth. He watches Geraldine's lips as they tremble with her sleep breaths. He asks himself why his own faith, that Jesus is the son of God, that His resurrection gives us promise of eternal life, should be the one true faith, and the others pale copies, or downright superstitious falsehoods. His gaze lingers on Geraldine's soft blond hair where the curls lie on her pale brow. Jesus said, 'I am the way, the truth, and the life.' So what of other ways, and other truths? Geraldine believes as he believes, she knelt beside him at Mass, her cheek shadowed by her lace mantilla. He would like to kiss her now, on the temple, just where the locks of hair fall away. He looks towards Tarkhan, dozing in the front seat, and thinks how much he likes him. How courteously he delivered his history lesson in the abandoned city, and yet how devastating its implications. You suppose yourself to be a modern man, free of the baseless prejudices of earlier generations, and then quite unexpectedly you catch a glimpse of your true self, and find it rests on an ocean of unexamined assumptions: that as an Englishman you inherit the civilised values that others will in time acquire; that as a Christian you possess the eternal truths that others will in time acknowledge. And all the time this slender girl lies trustful in your lap, and you long to kiss her, to slip off her dress, to enjoy her naked body.

Am I such a self-deceiver? Have I grown a mask that clings so tight I no longer know my own face? For whose benefit have I done so?

For the ones who look at me. For the ones who judge me.

So many masks. The mask of the gentleman. The mask of the man of culture. The mask of the good man. All worn for the onlookers, the judges, to appease them, to win their approval. But what is it that the maskless self wants? Who am I when no one is looking? Why do I care so much for goodness?

Fear, comes the answer. Fear, and love.

I'm afraid that if I'm not good, I won't be loved. And I want more than everything else, more than eternal life, to be loved.

This thought enters his mind in a flash, with the force of

revelation. Can it be true? He thinks back to his time of terror on Dieppe beach. That was true fear, fear of extinction. That was an animal instinct that overrode any other demands he could make upon himself. But what of the shame that followed, which he has lived with ever since? That's a different kind of fear.

I'm afraid that I don't deserve to be loved.

If this is true, is this all it is? All man's achievements, all acts of heroism, all acts of creation, no more than a plea to be counted worthy of love? Loved by whom?

Geraldine moves in his lap with the motion of the car, but she doesn't wake. There's something about her that's so contained, so quietly sure of herself, that makes her approval desirable and hard to win. And yet there was a man she loved, Rupert said, who broke her heart.

The driver honks loudly on his horn to disperse a flock of goats on the road ahead. Geraldine wakes, and sits up.

'Have I been lying on you? I'm so sorry. I do hope you don't mind.'

'No trouble at all,' says Larry.

He can see from the way she looks at him that she knows he liked it.

'You're very tolerant.'

The journey still has an hour or more to go. Tarkhan sleeps in the front. This time will not come again.

'You asked me why I came here,' Larry says. 'I came out to India because the girl I was in love with went off with another man. It seemed to be the end of the world then. Now it seems of no importance at all.'

'Why do you tell me that?' she says.

'I don't know, really.'

'It was the same for me,' she says. 'There was a man I loved very much. I thought we were going to be married. Then he told me he was going away. He never said why.'

'He's the loser,' says Larry.

'No,' says Geraldine simply. 'I was the loser.'

Tarkhan now wakes, and looks at the road, and then checks his watch.

'We'll be back in good time for dinner,' he says.

# 29

Ed Avenell descends the flank of Edenfield Hill, steadily tramping down the sheep path that cuts a diagonal into the valley. The evening sun, low in the sky, casts deep shadows over the bowls and billows of the Downs. As he goes the lines of the song run in his head, round and round.

*If I didn't care*
*More than words can say*
*If I didn't care*
*Would I feel this way?*

Sometimes he walks the Downs for hours looking and not seeing, wanting only to stop caring, to stop feeling. There's a state he can sometimes reach if he walks long and far enough that is very like intoxication, a state in which he loses all sense of himself. Rabbits scuttle into the gorse as he passes; sheep lumber away. He envies them their lives. You only have to look at a sheep to know it has no idea at all that it's a sheep, or even that it has an existence. It does what it needs to do, eats, sleeps, flees from danger, tends its young, all from instinct. People talk of animals as being innocent, and incapable of sin. Even when they see a fox eat a rabbit alive, they say it's obeying its nature. But animals aren't innocent, they're merely moral blanks. There's no more evil in a fox than in an earthquake. And no more good, either. This is what Ed envies. They have sidestepped the judgement. They know nothing of the speeding car that will crush them on the road, or the slaughterhouse at the end of the country lane.

Not to care. Not to feel. That's the trick. Then to return home as empty as a discarded wine bottle, and to see, beyond the opening door, her questioning eyes. How is he this time? Is he drunk or sober? Does he love me or does he not?

All it takes is a few simple words, but the words don't come. What paralysis is it that has him in its grip? If she could hear the crying in his head she would be reassured, but also dismayed. *I love you, I love you, I love you*, constant as the west wind. And relentless as the wind from the east comes the other cry. *All for nothing, all for nothing*.

The path leads him down to America Cottage, which has been unlived-in for many years now. The way to the coach road runs between the cottage and the collection of barns beside it, where the tenant of Home Farm stores his hay. Ed is passing round the end of the long barn when he hears voices, and comes to a stop to listen. There are two voices, a man's and a woman's. From where he stands he can't see into the barn, but the voices come clearly through the thin board walls.

The man's voice says, 'Baby wants cuddles.'

The woman's voice says, 'Bad baby wants spanky-spank.'

There follows a scuffling sound, mingled with gasping and

laughter. Then the man's voice says, 'Bare botty! Bare botty! Spanky-spank!' More scuffling and panting. Then the woman, 'What's Georgy got here? What's this then? Where's this come from?'

Ed is frozen to the spot, afraid of drawing attention to himself. If he walks on to the coach road he'll pass the open front of the barn and they'll see him. His only option is to retrace his steps as quietly as possible. Instead, he moves a little closer to the barn wall, where there's a gap in the boards. He doesn't mean to spy, and doesn't think of himself as spying, but he is compelled by a powerful impulse to understand.

'Baby wants cuddles,' the man is saying, more urgently now.

'Bad baby,' says the woman. 'Bad baby with his trousers down.'

Ed can see now, through the gap in the boards, through a fringe of hay, a large pink thigh, a rucked-up dress, a writhing half-undressed form beyond.

'Baby wants cuddles,' says the man, his voice choking.

'Bad baby,' says the woman, soothing, chanting, spreading her legs. 'Bad baby.'

After this there are no more words, only the gasping sounds of the man and the creaking and scratching of the hay that is their bed. Ed moves quietly away.

He knows both of them. The man is George Holland, Lord Edenfield. The woman is Gwen Willis, who comes twice a week to the farmhouse to clean and do the ironing. Ed knows her as a simple kindly woman in her mid-forties.

He reaches the sunken coach road and moves out of sight behind its fringe of trees. Here for no reason he comes to a stop. There's a fallen tree that offers its trunk as a bench, shaded by the canopy of the other trees. Ed sits himself down and waits.

What am I waiting for?

Not to shame poor George, that he's sure of. And yet he is waiting for George. He wants to touch and be touched by that simple urgent delight that he spied on in the barn. He wants to know that it's real. For all its absurdity, Ed senses that he has been a witness to a powerful force, one strong enough to override all convention, all good sense, and every instinct of self-preservation. George is riding the life force itself.

In time he hears voices again, then footsteps. Mrs Willis appears in the coach road, walking fast, alone. She throws him a startled look, and hurries past without a word. Some moments pass. Then George appears, strolling with an aimless air.

He too jumps when he sees Ed.

'Oh!' he says.

'Hello, George,' says Ed. 'Lovely evening for a walk.'

'Yes,' says George, going bright red.

Ed gets up off his tree trunk and joins George, ambling slowly down the track.

'Look, Ed,' says George at last. 'I don't know what to say.'

'You don't need to say anything, old chap,' says Ed. 'Nor do I.'

'Really?'

'None of my business.'

This evidently gives George much-needed relief.

'I appreciate that,' he says.

They walk on. Ahead through the trees loom the roofs and pinnacles of Edenfield Place.

'I say, Ed,' says George.

'Yes, George?' says Ed.

'It's not the way it looks, you know.'

'If you say so, George.'

'Look, stop for a moment, will you?'

They stop. George peers earnestly at Ed through his glasses, then looks equally earnestly at the stones of the track.

'This is nothing whatsoever to do with Louisa,' he says.

'I wouldn't dream of saying a word,' says Ed.

'No, I mean it really is nothing to do with her. I love her dearly. George Holland will always be a good and faithful husband to her. Always.'

'Right,' says Ed.

'But you see, there's someone else. There's Georgy.'

It's clear from the earnestness with which he speaks that George needs him to understand what he's confessing to him.

'Georgy's quite different. Georgy likes to play games. Georgy isn't shy or afraid of making a fool of himself, not with his Doll. Georgy is happy, Ed.'

'Right,' says Ed.

'Happier than I've ever been. And Georgy can do things I can't do. There's no real harm in that, is there? If Georgy can do it with Doll, then you never know. Maybe . . .'

'Why not?' says Ed.

'I expect I seem a bit of a joke to you. I'm a bit of a joke to most people.'

'No,' says Ed. 'Right now I'm thinking you're a bit of a genius.'

'A genius? I don't think I'm that, you know.'

'Tell me, George. When you go back to the house, now. When you meet Louisa. Will you be thinking about what you've just been doing? Will you be afraid Louisa might guess?'

'No,' says George. 'You see, I've not been doing anything. That was Georgy.'

'Yes, of course. Silly of me.'

They part outside the big house. Ed's opinion of George has undergone a reappraisal. He's impressed by the radical simplicity of his solution. Faced with irreconcilable demands upon him, by the world in which he lives and by his own needs, he has split himself into two people. Who knows through what accident he discovered this other self, the Georgy who finds his erotic fulfilment in the nursery? But having encountered him he has embraced him, made room for him in his life, and not judged him. This seems to Ed to be an act of great maturity.

Georgy is happy.

What greater achievement is there in any man's life?

Ed walks back across the park to the farmhouse, his thoughts occupied with this revelation. He too is pulled in opposite directions, by his love for Kitty and by his need to be alone. What if he were to split himself in two as George has done? One self could be the loving husband, while the other self remains untouched and untouchable.

He has never considered such a solution before, because he has assumed that there's a fundamental dishonesty to it. According to his own sense of integrity, his duty to Kitty is to tell her the truth about himself. Only then, surely, can he know that she truly loves him. But it strikes him now that this is selfish. This need to know that it's the real him who is loved: what is it but the child's fierce grip on the mother?

Baby wants cuddles.

Look at it from Kitty's point of view. What she wants is to know that he loves her. So why not construct, for Kitty's benefit, out of all the real love he has for her, a part-self, an Ed who can give her all she needs? This wouldn't be a falsehood, just an incomplete version. He imagines doing this, playing the part of an Ed who loves her and has no darker fears. To his amazement he finds at once he's released. He can say the words she so longs to hear.

But she'll see through his act, surely. She knows him too well. He considers what he'll say if challenged. He'll say, Yes, it's an act, but this loving Ed is real too. What will she say then? Will she say, Only all of you is enough for me?

There's Pammy too. And a new baby coming. This half-Ed can be a good father, in fact has been a good father for some time. The self he brings to his daughter is exactly that, a partial, edited self, suitable for children.

Think of it as a good Ed and a bad Ed. The bad Ed is weak or sick or mad. He drinks too much to numb all sensation, because the world to him is a dark and purposeless place. The bad Ed withdraws from contact with other people, most of all those he loves, because he knows his unhappiness is contagious. The good Ed is funny and brave and loving. The good Ed is the one Kitty fell in love with, the one who talks late into the night with Larry, the one who dances in the fields by moonlight. The good Ed has a shot at happiness.

He gets home, and pushing open the farmhouse door, calls out cheerfully, 'I'm back.'

Good Ed is back.

The kitchen is empty. He hears the sloshing of water upstairs. Bath time. He climbs the stairs to the bathroom. There's Kitty on her knees by the bath, and Pamela, pink and naked, squirming in the bath.

'Here you are,' he says. 'My two lovely girls.'

Kitty looks round in surprise.

'This is an honour,' she says.

'Do my story, Daddy,' says Pamela.

'I will,' says Ed, 'as soon as you're washed and dressed. But first I want to kiss my wife, because I love her.'

'Yuck!' says Pamela, impressed.

Ed kisses Kitty.

'What's brought this on?' says Kitty.

'Oh, nothing,' says Ed. 'I've been doing a bit of thinking.'

Pamela splashes in the bath water, wanting attention.

'Not about *you*,' says Ed. 'I never think about *you*.'

'You do! You do think about me!' shrieks the little girl, eyes bright.

'Well, whatever it is, it's much appreciated,' says Kitty, fetching a towel to lift Pamela out of the bath. 'Nice to have a husband who comes home and wants to kiss his wife.'

The good Ed is a great success. It turns out Kitty has noticed nothing amiss after all.

# 30

The Maharaj Rana of Dholpur drinks his tea with modest sips, then puts down the cup and sighs.

'I can't tell you that I like what is happening, Captain Cornford. This new India is a very recent invention. Dholpur's Paramountcy Treaty with Britain goes back to 1756.'

He's a small scholarly man, who wears a pink turban. In '21, during George V's tour of India, he and Dickie Mountbatten were ADCs together. Now, prince and ruler of his own state, history is about to brush him aside.

'Do me a favour,' Mountbatten told Larry earlier. 'Look after Dholpur while he's in Delhi. He's a decent man.'

'I suppose these days,' Larry says to the maharaj, 'it's harder to justify imperial rule by a far-off country.'

'Ah, these days.' Dholpur sighs again. 'That is the modern mind in action. The assumption that fundamental truths must change with time. Are you a religious man, Captain Cornford?'

'Yes,' says Larry. 'Catholic.'

'Catholic?' The maharaj brightens. 'Like the Stuart kings of England. Then perhaps you will understand when I tell you that

I believe most profoundly in the divine right of kings. The so-called Glorious Revolution of 1688, that drove James II into exile, was in my opinion both a disaster and an outrage. All the suffering that has followed springs from the false notion that the people can choose their own rulers. How are they to choose? What do the people know? Let God choose, and let the people be humbly thankful.'

'I see you're no believer in democracy,' says Larry.

'Democracy!' The maharaj gives him a look that combines melancholy with contempt. 'You think the people of India are choosing their rulers? You think when the British are gone the people of India will be free? Just wait a little, my friend. Wait, and watch, and weep.'

In these last days before the transfer of power the viceroy's staff work ever longer hours. They're planning the two days of ceremonial that will see the creation of two new sovereign nations. Sir Cyril Radcliffe, who has been shut away for weeks in a bungalow on the viceregal estate, has almost completed the award of the Boundary Commission. Everyone knows that once the details of the award are made public, the trouble will begin. Punjab and Bengal have now been partitioned; only Sylhet in Assam remains. Mountbatten makes it known that a late delivery on August 13th would be acceptable, fully aware that on that day he flies to Karachi for Pakistan's independence ceremony on August 14th. The following day, August 15th, India's Independence Day, is to be a national holiday, and the printing presses will be closed. In this way the precise details of the two new nations will not be made public until the celebrations are over.

The viceroy's staff spend the day of August 14th clearing their desks and contemplating the historic moment they are about to witness. The general feeling is that the British are making a dignified job of winding up the Empire, thanks in no small part to the charm, energy, and informality of the Mountbattens.

'He's an amazing chap,' Rupert Blundell says to Larry, as they break for a much-needed drink. 'He loves dressing up and prancing about with his medals, but actually he's the least stuffy man I've ever met. He's a member of the royal family, his nephew's marrying our future queen, but he's all for the Labour government. You know, in some strange way I think he sees himself as an outsider.'

'She's the one who amazes me,' says Larry. By this he means Edwina. 'They all adore her.' By this he means the Indian leaders.

'You know she and Dickie fight like cats,' says Rupert. 'But you're right. He adores her too.'

With the coming of independence, Mountbatten will cease to be viceroy, but will stay on as Governor-General of India. Viceroy's House is to become Government House. Some staff will remain, but many will go. Syed Tarkhan, a Muslim, plans to leave for Karachi, where he is to be an ADC to Jinnah. Rupert Blundell has decided to stay on for two more weeks, to assist in the transition, and then he and Geraldine will go home.

'What will you do then?' Larry asks him.

'Back to academia, I think. Charlie Broad says he'll have me at Trinity. How about you?'

'God knows,' says Larry.

On that same day, Independence eve, as the monsoon rains stream down over the Mughal Gardens, he has a conversation with Geraldine Blundell that focuses his thoughts. She's been talking to Rupert, and is curious to know about the banana connection. Unlike most others, she doesn't seem to think this is comical.

'So Fyffes is your family firm, is it?'

'In a way,' says Larry. 'We're actually a wholly owned subsidiary of the United Fruit Company. But they leave the UK operation to us.'

'Is it a big firm?'

'Before the war we employed over four thousand people. The war hit us hard. But we're building the business back up again.'

Hearing himself speak he's struck by his use of the possessive pronoun 'we'. Somehow here on the other side of the world his sense of separation from the family firm has diminished.

'And your father runs it?'

'Yes, that's right. My grandfather started it, in 1892. My father took over in '29.'

'And you'll take over from him?'

'Oh, no, I don't think so. I've not really ever been part of the firm.'

Geraldine's eyes open wide in astonishment.

'Why not?'

'I had other ideas. You know how when you're young you want to go your own way.'

'Yes, but don't you have a duty?' She looks at him so earnestly that he feels ashamed of his youthful dreams. 'You're born into privilege. You have to accept the responsibility that goes with it, don't you?'

'All I can tell you,' says Larry, feeling uncomfortable, 'is that it didn't feel that way.'

'So what was it you wanted to do?'

Larry shrugs, aware how inadequate his answer will sound to her; indeed, in this moment it sounds inadequate to his own ears.

'I wanted to be an artist.'

'An artist! You mean someone who paints pictures?'

'Yes.'

'I think that's wonderful, Larry. But it's not a job.'

Geraldine sees everything in a simple clear light, not distorted by vanity or illusion. She's strongly pragmatic, concerned to deal only with the realities of life, but she's also idealistic in her way. She believes in the grace of God.

She becomes more beautiful to him every day. Larry loves to look at her going about her work, unaware of his gaze. He has begun to think he would like to be more to her than a friend and colleague, but he hesitates to make any move. He's afraid of finding his overtures rejected. After all, what has he to offer?

He steals a moment to write to Kitty and Ed, which really means to Kitty.

> All is chaos and monsoon rain here as we prepare for Independence Day. There's much talk of England, the benign mother, looking on proudly as the child she has raised now comes of age. I do think this is perfect nonsense. The Indians have been civilised far longer than us. And speaking personally, when I'm in the presence of men like Nehru and Patel, and of course Gandhi, I'm the one who feels like a child.
>
> I've been puzzling mightily these last days over my own future. When am I to win my independence? I expect that sounds odd to you, after all I'm almost thirty, but since I've

been out here I've been having many new thoughts. What sort of life do I want to lead? Does what I want even matter all that much? I do so feel with you, Kitty, when you write that you want to be fully alive. I want that too. But at the same time I have this growing idea that chasing after what I want is not the answer. Perhaps I should think more of my responsibilities. A man my age, in my position, should do a useful job, and marry, and have children. Isn't that so? If I'm to remain unmarried, and without an occupation, then what use am I? This is what you call a mission in life, I think.

Anyway, I feel the world changing about me, in this historic moment, so maybe I'll change too. I think of coming home soon. To what? At least I can look forward to long talks with you and Ed, and Ed can tell me it's all luck and chance, and you can tell me I must learn to fly, and I'll sit there smiling and nodding, just happy to be back with you again.

After he's finished his letter it strikes him that he hasn't mentioned Geraldine, though she has never once left the forefront of his mind. Time enough to tell about her should there ever be anything to tell.

So the hour of midnight arrives, and with the dawn that follows the rains cease and the city is given over to parades and rejoicing. The national flag hangs at every window; saffron, white and green bunting festoons the trees. A huge crowd converges on Princes Park, where an arena has been built. In the centre of Princes Park stands a pagoda housing a giant statue of King George V; in a wide circle round it stand the palaces of the Nizam of Hyderabad, the Gaekwar of Baroda, and the Maharajas of Patiala, Bikaner and Jaipur. Today their windows gaze on a temporary dais and flagpole, where the flag of the new nation will be raised, and will thus eclipse the symbols of past power.

Larry sets off on foot to watch the grand moment, in a group that includes Rupert and Geraldine Blundell, Marjorie Brockman and Fay Campbell-Johnson. It becomes very obvious very soon that the crowd is far bigger than has been anticipated. The entire length of Kingsway, all the way to India Gate, is packed solid with cheering, laughing, flag-waving people, all eager to reach Princes Park. The group from Government House presses on, showing their tickets to beaming officials, but by the time they get to the parade ground all semblance of order has collapsed. The crowd has swarmed over the reserved stands and taken possession of the chairs, standing on the seats and arms and backs.

'Make way for the memsahibs!' call out happy voices, as Larry and Rupert attempt to squeeze their companions through the throng. They get within sight of the flagpole and then can go no further. The crush is so intense that women hold their babies over their heads. Nehru himself can be seen struggling to get through to the central dais. Unable to make progress he climbs onto a man's shoulders and walks in his sandals on the heads of the crowd.

There comes a great cheer. All heads twist round. Larry catches a glimpse of the ADCs in white, followed by the fluttering lance-pennants of the bodyguard, and then the state carriage itself, carrying the new governor-general. Mountbatten is in his white dress uniform, with Lady Mountbatten, also in white, by his side in the open landau.

Nehru, now standing on the central dais, waves his arms and calls for the crowd to let the procession pass through, but no one heeds him. Larry glances at Geraldine, held in the crush beside him, and sees that she has her eyes closed.

'Are you all right?' he says.

She doesn't answer.

The carriage and its escort come to a stop, some way from the flagpole. It's all too obvious that they can go no further. Mountbatten rises to his feet in the carriage, and gestures to Nehru to proceed. Nehru gives the signal, and the Indian tricolour rises up the flagpole. The crowd bursts into a giant roar. Mountbatten, trapped in the landau, takes the salute. A light rain begins to fall. The crowd discovers a rainbow in the sky: saffron, white and green. The cheering is redoubled.

In the midst of all the noise, Geraldine begins to utter low screams. She has her eyes tight shut, her hands over her ears, and she shakes her head from side to side.

'It's all right,' says Larry, putting his right arm round her. 'It's all right. I'll get you out.'

Holding her tight and close, he forces his way back through the cheering crowd, using his left shoulder to open up a space between the packed bodies. He feels Geraldine shaking, and hears her low screams, as he pulls her after him. At first their progress is slow, but as he works his way to the back of the crowd he finds they can move more easily. And so at last they emerge into a side street, where there is open space.

He holds her in his arms and lets her sob.

'There,' he says, soothing her. 'There, all safe now.'

The sobbing ceases. She remains in his arms, her face pressed to his chest. He feels the jerky shuddering of her chest as her breaths come slower and slower. Then she turns away, to dab the tears from her eyes.

'I'm so sorry,' she says. 'What a little fool you must think me.'

'Of course I don't,' says Larry.

'I don't know what happened. Suddenly I started to feel trapped. I couldn't bear it.'

'You were trapped. That's quite a crowd.'

'But you got me out.'

The light rain is still falling, bringing welcome refreshment on this burning day.

'Come on. Let's walk back.'

The next day Mountbatten hands Radcliffe's award to Nehru, and cables it to Jinnah in Karachi. Within hours, the Punjab is in flames. Ten million people are on the move, seeking safety on either side of the new borders. Three hundred thousand Hindus and Sikhs flee Lahore. In Amritsar Muslim women are stripped naked, paraded through the streets, and raped. Sikh fighting mobs, armed with machine guns and grenades, descend on Muslim villages and slaughter the inhabitants. Muslims at Ferozepur attack a train carrying Sikh refugees, and kill all they can reach. What begins as hysterical fear mutates into hysterical rage.

Hindu refugees begin to arrive in Delhi, bringing with them hunger, disease, and a poisonous lust for revenge. Within days the riots and the killings have taken over the capital. The main railway station, packed with Muslims trying to flee, is bombed by Hindus. In the subsequent riot police fire into the crowd. Looters smash Muslim shops in Connaught Circus. Muslim tonga drivers are dragged from their tongas and hacked to death. Arson attacks start fires across the city.

All flights in and out of Delhi are cancelled. Syed Tarkhan is unable to make his transfer to Karachi. Rupert and Geraldine Blundell, due to fly home on September 8th, are obliged to remain in Government House, one of the few islands of security. Lady Mountbatten learns that hospitals are being attacked, and the wounded massacred in their beds. She requests that the troops protecting Government House, who are the governor-general's bodyguard reinforced by the 5/6th Gurkhas, should add to their duties the protection of hospitals. She asks Larry and Syed Tarkhan to coordinate the allocation of guards.

'No need to go into the city yourselves,' she says. 'Just make sure we do the best we can with the men we have.'

Syed Tarkhan is deeply distressed by the violence.

'It's only what you said would happen,' says Larry.

Tarkhan shakes his head.

'I feel ashamed,' he says. 'I feel to blame.'

So many staff have left that there is a shortage of both cars and drivers. Government House rents three Buick Eights, and one is made available to transport hospital guards. Larry learns that Tarkhan proposes to drive the car himself.

'I'll come with you.'

'No, Larry,' says Tarkhan. 'There's no need.'

He means there's no need for Larry to put himself in danger. This is no longer Larry's country. But Larry too feels shame and blame.

'Think of it as a last hurrah for the motherland,' he says.

'Ah, I see.' Tarkhan smiles at that. 'A noble gesture.'

They pack into the Buick: a Gurkha lieutenant, three of his men, and Larry. Tarkhan takes the wheel. They drive across the city to Old Delhi. They encounter no trouble on the way, but here and there they see burned-out shops and overturned trucks.

At the Victoria Zenana Hospital the Gurkhas take up their post, and Larry receives a report on the latest casualties from the nurse in charge.

'Not so terrible.'

'The mobs will be out after dark,' says Tarkhan.

They drive back through the deserted streets of the Paharganj area as the light fades in the sky. Crossing the overbridge by New Delhi station they hear shouts. Then comes a burst of gunfire, and the windscreen explodes into fragments. Tarkhan gives a grunt and tips over to one side, then with a convulsive movement rights himself.

'Syed!'

The car lurches out of control, heading for the parapet of the bridge. Tarkhan struggles with the wheel, panting loudly. The car shudders to a stop. Tarkhan slumps forward, blood pouring from his right shoulder. The engine cuts out.

'Syed!'

Before Larry can make a move to help him, an army lorry comes screeching up, and eight or nine armed men jump out.

'Out of the way! Out of the way!' They point their guns through the shattered windscreen. 'This is for the Muslim scum!'

Larry can hear from their voices that they're beyond reason. They've come out hunting to kill, and they no longer care. The gun barrels jab at him.

'Out of the way!'

Half paralysed by terror, he realises dimly that he himself is not in danger. He is an Englishman. Their war is no longer with the likes of him. All he has to do is move aside and let the fratricidal rage take its course. These thoughts pass through his mind at lightning speed, even as his eyes fall on Tarkhan's hands, which still grip the steering wheel. He hears the wounded man groan. He sees the fingers of one hand open and close. This simple human gesture is all it takes.

'No!' he cries.

He throws himself across Tarkhan, embracing him, as if his arms have the power to shield him from gunfire.

'Muslim scum!' shout the armed men. 'We shoot Muslim dogs! You will die too!'

Larry pulls Tarkhan even more tightly into his arms, so that the blood from his wound runs down his own chest. He hears Tarkhan's choking voice.

'Go, Larry. Leave me.'

The men with the guns tug at his sleeves, shouting. He closes his eyes and rocks his friend in his arms and waits to die.

Now the shouting is loud and close. A gun fires, a single shot echoing in the night. He smells the smell of fresh blood. He hears Syed Tarkhan's low groans. Then he hears another sound: the growl of the army lorry driving away.

He draws a long deep breath. He becomes aware of the drumming sound in his ears, and knows it's his own pulsing blood. Have they killed his friend in his arms?

'Syed?'

Tarkhan turns to him, groaning. He can see no fresh wound.

'I'm taking you to the hospital.'

He drags the wounded man into the passenger seat, and wedges him between the seat and the door. He starts the engine. Hand trembling on the gear stick, he reverses onto the road, and turns to drive back the way they came.

At the Victoria Zenana Hospital the nurses stretcher Tarkhan into a ward and tear the blood-soaked clothing from his upper body. Larry stays by his side.

'How badly is he hurt?'

'He'll live,' they tell him. 'How about you?'

'I'm not hurt.'

Tarkhan has lost consciousness. A doctor comes and examines the single gunshot wound.

'Smashed the collarbone,' he says. 'Lucky not to have got the main artery.'

So that second gunshot missed its target. How could they miss, at point-blank range? Reliving its sound now in memory, it seems to Larry that the second shot was fired into the air. Why?

He drives the Buick back to Government House alone, careless of any further danger. The warm night air streams through the smashed windscreen, bathing his face. A strange lightness of spirit has taken possession of him. He feels as if he has died and risen again and is now immortal.

Entering Government House through the north door, he makes his way down the corridor, past the startled looks of servants, to the small office where Geraldine keeps her charts. He finds her there alone. She stares at him, mute with shock.

'It's all right,' he says. 'It's not my blood.'

He opens his arms. Responding instinctively to his gesture, she comes into his embrace.

He holds her tight, feels her trembling in his arms. He bends his head towards her, and understanding, she turns her face to his. He kisses her, clumsily at first. Then he feels her lips respond, and her body soften in his arms.

When they part, there are bloodstains on her dress, and she is looking at him wonderingly.

'Larry,' she says.

Suddenly it's all so clear. He could have died back there on the overbridge, but he didn't die. That second gunshot was a command that said: live. Time is so short, death comes so soon. While we have this precious gift of life we must cherish it. We must love each other.

'I have so much love to give you,' he says.

'Do you, Larry?'

'Will you let me love you?'

He doesn't ask for her love. That's for her to give. This isn't about his own needs or fears. This is about the life force within him, that's pouring from him in a ceaseless stream.

'Yes,' she says. 'Yes.'

Larry goes back to the Victoria Zenana Hospital the next day to find Syed Tarkhan sitting up in bed and drinking tea.

'Larry,' he says. 'My brother.'

'So you're going to pull through, are you?'

'I'm leaving, my brother. This afternoon I leave for Karachi.' He holds out his hand. His eyes have never left Larry from the moment he entered the ward. 'I will never forget you.'

His limpid gaze speaks to Larry, saying, There are no words.

'So you're off to build a brand-new country,' says Larry.

'If God wills.'

'I'll miss you.'

Tarkhan holds his hand tight, and nods and shakes his head at the same time, all the while looking into his eyes with his tender loving gaze.

'It truly was a noble gesture, Larry,' he says.

# 31

'Married?' says William Cornford.

'Well, we're not married yet,' says Larry. 'But we're going to get married.'

'Well, well, well,' says his father, nodding his head. 'This is very good news. Very good news. Cookie will be so excited. As am I. So who is she?'

'Her name is Geraldine Blundell. Her brother was at Downside a year above me. So she's a good Catholic, you'll be pleased to hear.'

'All I need to please me is to know that you're happy.'

'I'm very happy, Dad. You wait till you meet her. She's very lovely, and very special. She's been in India with her brother.'

'So we have poor India to thank, do we? I don't expect when you took yourself off there you thought you'd come back with a wife.'

'It was the last thing on my mind.'

'Well, my boy, I think this calls for a drink.'

William Cornford fusses about in his library, searching through his bottles for something suitably celebratory. He settles on a single-malt whisky.

'Now I know it's none of my business,' he says, his attention on the glasses, 'but have you given any thought to what you're going to live on?'

'Yes, Dad,' says Larry. 'I do realise I need a job.'

'I rather think you do.'

'I was wondering if you had anything going?'

William Cornford continues pouring whisky, but now his hands are trembling. He hands Larry his glass. Not trusting himself to speak, he raises his glass in a silent toast.

They drink.

'Welcome to the company,' he says at last, his voice throaty with emotion.

The Blundells live in Arundel. The marriage is to take place in the church of St Philip. Mrs Blundell has hopes that the Duke of Norfolk will attend, in his capacity as Earl of Arundel and head of the premier Catholic family in the land.

'You know he's also the first peer of the realm,' she tells Larry. 'As hereditary earl marshal he organised the coronation of the king. Not that Hartley and I care for titles as such. Really it's the sheer weight of *history* that we find so moving.'

Geraldine has warned Larry about her mother.

'She's one of those people who doesn't really believe in failure. She sees it as a lack of moral fibre, I think. I can hear her now, saying to us children, "Do it properly or don't do it at all."'

'She sounds terrifying,' says Larry.

But Barbara Blundell takes to Larry from the beginning.

'If you don't mind my saying so,' she tells him, 'you come as something of a relief after the last one. Geraldine is my special pet. You'll forgive my partiality, but I think you'd have to look far and wide to find her combination of beauty without and beauty within. She deserves a husband of true faith and ample fortune. And since Bernard Howard has sired only daughters . . .'

She gives a shrill high laugh, to show that this is a joke. Bernard Howard is the Duke of Norfolk. Larry is a little alarmed by the 'ample fortune' part, which seems not to be a joke. Geraldine tells him not to worry.

'Mummy knows you're only starting out. But she's tremendously reassured to know it's the family firm. Also I told her you have a best friend who's a lord.'

'Do you mean George?' Larry is surprised to find George in the role of asset. 'His grandfather sold patent medicine.'

'A lord is a lord,' says Geraldine placidly.

England has enjoyed a blazing summer, which extends into a warm dry autumn. The outlook is good for the wedding, now fixed for Saturday, October 25th.

'After all, we don't want to compete with the royal wedding, do we?' says Barbara Blundell with her high laugh. Princess Elizabeth is to be married on November 20th. This turns out to be the reason why the Duke of Norfolk can't come to Geraldine's big day. 'I am a little disappointed, but I suppose someone has to organise the wedding of our future queen.'

The honeymoon is to be in the Cornford house in Normandy, which has been fully refurbished after its wartime occupation. Louisa offers their house as a staging post for the Channel crossing.

'They're to stay the night of the wedding with the Edenfields at Edenfield Place,' Barbara Blundell tells her friends. 'Then they go on to the family estate of La Grande Heuze.' She lingers on the words *place*, *estate*, *grande*, with a light but pointed emphasis.

Larry bears all this with a good spirit. He sees Geraldine now in her element, quietly countermanding her mother's extravagances, making sure that the correct information passes down the chain of family, priests, guests and tradespeople who each have their part to play in the wedding. Her grasp of details astonishes him, as does her confidence in her own judgement in all matters of taste. She will wear her mother's wedding dress, the seamstress will adjust it to fit her. Larry will wear morning dress. There will be four bridesmaids, of descending size, and two very small pageboys. She suggests that George would make a suitable best man, but here Larry holds out. He makes it clear that he wants Ed Avenell.

'You've never met George,' he says. 'Ed is far more dashing.'

While Geraldine busies herself with plans for the wedding, Larry is given a crash course on the family company, Elders & Fyffes, in all its current aspects. The London headquarters has recently moved from the Aldwych to 15 Stratton Street in Piccadilly. The rooms are unfamiliar to Larry, but the faces are all the same. Everywhere he goes he meets a general smiling delight that he is to join the firm at last.

'You know why they're so happy?' his father asks him. 'It's not because of your pretty face. It's because they expect you to take over after me, and that means things will go on being run in the same way.'

'So they shall,' says Larry, 'if I have anything to do with it.'

'Subject, of course, to our ultimate masters in New Orleans.'

This means the mighty United Fruit Company.

'I thought they pretty much left us alone to run the show,' says Larry.

'They do. That was the understanding, back in '02, when the company nearly went under, and my father turned to them for help. Andrew Preston was running United then, and he was a man of his word. But Preston is long gone. There's a fellow called Zemurray in charge now. Very different kettle of fish.'

'Zemurray?'

'I think he began as Zmurri. Russian, I believe.'

'And you don't trust him.'

'I wouldn't want to get on the wrong side of him. But so long as we make money for him, I think he'll leave us alone.'

As part of his familiarisation process, Larry makes a tour of the main company facilities. He walks the quays of the purpose-built docks at Avonmouth, and at Liverpool. He inspects the purpose-built temperature-controlled railway wagons, and several of the huge depots where the fruit is kept in chilled storerooms until ready for delivery. He goes on board *Zent III*, the company's most recently acquired vessel, originally built in Norway and operated by Harald Schuldt, a German importer, before being seized as a war prize. The Fyffes fleet numbers fourteen ships, down from the twenty-one before the war, but more than enough for the current depressed level of trade. He studies figures that show the problems the company faces, due to shortages in Jamaica and government restrictions.

'We believe the answer may be to go back to the Canaries,' says William Cornford, 'which is of course where the company started.'

'The cargo side seems to be very modest,' says Larry.

'More trouble than it's worth,' says his father. 'Our ships are built as specialised bulk carriers.'

'Even so,' says Larry, 'we should take a look at it.'

The talk of tonnages and leaf-spot disease is familiar to Larry from his father's mealtime conversation. He finds that he slips into the company surprisingly easily, soon comfortable in the Stratton Street offices. He begins to understand how the company has become his father's family.

His father, noting this with some complacency, says to him, 'You see it now? You were born for this.'

The sun shines on the day of the wedding. George shows up in a grand old Rolls-Royce, accompanied by Ed and Kitty and Pamela.

'Where on earth did you get that?' exclaims Larry.

'It was my father's,' says George. 'I only get it out on special occasions. It uses far too much petrol.'

Barbara Blundell is thrilled.

'I do like the aristocracy to put on a show,' she says.

Louisa has stayed at home, feeling unwell. Kitty whispers the details to Larry.

'It's very early days, but she thinks she may actually be pregnant!'

Kitty herself is very pregnant.

'That's wonderful.'

'If it's true, it's a miracle,' says Kitty. Then taking his arm for support, she walks away to a spot where they can speak in private. 'I'm just so happy for you, darling. You deserve a family of your own. Is Geraldine as wonderful as I want her to be?'

'If I tell you she's the opposite of Nell in every way,' says Larry, 'that should give you some idea.'

'But I did like Nell's honesty. She had a way of saying just what she thought.'

'Oh, Geraldine's honest. But she's also moral, which Nell never was. You'll see when you meet her. She has high standards.'

'And she makes you happy?'

'I adore her,' says Larry. 'The more I know her, the more perfect she turns out to be.'

'She couldn't be too perfect for you,' says Kitty. 'You deserve the best.'

Ed in tailcoat and grey waistcoat and white tie looks as handsome as Larry has promised. Geraldine's father, older, shorter and plumper, looks almost decrepit by his side. 'Stand up straight, Hartley,' his wife says. 'You're not to sag.'

'Another one on the way, then,' Larry says to Ed.

'Mid-December, they tell me,' says Ed. 'An early Christmas present.' He looks round all the bustle of last-minute arrangements. 'Doing it in style, I see.'

'That's Geraldine,' says Larry. 'Or perhaps I should say her mother.'

Rupert Blundell wanders about looking uncomfortable in a morning suit, smiling but not fraternising.

'You look bewildered, Rupert. Is it really that bad?'

'Do I? I don't mean to. A great occasion.' His eyes are on Ed. 'That's Ed Avenell, isn't it?'

'Yes, of course. Come and say hello.'

Larry takes Rupert over to Ed and they shake hands and say yes, they remember each other, but it's clear Ed has no idea who Rupert is.

'Rupert was with Mountbatten,' Larry says.

'Good work on the VC,' says Rupert.

Rupert's father joins them, seeking the quiet haven of masculine company.

'What a lot of fuss,' he says with a sigh. 'Makes me wish I was a Quaker.'

'Look at you three!' Larry exclaims. 'Anyone would think you were all waiting to see the dentist.'

'Sorry,' says Hartley Blundell, straightening his posture. 'Attention! Ready for the salute!'

Ed smiles at that. Courage under fire.

'I really appreciate this,' Larry murmurs to Ed when he gets the chance. 'It's your idea of a nightmare, isn't it?'

'I'm not all that fond of people in crowds,' says Ed. 'But I'm rather fond of you.'

They move on in due course to the church in a convoy of cars. Larry's father travels with the bride's mother, and so gets the benefit of her close knowledge of the Duke of Norfolk.

'When he plays in the town cricket team, his butler is the umpire, and when he's bowled out, which he always is in no time at all, the butler raises his hand and announces, "His Grace is not in."'

William Cornford smiles polite appreciation.

'Class distinction means nothing to me,' Barbara Blundell confides. 'I take as I find. But I do love the quirky traditions you get in the great houses. They add colour to life.'

The church of St Philip, like Westminster Cathedral, like the Sacred Heart in New Delhi, is a new building conceived in an old style; in this instance French Gothic. As Larry stands at the altar rail waiting for the bride to arrive he finds himself thinking about English Catholics and their churches, and how odd it is that a faith that defines itself as rooted in tradition should have to function in new buildings. Of course in France, in Italy, all this is different. There the evocations of the saints ring out in pillared aisles once walked by the saints themselves. He thinks of his father's love of the great French cathedrals. Then, for no reason, he thinks how odd it is to be getting married.

Why am I doing this?

He asks the question not because he has any doubts, but because he's suddenly aware he doesn't know the answer. From the moment he took Geraldine in his arms, and stained her white dress with blood, he has known that this is what must happen. It has never presented itself to him as a decision. From the start it has been for him a solution to his puzzles about the future: puzzles of love, and sex, and status, and identity, and no doubt many more, all resolved by this one act. He is becoming a husband. He is forming a clearer picture of that misty realm that reaches before him, his grown-up life.

The organ booms out the wedding march. Geraldine enters the church in her mother's dress, on her father's arm. She looks fragile, and grave, and beautiful. The nuptial Mass begins.

The newly married couple pass that night at Edenfield Place. Louisa appears only briefly, white-faced, to apologise for her absence, and then retreats to her room. George, now proud, now fearful at her condition, makes an abstracted host. Bride and groom retire early to the principal guest bedroom.

Both are exhausted. The bed that awaits them has ornate barley-sugar posts holding a high carved wooden canopy, and curtains in a pink and blue floral fabric. The immense wardrobe has a mirrored central panel in which they see themselves reflected, smiling, uncertain.

'I'll go and use the bathroom first, shall I?' says Larry. 'I'll get into my pyjamas there.'

He understands that Geraldine is shy of undressing in front of him. He takes his time in the bathroom. When he returns, he finds Geraldine standing where he left her, but now in a white silk nightdress. The silk clings to the curves of her body.

'You look ravishing,' he says.

She smiles, and goes on tiptoe to the bathroom. He turns out the bedroom centre light, leaving on a bedside lamp. He gets into bed. The linen sheets are chilly.

Geraldine returns, and stands, hesitating, in the middle of the room.

'Would you rather have the light out?' says Larry.

'Maybe,' she says. 'Let's try.'

He turns out the bedside lamp. The room is plunged into total darkness. He hears her approach the bed, and pat her way up it to the head. She creeps under the bedclothes, barely disturbing them, and lies beside him without touching him. He hears her breathing.

'Tired?' he says.

'A little,' she says.

He reaches out his right hand towards her, and encounters her silk-clad hip. She gives a start.

'Hello,' he says.

'Hello.'

'Cold?'

'A little,' she says.

'Why don't I warm you?'

He shuffles alongside her and with some awkwardness takes her in his arms. She curls her body so that she's lying on her side, her head in the crook of his shoulder, her knees against his thighs. He strokes her back softly, to soothe the tension of her muscles.

'All a bit new, isn't it?' he says.

'Yes,' she whispers.

He kisses her, and she responds at once, in the manner of one who is determined to show willing. His caressing hands reach down her silk-clad back to the curve of her bottom. She moves a little, to release one hand, and finds his shoulder, and the back of his neck. In silence, in darkness, they touch each other lightly in safe places.

Then his left hand comes up her back to her neck and cheek, and down over her throat, over the lace ties of her nightdress, to her breast. He draws his fingers very lightly over her breast, feeling the nub of the nipple beneath the silk. While he does this she stops her own caresses entirely.

'Do you mind?' he says.

'No,' she whispers. 'You must do whatever you want.'

He runs his hand down her body to her curled-up knees, and softly presses them, making her straighten out her legs. She offers no resistance, but he feels her nervousness. For a little while longer he does no more than stroke her, from her cheek, down over her breast, to her hip. As he does so, discovering by touch alone the lines of her slender body, he becomes aroused.

Now he lets his caressing hand roam lower down her leg. His fingers tug at the fabric of her nightdress, drawing it up, until he can touch the bare skin of her thigh beneath.

'There,' he says. 'That's the real you.'

She lies still, trembling a little. He eases her nightdress up higher.

'Why don't you take it off?' he whispers.

Obediently she sits up and draws her nightdress over her head. As soon as it's off she wriggles back down under the bedclothes.

He takes her in his arms again, kisses her. Each stage is an experiment for him, its outcome unknown. Excited, he now realises she will indeed cooperate with his wishes.

But he understands he must proceed slowly.

'Shall I take mine off too?'

'If you want,' she says, her voice muffled beneath the sheet.

He sits up in his turn, and pulls off his pyjama top. Then he unties the cord of his pyjama trousers and pushes them down his body, kicking them off at the bottom of the bed. Now as naked as she is he draws her back into his arms, and feels her skin against his skin. He shifts the position of his hips so that his erection lies touching her body.

She stiffens with shock. For the first time he wonders how much she knows, and what she's expecting.

'It's all right,' he murmurs. 'It's all right.'

Slowly her body softens against him. He strokes her with long slow passes, all down her body, and timidly, she begins to caress him too.

He takes her hand and places it on his erection, wanting her to know that part of him and not be frightened. He moves her hand up and down, and she allows herself to excite him in this simple way. But when he takes his hand away, her hand stops moving.

He strokes her thighs, and runs his hand over the furry mound where her thighs meet.

'Do you know what it is we do?' he whispers.

'A little,' she says.

From the way she says it he realises that she doesn't know. He goes on stroking her, thinking now how brave she is to submit to this unknown ordeal. He kisses her.

'It's all right,' she says. 'You must do what you want.'

So this is her sacrifice, in her love for him. But once the unknown becomes known it will cease to be a sacrifice. It will become their shared delight.

Her naked body against his is having its natural effect. He wants very much to be closer still. But he wants her to know what's going to happen. So he runs his hand between her thighs and, easing them a little apart, he feels for the place where he will enter her.

As soon as his fingers began to probe, she stiffens once more. He withdraws his hand, and taking her hand again, causes it to move up and down his erection.

'When we make love,' he says, 'this has a special way of being close to you.' He takes her hand and places it between her thighs. 'In here. Inside you.'

She says nothing for a moment. Then, very low, she says, 'How?'

'It just does. It goes in.'

'Is that what you want?'

'It's just how it works,' he says. 'It's how love works.'

'Is that what love is?' she says.

'Oh, my darling. Your mother told you nothing?'

'She told me I must do whatever you asked of me. She said my wedding present to you was the gift of my body.'

'It is. It is. And mine to you.'

'Then you must do it, my love,' she whispers. 'You have only to tell me what it is you want of me. I belong to you now.'

Her submission touches him deeply. It also excites him. The idea that he can command her to pleasure him as he wills excites him.

He moves his body so that he's lying over her, and easing himself into position, begins to press to enter her. She opens her legs, now understanding his intent, but at the same time she holds her breath. He nuzzles against her, meaning to make no harsh move, aware that to start with she could feel some pain. But he makes no progress at all.

He pushes a little harder. From his lovemaking with Nell, he's familiar with the sensation of yielding and opening up, but this time there's no giving way. Her body is soft and exciting, almost too exciting, but offers him no right of entrance.

'Is there something I must do?' she says.

'Don't be afraid,' he says.

He wants to say, Open yourself to me, welcome me, love me. But he understands how frightening it must be to her, and that he must be patient. At the same time the desire is mounting in him, the simple hunger for satisfaction, and he wants to force himself into her before it's too late. He pushes more eagerly, and hears her utter a low gasp. Then comes a wave of guilt.

What right have I to put my own pleasure before hers? We have a whole lifetime ahead of us. I can surely afford to wait one more day.

He eases himself off her body, and lies on his back beside her.

'Have you done it?' she says.

He can't contain a short laugh.

'No, my darling,' he says. 'But it doesn't matter. We're both tired. There'll be other nights.'

She lies beside him in the darkness, in silence. After a while he thinks perhaps she's gone to sleep. But when at last she speaks he realises she's been crying soundlessly.

'I'm sorry,' she says.

'Darling, darling, sweetheart. It's not your fault.'

'I'm so stupid and ignorant,' she says. 'But I'll get better, I promise you. I'll be a good wife.'

'You are a good wife, my darling. The best in the world. You'll see. It'll all come right soon. It's my fault, I shouldn't be in so much of a hurry. But if I am, it's because I love you and want you so much.'

'And I do love you so much too,' says Geraldine.

After that they kiss, and put their night clothes back on, and settle down to sleep. Larry lies awake far into the night. Geraldine lies still and quiet beside him, and he's not sure if she sleeps or not.

Late October in Normandy is golden with sunlight. Geraldine, enchantingly pretty, stays close by Larry's side, smiling for him, touching him, leaning her soft head against his shoulder. The French staff of La Grande Heuze all fall in love with the young couple, and wait on them with tender care. Geraldine does her best with the servants, laughing at her own poor French, thanking them with smiling bobs of her pretty head. 'Qu'elle est charmante,' they say to each other. 'Vraiment bien élevée, cette petite Madame Cornford.'

At night, progress of a sort is made. Geraldine now understands fully what is required of her, and professes herself willing to do all that her husband wants; but her body is not under the command of her will. By the third night it seems to Larry that he is being too cautious, and that what is needed is a more powerful attack. He explains this to Geraldine and she accepts his analysis, saying as ever, 'If that's what you think is for the best.' However, when the theory is put into practice she suffers a violent reaction. She starts breathing in short rapid jerks, and almost faints. Alarmed, full of self-reproach, Larry abandons his attack at once, and spends the rest of the night cradling her in his arms. When they are found to be sleeping in late the following morning the servants smile at each other and whisper, 'Qu'il est doux, l'amour des jeunes.'

For the remaining days of their honeymoon Larry treats his young bride with great gentleness, and she shows him even more physical affection than before. They speak about the matter openly only once.

'It will be all right, won't it, darling?' she says.

'Of course it will,' he replies. 'It's just a matter of giving it time.'

'You aren't too horribly disappointed in me?'

'How could I be?'

He reaches his hand across the breakfast table and she takes it in hers. They smile into each other's eyes.

'I do love you so much, darling,' she says. 'I'm so proud and happy to be married to you. I promise you I'll make you happy too.'

'You make me happy already,' he says.

In so many ways she's so perfect. And of course, she's still young, only twenty-two. Easy to forget in view of the formidable efficiency with which she manages herself and those around her. If her body is young and fearful, that should be no surprise. All will come right in time.

# 32

Kitty's new baby is a good baby right from the start. She feeds well and sleeps well, and seems to be happy wherever she's put. Her name is Elizabeth. Her arrival changes everything for Kitty. Her life is now filled from morning to night with tending to the baby's simple and immediate needs. All other concerns withdraw to that shadowy space on the edge of consciousness. At the centre, pink-cheeked, smelling of warm milk, chirruping with contentment, lies little Elizabeth.

Pamela is less delighted.

'She looks like a monkey,' she says.

'But she's a dear little monkey, isn't she?'

'I suppose so,' says Pamela.

Somehow this name clings on, and the baby comes to be called the Monkey, which is later shortened to the Monk. Pamela, who has recently passed her fifth birthday, becomes aware that the Monk is often compared favourably to herself as a baby. Apparently she cried a lot, and wouldn't eat what she was given, and threw her toys out of the pram. The Monk's placidity is much remarked upon, always in highly approving terms.

'She was born with a good nature,' they say, gazing fondly on her as she sleeps.

'She might be dead,' says Pamela.

She takes to poking the baby surreptitiously, to make her cry.

Louisa comes calling most days. Her own pregnancy is now well advanced. The early sickness has passed, but she continues to give her doctors cause for concern.

'It's so unfair,' she complains to Kitty. 'I should be dancing for joy, but instead I feel like a cow with a hangover.'

George fusses round her, and tells her to sit down all the time. To Kitty's surprise, Louisa shows no irritation at this. She leans on his arm for support, and pats him, like a horse.

'George says if it's a boy he's to be William, after his father.'

'I think it will be a boy,' says George.

'Oh, you don't want a boy,' Ed says. 'Boys are always shouting and fighting.'

Ed is so much sweeter these days. Kitty knows very well that deep down he's not happy, but at least he's making a real effort to be friendly. She even has hopes that he's overcome his habit of drinking too much. Then one day Mrs Willis finds a stash of empty bottles while cleaning the small parlour. This is the room Ed calls his 'office', to which he often retires. The empty bottles were in a cupboard.

'Why hide empty bottles, Ed?'

'I wasn't hiding them. I was storing them. We reuse glass bottles, you know? Every bottle costs tuppence. That soon adds up.'

She can tell by the way his voice goes up in pitch that he's ashamed and defensive, so she lets the matter drop. But from now on, when he seems more silent and sleepy-eyed than usual, she suspects him of having been drinking. She knows she should talk to him about it, but the baby occupies all her time and care, and truth to tell she's afraid of raising the issue.

In May, when the hawthorn blossom is white in the hedges and the young leaves are bright on the trees, Larry and Geraldine come down for the weekend. This visit has been long promised, and at last a time has arrived when Ed is home, and Larry's business can spare him. The Cornfords motor down from London in a new Riley saloon, a shiny dark-red car with cream sides. This is only the first sign of Larry's new prosperity. He gets out to reveal he's wearing a tailored tweed suit, and a tie that looks suspiciously like an old school tie.

Kitty bursts into laughter.

'Larry, what's happened to you! You've turned into landed gentry!'

'That's Geraldine,' says Larry. 'She's taken me in hand.'

Geraldine is wearing a tight-fitting red wool coat with a long full skirt of a kind Kitty has never seen before. On Geraldine's slim and elegant figure the effect is stunning.

'Lord, I feel so dowdy and provincial,' Kitty exclaims. 'You mustn't be too disappointed by the way we live.'

'How could we be?' says Geraldine, looking round with the smile of one who has come determined to be pleased. 'It's bliss to be out of London. Just look at all this!' She means the trees, the Downs, the sky. 'It makes Kensington Gardens feel very poky, I assure you.'

Geraldine has perfect manners. She goes into raptures over baby Elizabeth, now almost five months old. She has a present for Pamela, a doll that isn't a baby at all but a lady, with clothes you can take off and another set of clothes to change her into. Pamela is mute with pleasure.

'Say thank you, Pammy.'

The little girl looks up at the beautiful lady and can't speak. Her eyes shine with gratitude.

'That's so clever of you,' says Kitty. 'You couldn't have got her anything she'd like more.'

There are presents for Kitty too, or as Geraldine puts it, 'for the house'. A box of chocolates from Fortnum & Mason and a bottle of Dom Pérignon.

'How in God's name did you get that?' says Ed, examining the label.

'From Larry's cellar,' says Geraldine. She and Larry have set up house in Campden Grove, along with Larry's father. 'It's a '37, which I'm told was a very good year. I hope you don't think I'm bringing coals to Newcastle.'

Over lunch Larry tells them about the source of his new-found prosperity, which is the family firm.

'The whole thing has been a revelation to me,' he says. 'You know how I was so dead set against going into the business, or any business, for that matter. And I'm sure you think the only reason I'm doing it now is for the big car and so forth. But the truth is, I've become almost passionate about the job.'

'Passionate about bananas, Larry?' says Ed, smiling as he watches him.

'Passionate about bananas if you like,' says Larry. 'But it's the firm itself I love. I'm so proud of what my grandfather and my father have built. Do you know we're just about the only company that provides retirement pensions for our employees? We've been doing it since '22. It's called the Staff Provident Fund. The company pays an extra ten per cent of salary every year into a special benefit account for each employee. Then they get a lump sum on retirement, and if it's not enough we top it up.'

Geraldine reaches out to touch his arm, stopping him in mid-flow.

'But I shouldn't go on like this about business. We're not in the office now.'

'No, do go on,' says Kitty. 'I love it that you love what you do.'

'The thing is,' says Larry, catching fire again, 'our people love the company. No one ever leaves. We have company sports grounds. In New Malden for the London-based staff, and in Avonmouth, and in Liverpool. We have an annual cricket match, Fyffes versus the MCC. Some of our men are county players.'

'I take it all back,' says Ed. 'This is more than bananas.'

'Well, of course the banana trade creates the wealth of the company,' says Larry. 'But the wealth of the company is spread round all our people, just as if every worker was a member of the family. Though of course' – he blushes as he realises he has perhaps gone a little too far – 'my father and I get a greater share of the wealth than most.'

'I'm impressed with wealth in any form,' says Ed. 'I know what damned hard work it is getting it.'

'Ed's doing so well,' says Kitty. 'He and Hugo now have crowds of people working for them.'

'If three counts as a crowd,' says Ed. 'But once all the restrictions are lifted I think we should make a decent go of it.'

'Don't talk about restrictions!' says Geraldine with a light laugh. 'I'm so tired of restrictions.'

Kitty wants to like Geraldine and tries to like her, but the truth is she does not like her. She's ashamed of this, suspecting that it springs from simple jealousy. Larry has always been her special friend, as she puts it to herself, choosing not to investigate further. She should be happy to see him settled at last, but she doesn't much care for the way he's changing. She doesn't like the tweed suit or the big car. She wants her old shabby Larry back, with his friendly puzzled face and his paint-stained fingers. She wants to have him to herself again, to talk about characters in books and how hard it is to make good people interesting.

Geraldine asks after the neighbours, which turns out after a little confusion to mean George and Louisa.

'Sometimes if it's not a bore I'd love to see Edenfield Place again,' she says. 'It is rather extraordinary.'

'Rather hideous is the word,' says Ed. 'It's the sort of monster that can only be created when money is no object. They say in his day George's father was the richest man in England.'

'We can walk over after lunch if you like,' says Kitty.

'I'd love that,' says Geraldine. 'Larry has such fond memories of being billeted in the big house.'

'No, darling,' says Larry. 'I was billeted here, in the farmhouse. Kitty was billeted in the big house.'

'Then how did you become so pally with Lord Edenfield?'

'Because of Kitty. George had a soft spot for Kitty. Kitty fell for Ed. Ed is my best friend.'

'Oh,' says Geraldine. 'I don't quite follow. But never mind.'

They walk across the park to the big house, Kitty pushing the Monk in her pram, with Pamela on one side and Geraldine on the other. Geraldine asks her about motherhood and babies. Kitty can't rid herself of the sensation that Geraldine has no personal interest in the topic, but chooses it out of politeness, supposing it to be Kitty's current central concern. In this she is correct, but that doesn't remove the faint polishy smell of good manners.

'And you manage it all without help!' says Geraldine.

'I do have someone to clean,' says Kitty. 'Two or three days a week.'

'Have you had any time at all away from her, since she was born?'

'No, not so far.'

'She doesn't do anything,' says Pamela from the far side of the pram. 'She can't talk or play or anything.'

'Oh, well,' says Geraldine with a smile, 'perhaps we'd better send her back.'

'Yes, that's what I think,' says Pamela.

'No, you don't, darling,' chides Kitty. 'She's your little baby sister. You love her.'

Larry walks ahead with Ed.

'Marriage seems to suit you,' Ed says to him.

'Yes, I suppose it does,' says Larry.

'I've always thought you were husband material. Unlike me.'

'Why aren't you?'

'You'll have to ask Kitty that. She's very patient with me, but I can be a bit much, you know? Or maybe I mean not enough.'

'Ed, Kitty adores you.'

'Yes, well.' He looks away, towards the steep rise of Edenfield Hill beyond the big house. 'It's a funny thing you going and getting married when you did. Just as well, I expect.'

'I've no idea what you're talking about,' says Larry.

'Nothing,' says Ed. 'Pay no attention to a word I say.'

They go into the house by the terrace door, Kitty calling as they enter.

'Louisa! George! It's only us!'

They find George on his own. Louisa has gone up to town to be examined yet again by her doctors. George is welcoming, but it's clear they've woken him from an afternoon nap. He keeps taking his spectacles off and rubbing them with an enormous pocket handkerchief, as if this will clear his fuddled thoughts.

'I'm so sorry Louisa's not here. We're very quiet when she's away. So this is your wife, Larry! I must congratulate you.'

'You were at the wedding, George,' says Kitty.

'Yes, I was. You're perfectly right.'

The butler appears, in response to a bell George has rung.

'Lott,' George says, 'we have guests. What are we to give them?'

'We don't need anything,' says Kitty. 'We've only come to let Geraldine have a peep at the house.'

'Our last visit was so rushed,' says Geraldine. 'I hardly saw a thing.'

'Maybe Mrs Lott could keep an eye on Elizabeth,' says Kitty.

The butler goes in search of his wife. The baby is sleeping contentedly. George becomes more animated at the prospect of showing off the house. He has done this many times, and finds himself on familiar ground. Ed and Larry opt out of the tour, and Pamela, who also knows the house well, runs off to the billiard room to play with the electric scoreboard. This leaves Kitty and Geraldine to follow in George's wake.

'The short tour please, George,' says Kitty. 'We don't want to bore Geraldine.'

'Oh, you won't bore me!' exclaims Geraldine. 'I adore old houses.'

'We'll start in the hall,' says George. 'You have to look up. The roof is the big thing here. The ridge beam is forty feet above us. All English oak. The architect was John Norton, who was a friend of Pugin. He built Elveden Hall in Suffolk, too. And this portrait here, this is my father, painted by Lorimer. He's wearing the uniform he served in, in South Africa. I've never been in uniform myself. I rather regret that.'

Meanwhile Ed and Larry settle down in the library.

'You've never told me about India,' Ed says. 'Was it fun?'

'You obviously don't know what's happening over there,' says Larry. 'Don't you read the newspapers?'

'Never,' says Ed. 'What's the point? I don't need a daily list of horrors to tell me what sort of world we live in.'

'Well, India's joined the horrors,' says Larry. 'God knows how many have died since independence. Hundreds of thousands.'

'Another glorious triumph for Mountbatten, then.'

'Actually I don't blame Dickie,' says Larry. 'It had all gone too far long before he got out there. But my God! The savagery. The hatred. It makes our war look like a gentlemanly scrap.'

'And your God looks on like a fat nanny, too lazy to get up off the park bench.'

'They've got their own gods. They don't need ours.'

'And here you are, still convinced of the essential goodness of the human race. I take my hat off to you, Larry. The triumph of hope over experience.'

'That's Dr Johnson on marriage.'

'The great doctor,' says Ed.

He's smiling at Larry, but his eyes are sad.

'I've had my own little brush with experience,' says Larry. 'As a matter of fact, it's one of the reasons I've ended up married. I was in a car with a friend of mine, a Muslim, when it was attacked by a Hindu mob. They wanted to murder my friend, just because he was a Muslim. They shot him and wounded him, but when they tried to finish him off I leaned over him and got in the way.'

'You saved his life.'

'I suppose so. I wasn't hurt at all. And afterwards – I don't know how to put it – I felt like I was floating on air. I got myself back, and went looking for Geraldine, and – well, here we are.'

'The intoxication of self-sacrifice,' says Ed. 'Strong medicine.'

'Don't laugh at me, Ed. That day on the beach in Dieppe left me thinking I wasn't worth all that much. Those few minutes in the car, holding Syed in my arms . . .'

He doesn't say any more. Ed is gazing at him now with nothing but affection in his eyes.

'You're a fine man, Larry,' he says. 'You always have been. I admire you. Did you know that? I wish I could be you.'

'You're the one with the VC.'

'Oh, that dammed VC! Can't you see you're worth a hundred of me?'

'What are you talking about? You were just telling me how your business is about to take off. You've got a beautiful new baby girl. Kitty loves you.'

'Has Kitty told you about my secret vice?'

'No.'

'She will. No need to look so alarmed, it's only good old booze. Not very original, I admit. Naturally I struggle against it. Naturally I lose.'

Larry gazes at his friend in sorrow.

'Why, Ed?'

'The horror,' says Ed. 'As told in the newspapers. Which I don't read.'

*

On their tour of the house, George and Kitty and Geraldine have reached the bedroom floor.

'You said you were billeted here in the war,' Geraldine says to Kitty. 'Did you have one of the grand rooms, like me and Larry on our wedding night?'

'Oh, no,' says Kitty with a laugh. 'Louisa and I were up in the attics.' She indicates a narrow servants' staircase. 'Up there.'

'You were in the nursery, weren't you, Kitty?' says George.

'Yes,' says Kitty. She remembers how she came back one evening to find Ed lying on her bed. 'We were in the nursery.'

'I haven't been up there for years,' says George. 'I've no idea what state it's in. Do you want to take a look, for old times' sake?'

'Why not?' says Kitty.

George leads them up the narrow stairs. They go along the passage, with its steep sloping ceiling and its peeling walls. Kitty remembers it all.

The nursery door is closed. George opens it and goes in.

'I used to sleep here when I was a little boy,' he says. Then he falls silent, staring at the room.

It's bright and clean. The beds are made with fresh linen. On one bed sits a smiling doll, on the other a teddy bear. Four tiny cotton hand-embroidered nightdresses hang from a rail. Four pairs of knitted bootees are lined up below them. A baby's basket, lined with rosebud-printed fabric, sits on the old rocking chair. A book lies open, face down, on the floor beside it. It's *The Common Book of Baby and Child Care*.

'How extraordinary,' says George. 'I had no idea.'

He moves round the room as if in a dream.

'Odd place to put the nursery,' he says. 'Up among the servants' bedrooms. But I was very fond of it. You see here, it has a tower window in one corner. I used to go in there and draw the curtains. I think I believed when I was in there no one could find me.'

'Such a pretty room,' says Geraldine.

'Yes,' says George. 'How extraordinary.'

'It's not so very extraordinary, George,' says Kitty. 'You are going to have a baby, after all.'

'The odd thing is,' says George, 'you don't quite realise it at first. I suppose he'll have this room, just as I did.'

'Isn't it more of a servant's room?' says Geraldine.

'No,' George insists. 'This is the nursery. I'm glad Louisa understands that.'

As they descend the main staircase they hear the sound of the gramophone coming from the drawing room. They go through the anteroom into the great room. Its red damask walls are brightly lit by the spring sunlight streaming in through the three tall south-facing windows. There on the red carpet between the sofas Ed is dancing with Pamela to the singing of the Ink Spots.

He looks round and smiles as they come to a stop in the doorway.

'Pammy found it,' he says. 'She insisted on a dance.'

Kitty watches them as they dance, Pamela gravely concentrating, looking up from time to time at her handsome father. Ed seems carefree, happy in a way that is all too rare these days.

'That is such a charming sight,' says Geraldine. 'Where have you hidden my husband?'

'I'm here,' says Larry, speaking from behind them.

'We should dance,' says Geraldine. Her dancing is generally admired.

'No,' says Larry. 'This is Pammy's dance.'

Kitty throws him a quick grateful look.

'Last time we played this song,' Kitty tells Geraldine, 'there was a foot of snow outside and we could hardly get out of the house.'

'Oh, that terrible winter,' says Geraldine, watching the dancers. 'Ed is a graceful mover, I must say.'

'Unlike me, she means,' says Larry.

'Not at all! You're a very good dance partner, darling. But Ed looks so relaxed, while at the same time being so very much in charge. He's the pure English type of hero, isn't he?' This is for Kitty. 'Going into battle as if he's taking a stroll in the park.'

Kitty doesn't answer. She's watching Ed and feeling how much she loves him, and how much it hurts.

PART FOUR

# A GOOD MAN

1950

# 33

Early May in London, and the last of the day's sunshine lingers over the city. Larry leaves the office early and walks home, as he often does, through the park. Past the Serpentine and the Round Pond where he sailed his boat as a child, just as other children are doing today; and so to the streets of Kensington.

There is a conversation waiting to be had, about which he is not thinking.

As he enters the house, Geraldine appears from the garden to greet him with a kiss, in the usual way, but he has learned to read the small signs. When under stress she retreats into efficiency, doing whatever is to be done with extra care and precision. This spring afternoon she has been weeding the rose beds in their town garden. She wears an apron, and carries a shallow basket to collect the weeds, and a small two-pronged fork.

'Do you mind if I carry on? I'm almost finished.'

'No, of course not,' says Larry.

He follows her out down the back steps, and settles himself on the garden bench. Geraldine kneels down on a rubber mat and digs away with her little fork, neither hurrying nor lingering over the task. She says nothing: waiting for him to begin.

'So how was the doctor?' says Larry.

'He was extremely thorough,' she replies. 'A very professional man.'

Larry waits for her to say more, but she seems intent on her weeding.

'Was he able to help?'

'Yes, I think so,' says Geraldine. 'He was able to reassure me on some points. There's no physical problem, he tells me. No' – her voice trembles for a moment – 'no physical defect.'

'Good,' says Larry. 'Good.'

'He told me that my situation is not unique. Far from it.'

She tugs out the weeds from the loosened soil and lays them carefully in her basket.

'And did he suggest that something can be done?'

'Time, he said. Time.'

'I see.'

Geraldine stops weeding. She rises to her feet and stands with her back to him, her head bowed. This is how she asks for affection. For a brief moment Larry rebels. He feels a pulse of anger go through him, that she should claim the role of the victim. Then he sees the way her basket shakes on her arm, and his anger melts into pity.

He gets up and goes to her, folding her in his arms. At once she turns round and presses herself to him.

'Oh, Larry. It was so horrible.'

She puts her basket on the ground and drops the gardening fork into the bed of weeds and begins to cry in soft gulps.

He holds her close, kissing her cheek, soothing her.

'All over now,' he says.

'I know he's a doctor, I know he does it all the time, but it was so horrible. I had to undress. I had to . . . I don't want to say it, I don't want to remember it.'

'But he told you there's nothing wrong, that's the important thing. It's good that we know that.'

She clings to him, sobbing.

'Nothing physical,' she says. 'Not physical.'

'Did he have some other suggestion?'

'He said if I wanted I could see . . . see a psychiatrist. He said it might help. He couldn't promise. He said some people benefit from talking . . . talking about it. Not everyone. Not most, even, he thought. He said sometimes these things just have to be accepted.'

'I see,' says Larry.

'Darling, I'm sorry, but I couldn't bear to talk about it with some strange man. I just couldn't. It would kill me.'

'Then you shan't,' says Larry.

'Oh, darling, darling.' She kisses him gratefully. 'I'll make it up to you in other ways. You'll see. I'll do everything for you. I'll be such a good wife to you.'

'You're that already, my love,' says Larry.

But his heart is heavy.

She wants to talk. She wants him to understand.

'I've been thinking about it so much since I got home. At first I was desperate, I kept telling myself how terrible it was, I couldn't see any way to carry on. So I did the only thing I could. I prayed about it. And while I was praying, I don't know why, I remembered what that Indian friend of yours told us, when we went to the abandoned city. Do you remember? He said it was the words of Jesus, carved on an arch. "The world is a bridge, pass over it, but build no houses on it." I don't really think they're the words of Jesus at all, but I think they're beautiful, and true. This is only a bridge, darling. What really matters is the world to come, on the other side. And when I thought that, I became calmer. I said to myself, this is the burden we're asked to carry in this life. This is our cross. But we still love each other. We're still married. We can still make each other happy. I'm right, aren't I, darling? So long as we've got each other, we're rich in love. Then I saw that there's a kind of vanity, or maybe it's greed, in expecting to have everything. Think how many cripples there are in the world, how many starving people. This is our cross, darling. Not so heavy a cross, once you get used to it. I know you want children. I know I do too. But if Almighty God is asking us to offer up to him that dearest hope of our hearts, then let's do it gladly! Let's not go about with sad faces, as if we've lost the one thing that makes life worth living. You at least understand, darling, and I so thank God you do, that this life isn't everything. This world is only a bridge. Eternity, my love. We must fix our eyes on eternity!'

Her beautiful eyes shine with a kind of ecstasy as she speaks, and she draws him into a kiss more passionate than any she has given him before.

After this Larry asks her no more. He is aware that she is more conscientious than usual, anticipating his wishes and deferring to his preferences, even when he hasn't expressed them. Having noticed the wordless tussle that takes place over *The Times* each breakfast between Larry and his father, she orders a second copy to be delivered: a simple solution that had not occurred to either of them. She discovers the date of Cookie's birthday and makes her a small present in Larry's name, and forewarns Larry so that he's prepared for Cookie's touching gratitude. She memorises the names of the humblest people in the Fyffes head office – the doorman, the cleaners, the junior secretaries – and makes a point of using them, knowing this will please Larry. She can tell almost before he knows it himself when his war wound starts to hurt him, and makes sure there are painkillers available. She's sensitive to his moods, and takes care to leave him alone when he wants to write letters, or read a book. She never criticises him, or interrupts him, or makes those sharp little jokes with which married couples sometimes pinch each other. And always, without exception, she looks lovely.

Larry's father thinks the world of her. His colleagues at head office are all half in love with her. Larry is universally said to be a lucky man. But Larry himself struggles with darker feelings.

He can't blame Geraldine, and yet he does. He knows that the physical side of love is not the most important, but he can't stop regretting it. He tells himself that this is his lower nature, his animal nature, and that he should rise above it. He reminds himself of all the priests of the Church, and the monks at Downside, who have taken vows of chastity the better to serve God. His mind admires them and wishes to emulate them, but his body aches with unsatisfied desire.

He can't blame Geraldine, and yet he does. Every time he's told how lucky he is to have such a perfect wife he flinches, stung by guilt that he doesn't appreciate her more. But what can he do? Somewhere buried deep within him, beyond the reach of faith or reason, lies the stubborn belief that she could love him better, with her body as well as her soul, but does not choose to. The matter appears to be closed as far as she's concerned.

'Let's not talk about it, darling. It makes me so miserable. We just have to be brave.'

The worst of it for Larry is that for all her concern for him, he doesn't believe she knows the price he has to pay. The few times they've talked about his 'sacrifice' it's always been in terms of the children they'll never have. Perhaps she doesn't mention the pleasures of sex because she's shy of the words she'd have to use. But what if she's never known or even guessed at such pleasures? How could she consider it a significant loss? Of course she will have heard that men keep mistresses and frequent houses of ill repute, but men have other pursuits that aren't shared by women. They play cricket and smoke cigars. A man may not wish to give up smoking, but if his wife's health requires that he do so, he'll surely surrender the modestly pleasurable habit with a good grace.

If this is so, if Geraldine is unaware of the strain she subjects him to, then that makes her all the more innocent and deserving of his love. But at the same time, in that deep secret place within him, it adds to the growing store of his anger. This anger frightens him, and shames him. The sweeter she is to him, the more he punishes himself for his ingratitude and his selfishness. The more he chastises himself, the more he longs to chastise her. And so, swept by fantasies of violence, he begins to fear himself.

He remembers Ed in the dark chapel at Edenfield shouting at him, 'Sex is a monster, Larry!' He remembers Nell, naked in his arms, saying, 'If you fuck me will God punish you, Lawrence?' He remembers the electric thrill of hearing her say the word *fuck*. He had no fear then of God's punishment, he knows sex is part of God's creation. But perhaps he's being punished now.

The longing is too strong. It must be controlled. All men

know this instinctively, that if released to do as they wish they would run amok, they would *fuck* and *fuck* and *fuck*. There's little love in this, only appetite. It's the dark side of love, perhaps it's not love at all, perhaps it's the absence of love. Which means that Geraldine is right, sex isn't what really matters. The good life can be lived without it.

So why does this capitulation feel like weakness? Because it does. Larry has felt the tug all his life of opposing forces: he wishes to be good, and he wishes to be a man. He wishes, in short, to be a good man. But when he's good he senses that he's weak, and a true man is strong. He has known himself to be weak countless times, most of all on the beach at Dieppe. He has been a good man just the once, in the midst of the Indian partition riots, when he held his wounded friend in his arms. In his exultation and relief he went, blood still wet on his clothing, to offer his newly purified love to a woman who wanted his goodness, but not his manhood.

When he thinks this way it half drives him mad. He wants to stamp and shout out, I'm a man! How does a man behave under these circumstances? He demands his rights. He satisfies his desires.

*You think she'd like it if I raped her?*

Ed's voice echoing out of the past.

No, she wouldn't like it. Nor would I. And anyway I could never do it. I'm too good, and too weak.

He begins to spend longer hours in the office. He studies the history of the business, and tries to understand the key factors that contribute to the good years and the bad years. Like all newcomers to a long-established business, he believes he can see better ways of ordering matters. He dreams of the day he'll be in charge of the company, and able to lead it into a new era of security and prosperity.

He talks over his ideas with his father.

'What's the biggest problem we have in the banana business? Uncertainty of supply. We have years when we just don't have the fruit to fill the ships, but we still have to maintain the fleet. These are the fixed costs that kill us. We *must* maintain the supply. So it all comes down to the producers on the ground. If they keep ahead of disease, if they replant rapidly after hurricane damage, if they manage the picking and packing as efficiently as possible, if they care as much as we do about the quality of the fruit – well, that's going to deliver a more reliable stream, isn't it? So it makes sound economic sense to get them to regard the company as *their* company. How do we do that? How do we make them understand we're all working together for the same goal? We extend to Jamaica and the Canaries and the Cameroons the benefits and the bonuses we give our people here at home.'

William Cornford nods his head in his slow way, that does not signify agreement.

'What you suggest costs money.'

'Of course. But my way, the company makes *more* money. If everyone on the payroll wants the company to succeed, then they work harder, they're more vigilant, they use their local knowledge and ingenuity to do the job better, they don't get into labour disputes, they don't fall sick, they see the fruits of their labour, and we all make money!'

His father nods his head again and frowns and sighs.

'We are a subsidiary of a larger company,' he says.

He goes to his shelves and takes down a book called *The Banana Empire*, by Kepner and Soothill, and opens it to a page he has previously marked.

'This is an investigation into the United Fruit Company,' he says. 'It was written and published before the war, in '35. In all fairness to the company I should tell you that the authors have been accused of making Communist propaganda.'

He reads from the book in his slow grave voice.

'This powerful company has throttled competitors, dominated governments, manacled railroads, ruined planters, choked cooperatives, domineered over workers, fought organised labour, and exploited consumers. Such usage of power by a corporation of a strongly industrialised nation in relatively weak foreign countries constitutes a variety of economic imperialism.'

Larry hears this in silence.

'I should also add,' says his father, 'that such practices have not been the norm in Jamaica, which has the great benefit of being part of the British empire.'

Larry gives a short laugh.

'One empire pitched against another.'

He reaches out one hand for the book.

'I'd better read it, hadn't I?'

'You'll only find one mention of our company, on page 181. I know it by heart. They write, "Elders & Fyffes from then on" – that is, from 1902 – "became the European arm of the United Fruit Company." That is not so.' His voice has risen. His face is flushed. 'Fyffes is an independent company, in spirit if not in fact.'

Larry stays up late that night reading the book. The next morning he speaks to his father over breakfast.

'I believe it even more strongly now. There is a better way of doing business.'

He has the book before him. He reads out his own chosen extract.

'If the United Fruit Company had been more concerned with the improvement of human relations and social welfare than with the mere obtaining of profits, it could have rendered extraordinary service to the Americas.'

William Cornford gazes at his son across his copy of *The Times* and says nothing.

'Just give me a chance to prove it,' says Larry.

'What is it you want to prove, darling?' says Geraldine, joining them at the breakfast table.

'That we can run our business for the benefit of all,' says Larry.

'All who?' says Geraldine.

Larry is watching his father. He answers Geraldine impatiently.

'All the employees.'

'But of course the business benefits the employees,' says Geraldine. 'It gives them jobs.'

'What do you say, Dad?'

'I'll tell you what I think you should do,' says his father. 'I think you should take a trip to Jamaica.'

Larry leaps up in excitement and strides up and down the breakfast room.

'The very idea I had myself! Of course I must go to Jamaica. I must see for myself. I must learn everything for myself. Of course I must go to Jamaica. I'm convinced we can produce and sell double the tonnage we're bringing in.'

'I've no doubt you're right,' says his father, smiling.

'When would you go?' says Geraldine. 'How long would you be gone?'

'You don't mind, do you?' Larry turns to her, his face bright at the new prospect.

'Of course not,' says Geraldine with composure. 'You are the breadwinner. Your work must always come first.'

The day before he sails, Larry receives a letter addressed to him as Lawrence Cornford, care of Fyffes head office. It's been opened by the office staff, who must have thought it was intended for his long-dead grandfather. The letter is from Nell.

> Darling, we're going to live in France, but I can't leave without writing to you. I expect you hate me but you shouldn't, if you had given me the chance I'd have explained. Darling I did it for you, and I was right, wasn't I? You were never sure about me. I told that story to see what you'd say and I was watching your face and saw how you were frightened and then a gentleman doing his duty so that was that really. I expect you were hurt and angry etc etc but I'm quite sure you've got over all that now and forgiven me. Tony Armitage and I are married, I expect you heard, I don't really know why he's such a pig most of the time and all this fame has gone to his head. He stamps and rants and calls everyone fools and how he can't bear fakes and posers, so we're going to live in France though I don't see why there shouldn't be fakes and posers in France too. I do love you darling and you mustn't mind about the story but come and visit us in France, it's called Houlgate just down the coast from Deauville and I'm going to be so bored I expect I'll kill

him. He won't care, all he cares about is himself and his painting which is actually quite restful for me. If I don't kill him we should get on all right. Remember we said we'd be friends so we have to go on being friends it's much better than being lovers. The other thing makes men so cross really I'm bored with it. Please write to me at the address above and tell me you forgive me.

# 34

After a day of driving down long straight empty roads, Ed reaches Narbonne, in the region of France called the Aude. He puts up in a modest inn, and eats a solitary supper of veal, accompanied by the excellent local red wine. Then as is his habit he questions his host about the vineyards of the region. He learns that the best wines are made in the land to the south, in the corner between the Pyrenees and the sea. He is advised to seek out the domaines round the village of Treilles; in particular the domaine de Montgaillard.

The next morning he drives south. On either side of the dusty white road lie shallow valleys planted with vines, sheltered by belts of almond and cypress trees. Low hills rise up beyond, the pink land studded with the grey of olive trees. Umbrella pines grow on the ridges, slanting under the pressure of the prevailing wind. The houses he passes are pink as the land, made of the same stone. He sees no one. The clusters of houses and barns have an air of abandonment.

He reaches a village at last, and stops by the church. A small bar seems to be open. In its dark interior, he finds a somnolent woman, who gives him directions to the chateau.

He follows the road, which becomes a rising track. He notes vines in their neat rows on either side. Then there at the end of the track appears the chateau, which is in fact little more than a fortified farm.

The house is big and square, with a single tower attached as if by some afterthought at one end. Two very old cars are pulled up in front of the wide door, which stands open. Ed knocks, and getting no response, calls out. After a while a girl of about ten appears, and stares at him, and runs away. After another while Ed hears a slow heavy tread, and a large elderly man presents himself. He has grey hair and grey skin that falls down his face in folds. He stoops, as tall men often do, which gives him a sad and defeated air.

Ed introduces himself and explains his business. His host, whose name is Monsieur de Nabant, is astonished to learn that an Englishman has arrived with a view to buying his wine. He keeps shaking his head, and rubbing at his cheeks. Then he invites his visitor into his house.

The interior seems to consist of one very large room, where all the affairs of the family are conducted at once. The shutters are closed against the heat, so the room is cool and dark. In the beamed and shadowy spaces Ed makes out a daybed, on which reclines an elderly lady; a kitchen table, round which sit several children; an immense fireplace, holding an iron cooking range; a grand piano; and some item of agricultural machinery on the floor, in the process of being mended by a young man. Assorted dogs gather round him to sniff at his legs.

Ed is shown to an upholstered chair in the part of the hall that might be called the sitting room. In a matching chair facing him there sits a second elderly man, small as a dwarf, with an entirely bald head, a smooth almost blank face, and remarkable grey curled moustaches. This person, who is not introduced to Ed, gazes at him with unsmiling intensity; exactly as if he supposes himself to be invisible.

M. de Nabant issues a stream of orders, and the children jump up and rush out. A middle-aged woman in an apron then comes in, makes a little bob of respect to Ed, and goes out again.

'Vous mangerez chez nous,' says M. de Nabant.

Ed thanks him.

Food arrives, carried in by the children. A bowl of olives, a *saucisson*, a block of pâté, a slab of *pain de campagne*, a cake of butter.

'Pour boire, il faut manger,' says M. de Nabant.

The wine arrives in unlabelled bottles. Ed and his host and his host's luxuriantly moustached friend eat and drink. The rest of the household and the dogs look on from the shadows. The wine is unusual, very ripe and gamy. M. de Nabant watches Ed as he drinks and notes his response with satisfaction.

'Notre premier vendange depuis la guerre.'

Ed asks what combination of grape varieties he uses.

'Carignan, Mourvèdre, Grenache Noir.'

Another bottle is opened.

'Seulement Mourvèdre,' says M. de Nabant.

Between the three of them they drink a bottle and a half of the wine. The woman comes and goes with the dishes. The boy on the floor grunts and mutters over his spanners. The children, no longer excited by the newcomer, return to giggling round the table. The dogs roll over and go back to sleep.

After they've eaten M. de Nabant rises, and with the same air he has projected throughout, that this is the way everything must be, he says to Ed, 'Maintenant nous allons visiter le vignoble.'

His moustached friend does not accompany them on their tour of the vineyard. Ed learns that his name is Vivier, that he is a scholar and a historian, and that he studied long ago at Oxford University.

The vines on closer inspection turn out to be extremely well maintained. The tiny green berries are just beginning to form. In all, the domaine extends to a little under five hectares, and produces ten thousand bottles a year.

Ed discusses quantities and prices and means of transport. He proposes an initial purchase from last year's bottling of ten cases, to test the market. The price is so low he finds himself suggesting a higher figure, which M. de Nabant accepts without comment.

On their return to the house, Ed is left by his host in the company of his silent friend while he searches out his account books.

'I understand you studied at Oxford,' Ed says in English.

The old man nods, and suddenly smiles a sweet smile that makes the ends of his moustache quiver.

'Is our local wine to your liking?'

He speaks softly and distinctly, with a charming accent.

'Very much,' says Ed.

'You are a long way from home.'

'I go where my business takes me,' says Ed.

M. Vivier studies him with an intent gaze.

'You have no need to travel so far to find good wine,' he says. 'The English are usually content to stop at Bordeaux.'

'Your prices are lower,' says Ed.

M. Vivier nods. Then after a pause he says, 'Are you aware that you are in the land of the *bons hommes*?'

'No,' says Ed. 'Who are the *bons hommes*?'

'Also called the Cathars.'

'Yes, of course,' says Ed.

Here in the Aude, as he knows very well, he's deep in what was once Cathar country: Carcassonne, Montségur, Albi. They say twenty thousand heretics were massacred in the siege of Béziers. But this is all ancient history.

'I haven't heard Cathars called *bons hommes* before,' Ed says.

'It was their own name for themselves,' says M. Vivier. 'They are a much misunderstood sect.'

M. de Nabant re-enters with his account book.

'They held heretical beliefs, I seem to remember,' Ed says. 'The pope launched a crusade against them.'

'That is so. May I ask, do you subscribe to a faith yourself?'

'I was raised a Catholic,' says Ed. 'But I've rather fallen away, I'm afraid.'

'Fallen away? You no longer believe?'

'I no longer believe.'

M. de Nabant, unable to follow the conversation in English, speaks rapidly to his friend in the local dialect. His friend replies, also in dialect. Then he turns to Ed.

'He tells me you have come to buy wine,' he says. 'I am not to bore you with dangerous nonsense from the past.'

After the wine and the music and the sunny tour of the vines, Ed finds himself in a mellow state of mind.

'What is this dangerous nonsense?'

'It is the creed of the *bons hommes*,' says M. Vivier. 'My own special area of study.'

M. de Nabant throws up his hands, as if giving up on his attempt to control his friend. He lays down his account book and reaches down to stroke his dogs.

'May I presume to ask,' says M. Vivier to Ed, 'why you no longer believe? Is it perhaps because you question how a good God could make an evil world?'

'Something like that,' says Ed.

'But you don't enquire further. You don't take the next step, obvious though it is.'

'I'm sorry,' says Ed. 'I seem to have missed it.'

'That this evil world was made by an evil God.'

Ed smiles, amused by what could indeed be called an obvious step.

'Ah, yes. That would follow.'

'Many things follow, once you open your mind. This world is a prison. In our hearts we know this is not where we belong. We seek freedom, sir. You seek freedom.'

'I'd gladly seek freedom,' says Ed, 'if I knew where to find it.'

'You do know. You have in you the divine spark. There is only freedom in the spirit.'

'It seems you know more about me than I know about myself.'

M. Vivier takes this as a rebuke.

'Forgive me. As my friend will tell you, I can forget my good manners once launched on this subject. The English care greatly about good manners.'

'Not me,' says Ed. 'I'm much more interested in this evil God.'

The little man is gratified.

'You are not shocked?'

'Not at all.'

'Then allow me to go further. All men have a natural instinct to look for meaning in their lives. We crave meaning, and love, and order. You too, perhaps?'

'Me too, perhaps,' says Ed.

'And do you find meaning, and love, and order?'

'No.'

'Of course not. You live in an evil world, made by an evil God. You are a *bon homme* in a *mauvais monde*.'

M. de Nabant utters a low groan and rolls his eyes. Evidently he has witnessed this performance by his friend before.

'I'm a good man?' says Ed. 'I'm a Cathar?'

'Names are unimportant,' says the old man. 'Only the truth is important.'

'And that truth is, that this world is evil?'

'This world is created and ruled by the power the *bons hommes* call Rex Mundi. The king of the world.'

'And this king of the world is evil?'

'We know it,' says the old man, 'by his works. This world is evil. All matter is evil. Our bodies are evil. But our spirit seeks the good, which is love. It is this suffering of the spirit, trapped in the prison of the body, which causes mankind so much unhappiness.'

Ridiculous though this should be, Ed finds himself taking the little man's words seriously. Partly it's the absolute confidence with which that soft earnest voice speaks. Partly it's because he seems to see into Ed's own heart with such uncanny accuracy.

'Do I understand,' says Ed, 'that you yourself follow this Cathar creed?'

'No. I follow no creed. I am a historian. I study the beliefs of those who are long gone. But my mind is open.'

'Did the Cathars have an answer? How did they seek to escape this trap?'

'The *bons hommes* taught that we must renounce this world, and set our spirits free.'

'How?'

'Must I tell you how? If the body is the prison of the spirit, how is the spirit to go free?'

'By death,' says Ed.

'The death of the body,' says the old man. 'The death of this world.'

'And after death?'

'After death is life.'

'How do we know that?'

'We know it because we have the divine spark in us. That is the source of our unhappiness. It is also our proof of eternal life.'

Ed is more struck by this than he cares to admit. For the first time he is being offered a version of existence that matches his own experience. The terror he feels, that he calls 'the darkness', is nothing more nor less than the world he lives in. The God who made it, in whom he could never believe, is an evil God. This he can believe all too readily. The pain he lives with every day is the longing to escape.

And yet surely this is all nonsense. Yet more superstition, cobbled together to meet man's bottomless hunger for meaning in a meaningless world.

'Why did the pope call the Cathars heretics?' he says. 'Why did they have to be exterminated?'

'Why does power hate freedom? Need you even ask?'

'Why did they call themselves *bons hommes*?'

'They believed themselves to be the true Christians. They believed the Roman Catholic church had become an abomination, and they were returning to the pure faith as preached by Jesus Christ. They sought no power, no glory. No hierarchy, no great churches. They wanted something that is very simple and very challenging. They wanted to be good.'

Driving away from Montgaillard, tracing his route back through Treilles and Narbonne and so on to Carcassonne, Ed laughs at himself for his partial surrender. There was a moment in which he almost thought he had stumbled on a truth that could set him free. And what does it turn out to be? Some warmed-up version of a long-dead heresy.

In Carcassonne he visits a library and finds a book about the Cathars. He learns that they were willing to die for their faith in their thousands. At the siege of Béziers their attacker, Simon de Montfort, mutilated a column of prisoners, sent them back into the town with their eyes gouged out, their lips and noses cut off, led by a one-eyed man, to frighten them into surrender. They all chose to die. At its height whole congregations converted en masse to the heresy, whole chapters of cathedrals, so compelling was the Cathar teaching. All Languedoc was infected, the highest born, the best educated, the most intelligent leading the way. It took the pope and the mercenary armies of northern France twenty-one years to crush the heretics. They never recanted. They had to be killed, by hanging or burning at the stake. Whatever else you might say of them, the *bons hommes* were brave and sincere.

Of course, he thinks; and laughs at the simplicity of it. Why should they fear death? Through death they found freedom.

# 35

Larry sails from Avonmouth on the company's newest purpose-built ship, the TSS *Golfito*. In the course of the two-week crossing he questions the captain on all aspects of the business, in particular the issue of how much cargo they carry on the westbound run. Larry finds it hard to believe the hold space can't be more valuably used.

'Everyone thinks that,' says the captain, 'but once you start running about here, there and everywhere, picking up a little of this and little of that, you've ended up paying out more than you're getting in. We carry bulk bananas. That's what our ships are built for.'

The *Golfito* has cabins for ninety-four passengers, sandwiched in the middle of the ship, between the giant refrigerated holds. It will make the return voyage with 1,750 tons of bananas.

One of the passengers, a colonial civil servant called Jenkins, takes it upon himself to dispel any illusions that Larry might have about the Jamaicans.

'Delightful people,' he says, 'friendly, happy, excellent company and all that. Just don't ever ask them to hurry up. They won't hurry up. I'm not saying they're slow-witted. Not at all. They're more what you might call easy. They like to take life easy.'

'But we don't. We take life hard.'

'That's one way of looking at it. We work hard. We get things done. We build railways, and shipping lines. So we end up in charge. But I'll tell you one thing, Cornford. If I'd grown up in Jamaica I'd be all for taking life easy. It's a very pleasant climate most of the time. I'm a subscriber to the climate theory of empire. Cold weather makes you active. So it's the nippy northerners who end up ruling the sleepy southerners.'

'Not in India any more.'

'True, but look what happens as soon as we leave. They all start massacring each other.'

'You don't think that's something to do with us?'

'How could it be?' says Jenkins, to whom this thought has obviously never occurred. 'They lived together happily enough under our rule for two hundred years.'

Larry decides not to tell Jenkins that he was in India at the time of partition. He still hasn't worked out in his own mind what he thinks about what happened.

'The killing of Gandhi,' he says. 'I was shocked by that.'

'That fellow lived in cloud-cuckoo-land,' says Jenkins. 'Did you know he drank his own urine? Mind you, it's coming here too. God alone knows how the place will run without us.'

By the end of the crossing Larry has had the opportunity to speak to many of the other passengers. They all tell him the same thing.

'You should have seen Jamaica before the war. It was a paradise. All over now, of course.'

When he tries to discover why, he learns that it's not just a matter of the damage the war years have done to the island's economy.

'The people aren't the same any more. What with the trade unions and the strikes, and Bustamante and Manley working them up to feel aggrieved about everything. The sugar strike in '38, that was the day old Jamaica died.'

They're all on deck as the ship sails round Port Royal and into Kingston harbour. The air is heavy and warm. The Fyffes manager, Cecil Owen, is waiting at the quayside. He's a red-faced comfortably built man in his fifties, who seems to know everyone he passes. He greets Larry with great warmth.

'Knew you as soon as I set eyes on you,' he says. 'Just like your dad, only with hair. How was the crossing?'

'Excellent. Very smooth.'

'She's a beauty, isn't she?'

He runs his eyes with satisfaction over the handsome new ship, then turns back to Larry.

'You'll stay with me, of course.'

'I don't want to cause you any trouble.'

'No trouble. I'm a bachelor. Glad of the company. Watch out, here it comes!'

A sudden downpour sends everyone on the dockside scurrying for cover. The warm rain dances on the paving stones, and the air fills with a rich sweet smell. Black dockworkers, careless of the rain, get on with unloading the passengers' trunks from the newly arrived ship. Cars roll by, splashing in the sudden puddles, rain overwhelming their windscreen wipers. Cecil and Larry stand under the cover of the long customs shed, waiting for the cloudburst to pass.

'Should be a driver somewhere,' says Cecil. 'He'll have seen the ship coming. He'll find us.'

That evening Larry finds himself sitting with Cecil on the wide porch of his house, drinking rum and fresh lime juice, gazing out over the dark blue waters of Hunt's Bay. The afternoon rain has left the roofs of the town below sparkling in the evening sunlight.

'They told me on the ship that Jamaica was a paradise once,' Larry says, 'but now it's all over.'

'All over, is it?' says Cecil. 'Who told you that?'

'A fellow called Jenkins. He thinks the people here aren't up to running things.'

'Johnny Jenkins? He's an idiot. I've lived here for thirty years and I love the place, but you have to look at it from their point of view. We bring them over from Africa as slaves. Then we set them free and tell them we're the mother country and they're our children, and they're to be grateful to us. Then we make a lot of money getting them to grow bananas for us. Then we get ourselves into a war and tell them we don't want their bananas after all. After all that, you'd want to run your own show, wouldn't you? But the difficulty is, if you spend three hundred years telling people they're children, they become afraid to go out alone. They need us, and they don't want to need us. So you see,' he concludes with a chuckle, 'what we've ended up with is an island full of angry children.'

Larry thinks of India, and the complicated mix of admiration and resentment he found there.

'Does everyone think the way you do, Cecil?'

'Good God, no! By everyone you mean the white men, of course.'

'Yes, I suppose I do.'

'No, no. Your average planter here thinks the Jamaicans are idle, ungrateful, and incapable of taking a piss without someone to unbutton their trousers. Happy children of nature and all that balls.'

'Children again.'

'There's the British Empire for you. Make the darkies work for you for nothing, then tell them you're all one big family.'

'There are other kinds of empire,' says Larry. 'What's your view of our American owners?'

'Gangsters, the lot of them!'

'So are we gangsters too?'

'Not in the United class. They wrote the book. You have to hand it to those boys. Did you hear about how Zemurray got Bonilla in as President of Honduras? One yacht, a case of rifles, three thousand rounds of ammunition, and a bruiser called Machine Gun Maloney. Those were the days.'

Larry relaxes in the warm evening air, tired after the long voyage, made dreamy by rum. A brown lizard scurries across the porch before him, to disappear over the side. The bougainvillea is in brilliant bloom on the slopes below the house. Then as he watches, a hummingbird passes, hanging briefly in the air before him.

'There,' says Cecil. 'That's a real Jamaican welcome.'

The bird has a tiny bright green body and a long red bill. As Larry watches, it jumps back and forth in the air before him, and then flits away into the purple blossoms.

'This is paradise, Cecil.'

Larry realises sitting on that porch that he is at ease in a way he hasn't been for many months. He chooses not to explore this realisation. Enough to enjoy it while it lasts.

*

Cecil takes him on a tour of the plantations. Many have been hit by Panama disease, a fungus that attacks the roots of the banana plants. He finds a vigorous programme under way of rooting out the diseased Gros Michel plants, and replacing them with the Panama-resistant Lacatan variety. He watches the plantation workers cutting the heavy stems of green bananas, and carrying them long distances to the collection points. He talks to them about the work, but can get very little out of them.

'They think you'll sack them if they complain,' says Cecil.

'I won't sack you,' says Larry.

'Sacking is nothing,' says Cecil. 'In Guatemala the United people shoot them if they complain.'

They laugh at that.

'I won't shoot you either, I promise. But I do want to know if you think the company's treating you fairly.'

They shrug and look down at the hard earth.

'It's a job,' says one.

The others nod in agreement.

'Could you get a better job?'

'Not today.'

'But maybe one day?'

They all give cautious nods, watching to see if he minds.

'One day Jamaica will be independent,' Larry says. 'Will everything be better then?'

They shrug and remain silent.

'Come on, Joseph,' says Cecil. 'You don't usually sit on your tongue.'

'Well, sir,' says Joseph. He strokes the fruit on the stem of bananas beside him. 'I don't see no one like me getting rich.'

'So when independence comes,' says Larry, 'you'll ask us to go.'

A great shaking of heads greets the suggestion.

'Fyffes leave Jamaica? Never!'

Rumbling across the island's rutted roads in Cecil's company jeep, the warm wind in his hair, Larry tries out the idea that has been forming in his mind for weeks now. He describes his vision of a company where every employee feels valued.

'Won't make a blind bit of difference,' Cecil says. 'They'll carry on just the same as ever.'

'But why? If we improve their pay, their benefits?'

'Whatever you give them they'll take gladly, but they've got people telling them every day that we get rich on their backs. They're comfortable being dissatisfied. They wouldn't know how to be content with their lot.'

'Why should they be so different to us?'

'Who says they're different to us? Hell, I'm dissatisfied. Improve my pay and my benefits if you want.'

Larry likes Cecil. He strikes him as a man who is at ease with himself. Sharing the evening meal with him, watching the pleasure he takes in his food, he returns to the subject of his dream company.

'There just has to be a way for people to work together in a business the way they work together in a regiment, or in a football team. Where every success is a success for all. Why does there have to be this feeling that one man's gain is another man's loss?'

'Because one man's richer than another.'

'I don't agree. I think everyone understands about differentials in pay. They don't expect everyone to get the same. They know some people are cleverer, or harder working, or more burdened with responsibility than others. Not everyone wants to be the boss. What everyone does want is to feel respected and valued in their work. They want to be proud of their company, and know that their company is proud of them. They want to be known as individuals, not bought and sold like cattle. They want their work to give meaning to their life.'

Cecil gazes across the table at Larry with a puzzled but affectionate look.

'I think you really mean it,' he says.

'Why shouldn't I?'

'Well, you're up against human nature, aren't you? Deep down, people are shits.'

'Are you a shit? Because I assure you I'm not.'

'You're a good man, Larry Cornford. Like your father before you. God bless you. I pray you don't get too hurt.'

Larry bids farewell to Cecil Owen and sails from Kingston to New Orleans, on a ship of the Great White fleet. New Orleans is now the headquarters of the United Fruit Company. Given Larry's position in Fyffes, inexperienced but marked for leadership, his father has thought it necessary for him to meet the president of the parent company, the legendary Sam Zemurray. However when Larry presents himself at United's handsome headquarters on St Charles Avenue, he finds he is scheduled to meet a vice-president of the company called James D. Brunstetter.

'Call me Jimmy. Great to meet you, Larry. We have a high regard for your father, as I'm sure you know. He doesn't go for the quick buck, but a slow buck is still a buck, right?'

He's a small man in his sixties who chain-smokes and talks fast.

'So you've been in Jamaica. Did you meet Jack Cranston, our

main man there? You'd like Jack, everyone likes Jack. So how old are you, Larry?'

'I'm thirty-two, sir.'

'Well now, I wasn't around when your grandfather did the deal with Andy Preston, but as I understand it, the deal went like this. Back us, leave us alone, and we'll make you money. Is that how you understand it?'

'Exactly how I understand it.'

'Then we'll get along just fine. There's only one rule in business. Just keep making money. That way no one's going to bother you. Now what can I do for you? You want to check out our operation here? You want to take a look at our docks?'

'I'd like that very much.'

'I'll take a stroll with you myself. The Thalia Street wharf is only a hop and skip away. Grab your hat, young man.'

Jimmy Brunstetter walks as fast as he talks. By the time they reach the wharf Larry is sweating freely in the humid heat.

The United wharf is three times the size of the Fyffes' wharf at Avonmouth. Lines of men walk one behind the other, each with a stem of bananas on their shoulder, forming a ceaseless stream from ship to store. Two ships are docked, each one being unloaded by specialist cranes.

'You know how many stems we bring in each year?' says Brunstetter. 'Twenty-three million. You heard of Miss Chiquita Banana? Sure you have. We're labelling the fruit now, every hand, with the Chiquita brand.'

'My grandfather did the same with the Fyffes blue label, in '29.'

'Okay! So you got there ahead of us. Good for you.'

They enter the welcome cool of the transit shed. All down

the long aisles stems of green bananas hang from racks as far as the eye can see.

'There it is,' says Brunstetter. 'That's where the money comes from. You want to know the secret of our success? Control. Ask Sam, he'll tell you the same thing every time. Control. Control every stage in the process. Planting, growing, transporting, shipping, marketing. And how do you get control? Ownership. Own the plantations, own the railroads, own the ships, own the docks.'

'Own the countries,' says Larry.

Brunstetter gives a hoot of laughter.

'You got it! Own the countries. Damn right! Only we don't do it the way you guys do it, with your empire. We don't put our name over the door. That way everyone hates you. No, we leave the local boys to run the show. All we ask is that they run it our way.'

'So I hear,' says Larry.

Before he sails for home Larry writes two letters, to Ed and Kitty and to Geraldine, even though he knows they'll reach England only a few days ahead of his own return.

> This trip has taught me so much about this strange business I'm in, and a lot of it's not very edifying. The general idea seems to be that if it makes money it's good. There is a kind of logic to this, we all need money to live, so making it is good however you go about it. But the more I think this through, the more it seems to me that the world of business is missing the bigger picture. Man does not live by bread alone. I can hear Ed utter a groan. But you don't need to bring in God for this. Surely it's obvious. We need bread to

stay alive, but bread is not *what we live for*. And so it is with money. It's not an end, it's a means. The goal we're all after is the good life. So you see, Kitty, all our talks about goodness turn out to be important after all. Even in the hard world of business, goodness matters. It's the heart of the good life. To be honest I'm not sure what I mean by this, I'm working it out as I write. What has goodness to do with the good life? I suppose what I call the good life means life that is both happy and valued. We all want to feel our existence has some purpose. And I don't see how we can feel that if we live in such a way that all our comforts come from the suffering of others. So we need to believe that we're fundamentally good, on the side of the angels as we say, in order to lead a good life. And yes, we need money too. So the business of business must be to *make good money*. As soon as businesses introduce a split between their profits and their morality they lose the point of the whole enterprise. You can say, like St Augustine, 'I'll be wicked for twenty years and then when I've got enough money I'll be good.' But in those twenty years you've poisoned your world and lost your soul. Yes, Ed, I know you haven't got a soul. But you've got a heart, you live among people you love. Kitty, you tell him. Love is goodness. Love is people being good to each other.

Maybe I'm missing something here. It's hot as hell and I sweat like a pig. Do pigs sweat? Better say I sweat like a horse. So my brain may be softening. But here's my confession. I'm excited. I can see a way to use something as mundane as selling bananas to create the good life for several thousand people. I'm sure the company will grow over the coming years. What if it were to be a force for good? We're so accustomed to think of making money as the devil's work. I want to reclaim it for God. I expect by now you're both smiling tolerantly. Poor old Larry, he can't cross a road without looking for a greater purpose. It's true, I admit it. I want meaning in my life. But so do you in yours. So does everybody. And that's what we want our work to give us, more than money, more than status. We're hungry for meaning.

There, I've rambled on for too long. I shall be home in two weeks and four days. I miss you both and long to see you again. Give Pammy and the Monk a kiss each from me, of equal size. We never seem to have enough time together. Why don't you and the girls join us this summer in our house in Normandy? Seriously, do think about it. We plan to be there all of August.

To Geraldine he writes:

My dear darling. Only two weeks or so before I'm with you again, and by the time you're reading this it will be only a few days. New Orleans is beautiful and lush and dirty and hot and half-mad, I think. The whole city feels like an over-ripe fruit about to burst. I've met our parent company, but I think they're not very good parents. All they tell me is, Make money. Oddly enough this place reminds me of India. The same brightness and energy and noise, but underneath, the savagery. I trust you got my second letter from Kingston. I've heard nothing from you since Kingston, so I expect your last few letters will follow me home. I've had an idea to ask Ed and Kitty and their girls to La Grande Heuze this August. It would be jolly to have children running about, don't you think? I can't wait to be home again, and to hold you in my arms again. I feel as if I've been away half my life, and when I get home everyone will be wrinkled and stooped and ninety years old, all except you, darling, who are ageless and whose beauty never fades.

# 36

Pamela falls in love with La Grande Heuze at first sight. Larry watches her running from room to room, and out into the garden where the great forest begins, and sees in her wide excited eyes the same wonder that possessed him twenty-five years ago and more, when he first came here. That was the summer before his mother died. He was five years old, two years younger than Pamela is now. He has clear memories of his mother sitting in the shade of a giant parasol on the terrace, and walking rather too slowly down the long straight *allées* that cut through the endless world of the forest.

'Is it your house?' Pamela says. 'Do you really live here?'

'When I'm on holiday,' Larry says, smiling down at her.

'I love it!' she cries. 'It's so beautiful. It's a secret house in a forest. Can I come and live here with you?'

'You are living here with me.'

'No, I mean for ever and ever.'

'I'm not sure your mother would approve of that.'

'She could come too. But not the Monkey. She wouldn't understand.'

In this way Pamela appropriates the house and its garden and its surrounding forest as her rightful domain. She announces that its name, La Grande Heuze, is a reference to herself.

'It's *hers*, you see, Mummy. That means it's mine.'

'Well, darling,' says Kitty, 'you'll have to fight it out with Larry and Geraldine. I rather think they think it's theirs.'

'Geraldine!' Pammy is indignant. 'It's Larry's house, not Geraldine's house.'

Geraldine is looking lovelier than ever. In her light cotton dresses, her sunglasses perched on her blond curls, she looks like summer itself. Under her management, the old house is filled with softly coloured light. She makes sure there are fresh flowers in the rooms every day, and fruit in shallow blue and white bowls, and a large glass jug of lemonade on a table on the terrace.

She asks Ed and Kitty for news of their neighbours in the big house at Edenfield.

'We haven't seen them in such a long time. How's the new baby?'

'Not a baby any more,' says Kitty. 'He's walking now. But Louisa still isn't right. I do worry about her. You remember how she was always so jolly? These days she seems much quieter. I don't think she's as strong as she should be.'

'Why does everyone want babies so much?' says Pamela, scowling at her little sister. 'I don't see the point of them.'

'You were a baby once,' says Ed.

'*One* baby is all right.'

She jumps up and goes over to Elizabeth, who is toddling out through the open garden doors.

'No, Monk. Don't go outside.'

'Leave her alone, darling,' says Kitty.

'That forest out there,' says Ed. 'How far does it go?'

'A long way,' says Larry. 'You can walk for miles and see nothing but trees.'

'It frightens me,' says Geraldine. 'I've been telling Larry we should sell this house and buy somewhere on the coast. Étretat, maybe, or Honfleur. I love to look out over the sea.'

Pamela stares at Geraldine in astonishment.

'It's not mine to sell,' says Larry lightly. 'Not for many years yet, I hope.'

Their guests have hardly been installed for a day before Ed finds his way into one of the forest paths. He's gone for hours.

'Don't worry about him,' says Kitty. 'He'll be back for dinner.'

Geraldine takes pride in her dinners; not just the food laid on the table, but every detail of the table settings. She speaks poor French and has difficulty communicating with Albert and Véronique, the young couple recently hired by Larry's father to cook and clean and tend the garden. This produces many moments of frustration.

'Larry, could you tell Albert not to put out bowls for coffee in the morning. Why do the French drink coffee from a bowl? When it's hot you can't pick it up, and before you know it the coffee's stone cold.'

And, 'When will Véronique get it into her head that I want the vegetables served at the same time as the meat? I told her, I said, "Toutes ensembles", but she just gaped at me.'

The standard of service at La Grande Heuze, under Geraldine's watchful eye, is in fact very high. The bread, crusty and fresh, arrives on a bicycle each morning from the *boulangerie* in Bellencombre. The coffee, made in a glass retort as if in a science lab, is dark and smooth and strong. The plain unsalted butter comes in a large cake, white and creamy, too good to need jam.

'You have no idea what a luxury this is for me,' says Kitty to Geraldine. 'It's simply heaven.'

'My mother always says guests are like horses. You have to keep them warm and watered and well fed.'

'I'm a very happy horse. You think of everything.'

'It's all about putting yourself in other people's place, isn't it?' says Geraldine. 'I think that's all that good manners comes down to.'

In the evenings the Monk is fed early, in the kitchen, where she is much fussed over by Véronique. Pamela is allowed to stay up to dinner with the grown-ups.

Larry can tell that this agitates Geraldine.

'Shall I say we'd rather the children both ate in the kitchen?'

'No, no,' says Geraldine, giving him a quick guilty look. 'If that's what Kitty wants. I'm just worried she'll find the food a bit much for her. Do you think I can serve *moules*?'

Pamela is aware that this privilege is also a test, and is undaunted by the *moules*.

'I like this,' she says. 'I expect I shall ask for more.'

'Oh, it's too bad!' exclaims Geraldine, taking her napkin out of its ring. 'I told Albert the napkins must be clean each evening. What am I to do, Larry? They don't pay any attention to a single thing I say.'

'I'll make sure they understand,' says Larry.

Geraldine smiles at Ed and Kitty, and smooths the offending napkin on her lap.

'I know it doesn't really matter, but one might as well get things right. Otherwise why don't we all sit on the ground and eat with our fingers?'

'Like the Monk,' says Pamela.

Kitty wants to know what's happened to Larry's painting.

'I don't have the time any more,' says Larry.

She looks at him with a puzzled smile, trying to guess what he really feels. Returning her gaze, lingering on her long-loved features, he realises that there's no one else who knows what this renunciation has cost him. Since that day he threw his canvases into the Thames, he has resolutely turned his back on his artist-self. He tells himself this is honesty, this is realism. But seeing Kitty's troubled look, he remembers the pain of it.

'To tell you the truth,' he says, 'I realised I just wasn't good enough.'

'But you sold your paintings! You told me so.'

'To George, because Louisa made him.'

'No. The others too.'

'Yes, there was a genuine buyer. I never knew who. That was my moment of glory.'

Kitty appeals to Ed.

'He was so good. Wasn't he, Ed?'

'I've believed in Larry since school,' says Ed. 'But we all have to live.'

'Don't you love his paintings?'

Kitty says this to Geraldine, innocently confident of support.

'I've never seen them,' says Geraldine.

'What?'

Kitty's bewilderment is devastating. Geraldine blushes, and turns to Larry.

'Why haven't I seen them, darling?'

'Because there are none to see,' says Larry. 'I threw them all away.'

He speaks flatly, meaning to remove any emotional weight from his words. Instead he communicates to all of them how much he cares.

A silence follows. Véronique comes in to clear the plates. The clatter of crockery releases them.

'Have you ever heard of a painter called Anthony Armitage?' says Larry, his voice now bright again, conversational. 'He's younger than me, but he's become quite a legend already. I knew him at art college, before he was famous.'

It's clear from their faces that none of the others have heard of him.

'It was my bad luck,' Larry goes on, 'to come up against a true talent. I looked at Armitage's work, and I looked at mine, and I knew I was fooling myself.'

'Oh, Larry.' Kitty soft with compassion.

'It's not all bad luck,' says Geraldine. 'That's one of the reasons why Larry came out to India.'

'That's quite true,' says Larry, smiling at her.

'This Armitage,' says Ed. 'Is he really so wonderful?'

'You can see for yourself if you want,' says Larry. 'He lives not very far away. A little place on the coast called Houlgate.'

'You never told me that,' says Geraldine, caught by surprise.

Nor has Larry told her that Armitage lives there with Nell. There has seemed to be no point. But now he finds he wants to see Nell again, and Armitage, though for very different reasons.

'And guess who he's married?' he says to Kitty. 'Nell.'

'Nell! Your Nell?'

'Not mine for a long time.'

'Oh, do let's go and visit them!'

That night going to bed Geraldine is silent in the way she

goes when she feels ill-treated. This annoys Larry, but he also knows she's right.

'Look, I'm sorry,' he says.

'Oh, you're sorry. I wonder what for.'

'I shouldn't have sprung all that on you.'

'So we're going to go and visit them, are we? Your ex-girlfriend who you asked to marry you, and her famous artist?'

Larry knows he should say that Nell means nothing to him, that of course they won't go if she doesn't want them to. Then she'll cry a little and say she only wants him to be happy. But a stubbornness takes hold of him.

'I think it would be fun,' he says. 'And Kitty wants to.'

'Oh, well then, we must go.'

They lie down on the bed side by side, not touching, in silence. After some time, neither of them asleep, Geraldine wriggles close and kisses his shoulder.

'Sorry,' she says. 'I'm being silly. Of course we can go.'

The Monk is happy to stay behind and help Véronique cook. The rest of the house party set off, squeezed into the sand-coloured Renault 4CV usually driven by Albert. They drive through Rouen and Pont-Audemer, passing war-damaged buildings all the way. Larry tells the others how La Grande Heuze was occupied in the war first by German officers, then by Americans as the front advanced, and finally by former prisoners-of-war en route home.

'There's supposed to be compensation for all the damage,' he says, 'but I don't expect we'll ever see it.'

They look out for the sea all the way from the outskirts of Houlgate, but it remains out of sight until they're winding their way through the little town itself. Then all at once there it is, at the far end of the narrow street, trapped between the grey shuttered houses: a band of dull gold, a band of blue. They turn onto the Rue des Bains and drive slowly past the half-timbered houses, with the wide sands and sea stretching out to their left.

'Oh, I do so love the sea,' says Geraldine. 'Why do we have to be shut up in a forest? Don't you feel when you can see all the way to the horizon that anything is possible?'

'Mere illusion,' says Ed. 'Very few things are possible. Most of the time we do as we must, not as we would.'

'Pay no attention to him, Geraldine,' says Kitty. 'He's a terrible Eeyore.'

The Armitages live on Rue Henri Dobert. Larry pulls up and asks a man pushing a bicycle for directions. Driving on, he finds the road and crawls along it hunting for the house.

'Good God! I think that must be it!'

The house is high and narrow, stuccoed, with brick edging round the windows and ivy climbing to the second storey.

'That's not an artist's house,' says Ed. 'That's a bank manager's house.'

They drive onto the forecourt. On closer inspection the house can be seen to be run down, with weeds fringing the paving stones and the paintwork on the door crazed and flaking.

'They are expecting us?' says Geraldine.

'Possibly,' says Larry. 'If the post works.'

Larry doesn't show it, but he too is nervous. They get out and kick their legs, stiff after the long drive.

'What'll be for lunch?' says Pamela.

'Hush, darling,' says Kitty. 'It's rude to ask.'

'Why?' says Pamela. 'Why can't I ask?'

*Those that don't ask don't get*. Larry's mind echoes with the last words Nell ever spoke to him.

The door opens before they can knock, and there's Nell.

'You beautiful people!' she cries, bounding out. 'I'm going to kiss every one of you!'

She's just the same as Larry remembers, perhaps a little plumper, her hair longer, pulled back and held under an Alice band. She's wearing a bright check blouse and trousers. The same ease with her body, the same uncompromising meeting of eyes, the same lack of restraint.

'So you're Geraldine! Oh, you're perfect! What did Lawrence do to deserve you?'

Larry sees Geraldine flinch in her embrace. Then it's his turn.

'Darling Larry. Don't you look prosperous! My God, Camberwell feels like it was a million years ago. Come in and meet the monster.'

She ushers them in to a cluttered hall, and on to a big room at the rear of the house. Here windows open startlingly onto the sun-dazzled sea.

'There!' says Nell. 'The house is hideous, but you could hardly get closer to the sea, could you?'

She turns and yells, 'Tony, you mannerless shit! Come and greet your guests!'

She gives a laugh as she throws open the windows.

'He's completely unshameable. Now that he's an officially proclaimed genius he behaves as if none of the usual rules apply to him.'

She loops her arm through Larry's and leads him out into the bright sunshine.

'Come on, darling. We have some catching up to do.'

They walk arm in arm down a path that runs beside the beach.

'So are we still friends, Lawrence?'

'Yes,' says Larry, marvelling at the ease he feels in her company. 'Of course.'

'I know I'm a bad girl.'

'It doesn't matter. All in the past.'

'The thing you have to understand,' she says, 'is that when people say things to each other they aren't always saying what they're saying. They're saying something else, that's harder to say.'

'Like, Do you really love me?'

'Exactly.' She gives his arm a squeeze. 'You are such a sweetie-pie, Lawrence.'

'So how are things with Tony?'

'Oh, Tony! He'll do for now. How are things with Geraldine?'

'Very good.'

'Liar, liar, pants on fire.'

Back in the house the others, abandoned, look at each other, unsure what to do.

'Speaking purely personally, I need a drink,' says Ed. 'Do you think we forage for ourselves?'

'I want to go out on the beach too,' says Pamela.

At this point the artist himself appears, looking as if he's only just got up.

'Who the hell are you?' he says.

'Friends of Nell's,' says Kitty. 'She's out on the beach with Larry.'

'Oh, Larry.' He rubs his eyes. 'So what am I supposed to do with you?'

'You're supposed to greet us in a friendly manner,' says

Geraldine, 'and make us feel at home, and offer us a drink.'

She utters this advice with a charming smile. Armitage is unnerved by the direct assault.

'Am I?' he says, looking about him as if seeking a way out. 'A drink, you say?'

Abruptly he withdraws to some other part of the house. Ed and Kitty both applaud Geraldine with softly clapping hands.

'Bravo, Geraldine!'

'Well, really!' says Geraldine, going pink.

Armitage reappears with a bottle of pastis, a bottle of water, and three glasses.

'Couldn't find any more glasses,' he says. 'Not clean ones.'

'You can even pour it if you want,' says Geraldine. 'But not for me, thanks.'

'Nor me,' says Kitty.

'I'll do it,' says Ed.

He mixes the pastis half-and-half with water and drinks it down. Armitage leans out of the window.

'Nell, you great cow! Get back here!'

The guests act as if they haven't heard him.

Nell returns, with Larry in tow.

'You behave yourself,' she says to Armitage, 'or no jiggery-pokery for a week.'

'What have I done?' says Armitage in an aggrieved voice. 'Hello, Larry. What's wrong with you?'

'I don't know. What is wrong with me?'

'You look all shiny. Have you been varnished?'

'I told you,' says Nell. 'He got rich.'

It turns out there is lunch of a kind waiting for them. Nell has planned a picnic on the beach. She's filled a big basket with bread, tomatoes, and pork *rillettes*. To drink, there's a flagon of the local cider.

'The whole idea of living here is that we have the beach on our doorstep. Tony spends hours staring at the sea. I can't see what there is to look at, myself. It's just a lot of nothing.'

'You're an empty-headed fool,' says Armitage.

'I think he stares at the sea to clear his mind,' says Nell as if he hasn't spoken. 'Like preparing a canvas.'

'That is perfectly true,' says Armitage.

He goes to her and kisses her in front of them all.

They sit in a ring on the sand in the shade of a large beach umbrella, and make themselves sandwiches by tearing the baguettes apart. Pammy loves it.

'We're sitting on the ground and eating things with our fingers,' she says.

Armitage stares at Kitty as he eats.

'Don't mind him,' Nell says. 'It just means he wants to paint you.'

'Yes, I do,' says Armitage. 'You have an interesting face.'

'So where do you paint?' says Larry.

'Over there,' says Armitage.

'He's got a studio in the house,' says Nell. 'No more crouching in bed-sitting rooms. But it was fun in those days, wasn't it?' She turns to Geraldine, wanting to include her. 'Larry and Tony and me used to walk along the river in the small hours of the morning and drink hot sweet tea from the cabbies' café by Albert Bridge.'

'More cider?' says Ed, pouring from the flagon.

An extended family goes trudging by, grandparents, parents, children, dog, carrying baskets, rugs, umbrellas. A steamer crosses the horizon, moving without seeming to move. From time to time Nell strokes Armitage's arm, as if to reassure him she's still there.

Then they have a sudden violent row. It's about letting their visitors see his studio.

'I'm not a zoo animal,' he says.

'You *exhibit*, don't you?' demands Nell. 'You're an *exhibitionist*, aren't you?'

'I don't care if no one ever sees my work.'

'That is such shit! You hypocrite!'

'Cow!'

'You're afraid, aren't you? Bloody hell!' she appeals to the others. 'He sells everything he does. He's got famous people begging him to paint them. He gets compared to Titian. And all along he's wetting himself with fear.'

'Bitch!'

'Oh, yes! Very effective! That'll shut me up, won't it? That's a really conclusive argument!'

Armitage gets up and stalks away down the beach.

'Go on!' Nell shouts after him. 'Run away! Coward!' Then in a suddenly normal voice to the others, 'Don't worry. I'll take you to see his studio.'

'But if he doesn't want it,' says Geraldine.

'Why should he be the one who gets what he wants? What about what I want?'

They gather up the picnic and brush the sand off their bottoms and troop back to the house. Armitage is nowhere to be seen. Nell leads them up the stairs to the back room on the first floor. Here what was once a large light bedroom has been transformed into an artist's studio. Canvases lean against the walls and stack up on a long paint-spattered table. Two easels, both bearing works in progress, stand by the window. An armchair draped with a multicoloured shawl occupies the middle of the room. The portraits taking shape on the easels are of an old man and a stout middle-aged woman.

Larry and the others look round the studio in silence, examining the paintings.

'I hate to say it,' Larry says, 'but the bastard's got even better.'

'Why are they all so sad?' says Kitty.

'Tony would say he just paints what he sees,' Nell says. 'The way he sees it, most people are disappointed by their lives.'

'Do you think he's right?'

'Probably,' says Nell.

'I think that's ungrateful,' says Geraldine.

'Ungrateful to who?' says Nell.

'To God, actually.'

Nell gives her an incredulous look.

'We're supposed to be grateful to God?' she says. 'What for?'

'For being our Creator,' says Geraldine. 'I know it means nothing if you don't have faith.'

'Take it from me,' says Nell, 'I know about creators. It's all vanity. It's all look at me, aren't I wonderful? As far as I'm concerned God is just another immature egotistical artist whining on about how no one appreciates him.'

Driving back to Bellencombre, Kitty says, 'You've got to admit they're not dull.'

Geraldine says, 'I thought they were pitiful.'

In their bedroom that night she says to Larry, 'I don't understand how you could ever have loved her. I just don't understand.'

'I was young,' says Larry.

'It's only five years ago. You weren't a child. She's just so . . . so crude. So loud. So coarse.'

'She's fun as well. You must see that.'

'Fun! Is that your idea of fun? All that childish swearing?'

Larry feels the stirrings of anger.

'It's late,' he says. 'That was a long drive.'

'No, Larry. I want to know. Did you really love her?'

'I thought I did. For a time.'

'Was it just because of . . . you know?'

This is the closest she can come to talk of sex.

'Maybe it was,' says Larry.

'I could understand that,' says Geraldine. 'I know that makes perfectly sensible men do really stupid things.'

'Not really stupid,' says Larry. 'Don't say it was really stupid to love Nell. Don't say that.'

'Well, what am I supposed to say? Why else would you give a creature like that more than a glance?'

'A creature like that.' He feels his heart pounding. 'What do you know?' His voice is rising. 'Who are you to criticise her? Who are you to tell me why I do what I do? You think you do everything so bloody perfectly. Well take it from me, you don't!'

Geraldine lies perfectly still beneath the bedclothes.

'Please don't swear at me,' she whispers.

'I'll bloody well swear at you if I want!' shouts Larry.

'Hush!' she says. 'Keep your voice down.'

'No! I won't! And don't shush me! I'm not a child.'

'Then I don't know what to say.'

'Then don't say anything at all. If all you can do is insult my friends I'd rather you said nothing. Why should everyone be like you? What makes you so right about everything?'

Geraldine says nothing.

'And in case you haven't noticed, we're not in Arundel any more. We're in France. They do things the French way in France. And why the hell shouldn't they?'

He feels her shudder, but still she says nothing.

'Well?' he demands.

'I was told not to speak,' she whispers.

'Oh, for God's sake, Geraldine!'

Robbed of opposition, his anger trickles out of him. They lie side by side in a wretched silence, both feeling sorry for themselves. After some time, wanting to go to sleep, Larry attempts a half-hearted resolution.

'Sorry,' he mumbles.

'It doesn't matter,' she says. 'I just didn't know.'

'Didn't know what?'

'That you don't love me at all.'

'Oh, please.'

'It's all right. It's not the first time.'

'Geraldine, you're taking this far too seriously. It's just a row. People have rows. It's not the end of the world.'

'I'm not blaming you. I know it's my fault. I try so hard, but somehow I'm never good enough.'

'No, darling, no.' He feels only a heavy weariness now. 'You know that's not true.'

'I've always known I'm not good enough, deep down.' She goes on whispering to herself, hearing nothing he says. 'I've never felt anyone's really loved me. Not Mummy or Daddy. Not even God.'

'Oh, darling.'

'There's something wrong with me. I don't know what it is. I try so hard. It's nothing physical. Not physical. I say to myself, I must just try harder. I must do better. And I will. I promise you. I'll be a good wife.'

'Of course you will. You are.'

But as he lies beside her in the night Larry is overwhelmed with desolation.

'This life is such a hard journey,' she whispers. 'All I ask is that from time to time you hold my hand. So I know you're still there.'

He reaches out under the bedclothes and holds her hand.

'Thank you,' she says, her voice almost inaudible.

Next day Geraldine appears as charming and elegant as ever. She's especially attentive to Kitty, teasingly aligning herself with her against the boorishness of the men.

'What are we to do with them, Kitty? Sometimes I think men have no manners at all. You see how Larry leans on the table, and reaches for whatever he wants, as if he's the only person at breakfast?'

'You should pity me,' says Larry, smiling. 'I had no mother to teach me manners.'

'Ed has a mother,' says Kitty, 'but he might as well have been raised in the jungle.'

'I've no idea what you're talking about,' says Ed, deep in the morning edition of *Le Figaro*. 'You may like to know that Princess Elizabeth has had a baby girl. The princess is naturally radiant, and naturally she repeated the words she uttered on her marriage, and on the birth of her son. "Nous sommes tellement chanceux,

Philip et moi." Odd that she said it in French.'

'You see what a beast he is,' Kitty says to Geraldine. 'He makes fun of all good news.'

'I'm so impressed he understands French,' says Geraldine.

'Oh, he practically lives in France these days.'

'I'll tell you what,' says Larry. 'Why don't we beasts clear off for the day?'

'Clear off where?'

'I thought Dieppe.'

Ed looks up from his newspaper.

'Why on earth do you want to go there?'

'I don't know. Lay the odd ghost.'

'I think you should, Ed,' says Kitty.

'All right,' says Ed abruptly. 'We'll go.'

They park in front of one of the hotels, and walk down the concrete pathway between strips of grass where boys are playing soccer, to the broader strip of concrete that is the promenade. They stand here gazing over pebbles to the sea. It's a sunny August afternoon, and the long flat beach is dotted with families stretched out on towels, and children flying kites.

'Do you dream about it?' says Larry.

'Sometimes.'

'Once I woke from a dream of it, and I'd wet myself.'

Ed shakes his head.

'What a fuck-up that was,' he says. 'What an utter God-awful fuck-up.'

They reach the shiny strip of pebbles, washed by the waves as they roll in and roll out. Here they turn round. Now they're looking up the beach to the promenade and the town, just as they looked when they came off the landing craft eight years ago.

'Am I supposed to be feeling something?' says Ed. 'Because I'm not.'

'Remembering,' says Larry.

'I'd rather forget.'

'This is where you won your VC, Ed. Right here.'

Ed scans the beach, with its scampering children and its barefoot bathers picking their way over the pebbles.

'I should have died here,' he says.

'Maybe you did,' says Larry. 'Maybe I did.'

He walks up the beach a little way, fancying that he follows the path he took eight years ago.

'There was a wrecked tank round about here,' he says. 'I sat down against it and prayed it would protect me.'

'You prayed?'

'No, you're right. I don't remember praying. I just remember the dead feeling of terror. You never felt that, Ed. I saw you. You weren't afraid.'

'I've always been afraid,' says Ed. 'I've been running away all my life. I'm still running.'

'But why? Why are we so afraid? What is it we're afraid of?'

No need to tell Ed he's not talking about sniper bullets and mortar shells.

'God knows,' says Ed. Then he laughs. 'Afraid of God, I expect. The God we've constructed so that we're bound to fail in the end.'

'Who says it has to be in the end?' says Larry. 'Some of us are failing right now.'

Ed turns on him, almost angry.

'Don't you talk like that! You're the one who's got it right. I need to know at least someone's come through.'

'You've got eyes, Ed.'

'Geraldine?'

'Yes.'

They walk on up to the promenade and sit down on the concrete wall. Below them bewildered farm boys from Alberta and Ontario died in their hundreds, on that day that happened somewhere else, long ago and far away.

'Geraldine isn't great on the physical side of things,' says Larry.

'Maybe she just needs time.'

'Ed, it's nearly three years.'

'How bad is it?'

'There is no physical side of things.'

'Bloody hell,' says Ed softly.

'She tries, but she can't.'

'Bloody hell,' says Ed again.

'It's not going to change. I know that now.'

'So what do you do?' says Ed.

'What do you think? I don't have a whole lot of choice.'

'Are we talking tarts or wanking?'

'Good old Ed. The latter.'

Ed gazes out over the sea to the horizon.

'Remember the smoke?' he says. 'Bloody smoke over everything, so you didn't know you were coming off the boats into the end of the world.'

'I remember the smoke,' says Larry.

'You're going to have to get out of this, my friend. Time to beat a retreat. Back to the boats and sail away.'

'I can't.'

'Why not? Oh yes, your dumb religion.'

'And yours.'

'It's a fairy story, chum. Don't let them bully you.'

'It still means something to me,' says Larry. 'It's just too deep in me.'

'Do you still go to confession?'

'From time to time. I like it.'

'Do you tell the priest about the wanking?'

Larry laughs.

'No, not any more. It got too boring. And I knew I wasn't going to stop.'

'There's faith for you. You know it's nonsense but you let it ruin your life. Sometimes I swear to you I think the human race has a built-in need to suffer. When there aren't enough plagues or earthquakes we have wars. When we run out of wars we turn our daily lives into misery.'

'So what do you advise me to do?' says Larry.

'How would I know?' says Ed. 'I drink. But I don't recommend it.'

Larry sighs.

'Remember sitting in the library at school, with our feet up on the table, and you reading out the dirty bits from your illicit copy of *Lady Chatterley's Lover*?'

'Sex in the gamekeeper's hut. As far as I can remember she had no underclothes, and slept through the whole thing.'

'It was still exciting.'

'That's the trouble with sex. It's never as good as when you're sixteen years old and haven't had it yet.'

'So what do we do, Ed?'

'We stumble on, chum. Stumble on in the smoke until that one merciful bullet finds us at last.'

# 37

Louisa is back home and a lot better, but one look at her and Kitty knows she's not yet her old self. Little Billy hangs about her, clinging to her skirts, but she makes no objection when his nurse comes and carries him off for his tea.

'I'm all right really,' she tells Kitty, 'but everything's so tiring. I want to have Billy all the time, but I can't manage it. Aren't I hopeless?'

She gives Kitty one of her old mischievous smiles, but ends with a grimace.

'Oh, Kitty. Were your babies such hard work?'

'Of course,' says Kitty loyally. 'Having babies is hell.'

'It's like being disembowelled, isn't it? But I should be over it by now.'

'What do your doctors say?'

'They can't find anything wrong with me, which should be cheering but somehow isn't. If only I could cough blood or something. At least then I'd know it wasn't my own fault.'

'Of course it's not your own fault.'

Louisa is sitting on a sofa in the big drawing room with cushions all round her and a little table by her side. Mrs Lott brings through a pot of tea and some home-made scones. Kitty offers to pour the tea.

'Still, it's good to be home,' says Louisa.

Then she shakes her head and bites her lip and says, 'No, it isn't.'

Suddenly she sounds like a frightened child.

'I've become so useless.' She's on the point of tears. 'In the nursing home I sit about all day, doing nothing, and it's restful. Here I sit about all day, not doing things I should be doing, and I feel terrible. What's gone wrong with me, Kitty?'

'It'll pass,' says Kitty. 'You'll get better.'

'Darling Kitty. Do you mind if I tell you a secret?'

'You say anything you want,' says Kitty.

'I'm so afraid I might never get better.'

'Oh, rubbish!' exclaims Kitty.

'There is a good side to it, though. I've become much nicer to George. He turns out to be such a lovely man. And of course, he adores little Billy.'

'You're just feeling tired,' says Kitty firmly. 'People don't just not get better for no reason.'

'Well, I've thought about that,' says Louisa. 'Really, most things happen for no reason. We die for no reason. It's not a punishment or anything. It's like in the war. It's all just chance. Remember Ed saying how he believed in luck?'

'Yes,' says Kitty.

'We've had good times along the way, though, haven't we?'

'Yes,' says Kitty.

George comes in to join them, and it's marvellous to Kitty to see how his presence cheers Louisa. He sits by her side on the sofa and fusses over her.

'Have another scone. You're to be stuffed like a goose, doctor's orders. She's so much better, isn't she, Kitty? Getting her colour back.'

'She's going to be just fine,' says Kitty.

'In the spring we're going to go to the South of France,' he tells Louisa. 'To Menton. You and me and Billy. We'll sit in the sunshine and watch the boats in the harbour and get lazy and fat, all three of us.'

'Will we, George? I shall like that.'

Kitty collects Elizabeth from the kitchen, where she always goes when they visit the big house, and they walk back home across the park. Kitty is filled with troubled thoughts. Louisa has always been the one who laughs away such moments, the living proof that even as life lets you down there are good times to be had. Now the good times seem to be receding into the past.

I'm thirty years old, Kitty thinks. Don't tell me it's over.

They stop at the kissing gate out of the park and Elizabeth puts up her face to be kissed.

'I do love you so much, darling,' says Kitty.

When they get back to the farmhouse, there's Hugo's van in the yard, and Hugo himself in the kitchen. His presence is not welcome. Kitty is feeling too fragile to deal with his boyish flirtations.

'What are you doing here, Hugo? You know Ed's away.'

'That's why I'm here,' he says. 'To talk about Ed.'

'I don't want to talk about Ed.'

'I want tea,' says Elizabeth.

Kitty looks round a little distractedly, glancing at the clock, trying to calculate how long it will be before Pamela gets home from school. She likes to have her tea ready on the table.

'Soon, darling.'

Elizabeth runs off. Kitty puts the kettle on to boil.

'You know it and I know it,' says Hugo. 'We've just never said it aloud.'

'Know what?'

'Ed's drinking too much.'

'Oh, God.'

Kitty knows she should sound surprised, even angry, but she can no longer summon up the energy to defend Ed.

'He's not really capable of doing the job any more,' says Hugo.

She turns to look at Hugo, so serious, so earnest; the boy become a man.

'I didn't know it had got that bad,' she says.

'I'm getting calls from producers saying he's showed up hours late, or not at all. The orders he places have to be rechecked by someone else, we've had so many errors. Last week we received a shipment of a hundred cases of rosé we've never stocked before. Ed couldn't even remember placing the order.'

Kitty stares at him hopelessly.

'Why are you telling me this, Hugo?'

'As chairman of the firm,' he says. 'I'm going to have to ask him to take a leave of absence.'

Chairman of the firm. Leave of absence. And he's still in his twenties.

'Is that a nice way of saying you want him to go?'

'That depends on whether he can sort himself out,' says Hugo.

Kitty says nothing. The kettle boils. She takes it off the stove, but she stays standing there, one hand resting on its handle, as the steam dissipates into the air.

'Look, Kitty, I like Ed. And I'm grateful to him. He's worked like a Trojan building up the business. We probably have more contacts in provincial French vineyards than any other importer. But his heart just isn't in it any more. I can't let him damage the reputation of the firm.' He pauses, looks down, gives a quick shake of his head. 'And I hate seeing him hurt you.'

'Hurt me?'

'Come on. I'm not blind. He's killing you, Kitty.'

'Killing me?'

She repeats his words like a fool to play for time. Nothing Hugo says comes as a surprise, except for the fact that it's Hugo who says it. If anything it's a relief to hear it spoken aloud.

'He's stealing your life away from you. You're so lovely and so kind-hearted and so . . . so full of light. And now, it's as if he's dimmed you. He's letting your light fade. He gives you nothing, Kitty. You must see that. He's stealing your spirit, because he has none of his own left.'

Kitty bites her lower lip to hold back the tears. This is so exactly what she feels that it frightens her.

'But I love him,' she whispers.

'But he's no good for you. You must see that.'

Tears brim in her eyes. Hugo jumps up and takes her in his arms.

'You know how I feel about you,' he says. 'You've known from the beginning.'

'No, Hugo— '

'Why not? Aren't you at least allowed to live?'

It's too much for Kitty. The tears flow, and as she weeps he kisses her: at first as if to brush away the tears, and then on the mouth. She doesn't push him away. She has no resistance left.

And it's good to be wanted, and held in a man's arms, if only for a moment.

A clatter at the door. She looks round. There's Pamela, frozen on the threshold, staring at her.

She backs away from Hugo and wipes her eyes.

'And I haven't even got the children's tea on the table,' she says.

'Hello, Pammy,' says Hugo.

Pamela says nothing. Elizabeth comes pushing into the kitchen from behind her.

'I'm so hungry,' she says, 'I'm going to die.'

'You shut up, Monkey,' says Pamela, her eyes still on her mother.

'I won't shut up!' says Elizabeth. 'And don't call me Monkey!'

Kitty is now in motion, putting out bread and butter and honey, milk and biscuits.

'Monkey, Monkey, Monkey,' says Pamela.

'Now, Pamela,' says Hugo.

'You're not my father,' says Pamela.

'Tell her not to call me Monkey,' Elizabeth cries, tugging at her mother's skirt.

'You know she doesn't like it, Pammy,' says Kitty.

'Why do you side with her always?' Pamela is suddenly furious. 'Why is it always me who's wrong? Why do you hate me?'

'I don't hate you, darling.'

Kitty is overwhelmed. It's all too much. She wants to sit down and cry until she can cry no more.

'You know I don't like Rich Tea biscuits, so why do you get them?' Pamela senses her mother's weakness, and attacks with all the cruelty of a self-righteous seven-year-old. 'I don't know why I even come home. The food's always dull or horrid. We never have cakes with icing, like Jean has, or chocolate milk. I wish I lived in Jean's house and Jean's mummy was my mummy.'

'Pamela!' says Hugo sharply. 'That's enough.'

Pamela turns her burning eyes on him.

'Oh, yes,' she says. 'It's enough.'

She goes back out into the hall and can be heard running up the stairs.

Kitty proceeds with the automatic tasks of slicing and buttering bread, and pouring milk into glasses.

'You'd better go, Hugo,' she says. 'I'll talk to Ed.'

'Are you sure?' says Hugo. 'You don't want me to go to Pamela?'

'No. It'll only make things worse.'

She puts out the tea for Elizabeth.

'Here you are, darling. Do you want me to spread the honey for you?'

'I'll do it,' says Elizabeth happily. Then as she spoons out unwarranted amounts of honey, 'I don't want to live in Jean's house. I want to live here.'

Kitty meets Larry off the train at Lewes. Driving back, she asks after Geraldine, who is spending a week in Arundel with her parents.

'Geraldine's fine,' says Larry.

Pamela and Elizabeth greet Larry with cries of joy, and fight over who's to sit on his lap. Kitty looks on with a smile.

'Sometimes I think they see more of you than they do of Ed.'

'Pure cupboard love,' says Larry, searching his weekend bag. 'Now what have I got here?'

He takes out two small packets of sweet buttery biscuits from Normandy.

'And the bananas!' cries Elizabeth.

'Bananas?' says Larry. 'What bananas?'

His gifts are always much anticipated, always the same. He takes a bunch of ripe bananas from his bag and hands them over. The girls retire to gorge.

'How are bananas?' says Kitty, meaning his work.

'Challenging,' says Larry. 'My father has just decided to retire. Which puts me in the driving seat.'

'But that's wonderful, isn't it?'

'As I say, challenging. After all these years of having the market pretty much to ourselves, it looks like we're about to get some serious competition. A Dutch firm called Geest.'

'Geesed? As in goosed?'

'Almost.'

'You've been wanting to take over for ages, Larry. Now you can do all those things you've been dreaming of doing.'

'Yes, that's the exciting part.' He looks round. 'I take it Ed's away.'

'As usual. I want to talk to you about that. Later, when the girls are in bed. Oh, Larry, I'm so glad you've come.'

The guest bedroom above the kitchen is known as 'Larry's room', because whenever he comes, with or without Geraldine, this is where he sleeps. He's in the room, hanging up the modest changes of clothes he's brought for the weekend, when he hears a soft tap-tap on the door.

'Come in!' he calls.

No one comes in. He opens the door himself. There stands Pamela, looking unsure whether she wants to come in or run away.

'Pamela?'

She twists about on her toes and turns her head this way and that, but says not a word.

'You want to talk to me?'

She nods, not meeting his eyes.

'Come on in, then.'

She comes in. He closes the door. Realising she might find it easier to speak if he isn't looking at her, he continues with hanging up his clothes.

'Larry,' she says after a while, 'do you think Mummy would ever leave us?'

'Leave you?' says Larry. 'No, never. Why would you ever think such a thing?'

'Do mothers ever leave their children?'

'No, they don't, sweetheart. Hardly ever.'

'Judy Garland got divorced. She's got a little girl.'

'But she didn't leave her daughter, did she? And anyway, film stars aren't like us.'

'So Mummy wouldn't ever go off with another man?'

'No, Pamela, never.' She has his full attention now. 'Why are you asking me this?'

'I can't tell you.'

'Then tell your mother. You can tell her.'

'No!' says Pamela. 'I could never tell her!'

'Pammy, this must be some silly muddle you've got yourself into.'

'It's not a silly muddle! You don't know. But I jolly well do know.'

Larry can see that she wants to tell him, but holds back for fear of the consequences.

'How about I promise not to tell anyone else, if you tell me?'

'No one else at all?'

'No one in all the world.'

'Not Mummy or Daddy?'

'No one. Cross my heart and hope to die.'

'You have to do it,' Pamela says.

'What?'

'Cross your heart.'

Larry makes the sign of the cross.

'No, not like that!' Pamela demonstrates, describing an X across her skinny chest. 'Like that.'

Larry complies. There follows a silence. Then Pamela bursts into tears, and mumbles some indistinct words that Larry fails to catch.

'Come here, sweetheart,' he says gently, opening his arms. 'Whisper it in my ear.'

She presses her lips to his ear and whispers.

'I saw Mummy kissing Hugo.'

He moves her round so he can look her in the face.

'Hugo?'

She nods, snuffling.

'You're sure?'

Another nod.

'Where?'

'In the kitchen. When I came back from school.'

'They were probably having a friendly hug.'

'No! It was mouth kissing!'

Larry says nothing. He's not sure what to think. He's not sure what he feels.

'You don't believe me.'

'Yes,' he says. 'I believe you.'

'So you see. It's not a silly muddle I've got myself into.'

'No,' says Larry, 'but it may be a silly muddle all the same.'

All through the remainder of that Saturday Pamela's revelation fills Larry's mind. He knows he must talk to Kitty about it, but doesn't know how. His promise to Pamela seems to him to be overruled by the seriousness of the situation. Kitty is clearly in trouble. Apart from Louisa, who's not at all well, he's her best friend. Who else can she confide in?

All day long his thoughts bounce back and forth, from Kitty to Ed to Hugo and back, missing out only himself and his own feelings for Kitty. So long controlled if not denied, he dares not unlock the secret room in which he has hidden away his love for her. Kitty is married to his best friend. He himself has a wife. Things are as they are, and must be lived with.

But Hugo?

It makes no sense at all. Behind the locked door waits the secret cry: if Hugo, why not me? Except he knows why it can't be him.

But Hugo!

One case reported by a child, one kiss that may never have happened, has rocked the fragile equilibrium with which he's been living for so long. The old self-accusation rises up to taunt him.

I've been too weak. I've been too afraid. If I'd spoken out long ago. If I'd made demands. If I'd been a man.

If you don't ask, you don't get.

Evening comes. The girls are tucked up in bed, presumed asleep. Kitty talks freely now, telling him about Ed and his absences and his drinking. All the time she's talking, Larry looks on her lovely face and asks himself, Is it possible she has sought consolation elsewhere?

'Hugo was here the other day,' she says. 'He told me he wants Ed to take leave of absence from the firm. That's how bad it's got.'

Hugo was here the other day.

'What will you say to him? To Ed, I mean.'

'I don't know, Larry. I don't know what to do with Ed. He knows I hate his drinking. So now of course he does it in secret. But there's something I hate more than the drinking. Why is he so unhappy? Have I failed him? What have I done wrong? He's got me, he's got the girls. I've never asked him to do anything he doesn't want. I don't ask him for smart cars or fur coats. I'm a good wife to him, aren't I? He knows I love him. And I do, I do love him. Sometimes he can be so sweet and I think I've got him back, the old Ed. But then it's like a door closes, and I'm on one side, and he's on the other, with his unhappiness.'

She speaks rapidly but calmly, long past the stage of incoherence and tears. Larry understands that what he's hearing is the cycle of thoughts that go round and round in her head.

'Of course I blame myself, how can I not blame myself? But I'm so tired of it all, Larry, it wears me out. And there's something worse. I get angry, too. Angry with Ed. Why is he doing this to us? Why can't he see how good his life could be? Why can't he see how unhappy he's making me?'

'I think he knows that,' says Larry.

'Then why doesn't he do something about it?'

'I don't know,' says Larry. 'But I'm sure of one thing. It's not your fault. I know he'd say that too. It's something in him.'

'What?' she says, searching his face as if to find it there. 'What in him? Why?'

'I think he'd call it the darkness,' says Larry. 'I don't understand it. But it's been there as long as I've known him.'

'Even at school?'

'Oh, yes.'

'If only he'd talk to me about it.'

'I think the problem there,' says Larry slowly, 'is that he feels he's already let you down. He feels so much guilt about you, he doesn't want to burden you with even more. He loves you so much, it must be torture to him, knowing he's making you unhappy too. I think he's trying to keep it away from you, his unhappiness. Like a contagious disease, you know? He's quarantining himself.'

'Then what am I to do?'

'I don't know,' says Larry. 'I suppose you could seek consolation elsewhere.'

'Elsewhere? Where?'

'Hugo, maybe.'

'Hugo?' She laughs at the sheer absurdity of it. 'Why Hugo of all people?' Then she guesses. 'Pamela told you.'

She sees from his face that she's right.

'Oh, God! I should have talked to her. I just couldn't think how to explain. Poor Hugo has had this idea he's in love with me for ages and ages, and when he was telling me about Ed and how he had to stop work I got upset and cried a little, and he kissed me. Pamela had just got back from school and she saw. What did she tell you? Is she terribly upset? Oh, what fools we all are.'

'She thought you might leave her to go off with Hugo.'

'Go off with Hugo? He's a child! It's all a fantasy of his. No, I'd never go off with Hugo.'

'That's what I told her.'

Even so, the sweet relief is running through his veins, making his skin tingle. He hadn't realised how afraid he had become of that kiss.

'Anyway, I never kissed Hugo. He kissed me.'

'What does he think of it all now?'

'Oh, he's fine. We're still good friends. I just told him to stop being silly. He's so used to his little game of unreciprocated love that I think he was almost relieved to go back to the way things were.'

His little game of unreciprocated love. There's more than one of those.

He sees that she follows his thoughts. How could she not? It's been so many years now.

'How's Geraldine?' she says; even though she asked in the car, and he replied then, 'Geraldine's fine.'

'Geraldine and I,' he says this time, 'are as unhappy together as you and Ed. Different couple, different problems, same misery.'

Kitty's face shows sympathy but not surprise.

'I did think, in France.'

'We keep up appearances. But we more or less lead separate lives now.'

Kitty reaches across the table and takes his hand.

'How do you cope with it?' she says.

'I work. Work can take up all your time, if you want it to.'

'Like Ed.'

'Ed's angry with himself. The worst of my situation is I'm

angry with Geraldine. I know I shouldn't be. I half understand why she is the way she is. I'm sorry for her. But more than everything else I'm angry with her. She won't do the one simple thing that makes marriages possible. She won't love me.'

'Does that mean what I think it means?'

'We sleep in separate rooms.'

'Oh, Larry.'

'I'm ashamed of myself for minding so much. But I do.'

'Oh, Larry.'

'So one way or another, we've both made a bit of a botch of our lives, haven't we?'

She goes on stroking his hand, gazing into his eyes.

'You were the one I wanted,' he says.

It seems so easy to say it now.

'I know,' she says.

'Have you always known?'

'Yes,' she says. 'I think so.'

'But you love Ed. Even though he doesn't know how to be happy.'

'Sometimes I think that's why I love him.'

'So if I'd just been a bit more miserable, might you have gone for me instead?'

'Probably,' she says, smiling.

'I could start now.'

He pulls a sad face.

'Darling Larry.'

'Don't be too nice to me. I don't think I can take it.'

'I could have been happy with you,' she says.

'Well, there it is,' he says. 'What might have been.'

She goes on looking at him, and he sees so much love there

that he doesn't want either of them to say any more. This moment is so sweet to him that he'd ask for nothing else in life if only it would go on for ever.

Then she says, 'If Hugo can kiss me, I don't see why you can't. I've known you far longer.'

He gets up from his side of the table and goes round to hers. She stands, and puts her face up to his, timid but willing, like a young girl. He kisses her very gently at first. Then he draws her into his arms and they kiss as he has longed to kiss her ever since the first moment he set eyes on her, ten years ago.

And so they part at last.

'I can't help it,' he says. 'I've always loved you, and I always will.'

'Dearest darling Larry. Don't ask me to say it. I'll never do anything to hurt Ed. You know that.'

'Of course I do.'

'But this' – she strokes his arms, smiling at him, meaning the acknowledgement of his love – 'this makes it easier.'

'For me too.'

And it does. Nothing can change. Their circumstances make anything more between them impossible. But everything has changed. Larry feels filled with a joyful lightness. Now, and to the day either he or Kitty dies, he will never be alone.

'That was it,' she says. But she looks so much happier. 'That was what might have been. Now back to what is.'

# 38

'What system of budgetary controls do you operate, Mr Cornford?'

'I'm sorry,' says Larry. 'I don't follow you.'

Donohue, the young man leading the McKinsey team, frowns and leans back in his chair. He exchanges glances with Neill and Hollis, his colleagues. All three wear dark suits and white shirts with dark ties. All three are younger than Larry.

'Purchasing, transport, stock management, maintenance contracts – every part of the running of the company incurs costs, and these costs have to be managed. But of course you know that.' Donohue smiles suddenly and brightly. Larry waits to be told something he doesn't know. 'I'm simply asking what systems you have in place, as managing director, to ensure that your costs are kept as low as possible.'

The question annoys Larry. Donohue annoys Larry. The team from McKinsey & Co, brought in by the parent company in New Orleans, annoys Larry.

'I don't assume,' he answers carefully, 'that the lowest costs will always deliver the greatest benefit.'

'But you must have some system for monitoring costs,' says Donohue.

'It's called my staff,' says Larry. 'Each purchase is made by a member of staff who knows his business and has the best interests of the company at heart.'

'I see,' says Donohue, making a note. 'Would it be correct to say that your staff are only lightly supervised?'

'You could say that,' says Larry. 'Or you could say our staff are greatly trusted.'

'And what if it were to turn out that your trust had been abused? Indeed, has it ever so turned out?'

'We all fall short of the glory of God, Mr Donohue,' says Larry. 'The question is, what are we to do about it? We can set up what you call a monitoring system, which tells people what they should be doing, and detects when they're failing to do it, and presumably punishes them in some way. Or we can give them an area of responsibility, and ask them to work out how best to operate for themselves, and rely on their pride in their work and their loyalty to the company to deliver the best possible results.'

'And if they're incompetent, or idle, or corrupt?'

'Then the failure is mine. I've failed to make them see that the company's good is also their good. Perhaps we need a system for monitoring me.'

Donohue exchanges looks with Neill and Hollis.

'I think you're talking about the ethos of the small family firm, Mr Cornford,' he says. 'What you might call the paternalistic model. But Fyffes is neither family owned, nor' – he checks his notes – 'small. You have over three thousand employees.'

'Yes,' says Larry with a sigh. 'You're quite right. And of course if you and your team can show us ways to operate more efficiently, we'll gladly implement them.'

'That's what we're here for,' says Donohue.

'One question, Mr Donohue. In all your calculations, do you have a column for the life satisfaction of the staff of the company?'

There follows a pause.

'I understand you, of course,' says Donohue at last. 'But firstly, there's no easy way to measure it. And secondly, without profits there is no company, and without a company, there is no life satisfaction for its staff. Or, to put it plainly, you all sink or float together.' He rises, and Neal and Hollis rise with him. 'With your permission, we'll get to work.'

At home after dinner that evening, Larry paces the library and vents his frustration on his father.

'What do they know about our business? They've never run a business. All they can do is add up numbers and spread insecurity. God only knows how much they get paid! And what revelation will come out at the end? That we'd be advised to make a profit rather than a loss.'

'We've been through this sort of thing before,' says his father. 'In our business there are lean years and fat years. Once we're back paying a healthy dividend all this nonsense will go away.'

'I hope you're right. The Geest operation changes things.'

'Geest came into the market because we've not been able to meet the demand,' says William Cornford. 'We'll lose market share, that's inevitable. But there's enough out there for both of us.'

'Of course there is! And of course we'll diversify. And of course we'll modernise the distribution network. I don't need consultants to tell me that.'

His father smiles to hear him.

'It makes me very happy to know you're with us, Larry. I could never have stepped down for anyone else.'

'Don't worry, Dad. I won't let them rape the old firm.'

'I think I always knew you'd come back to us.'

Geraldine looks in at the library door.

'I'm going up, darling,' she says. 'Good night, William.'

Larry gives her a kiss on the cheek.

'Don't stay up too late,' she says.

Alone again, William Cornford watches his son return to his agitated pacing.

'Larry, I've been meaning to ask you,' he says. 'Wouldn't it be easier for you and Geraldine if I were to get myself a place of my own somewhere?'

'But this is your house. We can't turn you out of your own house.'

'I would make the house over to you.'

'No, Dad. I don't want you to go.'

'How about Geraldine?'

'She's very fond of you. You know that.'

'She's very good to me,' says William Cornford. 'She's always charming, and considerate. I'm not sure I know that she actually likes me.'

'Of course she does! Why wouldn't she?'

'I don't know. I'm sure it's all nothing. Forget I mentioned it.'

Larry is silent. He has stopped pacing. Some private train of thought leads him to ask a question he's long meant to ask.

'Dad, why did you never marry again?'

'Oh, Lord,' exclaims his father. 'What a question.'

'All I mean is, was it by choice?'

'These things are mostly a matter of chance, aren't they? You don't meet the right person. You work hard. You grow to like the life you have.'

'So it's not because you found your marriage was . . . was not what you'd hoped?'

'No, not at all. Your mother and I got along better than most. Her death was the most terrible shock. When something like that happens, you remember only the good times. I suppose it all depends what you expect marriage to be. It can't be everything, you know.'

He says this gently, sensing his son's reasons for raising the topic.

'No, of course not,' says Larry.

'Your mother never really understood why the company took up so much of my time. I expect Geraldine finds that, too.'

'No, I don't think so,' says Larry.

'Well, then. You're doing better than I did.'

'No,' says Larry flatly. 'I'm not.'

His father says no more.

'The truth is, Dad,' says Larry after a long moment, 'my marriage isn't working out at all.'

'I'm very sorry to hear that.'

'Perhaps I should get the McKinsey men in.' He gives a bitter laugh. 'They could install a monitoring system to make my marriage more efficient.'

'Are you quite sure you wouldn't rather have me out of your hair?'

'No, Dad. It wouldn't help. Things have gone too far.'

He looks up at the clock on the mantelpiece.

'I should be going on up.'

He turns and sees his father's familiar face, loving as always, puzzled as to what to say or do. It strikes him then how his father has been there all his life, the constant presence that has watched over him and protected him. There was a time when all he wanted was not to turn into his father, not to lead his life. There seemed to him, in his youthful arrogance, so little to show for it. What did the world care if a few more bananas were sold, or a few fewer? What sort of enterprise was that for a life? But now he sees matters differently. Not just because he's joined the company. It seems to him that every sphere of life can offer meaning, if lived properly. That there is as much nobility in living rightly among bananas as in an artist's studio. And that his father has lived rightly.

'Good night, then, son,' says William Cornford, lightly clasping Larry's shoulder with one hand.

Larry thinks then he would like to hug his father, but he doesn't make the move. He thinks he'd like to say something to him, along the lines of, 'I admire you so much, Dad. Any good there is in me I owe to you.' But the two of them are not accustomed to such exchanges, and the words don't come.

'Good night, Dad,' he says.

The report on Fyffes by McKinsey & Co recommends the closure of the current seventy-four store branches and their replacement with nine new strategically placed large modern facilities. It proposes that the current thirteen departments be rationalised to five, and that a unified budgetary control system be rigidly enforced across the company. Overall the report identifies potential savings of a remarkable 39% on current operating costs, largely by what it calls a 'shakeout of excess personnel'.

Larry presents the report to his board in Stratton Street.

'I calculate,' says Larry, 'that if we were to accept this report as it stands we would have to terminate over one thousand of our people. That is not the Fyffes way. I will not do it.'

The board applauds him. He invites his colleagues to work with him in the creation of a new report.

'If costs are too high we can bring them down. If there is over-manning in some departments, we can reallocate staff. But you know and I know this is a cyclical business, and it would be madness to lose experienced staff, staff we will dearly need later, just because we're at a low point in the cycle. There is another aspect to this also. These employees who we're advised to sack are men who have given their working lives to the company, men who've made it successful. They have families. We all know them. They're our friends. I measure the success of Fyffes not just by the profits we make, which vary year on year, but in the well-being of the families that our company supports. They have trusted us. I will not let them down.'

The board applauds again.

Larry is invited to present his response to the parent company's management in New Orleans.

Jimmy Brunstetter greets him as an old friend.

'Too long, Larry, too long. I'm going to take you out tonight and give you a dinner that will knock your socks off. Now you go and freshen up, and do what you have to do, because I have to run.'

Larry has brought his report, and holds it in his hand.

'Maybe you'd like to take a look at this.'

'Sure, sure I would. Only right now I'm late for the meeting I cancelled another meeting for on account of being late for that one, if you get my drift.'

And away he trots, head bobbing, smoking as he hurries to the elevator. His assistant takes over.

'Mr Brunstetter has booked a table at Broussard's for seven p.m., Mr Cornford. Is there anything more I can do for you now?'

Broussard's, in the heart of the Vieux Carré, is very grand. Ornate gold-framed mirrors line the walls. A statue of Napoleon holds pride of place.

'I got us a table in the courtyard,' says Jimmy Brunstetter, arriving fifteen minutes late. 'They looking after you okay?'

'Excellently, thank you,' says Larry.

The courtyard is wisteria-covered, mild in the evening air, and grandly relaxed. Brunstetter seems to know everybody, most notably the proprietor-chef Joe Broussard.

'So, Papa,' Brunstetter tells him, 'I got a VIP guest from England, and we're going to do him proud, right?'

'You said it,' beams the chef.

Brunstetter takes personal charge of Larry's menu choices.

'Fried oysters. You ever had fried oysters? You have not lived. So you'll have Oysters Broussard, you will die and go to heaven. Then, let's see, oh sure, Creole Ribeye, that's the one. You ever had Creole cooking? You have not lived. So what are you drinking? Tell you what, my friend. You order a Brandy Napoleon here, you know what they do? They bring it out and all the waiters sing the 'Marseillaise'. Gives you one hell of a kick the first time, but after that it's a pain in the ass, to be frank with you. But if you'd like? No? That's good for me.'

'So what's the Napoleon connection?' says Larry politely.

Brunstetter looks at him as if he's mad.

'This joint is French,' he says. 'Joe Broussard is French. Napoleon was French, right?'

'Yes,' says Larry. 'I believe he was.'

The food is superb. Two courses come and go and no mention is made of the reason for Larry's trip.

'So you heard Sam retired?' says Brunstetter.

'Yes,' says Larry. 'What's the new man like? I hope to meet him.'

'A good man. A good man. But Sam was something else. Big shoes to fill.'

'So is there a meeting planned for tomorrow? They didn't seem to know in your office.'

'Meetings? Don't tell me about meetings! My life is meetings. But we're here to enjoy ourselves, right? How about the brandy without the singing waiters?'

'I left a copy of my report with your assistant,' says Larry. 'Can I be sure he'll get it to the president?'

'Don't you worry about that. Don't you worry about anything. This is the VIP treatment. You're having a good time, right? Have a cigarette. You like something sweet? They got crêpes here, they roll 'em round cream cheese and brandy pecan stuffing, they float 'em in strawberry sauce, and all you have to do is open your mouth. You will die and go to heaven.'

The next day is a frustrating one for Larry. He waits in his hotel but no message comes. He calls Brunstetter's office, only to learn he's out of town for the day. He calls the president's office to confirm that they received his report, and is assured the matter is being attended to. Left to his own devices, reluctant to walk the streets in the sultry heat, he stays in his hotel room and thinks about Kitty. He thinks about how he kissed her and how he told her he loved her, and the petty annoyances of the day fade into nothing. Something so big has come so right that now all he can do is rest silent, grateful, in its presence.

In the end, because thoughts of Kitty so fill his mind, he writes her a letter. All his letters to her have been love letters, but this is the first time he has written openly about his love.

> I don't know how to begin this letter. Whatever I write will sound either too faint to express what I feel or too presumptuous. What am I to you? One who has loved you for ten years and only kissed you once. One who wants only to spend the rest of his life with you and knows it's impossible. What a mess it is. What a wonderful ridiculous joyful mess! Everything is wrong but all I feel is happiness. I suppose from now on we're to lead lives of guilt and subterfuge but I don't care. It turns out I don't care about anything or anyone but you. I suppose this is how crimes of passion come about. As you see from the letter paper I'm in a grand hotel in New Orleans. They give me grand dinners, and a car and driver to take me wherever I want. And all I want is you. I long to say to my driver, Take me to Kitty. Then an immense American car would come swishing down the track to your house, and you'd get in the back seat with me, which is deep and soft and long, and . . .

He doesn't finish the letter. Nor does he send it. He knows he can't involve Kitty in a secret life she has to hide from Ed.

But he keeps the letter, just in case the time should ever come when he can show it to her.

The next day a message comes from Jimmy Brunstetter. He would like to meet Larry at ten a.m.

Larry finds Brunstetter has the McKinsey report on his desk, but sees no sign of his own report. There's another man in the room who is only introduced as 'Walter'. This time Jimmy Brunstetter gets straight down to business.

'So the McKinsey boys did a fine job, right? We were pretty pleased with what they turned up. There's your company future right there, Larry. You seen the latest figures? We didn't see Geest coming, did we?'

'No, we didn't,' says Larry. 'But the market's potentially big enough for both of us.'

'Potentially.' Brunstetter glances at Walter. 'We like *actually*.' He taps the McKinsey report. 'This is *actually*.'

Larry made up his mind before leaving London to show no signs of his real feelings about the McKinsey report. After all, United have paid for it.

'The report is excellent in its analysis of costs,' he says. 'But it doesn't take account of company culture. You'll find in my report that there's another approach.'

'That's good, that's good,' says Brunstetter. Once more he taps the McKinsey report. 'The president and the board have signed off on this.'

'Signed off? I don't understand.'

'The recommendations of this report will now be implemented.'

'Implemented? I'm sorry, Jimmy, there's some misunderstanding here. I don't accept the McKinsey findings, and nor does my board.'

'I don't think you mean that, Larry.'

Walter is taking notes.

'Give me a year,' says Larry. 'You'll see in my report how I plan to tackle the issues the McKinsey report raises.'

'You'll make the redundancies?'

'I'll do all that's necessary.'

'Come on, Larry. We're old friends, we don't need to bull around. Fyffes needs to lose at least half its people. You know that. I know that. Are you going to do it?'

'I don't accept that cuts on that scale are needed,' says Larry. 'The company's in good health. In a year we'll be back in profit.'

Brunstetter turns to Walter.

'What do you reckon, Walter?'

'The question is very simple,' says Walter. As soon as he starts talking Larry knows he's a lawyer. 'The board of the parent company requires the report here to be implemented in full. Is Mr Cornford willing to do that or not?'

'Of course I'm not,' says Larry. 'I'm here to talk about the report. I'm here to talk about the best way forward for Fyffes. After all, I was born into this company. My grandfather created it. My father made it successful. I think I can claim to know more about how Fyffes works than either McKinsey or your board.'

'Well, there you have the problem,' says Brunstetter. 'You just put your finger right on the button, Larry. You were born into the company. Maybe the time has come for fresh blood.'

'Fresh blood?'

'The question is very simple,' says Walter. 'Will you or will you not implement the recommendations of this report?'

'Why should I?' He can't help himself. 'It's narrowly based, error-riddled, ill-conceived, and concerned with nothing but the bottom line.'

'We are concerned with the bottom line, Larry,' says Brunstetter.

'The company is greater than its profits.'

The two Americans greet this with silence.

'The question is very simple,' says Walter doggedly.

'No! It is not!' Larry is angry now. 'It's complex, and there are many ways forward. I will not accept this corner shop chiselling as any way to run a company.'

Another silence follows.

'Are we to understand,' says Walter, 'that you are offering your resignation?'

That's when Larry gets it at last. They want him out.

'No,' he says. 'Fyffes is my family. How do you resign from your family?'

He looks from one to the other. He realises now that it's Walter who's the power in the room.

'Are you telling me that if I don't agree to implement this report, I'm out?'

'Are we to understand,' says Walter, 'that you're offering your resignation?'

'Can I have time to think about this?'

'No, sir,' says Walter.

'No time? You ask me to choose between the jobs of a thousand employees of my company, and my own job?'

They give no answer to that.

Larry gives a laugh.

'It seems the question is very simple after all,' he says. 'You've already made up your minds. Half the staff are to go. The only remaining question is whether I go too.'

He turns and looks out of the window, seeing nothing of the street below, not wanting to see their faces.

'I believe this strategy to be profoundly mistaken,' he says. 'I can't run the company on this basis. If so many lives are to be destroyed by the shortsightedness and greed of you gentlemen in the United Fruit Company, then let mine be destroyed too. You're choosing to sink a fine company. As captain, I choose to go down with the ship.'

'Are we to understand,' says Walter, 'that you are offering your resignation?'

'Yes,' says Larry. 'You are.'

# 39

On landing at Heathrow, Larry finds his driver is not there to meet him. Exhausted by the flight, he considers taking a taxi home, but chooses instead to ask the cabbie to take him to Piccadilly. The company is in crisis and he feels an urgent need to be with his colleagues; almost as urgently, he does not want to have to explain to Geraldine how everything will now have to change.

London looks drab and poor after New Orleans. A smattering of rain brings out the black umbrellas on the pavements. Larry sits in the jolting cab, eyes closed, preparing himself for the shock he is about to deliver. He remains sure he has done the right thing, and is ready to pay the price. But so many others will pay too.

It's just past three in the afternoon when the taxi pulls up outside 15 Stratton Street. Larry hauls his suitcase through the heavy door into the dark lobby where Stanley the doorman has his cubbyhole.

'Mr Lawrence, sir!'

'Hello, Stanley. Sorry if I look like a tramp, I've come straight from the airport. I'll leave this with you.'

He drops his suitcase and makes for the stairs.

'Sir!' cries Stanley. 'Sir! I'm sorry, Mr Lawrence!'

Larry turns round.

'What is it, Stanley?'

'I'm not to admit you, sir.'

'Not admit me?'

'Your things have all been sent to the house, sir. Mr Angelotti is in your office now.'

'Mr Angelotti?'

'The new boss, sir.' Stanley can't meet Larry's eyes. 'He came Thursday.'

'Thursday!'

'And sir. Mr Lawrence, sir. We was all so sad to hear about Mr William, sir.' Now he looks up at Larry, and his eyes are blurry. 'They're saying it's all over for us, sir.'

Larry struggles to keep a grip on what he's hearing. As gently as possible he responds to the doorman.

'Nothing's over,' he says. 'Now tell me what's happened to my father?'

'Your father, sir? Didn't no one tell you? He passed away, sir. We heard this morning. I'm sorry, sir. He was a gentleman.'

Larry returns to the house in Campden Grove to find the situation entirely under control. Geraldine is superb in a crisis. Undertakers have been called. The library has been turned into a lying-in room. All the necessary people have been informed.

'I tried to reach you,' she says.

Larry is almost mute with shock and grief. Coming on top of the stress induced by his resignation, and the long flight home, this news comes close to breaking him.

'When? How?'

'Yesterday evening. They phoned with the news from the office. We were in the middle of dinner. Cookie called him to the phone. He spoke on the phone, then he came back to the dining room and said, "They've brought in an American to run the company." Then he put his hands forward on the table, as if to steady himself. Then he fell to the floor.'

'Dear Lord!' groans Larry.

'The doctor says it was a single big stroke. They say it must have been instantaneous.'

'Oh, Dad,' says Larry. 'Oh, Dad.'

'I'm so sorry, Larry. What can I do? Just tell me how I can help you.'

'You've been wonderful. You've done everything. I don't know. I can't think.'

Timidly she says, 'There'll have to be a funeral.'

'Yes. Yes, of course.'

'I can arrange it if you like.'

'Please. Arrange everything.'

He goes into the library, where the curtains are closed, and two candles burn on either side of an open coffin. His father lies in the coffin, looking like a poorly executed dummy. Larry kneels and prays, briefly. But his father is not here.

He climbs the stairs to the suite of rooms on the second floor his father has used for the whole of his life. The small sitting room opens onto a bedroom, a bathroom, a dressing room. Everything here is neat and tidy, as his father liked it. Larry came into this suite of rooms from time to time as a child, but has not been through the doors for twenty years or more. He closes the door onto the stairwell behind him, wanting to be alone in his father's presence. Almost delirious with exhaustion, he walks about the rooms, touching the items his father touched every day: his quilted dark-red bath robe, his badger-hair shaving brush, the pomade with which he added a discreet shine to his greying hair. On the bedside table lie his rosary and his breviary, its silk marker in yesterday's place. He read Compline to himself every evening, Matins every morning. How can he be dead?

His father kept a prie-dieu in the little sitting room, though Larry never saw him kneeling at it. He must have done so in the night, the kneeler cushion is deeply indented.

Larry kneels, resting his elbows on the armrest, letting his head sink into his hands.

'Lord Jesus Christ,' he prays, 'take my beloved father into your loving arms. Let him know the peace and rest he deserves. Tell him I admired him so much. Tell him he was the only truly good man I've ever known. Tell him I loved him all my life. Tell him . . . tell him . . . Dad . . . don't leave me now. Don't leave me. Dad, I need you so.'

Then he lets himself cry, wetting his jacket sleeves with his tears.

In time the tears pass. He looks up and sees, through the open dressing room door, on the wall above the chest of drawers, a blur of colour. He blinks and dabs at his eyes. He rises from the prie-dieu and goes into the dressing room. There, close beside the rail of suits his father wore that still carry his familiar smell, hang two small pictures on the wall. Two views of Mount Caburn, with Edenfield church in the foreground. Two pictures painted by a son who had disappointed his father. Bought from the Leicester Galleries five years ago, by a father who wanted only that his son should be happy.

*

*Requiem aeternam dona eis Domine.*

The Carmelite church is packed for the funeral. Looking around the pews Larry sees board members, directors, managers, storemen, porters, maintenance workers; ships' captains and crew men; company representatives from Jamaica, Honduras, the Canaries, Cameroon. These are the people his father served. These are the people he too has served in his turn. And now it's all over.

This is not how it should have been. His father's death should have been celebrated as the end of a good life, his achievements recognised and perpetuated. He built a company that he meant to outlast him. And when he took his leave, honourably, asking for nothing for himself, looters and wreckers rose up to destroy his heritage.

Who are these mighty masters of the world, these presidents of a far-off empire who look with their cold eyes on balance sheets and turn them into shrouds? Zemurray and Brunstetter and McKinsey and the rest, what God do they worship? In the name of what grand design do they exploit their workers and corrupt their governments?

*Dies irae*!

'Oh what fear man's bosom rendeth, when from heaven the Judge descendeth, on whose sentence all dependeth!'

So while others mourn, Larry rages. His anger is directed against himself, too. His father entrusted the company to him, and he promised to keep the company safe, and he failed.

I have killed my father.

*Libera me, domine.*

'Deliver me O Lord from eternal death on that awful day

when the heavens and the earth shall be moved, when Thou shalt come to judge the world by fire.'

Sitting in the car following the hearse, with Geraldine by his side elegant in black, leading a convoy of cars from Kensington to Kensal Green, he feels entirely alone. Standing by the graveside, watching the priest sprinkle the coffin with holy water, he wants to laugh at the absurdity of the whole charade.

My father isn't here.

'May his soul and the souls of all the faithful departed through the mercy of God rest in peace.'

What mercy? The good men are broken and the hard men endure. Here lies a man abandoned by God. He built a business, and that business was the well-being of others. They told him a slow buck is still a buck. But they lied.

No, don't rest in peace, Dad. Stand up before that heavenly throne and rage. Waken the anger of the Lord of Hosts. The time has come to judge the world by fire.

'What I don't understand,' says Geraldine, her voice soft and insistent, 'is why you resigned?'

'Hardly a resignation,' says Larry. 'Even while I was in that meeting, back in London they were clearing my office.'

'But you said you resigned.'

It's true. Larry clings to this version of events to salvage something of his honour. When asked to preside over the butchery of his father's company, he declined.

'I had no choice,' he says wearily.

The funeral is over. The guests are gone. The tall dark house is left to Geraldine and him.

'I'm sure you're right, darling,' says Geraldine, 'but I wish I could understand. Why couldn't you have stayed on, and done your best to make it not be so bad? I don't see what you meant to achieve by resigning.'

'Why should I keep my job and my comforts when the rest lose theirs? Because that would be all I'd be left with. The title, the salary, the car. Do you think I'd have been able to look my colleagues in the eye, as they cleared their desks and crept away?'

'Yes, I do see that, darling. But how are things any better this way? I don't see how it helps them having you out of a job too.'

Larry contemplates his wife. She seems to him to be living in another universe, far away. Nothing touches her. She remains perfectly groomed.

'You miss the title, and the salary, and the car?'

'Am I wrong to worry?' she says. 'What will we live on? Do we even own this house?'

'Yes, Geraldine,' says Larry. 'We own this house. And the house in France. We have some shares in the company. We won't starve. And anyway, we're young still. We can work.'

'What will you do?'

'I don't know.'

Then he realises he does know; or at least a part of it. With this knowledge comes a release of kindness for his wife.

'Geraldine. Please. Let's not pretend any more.'

'Pretend what?'

But she's frightened. She knows too.

'Our marriage hasn't worked. It doesn't work. We don't make each other happy.'

She looks away. She's trembling.

'I've done my best,' she says in a whisper. 'I've tried and tried.'

'I know you have. It's not your fault. It's just who we are.'

'But Larry, we're still married. Nothing can change that.'

'We can divorce.'

She gasps, as if he's struck her.

'Divorce! No!'

'Then you can find someone you can really love. You're young. You're beautiful. You don't want to spend the rest of your life here, with me. You know you don't.'

'But Larry. The sacrament. We can't break it.'

'It's only words.'

Again that quick sharp gasp.

'Only words! And is the Church only words? Is the love of God only words? Are we all to do as we please, and think only of our own pleasure, and live and die like animals?'

'But Geraldine— '

The words pour out of her in a fervent stream, overwhelming him.

'What does it matter if you and I aren't as happy as we'd like to be? We can bear it. We know how to do our duty. We're married. For better, for worse, till death us do part. You swore it, and so did I. That's real, Larry. That's the rock on which we stand. Nothing can ever change that.'

She clasps his hands, willing him to join her.

'We're bound for eternity, Larry.'

'It's too late,' he says.

'Too late? How can it be too late?'

'I've gone too far. I'm sorry. I just can't go on any more.'

She lets go of his hands. Her voice changes, becomes bitter.

'It's Kitty, isn't it?'

'No— '

'You can never have her! She's another man's wife. I know

you love her, I've always known, do you think I'm blind and deaf?' Now in her pain and anger her face contorts, becomes ugly. 'What do you think it's been like for me, seeing you dangling around her, playing your childish little games? But have I ever said a word? Not one word! How do you think I feel, knowing my husband loves another woman? But have I ever told you not to insult me with her presence in my house? Never! Not once! I am your wife. I know my duty. But do you know your duty? Because believe me, at the peril of your immortal soul, you must do your duty! You can't have her, Larry. Would you lose your immortal soul, would you burn in hell for ever, for one silly little woman?'

'Yes,' says Larry.

'Oh!' She buries her face in her hands. 'What's happened to you? What have you become?'

'You're right,' says Larry. 'I can't have Kitty. Even by losing my immortal soul. But this isn't about Kitty. It's about me, and you.'

She waits, her face in her hands. He no longer has any doubts. Somehow his father's death, the loss of the company, have set him free.

'You and I must part. For my sake, and for yours. I'll share all I have with you. I'll give you this house. You'll not be poor. We must each make new lives for ourselves.'

Geraldine begins to weep.

'I'm sorry that I'm not the man you thought I was,' says Larry. 'I'm sorry to let you down. I've let many people down. I'll try to do better in future.'

'Please, Larry.' The ecstasy gone now, and the bitterness. 'Please promise me one thing. Talk to a priest.'

'About my marriage? What does a priest know of marriage?'

'A priest knows the mind of God.'

'No one knows the mind of God,' says Larry. 'Not priests. Not the pope. Not even God. God has no mind. God is just our word for everything that is, and our hope that it has some meaning. But that's all it is. A hope.'

'You know you don't believe that.'

'Do I? Maybe I do, maybe I don't. Who knows what I believe any more? Everything's changing.'

She says nothing. He's not been looking at her, ashamed and afraid to meet her eyes. His whole body feels knotted and hard.

'Larry?'

'Yes?'

'I'm frightened.'

He looks at her then. She stands with her hands clasped before her, her head bowed, like a child come for punishment.

'There's no need,' he says sadly. 'No need.'

'What is it that's wrong with me? Why does no one love me?'

'That's not true. Not true.'

'Why am I all alone? What have I done to deserve such a punishment? Please tell me. I'll try not to do it again.'

'There's nothing, sweetheart. There's nothing.'

No offence. No remedy. The gentleness forced out of him by pity. But it changes nothing.

'Sometimes things don't work out. That's all.'

# 40

Kitty goes ahead of the others, with the girls running ahead of her.

'Is it here?' shouts Pamela. 'Is it here?'

Ed and Larry come behind, carrying the baskets with the food and the rugs. The car is parked in the lane in Glynde below. They are hunting out the place where they picnicked ten years ago.

'No,' calls Kitty. 'Further on. In the trees.'

It's a golden October day, and on all sides the tawny Downs reach rolling down to the patchwork of russet fields. Kitty is happy, because Larry has come, and because Ed is light-hearted. She looks back down the hill to see them climbing slowly after her, laughing together; just as it was all those years ago.

'Here!' cries Elizabeth. 'I've found it!'

The little girl stands on one side of the copse.

'It's all nettles!' says Pamela. 'Yuck!'

'A little further,' calls Kitty.

She remembers the place exactly. Nothing has changed. The trees rise up from the sloping land, their leaves more faded than they were then, but that was June and summer had just begun. She catches up with the girls and confirms the spot.

'I found it!' says Pamela.

'You did not!' says Elizabeth.

But the girls aren't really quarrelling. They're happy too, excited by the prospect of the picnic, and their father's company, and Larry's too.

The men join them, and lay out the tartan rug. Elizabeth at once sits down, right in the middle. The food comes out of the basket to whoops of delight.

'Treacle sandwiches! Meat!'

'It's cold lamb, darling.'

'Can I have cider, Mummy?'

'No, Pamela. There's orange squash.'

'Are you sure this is where we came?' says Larry.

'Totally sure. You were over there. I was here, with Louisa here.'

'Poor Louisa. It doesn't seem fair.'

'It isn't fair,' says Ed. 'When will you get it into your head that life isn't fair?'

Larry grins at Ed.

'What was it?' he says. 'Impulse and glory?'

'Something about an arrow in flight,' says Kitty.

'Dear God!' exclaims Ed. 'Did I really talk like that?'

Larry pours them all drinks and stands to make a toast.

'My dear friends,' he says. 'My dear friends' children.'

Pamela smiles up at him.

'You are funny, Larry.'

'You see me now, a poor bare forked animal— '

'You're not bare,' says Pamela. 'You've got your clothes on.'

'Be quiet. That's King Lear upon the heath. He's lost everything, just like me. No job. No father. No wife.'

'Did King Lear have a wife?' says Ed. 'I suppose there must have been a Queen Lear to produce those daughters. You don't hear much about her.'

'For heaven's sake!' complains Larry. 'Here I am baring my soul, and you keep interrupting.'

'Go on, Larry,' says Kitty.

'I am the thing itself,' says Larry, waving his mug of cider in the air. 'Unaccommodated man. Off, off, you lendings.' He looks down at the girls. 'In the play he actually does take off all his clothes at this point. I'll spare you that. My toast. Raise your glasses!'

They all do so.

'My toast is – to freedom!'

'To freedom!' they cry.

Then they settle down to eat their picnic.

'But Larry,' says Kitty, 'it's terrible about your job. You loved it so.'

'Gone,' says Larry, his mouth full of hard-boiled egg. 'Gone with the wind.'

'He's demob happy,' says Ed. 'It's because he's got away from Geraldine.'

'Eddy!' says Kitty.

'You know we couldn't stand her,' says Ed, unashamed.

'Geraldine was,' says Larry, waving a fork in the air. 'Geraldine is. Geraldine will be.'

Kitty bursts into laughter.

'So much for Geraldine.'

'So what are you going to do now?' says Ed. 'Live the life of the idle rich?'

'Not at all,' says Larry, indignant. 'I'm not idle enough. And actually, I'm not rich enough. I shall find work. I shall offer the sweat of my brow.'

'Yuck!' says Elizabeth, looking at Pamela to check she's got it right.

'Well, here's an idea,' says Ed. 'Kitty may have told you that my labours in the wine trade appear to have reached their natural end. So why don't you take over? You could buy me out of the partnership. I'd have money, you'd have a job.'

'When did you dream this up, Ed?' says Kitty, surprised.

'When Larry told us he'd been sacked.'

'I don't know anything about wine,' says Larry.

'Much like bananas,' says Ed. 'Except it grows in France, and ripens more slowly.'

'Well, I suppose it's worth a thought,' says Larry. 'But what will you do?'

'Oh, I'll find something.'

'Larry,' says Pamela, climbing onto his lap. 'Is it true you're not married to Geraldine any more?'

'I won't be soon,' says Larry.

'Does that mean you can marry me? When I'm older, of course.'

'I suppose it does.'

'You have to wait till I'm sixteen. That's only nine years.'

'But sweetheart, won't I be too horribly old by then?'

'Maybe,' says Pamela. 'We can decide then.'

'Yes, I think that's probably wise.'

'What about me?' says Elizabeth. 'Who can I marry?'

'You can marry Hugo,' says Ed.

'No,' says Pamela, 'I want Hugo as well.'

Everyone laughs except for Elizabeth.

'She always does that,' she says. 'She always takes everything for herself.'

When they've had all they want of the picnic they lie on their backs on the rug and gaze up at the passing clouds. Kitty lies between Ed and Larry, with Elizabeth half on top of her.

'We should go to the top of Caburn,' she says.

'You and Ed go,' says Larry. 'Like last time.'

'Would you like that?' Kitty says, turning her head to smile at Ed.

'Of course,' says Ed.

'I'm coming too,' says Pamela.

'Me too!' cries Elizabeth.

'No,' says Larry, 'I want all those who are going to marry me to stay here and practise.'

'Practise what?' says Pamela dubiously.

'Being married,' says Larry. 'I tell you to do things, and you don't do them.'

This goes down well. Both girls stay with Larry. Ed and Kitty climb the hill. As they go they hear the game begin.

'I go first,' says Larry. 'Pamela, make me a cup of tea.'

'Shan't!' cries Pamela joyfully.

They climb on, out of earshot.

'That's a good friend you have there, Ed,' says Kitty.

'I know it,' says Ed.

They walk to the end of the long ridge, and down the steep side of the ditch at the top, and up the other side to come out onto the summit. Here they stand, side by side, holding hands, looking over the immense view towards the sea.

'Remember how the park was full of huts,' says Kitty.

'And the harbour full of ships,' says Ed.

'I've never forgotten what you said.'

'What did I say?'

She looks at the looping river, and Newhaven beyond.

'You said the river's always running, until it meets the sea and can rest.'

'Well, I suppose that's true enough in its way.'

They gaze over the great sweep of Downs and sea in silence. Both are thinking how they kissed for the first time, standing here in the warm wind.

'I'm sorry you've not been happy,' Kitty says.

'Not your fault,' says Ed. 'Just how I'm made.'

'It feels like my fault.'

He takes her in his arms and smiles for her, just like the old Eddy did.

'You're my lovely angel,' he says. 'I love you so much.'

'And I love you, my darling.'

'I want you to be happy more than I want anything.'

'That doesn't matter,' she says. 'And anyway, I am happy now.'

'Will you kiss me?'

'Of course I will,' she says.

He kisses her. For a long time after the kiss has ended he holds her close, his head bent over her shoulder, his eyes closed.

Back at the farmhouse, the car unloaded, Ed wheels out his old bike.

'Just going for a spin,' he says.

He follows the road to Newhaven and through sleepy Seaford, down the long hill to Cuckmere Haven and up the other side, heaving on the pedals, to the high ridge over Friston. Then down again into the forest, and up again, tired now. He gets off halfway and pushes the bike. At the summit he climbs onto the saddle again and pedals down the road to Birling Gap. It's a long ride, the sun dropping slowly in the sky behind him, throwing his shadow before him. From Birling Gap the track runs unmade along the clifftop to Beachy Head. Here he dismounts and wheels the bicycle over the close-cropped turf. He lays the bicycle down, and takes off his jacket, and bundling it up, pushes it into the bicycle basket. In the breast pocket of his jacket there are two letters.

He stands looking round. Behind him the soft roll of Downland; before him the sea, ruffled by the wind, brownish-yellow near the land, grey-blue further out. There's a low brick structure by the cliff edge, the remains of a Lloyd's shipping watchtower, now converted into a viewing platform. Wooden benches are set inside its octagonal walls. On the outer wall there's a new metal plaque.

> On this headland and the surrounding Downs in the years of the Second World War between 1939 and 1945, the men and women of the Allied Forces helped defend their country.

The plaque is in honour of the Royal Observer Corps, the RAF, the WAAF, the Home Guard, the Anti-Aircraft Defences.

> This plaque also commemorates the epic Dieppe Raid in 1942, which was partly controlled from the radar station on this headland. Beachy Head is once more in peace. But the devotion and patriotism of those who operated on this stretch of Downland in Britain's greatest time of suffering will not be forgotten.

The plaque is dated October 16th 1949.

He reads, and gives a small wry smile, and moves on. He follows the cliff edge to a point where the chalkland forms a jagged projection. He stands here for a moment looking down at the red and white lighthouse. The breakers splash softly at its concrete base. The tide is in, the sea pushing against the foot of the great white cliffs five hundred feet below. He looks up, over the sea to the hazy horizon. Somewhere over there is Dieppe, and the beach where he thought he would die, but did not die.

Beachy Head is once more in peace.

He has been happy today for the first time in months; perhaps years. That's something.

There's a light wind blowing off the sea. He breathes in the salt air. He feels young again, and strong. The late afternoon sunlight gleams on the water, forming a bright broken road to the horizon.

Live like an arrow in flight. How he must be laughing, Rex Mundi, the king of the world. Only a few short steps to freedom.

He walks briskly towards the edge and jumps. As he falls, accelerating all the time, his arms reach out as if to slow his descent. Halfway down his body strikes the cliff, lacerating his side, tumbling him over. Near the bottom his flailing body hits the cliff again. So he hurtles on down to meet the yielding water and the unyielding rocks.

The letter to Larry reads:

> Dear Larry. I'm sorry but I can't do it any more. I've done all I can to provide for Kitty and the girls. Believe me, I've worked like a very devil. The business is in good shape. I don't expect most people will understand, but I think you might. You've known me long enough. The simple truth is

life has long been a torment to me. I don't know why this should be so. The darkness is always there, waiting for me. I try to keep away from other people. I know my unhappiness is a burden and a sadness to them. In the end, this is the only way I know to keep away for ever. And dear old friend, don't be angry with me for writing what I'm about to write. I want you to believe that I'm doing the little I can to make amends. I know you love Kitty, and have loved her from the first. I believe she loves you, without lessening her love for me. I've always known you could make her happy, and that I never will. In my selfishness I held on for too long. But now I know you're free to be with her, I must go. Don't pity me. Be happy for me. You have no idea how many times I've dreamed of this. Thank you, my friend, for your endless kindness to me. You're a good man, and a braver man than I can ever be. Love Kitty and my girls for me. You'll make a better job of it than I've ever done. Goodbye, dear friend. I'm not afraid of the darkness any more. Rest at last.

The letter to Kitty reads:

My only darling. Loving you has been the one good thing I've done in my life. Being loved by you has been a miracle to me. But we each have to live our own lives. I won't drag you down with me any more. Don't believe that your duty is to save me. I know how much I've hurt you. There's no remedy for that. So now I've decided to go. My dearest darling, you're so beautiful, so young, you have so much of your life ahead. Why should you live in the darkness with me? I don't do this for you, I do it for me, to be free at last.

But now you will be free too. My dearest, I know you love me. I've known it from the start. But I know you love Larry too. No shame in that. Who could not love Larry? Now that he too is free, I can go. Love Larry, darling, he deserves your love, and remember me, and love me too, and know that I've found rest at last. Don't hate me for leaving you. Don't be angry. Just say he did his best, and when he could do no more he laid himself down to sleep. Kiss the girls from me. Tell them if there's a heaven after all, I'll be waiting for them. Tell them I go with my head held high, still storming the fatal beach, still the war hero. Tell them I'll love them for eternity. As I'll love you. If we meet again it'll be in a place where all things are known, and you'll forgive me. Good night, my darling. I shall fall asleep in your arms, and the hurting will be over.

# 41

Larry stays on at River Farm, taking charge of all the necessary arrangements. Ed's body is recovered by the coastguards. After a short service in Edenfield church, throughout which Kitty remains silent and dry-eyed, the body is buried in the churchyard. The obituary notice in *The Times* is entirely taken up by the events of one day in August eight years ago that won Edward Avenell the Victoria Cross.

Pamela cries in her mother's arms, but Kitty hardly cries at all. Grief has paralysed her. At the same time she finds she can't forgive Ed for what he's done to them. She's angry that he believed what he was doing was best for her. Alone in bed at night she speaks to him, not shouting, bitter in her insistence.

'What gave you the right to walk away? What makes your suffering so much greater than everyone else's? How can you not see the damage you've done? You have oblivion. What about us? We have a sorrow that won't end. We have our failure to love you enough. We have your example before us for the rest of our lives, that unhappiness wins in the end.'

Larry makes no attempt to console Kitty, nor she him. He concentrates his energies on securing the family's finances, and helping Hugo with the wine import business. By the time Hugo asks him to become a legal partner in the firm he has already made himself indispensable.

'So now Ed's got what he wanted,' says Kitty. 'You're obliged to look after us, whether you want to or not.'

She doesn't refer to Ed's other bequest to them. Kitty feels numbed, trapped by Ed's final act, rendered powerless. The thought of profiting from his death is repugnant to her. Such a hurtful wasteful denial of life can have no good consequences.

Elizabeth, three years old, placid and good-tempered, cries for a while and then returns to her daily concerns. Her father had always been away for such long periods that little in the daily routine changes. Pamela moves on from grief to incomprehension. Neither of the girls has been told the truth about their father's death. He was out walking, they've been told, and he had an accident, perhaps a heart attack, and fell to his death.

'How is it an accident?' says Pamela. 'Why was he so close to the edge? I don't understand.'

There are no answers.

'We just don't know,' Larry tells her. 'It's a terrible thing to have happened. All we can do is help each other.'

'How?' says Pamela. 'How are we to help each other?'

'By loving each other,' says Larry.

'Will you love me and Elizabeth? Will you love Mummy?'

'Yes,' says Larry.

'Will you marry Mummy?'

'I don't know,' says Larry.

'I don't want you to,' says Pamela. 'I'm waiting till I'm grown up, then you can marry me.'

'All right,' says Larry.

Larry makes a pilgrimage of sorts to Beachy Head. He goes on his own. He has no way of knowing where Ed stood in that last moment of his life, but this seems to be the closest he can get to him now.

There are other walkers out on the bald grass. They throw him furtive looks. He knows what they're thinking. Is he a jumper? Will it happen now, the unstoppable unforgivable act of self-termination?

I could do it. They could do it. That's what grips the imagination. Just a few steps, and then a few more, and the story ends.

But for us the story hasn't ended.

My best and oldest friend. I dream of running after you, of arriving here on the cliff top just in time. There you stand, the deed not yet done, and I shout out to you, 'Wait!' You turn and see me, and you wait for me. I take you by one arm, I hold you tight, I say, 'Come home.' You smile that half smile of yours and step away from the cliff edge and we walk home together, you pushing your bike. There are two letters in your jacket pocket that will never be delivered.

I've loved you for so long. How could you leave me?

Larry has a visit from Rupert Blundell. He seems uncomfortable, which is to be expected, since they haven't met since the break-up of Larry's marriage to Geraldine. It turns out he's seen Ed's obituary.

'I was so shocked,' he says. 'I don't quite know why, but he always seemed to me to be immortal.'

'I sometimes felt that too.'

'He was' – Rupert reaches for the right word – 'debonair.'

'Some of the time,' says Larry.

'I suppose he meant to do it.'

'Yes.'

'Dear God. The poor boy.'

There seems to be nothing more to say.

'How's Geraldine?' asks Larry.

'Geraldine?' Rupert takes his glasses off and cleans them with one end of his tie. 'She's as you'd expect. Miserable. Angry.'

'I'm sorry.'

'She says there's another woman in the case.'

'Yes.'

Rupert puts his glasses back on and looks up at Larry.

'She feels what you've done is breaking one of the fundamental laws of the Church,' he says.

'I don't want to duck my share of the blame,' says Larry. 'But if you go by the laws of the Church you could say I have grounds for annulment.'

'Right.' Rupert passes one hand across his eyes. 'There was something of that sort before.'

'So I gather.'

'Just to be clear,' Rupert says after a pause. 'You're saying the marriage was never consummated.'

'Yes,' says Larry.

Rupert bows his head as if in prayer.

''Tis a consummation,' he murmurs, 'devoutly to be wished.'

He shakes his head. 'Hamlet's talking about death, of course. Ed Avenell, of all people.'

He looks up and meets Larry's puzzled gaze.

'People always turn out to be so much more complicated than we imagine.'

He rises.

'Well, I'd better be off.'

Larry walks with him to his car.

'One question. I ask because it rather obsesses my sister. What's become of your faith?'

'It seems to have fallen off the back of the truck,' says Larry. 'It's been a bumpy ride.'

Larry tells Kitty about Rupert Blundell's visit, and how Geraldine said there was another woman in the case. For the first time since Ed's death she bursts into laughter.

'Another woman in the case? Meaning me?'

'Who else?'

'Oh, Larry. I've never been the other woman before.'

'I've no idea where Geraldine got the idea from. I never said a thing to her.'

'Things don't need to be said.'

'Yes, they do,' says Larry.

Kitty smiles for him, and he knows then that the sadness will pass.

'I love you,' he says. 'All I want is to be with you. I want to go to sleep with you at night, and I want to wake up with you in the morning.'

She takes his hand and raises it to her lips and kisses it. Such an odd old-fashioned gesture, that speaks of her humility, her sadness, her gratitude.

'Here I am,' she says.

He folds her into his arms and they kiss, a true lovers' kiss that doesn't have to end, the kiss that has been waiting for so long. Then she remains warm and close in his arms, and lets herself cry. It's the first time she's cried since Ed died.

'I really did love him,' she says.

'So did I,' says Larry.

# EPILOGUE

## 2012

Alice comes down on the morning of her last day to find the house silent, bathed in sunlight. Breakfast is laid on the terrace. Gustave appears with coffee and fresh bread. Alice eats and drinks alone. She wonders where her grandmother is.

When she's had her breakfast she gets up and walks across the grass to the trees, as she did on her first day at La Grande Heuze. Ahead of her stretches the forest, as far as the eye can see. There are no paths, or many paths. She walks a little way between the smooth trunks over the crunching ground. Her mind is lost in the past, haunted by ghosts.

Alone now among the trees, seeing only the same patterns of light and shade in every direction, it seems to her that with her new deeper past has come a deeper future. Her life extends infinitely backwards, but also forwards. The story her grandmother has told has shown her, as if from a great height, her own place in time. This immensity is consoling. One life can contain so much.

She returns to the house, and finds Pamela taking her breakfast on the terrace. She joins her, and drinks another cup of coffee.

'I was thinking,' her grandmother says, 'before you go home maybe we should visit the graves.'

'The graves?'

'They're buried here, in Bellencombre. My mother, and Larry. Larry made it to eighty-four, not such a bad age. I was with him when he died.'

'Here?'

'Yes, here. This was his house. This is where they lived in their later years.'

Somehow this comes as a surprise. After the long story of the distant past, it brings them shockingly close. I could have met them, Alice thinks. I could have known them.

'I adored Larry,' says Pamela. 'Really he was the one I wanted to marry.'

'But you married Hugo.'

'Yes. Poor Hugo. All frightfully Freudian, I suppose. Except I can't help thinking Freud got it all wrong. I was never in competition with my mother. I loved her far too much for that. No, it was all the other way about. I wanted to *be* my mother.'

They drive in to Bellencombre and visit the graveyard by the side of the church of St Martin. Here Kitty and Larry lie buried in the same grave. The headstone, looking disconcertingly new, bears only their names and dates. Kitty is named as Katherine Avenell.

'They were together for just over fifty years,' says Pamela.

'Were they happy together?' says Alice.

'Yes, they were very happy.'

'They deserved to be happy.'

'Why do you say that? Because Larry had waited for so long?'

'I suppose so,' says Alice.

'He wasn't just a sweet patient man waiting in the wings, you know. His love was the biggest thing in all our lives. It was like a blazing fire in the room. Love can be so ruthless, can't it?'

They walk back between the headstones to the waiting car. Alice is silent, thinking.

'Has any of that helped you?'

'In a way,' says Alice.

Why should love end? Once you start loving someone the love continues to grow and change for the rest of your life. But we're all so afraid, so unsure we're lovable, so fragile. We want love never to change.

I'm growing stronger now. I want a life of my own. I want adventures of my own. If one day I marry and have children, I want to be able to make that commitment as a woman who knows she deserves to be loved.

I come from a long line of mistakes. And one true love story.

# AUTHOR'S NOTE

The historical background to the events in *Motherland* is as accurate as I have been able to make it. The account of the Dieppe raid is based on several first-hand reports, in particular by the war journalists A.B. Austin, Quentin Reynolds, and Wallace Reyburn.

My knowledge of the events surrounding Indian independence began when I was asked to write a screenplay based on Alex von Tunzelmann's excellent *Indian Summer*. For the details I have relied heavily on Alan Campbell-Johnson's diary of that time, published in 1951 as *Mission with Mountbatten*.

For background on William Coldstream and Camberwell College of Art in the post-war period I have been greatly helped by the first-hand memories of my mother-in-law, Anne Olivier Bell.

For the tale of Fyffes and the banana business I am indebted to my old friend David Stockley, whose father, grandfather and great-grandfather managed Elders & Fyffes for so many successful years. The business details are accurate; the character details of the fictional Cornford family are of course invented. I have relied also on A.H. Stockley's privately printed autobiography *Consciousness of Effort: The Romance of the Banana*, 1937; *The Banana Empire* by Charles Kepner and Jay Soothill, 1935; and *Fyffes and the Banana* by Peter N. Davies, 1990.

In matters of historical fact and tone of voice I have relied throughout on my wife, the social historian Virginia Nicholson, whose own books, particularly *Millions Like Us*, her account of the lives of women in the Second World War and after, have been an inspiration to me.

Readers may be interested to trace the links between the characters in *Motherland* and characters in my other Sussex-based novels. Alice Dickinson appears at the age of eleven in *The Secret Intensity of Everyday Life*, and again aged nineteen in *All the Hopeful Lovers*. Her father Guy Caulder also plays a part in both novels. George Holland's curious love life is discovered long after his death in *Secret Intensity*, where a very old Gwen Willis makes an appearance. Louisa, George Holland's wife, dies in 1955, after *Motherland* has ended and many years before *Secret Intensity* begins, but her son Billy has a large part to play in the later book. Anthony Armitage, the artist, appears as an angry old man in *All the Hopeful Lovers*. Rex Dickinson, briefly encountered in *Motherland*, is the absent husband of Mrs Dickinson, who appears in *Secret Intensity* and *The Golden Hour*. The farmhouse where Larry and Rex are billeted, and where Kitty and Ed later live, appears in all three earlier novels as the home of the Broad family. Edenfield Place appears in all four novels, at different stages of its existence. This great Victorian Gothic house is based on Tyntesfield, the Gibbs family mansion near Bristol, now owned by the National Trust.